# Advanced Praise

*Behind Silent Smiles* is an addictive read that somehow manages to be both uplifting and tragic at the same time. Tanya J. Peterson has once again crafted a novel that gives the reader an unpredictable roller-coaster ride through a vast array of emotions. Not many books include Domestic Violence, and the story also gently touches on the subject of childhood sexual assault. As a survivor of both circumstances I found that it was incredibly well done and not greatly triggering. For me personally it gave me the wonderful gift of not feeling alone in my experiences. I can't love this book enough!

> — Charlene Martel – *The Literary Word*

Another compelling novel by Tanya J. Peterson that will push your mind in new directions. *Behind Silent Smiles* bends time and place to expose the human condition. Catie is a character that will stick with you for a long time. A multilayered, immersive, must read!

> — Dr. William K. Lawrence, author of *The Punk and the Professor*

Tanya Peterson depicts in excruciating detail the horrors of an upbringing in Communist Romania, illuminating the trauma experienced by Catie and the genesis of her physical suffering and inability to love herself. The present-day story takes place in Sacramento, California, a refuge to which Catie and her two children have recently fled from her abusive husband. We watch as the children adjust in their own ways but Catie remains tormented by her past, gradually learning to trust others. A heart-wrenching but beautifully written story that finally leaves the reader with hope born of faith, love, and human kindness.

> — Linda Franklin, former editor, Inkwater Press

# BEHIND
# SILENT SMILES

# BEHIND
# SILENT SMILES

*A novel by*
*Tanya J. Peterson*

Apprentice
House Press
*Loyola University Maryland*

Names: Peterson, Tanya J., author.

Title: Behind Silent Smiles : a novel / by Tanya Peterson.

Description: Identifiers: Subjects:First edition. | Baltimore, Maryland : Apprentice House, Loyola University Maryland, [2018]

ISBN: 978-1-62720-176-6 (casebound) | 978-1-62720-177-3 (paperbound) | 978-1-62720-178-0 (ebook)

LCSH: Struggle--Psychological aspects--Fiction. | Self-acceptance--Fiction. | Self-esteem--Fiction. | Romania--Fiction. | Communism--Romania--Fiction. | California--Fiction. | Emigration and immigration--Fiction. | Mental illness--Fiction. | Psychological abuse--Fiction. | Family violence--Fiction. | Families--Fiction. | Mentally ill--Fiction. | Mentally ill--Family relationships--Fiction.

Classification: LCC: PS3616.E8478 B44 2018 | DDC: 813.6--dc23

First Edition

Casebound ISBN: 978-1-62720-176-6
Paperback ISBN: 978-1-62720-177-3
Ebook ISBN: 978-1-62720-178-0

Design: Margaret Sandorse;
Marketing: Meredith Wardell
Development: Alessia Hughes

Printed in the United States of America

Apprentice
House Press
*Loyola University Maryland*

Apprentice House
Loyola University Maryland
4501 N. Charles Street
Baltimore, MD 21210
410.617.5265 • 410.617.2198 (fax)
www.ApprenticeHouse.com • info@ApprenticeHouse.com

# Dedication

For N. I'm deeply grateful for our friendship and honored that you trusted me with your story.

Behind Silent Smiles is a novel inspired by the story of an incredible woman. From childhood through adulthood, she has experienced the depths of pain while at the same time possessing the height of a beauty that she has a difficult time seeing.

To protect the woman's privacy as well as generalize this story that is lived by too many, I have retained the essence of her story, its emotions and themes and important components, but I have changed all details. For example, her country of origin is different, as is the country to which she escaped. The number of children she has is different, but she does indeed have children. The Catie of the story didn't live through war like the real-life woman did, but Catie experienced the harsh conditions of poverty and devastation in a communist country. This holds true for all the specific details in the story. What isn't fiction, however is that people do live through horrific experiences to come through on the other side and learn to thrive.

When I first learned of this incredible story, incredible life, I knew it needed to be told. It's my hope that this woman see her own worth and strengths. It's also my hope that we all see a bit of ourselves in this character, this person. People seem to be easily self-critical without pausing to look in the mirror to see all that lies behind silent smiles…

# A Foreword by the Woman Who Inspired Behind Silent Smiles...

·················································

It all started on social media.

I have not yet had the opportunity to meet Tanya J Peterson but that does not stop me from considering her to be one of my best friends. You see, I love books and admire authors.

I saw a tweet about a book called 'My Life in a Nutshell' which I retweeted and saved with a view to adding it to my 'To Read' list. The title was eye-catching but what also piqued my interest was the fact that it was about anxiety. Tanya responded to my retweet, saying she liked my profile picture.

I read 'My Life in a Nutshell' and fell in love with the characters. This book impressed me because I am so used to seeing the world portrayed as being divided between the good and the bad characters, and in this book, they were ALL good people.

One day, after reading a second and a third book by this author, and after having some conversations with Tanya, I wrote to her and said 'Something weird is happening: I am truly falling in love with the characters. I admire them, even in their weakest moments. I find myself missing them and wishing there were more like them in this world. She said 'I wish you could see your own worth and courage. I wish you could see how strong you are. I would like to write a story about you, hoping that you would fall in love with the character and realize it is you.'

Learning to read was my first escape from the realities of life and my ambition from an early age was to write books, hence my own first book, written at the age of ten. I never truly believed, however, that I was good enough to write either fiction or memoir.

I had blogged for a couple of months: I liked that, I enjoyed doing it and I consider that phase as being one of the most therapeutic things I have done. Blogging and writing gave me some visibility in a virtual world when I felt completely invisible in my real world. Before 2011, I didn't even know what a blog was: I was far too deep in the darkness and too involved in struggling to manage my life and survive as best I could. My new life began when I stumbled over the first blog post by accident one day. Writing gave me friends, empathic people who supported me when I was in need and cheered my accomplishments. It opened my eyes to the reality I was living and helped me to realize I wasn't alone in my pain. The most important thing was that it showed me there are people out there who care, who believe you and who believe IN you.

Many times, other bloggers pointed out that my story needs to be told, that my writing was powerful and that I should write a memoir. Someone offered to buy my story for a book, but this did not interest me; I wasn't ready to write it then and I'm still not ready now.

However, having someone as good as Tanya telling a tale inspired by mine is amazing. The big lines and the essence are there although the rest of the characters are all fictionalized. It is good, not only because I am not ready yet to go public but also because I do not want it to be too raw, too hard for readers to deal with.

When I read Khaled Husseini's book, 'A Thousand Splendid Suns', I could relate so much to a lot in Leila and Mariam's stories. I could relate to both the war experiences and the abuse. It was a heartbreaking story but beautiful at the same time. 'Behind Silent Smiles' is dealing with similar themes in a different way, but instead of being heartbreaking, it is empowering.

Who saved my life? I don't know.

Living through a war is not an easy thing. We lived in a very dangerous neighborhood and therefore were much more exposed than others in that country. My childhood memories are mainly about the shelter: running away, listening to the radio, the breaking news while hearing all about the horrors and victims, wondering 'When will it be us? Will it be me? What is it that is making me survive while others die? WHY ME?'

Catie's mother in this book is not like my mum. My mother was my idol and she still is but, Catie's mother in here is more like what I was telling myself in my own inner voice. There are things I can understand now, as an adult, that I could not understand back then. Life, for me, was a long struggle to fit in, to feel enough, to feel accepted and loved by my family. In reality, I did fit in and I was loved but it was all stories that I fashioned inside my head that no one else could hear. I thought I was unloved and abandoned, I believed I did not matter and, what's more, I knew I was by far the ugliest of us girls and that I was timid and stupid. When I expressed my feelings, I was laughed at for being stupid. Being molested as a child did not help because I felt that I had to accept this treatment in order to protect my younger sisters and cousins.

Years passed, I grew up and married.

Somehow, something did not feel right at home but I could not quite place my finger on whatever it was long enough to identify it. I had no friends of my own and he would say 'You should be friends with my friends' wives - why would you need others?' Whenever I wanted to see my own family, he would criticize them all and say 'Now WE are your family - what use are THEY?' Whenever he was aggressive with the kids it was always my fault because I kept forcing him to teach me a lesson.

(Why can't I be a good wife and a good mother? Why am I such a bad person. He is such a nice man and everyone loves him as much as I do, he deserves so much better)

Every time I got a friend he would push them away. The first time I was asked whether he ever laid a hand on me I was shocked and didn't answer because how could I say that he did without having to confess that I kept on driving him to it?

I continued to deny for a very long time.

My internet friends saved my life.

I was desperate and asked for support because the only person I was close to, my only friend who knew the truth, who witnessed the abuse, taking me to hospital, mopping my tears, coming whenever I needed her, had decided to cut the ties. I could not blame her ... after all, who would want to be my friend? She was amazing because she had lasted over three years, but as for me, my life had come to the end. I had my children, my own family and that husband I adored despite everything but I could not imagine living one more day without her support. I didn't have the energy to leave them a letter of any kind but I did feel the need to justify my actions to someone out there. I turned to strangers on social media. These people had believed me and offered lots of support and advice, even if they did not understand the laws of my country; did not realize that the laws of the western world did not apply here.

The only organisation that deals with domestic abuse in my country could not help me. In fact, they could have helped me if I had been prepared to leave my kids with their father. That wasn't good enough for me because he had also started abusing the kids in sly, sideways steps.

I turned to the priest and he was great until he met my husband and chose to believe his version of events instead of mine.

I can also say that my kids saved my life.

I would still be there (or in my grave) if it wasn't for them. My friend told me that I should set an example for my daughters, that they might find themselves in a similar situation in the future because mine is the only example they had. She also pointed out that my son might grow up to be abusive as that was his sole example. Now I decided it was time to escape. It was no longer about me but was very much about them. I had a purpose at last and that was to protect my kids.

I started planning it secretly, or maybe planning it is the big word for what it was. Maybe I can say that I started believing that it might be possible, that I might have a chance of escape, and that is when I feel that the whole universe has worked with me instead of against me. It is when I believed that things could be positive that they became. It wasn't an easy time, far from that, but things were moving in the right direction. I say the Universe but it is mainly the people around me. My boss and colleagues helped logistically and gave me support and understanding. My sister and family helped enormously, and my friends online kept me alive. The daily words of support, the presence when I needed them, the courage when I thought it was too much. I don't think I could have done it without them all. All of them are Miracles in my life.

Every day is a miracle to me. This is how I choose to see life. I was on a website once where I shared parts of my story. I was accused of lying because they found it hard to accept that one person could go through so many different unrelated traumatic experiences. I was told to make up my mind whether I was a war survivor, a sexual abuse survivor or a domestic abuse survivor? Was I just grieving or depressed or anxious? I am none of these. I am just a person who witnesses life as it is and who finds the miracle in every episode of her life. When going through them life seems so hard that we might complain and share our issues, expecting support and understanding but once the problem is solved I can look back and see the miracle in each moment.

War taught me to value life and appreciate every moment. War taught me that if I eat today, it doesn't guarantee I will have food tomorrow. I also learned that sleeping in my comfortable bed tonight does not guarantee that I won't be shivering in a cold shelter the next night. It taught me to never be in conflict with anyone and to never criticize anything and just take it as it is. War taught me that I have my parents with me, my sisters and my family now but I might not have them around forever. Instead of fighting and arguing about futile things it is better to share the love. After all, love is all that matters. War told me to live in the moment and never go to bed with an unresolved issue with anyone.

Sexual abuse taught me about human weakness, my weakness and my abusers'. It taught me that being abused didn't have to define me and who I am. I tolerated the abuse strictly believing that if I didn't he would attack my sisters instead. I learned that putting myself in a victim position, accepting being the victim of something doesn't really protect anyone else.

Domestic abuse taught me that my life is not mine alone, that I am connected to everybody and everyone. When I was told at first that I am being abused and that it wasn't OK, I used to answer that I don't mind. He can hit and curse, but it's OK, I'm OK with it since I can handle it. It took me many years before I learned that if I can handle it, it doesn't mean that my kids have to or my family have to endure it with me. I didn't realize that allowing myself to be a victim was harming everyone I love and not only me.

Being raised catholic and very close to God gave me false ideas of how life is or should be. I was still a child when the nuns used to teach me that to be a good person who deserves God's love I had to accept and say yes to every little challenge. I was taught that the more you suffer, the closer you are to God. The more you suffer, the more God loves you and you become his favorite child. I was told stories of Saints who inflicted pain on themselves to suffer like He did and I believed that that was it. I had to go through it all and feel grateful about it. I thought that if I was suffering it meant I was loved and it's the love I wanted from everyone that I could get just from God by suffering.

Now I know the truth. Now I know that God loves me for who I am and not for the suffering I can endure. God loves me to be happy and healthy. God loves me despite all my imperfections. God is not what we are taught he is. God is in every little miracle I have witnessed and continue to witness.

For so many years, I believed that I was alone, that no one cares and that no one will ever help me, but also that it was impossible to escape. I believed it and had so many proofs. Whatever I saw or read was about how "impossible" it was to run away. Once I decided I wanted to do it, all the doors have opened and I was no longer alone. This is something I keep reminding myself of when I am having a hard time. Good people exist. Real friends exist. Loving family exists. Resources and help are available for anyone all the time but you can only see it when you are ready. No one will help if you don't know or say that you have a problem. If anyone reading this is struggling in any way, please reach out. There is help and support as long as you do the first step towards it.

# Sacramento, California
## *2018*

# Chapter 1

· · · · · · · · · · · · · · · · · ·

"Mother!"

Catie groaned and burrowed under her quilt. She did it partially for warmth; she was always cold no matter the time of year. Even though her quilt was thin, it warmed her soul, if not her body, when she surrounded herself with its serene images of Christ Jesus, the Virgin Mary, and St. Basil. The tranquil icons reminiscent of Byzantium in Medieval times beckoned from the past and promised a peaceful future in Heaven, and this was a source of comfort in a present she could hardly bear.

"Ugh. Mother. Get up. I need to leave, and you forgot to sign my grade report last night. I'd do it myself, but I'm not in the mood to get busted for forging your signature again. God. It's such a stupid school." She pushed her mother's shoulder. "Mother! I know you heard me. Seriously, just get up already. It's not that hard."

Catie rubbed the shoulder that her daughter had just shoved. Her joints ached terribly, and the pain of the nudge sparked hot needles that angrily jabbed at her skin as if they wanted to punch their way through. Maybe they could sew her to the sheets and give her a legitimate excuse to stay put. As much as she wanted to lie in bed, she had a duty to rise and get moving. She loved her daughter, and she loved God, and it saddened her heart to know that she was a constant source of displeasure to them both.

"I'm sorry, Florina. I didn't sleep well again last night." Catie smiled tenderly. "You look beautiful as always, my daughter." Florina didn't smile back. Catie knew she wouldn't. She never did. The fiery pain in her shoulder receded as a different type of pain flared within her. She sighed. "All right. Let's go get that form signed so you can get to school on time." Catie shivered as she stood, adjusted the twisted robe that she wore through the night for added warmth, and shuffled to the kitchen behind Florina.

The state of the kitchen made her want to slink back into her bed. Last night's dishes, including a greasy frying pan, were stacked haphazardly beside the sink. The dishwasher's open door partially blocked the path into the kitchen. A bowl and a plate had been removed; otherwise it was full of clean dishes. Cupboards were open. The garbage can was out. A loaf of bread lay on the counter, a few pieces peeking out of the open wrapper, deciding if they should jump onto the floor. Catie thought that if she were one of those pieces of bread, she wouldn't have to think about it. She'd just jump.

She shook her head and resumed her survey of the kitchen. A jar of peanut butter sat on one side of the counter, illogically far from the bread. The jar's lid was nowhere to be seen. A knife, gooey with a glob of peanut butter, lay on a different counter, oozing its burden onto the surface. The milk and juice were out of the refrigerator, and even though Catie was cold, the day and the room were both warm, too warm for milk and juice to be out. That much was evident from the little beads of water that rolled down each container, leaving wet ruts behind. Some of the moisture dripped onto one of the rolled-up newspapers that mocked her because, as much as she wanted to, she never had the time or the energy to read them. She truly did want to know what was happening in the world as well as learn more about her country, the United States of America, and about California and Sacramento, where she now lived. Day after day she promised herself that she'd read the paper, but somehow, she never did—just like she obviously didn't get to the kitchen last night or this morning. The little energy she possessed fell down to her feet and left her body, probably seeping down into the floor. She looked down to see if it was a visible pool beside her feet, but she saw nothing. The energy was invisible; she wished she were invisible, or better, beyond invisible—nonexistent. But here she was. She felt like a deflated, wrinkly, worn-out balloon, and the day had barely begun. She looked up and sighed.

Florina must have seen her surveying the kitchen, for with self-important disgust, she spat, "I know what you're thinking, mother, and you can get it out of your head. This isn't my fault." Florina gestured sharply at the mess beside her. "You only have yourself to blame for this mess. You were too lazy to clean up last night and too lazy again to get up this morning and get us breakfast and make our lunches. So this is what you get." When she gestured this time, she looked like a self-righteous princess showing off a crystal palace rather than a sixteen-year-old girl barking a tirade at her mother.

Catie's voice was limp. "Florina, I doubt you know what I'm thinking. What I'm thinking is that it *is* my own fault that I have this kitchen to clean up before work. What I'm thinking also is that I love you and your brother and I'm very sorry that I wasn't up early enough this morning."

Catie looked into Florina's eyes. Florina looked away. "Will you just sign my grade report so I can go?"

Catie moved her lips up as much as she could. At least she could form a small smile. And at least Florina hadn't rolled her eyes and said something sarcastic. She just needed her form signed. "Of course. Where is it?"

Florina strode to the table and rifled through books, binders, and various school supplies. She lifted up a bulky cardboard box that her brother was transforming into a diorama about Betty Smith's *A Tree Grows in Brooklyn*. She slammed it back down as she bellowed, "Alexandru! What did you do with my grade report?"

A gangly boy wearing baggy athletic shorts and a hooded sweatshirt sporting the San Francisco Giants logo sauntered into the kitchen. He laughed. "Chill out, Florina. Our house is small; you don't have to yell. It's just a grade report. And I didn't touch it, by the way." He walked to Catie and stood beside her. "Good morning, Mamă."

"It's important. Not that you would know. You're just in middle school." She returned to rifling around the kitchen.

"I may only be in middle school, but I know where your report is."

"I knew you did something to it! Go get it, Douchebag." When Alexandru only laughed, Florina squawked, "Mother! Make him give me my report!"

Catie squeezed her eyes shut and rubbed her temples. She held up her hands, palms out to emphasize her words. "Stop. Just stop, both of you. Okay?" She looked at her son. "Good morning to you, too, Alexandru. Please, will you tell your sister where her paper is?"

He looked at Florina and shrugged nonchalantly. "It's on the bathroom counter buried under a bunch of your crap." Without a word, Florina stomped away, rushed back, thrust the form and a pen at Catie, and left the house in a huff.

"I guess I'd better get going, too." He looked at his watch. "I'm glad the school isn't far from here." When he walked into the living room, Catie followed him. He grabbed his backpack from its residence beside the door and shrugged into it. He studied his mother and frowned. "You look tired again, Mamă." He looked at her and seemed to notice for the first time that she wasn't showered and dressed. "Are you going to miss work again today?" His forehead creased. He was too young for the tender skin on his forehead to crease so much, Catie thought. She didn't want to make him worry so, but she didn't want to lie to him, either.

She patted her unruly hair self-consciously and sat down on the couch. It was as if that act of smoothing her hair was all the activity she could muster for the entire day. She lay back and closed her eyes. "I know I should go, Alexandru. And I feel so blessed to finally have a job again. We need the money. I do like working, too, but I'm just so tired and in pain. And..." She trailed off.

"And what, Mamă?" He wiggled his thin shoulders, and the ratty backpack dropped to the floor with a thud. Startled, Catie jumped, and her eyes flew open. Embarrassed by her response to the harmless thump, she looked at the backpack rather than at her son. The corner of his binder poked out of the space where the zippers didn't come together. Alexandru nudged it gently with the toe of his sneaker, and the binder disappeared into the bag. Catie watched his feet slide toward her and turn to face the other direction as he sat down beside her.

Her heart kept pounding from the thump of Alexandru's backpack. She was still exhausted to the bone, but she was now keyed up and uneasy. Alert, almost too much so, she looked around the room to check for something vague, some threat she wasn't quite certain of because it really shouldn't be here.

Tell that to her soul, though. Her soul knew the threat, and her soul knew that she had it coming.

"Mamă, look at me. It's okay. Just tell me what you were going to say."

Catie forced herself to attend to her second-born child. After making herself look directly at him, it wasn't so very difficult to make a little smile come to her face. When she saw the smile spread across his face, she knew she couldn't tell him the rest of what she had almost said. How could she burden this boy with the "and?" She took his hand in hers and squeezed it. After wincing at the pain of it, she said. "And now not only am I going to be late for work, you are late for school. You are sweet to care about me," she leaned over and pecked him on the cheek, "but off with you now. I will call your school and explain that you were helping your mother."

She watched Alexandru study her and nod slowly. "Okay." The worry wrinkles appeared on his face again. "But if I go to school now, do you promise you'll go to work? It's important for all of us, Mamă."

"I know it is, son. I will go. And so must you." She pointed toward the door. Alexandru grinned, jumped up, took only two steps to reach the door—his legs were growing longer every day, which meant that he would soon need new clothes and shoes again, Catie mused—swooped up his backpack, and wriggled back into it as he shot out the door. With a heavy sigh, Catie rose slowly, crossed the room in more than two steps, shut the door behind her son, and, dragging her feet, made her way into the kitchen. Her eyes filled with tears when she saw the disastrous mess for the second time. She picked up the peanut butter. It felt heavy despite the fact that it was over half empty. She put it down and searched for the lid, to no avail. She gave up on her effort to clean the aftermath of the barbarian invasion and instead picked up the phone.

She accidentally dropped it when her hands began to shake. She was suddenly dizzy and couldn't breathe well; it seemed as though she couldn't get enough air no matter how much she gasped. What had she done this morning? Why couldn't she have risen from her bed when she was supposed to have done so, when it was dark and the children were still asleep? Now she would be late for work and be fired. Then what would happen to her and her kids? And Alexandru was late for school because he was being a good son and looking after his mother. American schools didn't like tardiness any more than Romanian schools did. What was she doing to them all? Everyone was right. She was completely and totally worthless, to people and to God himself. She had to try to be better, and that meant doing what she had to do. Angrily, she swiped the tears from her eyes. She picked up the phone once again and called Alexandru's school and her work.

She gazed out the kitchen window to her tiny backyard as she spoke, and when she hung up, she stepped outside. The smell of freshly mowed grass made her nose itch, but it was a nice sensation. It reminded her that she had done the yardwork yesterday. That was likely why the pain was so intolerable today, but that was no excuse for being lazy and irresponsible. Even things she did right, like taking care of the lawn and flowers yesterday, led her to be a horrible person who deserved every one of her punishments.

She knelt down beside a patch of bloodroot flowers growing in her flower bed against the house. Catie loved these cheery spring flowers dancing gently in the breeze, pure white petals stretched open from a sunshine center to welcome the fresh air and rays of sun. She brushed her hand over the flowers. Her fingers found one that was drooping; she must have missed this one when she pruned yesterday. Either that, or when the sun rose this morning, it decided that it simply couldn't face one more day of sunshine that penetrated the surrounding flowers but didn't want to shine on it. She knew how it felt. Tenderly, she pinched it off of the plant. She rolled the stem in her fingers and watched the flower spin before holding it still. Holding the flower in her left hand, she moved her right hand toward it and grasped a petal between her thumb and index finger. "I love me." She plucked the petal and let it fall on her lap. "I love me not." The second petal fell beside the first. "I love me." The tears came as this petal fell. One by one, until only the little yellow button remained on top of the stem, Catie removed the petals and repeated, "I love me not. I love me not. I love me not." She let the stem with its little lone button drop to the ground, and when she stood, the petals on her lap floated down to join it. She looked at the pile. "I love me not!"

She couldn't move well or fast, but Catie worked her way back into the house to prepare to face the day.

# Chapter 2

Catie was on her feet and inching toward the door blocks before the bus stop. Part of her knew that she would be able to get to the door in time, because even though passengers stood while riding these American busses, there was enough room for people to reach the door. Here in Sacramento, nobody was smashed, trapped and nearly suffocating, against windows and the door itself. That same part of her also knew that the bus driver would wait for passengers to disembark before roaring away. But another part of her wasn't so sure that the bus system was really like this or that it would stay this way. Maybe her experience with American busses thus far had been a fluke. She was accustomed to overcrowded buses jammed with people packed more tightly than all of those hundreds of bats clinging to a little patch of ceiling deep within that cave in the Apuseni Mountains. She felt a smile creep across her face at that analogy, and even without the benefit of the little mirror in her bag she knew it was a wicked one. She pinched her thigh hard. While it did the trick to rid her face of the sneer, it couldn't erase the memory of Dumitru losing his rigid control and collapsing in panic. She sighed and silently asked God to forgive her for taking selfish delight of the memory of a traumatized Dumitru. She truly didn't like anyone to suffer. Even him.

The jar of the bus jerking to a stop jolted her out of her twisted reverie. She hurried to complete her trek to the front, and when the bus's big mouth finally whooshed open, folding outward and spitting passengers onto the sidewalk, Catie rushed down the stairs and, ignoring the pain in her joints, ran the three blocks to Hey Little Diddles Childcare Center— the place she had worked for only three weeks and the place she wanted to keep working for a very long time.

She came to a halt just outside the door. Briefly, she studied her reflection in the glass. She had done her best to get ready quickly but still look nice. As usual for her no matter what she did, she had failed miserably. She was inexcusably late. She had let everyone down. She looked like a mess, unfit to present herself to people. She lifted her hands to her head and ran her fingers through the long waves. It did no good at all; errant sprigs insisted on popping back up in random directions. Oh, what had she done by staying in bed so long?

She squeezed her eyes shut and sighed deeply. She made a quick sign of the cross, bowed her head, and prayed, "Please, God, let this be okay. Please let me keep my job. I don't mean to be selfish, and I am only asking because I need this job so I can take care of my children. I promise to serve you better." She made the sign of the cross again, looked up, promptly looked back down, and speedily made another sign. "Lord, please forgive me that this prayer was so brief. I will make it up to you tonight." After one final sign of the cross, she entered the building and steeled herself for a berating from her boss.

Catie didn't think anyone could scare her ever again. Irene McIntyre, however, frightened her. Catie had thought that someone owning and operating a child care center here in the United States of America, a place to nurture and care for babies, toddlers, and older children after the school day, would be warm and loving and open. But not Irene. Irene almost reminded her of the supervisors at the center where she had worked in Romania. How sad and tragic for Irene and for the children in her care, thought Catie. It shouldn't be this way, but maybe she was being naïve. Maybe it was just a dream and a hope she clung to after working in those horrible orphanages all those years. As always, tears sprang to her eyes as terrible images of miserable, suffering children began to swirl in her head. She pressed the heels of her hands hard into her eyes until flashes of lights replaced the horrific images that invaded her consciousness. Her chest constricted painfully

No. Not now. She forced herself to hone in on her surroundings and to concentrate hard on what she saw and heard. What she saw were small backpacks on low-to-the-ground pegs, full cubbies above them, and empty alphabet-block rugs in an unoccupied waiting area. The day had begun. Adults were off in different areas of the building caring for people of various young ages. Marcy, her partner in the infant room, was likely with a floater because she, Catie, was too lazy and incompetent to get out of bed on time. She heard a loud click that seemed to echo ominously in the spacious greeting area. A brusque, nasal voice summoned her.

"Catie, would you like to continue to study the contents of the cubbies, or would you like to step into my office to begin your workday?"

How about neither? But she didn't dare to utter a word, let alone such a disrespectful, hostile statement. She silently chastised herself for even thinking such a thing. She didn't want Irene to think she was weak, so she hoped she moved without a limp as she walked rather than hopscotched along the path that sported the classic children's game.

"Catie, I'm sure you want to get right to the infant room, but I need to check in with you first. You've been here only a few weeks, and you've been doing a fantastic job." At this, Catie felt her heart skip happily. It returned to its ordinary tha-thumps when Irene asked, "But no matter how good you do your job, you can't do it when you're not here. Do you understand the importance of coming to work on time? I don't know what people do in your country, but here it's important to pay attention to schedules and clocks."

Catie's cheeks burned, and she quickly looked at her feet. She didn't want Irene to see the ugly color of humiliation on her face. Florina's rant this morning about needing to be on time for school reverberated in her head. Even her teenage daughter, and son, too, adhered to schedules better than she did. "I do understand, ma'am, and I'm very sorry. This is no excuse, but there was an issue with my daughter needing something signed for school. I will make sure to always be on time from now on." She chewed on her thumbnail, a nervous habit that she loathed, and the second she caught herself, she forced her hand down to her side.

Catie could hardly bear the silence that followed. Her muscles tensed in anticipation of what her mind knew would follow. When no blows came, no scathing words, and she realized that while Irene had power over her, she was unlikely to beat her, she looked up. She wanted to squirm under Irene's intense gaze, but fear held her still. Finally, Irene uttered, "Good. I'm glad you understand the importance of punctuality. The people here depend on you. And speaking of that, Marcy is waiting for you. You'd better get in there before even more time passes."

"Of course. Thank you." When Catie opened the door to go, she positioned herself in such a way that Irene wouldn't see her hands tremble should she look. Without turning back, she hurried into the infant room and didn't even have time to catch her breath before someone thrusted a wailing baby into her arms.

"Catie, thank God you're here. This—"

"Marcy, I'm so sorry. I—"

"Oh! No. Don't apologize." Marcy was changing between shaking out her arms and poking at her ears, as if the shrieks could be coaxed out like pool water.

"But I'm late, and that's not okay."

"What? You think you're the only one who has ever been late?" Catie lightly swayed with the distraught baby as she rubbed his back. She kissed his head when he hiccupped between cries. She didn't answer Marcy's question because Marcy went on without giving her a chance. "Lemme guess." Catie watched Marcy straighten herself tall, square her shoulders, and pinch her face as if she had just eaten a heaping spoonful of the sweet and sour cherry soup Catie's sister had made all those years ago; accidentally omitting the cup of sugar that was to account for the "sweet" part of the dish made the soup painful to the cheeks. Now fully in a school-marmish pose, Marcy wagged her finger and spat, "Now, now, Missy. You must behave if you want to work in my daycare. I will not stand for naughtiness, you see."

Catie couldn't help it. She laughed. Making fun of another person wasn't all that funny, but there was a playfulness about Marcy that made her more spirited than malicious. Marcy slouched back to her own posture and said, "Yeah, don't worry about Irene. She's a grump to pretty much everyone."

This did nothing at all to ease Catie's discomfiture, but she didn't want to say more and risk alienating her partner.

Catie found herself at once both enervated and anxious. She wasn't witty or chatty like Marcy; she had nothing of value to offer Marcy or even this brief conversation. She felt awkward and needed to distance herself from Marcy right now; thus, she began a slow, swaying saunter around the room with the colicky baby in her arms. As she moved, she sang a soft Romanian lullaby. Gracefully, she shifted him so that, rather than resting over her shoulder, he nestled into her arms. Once he was snuggled into the crook of her left arm, she massaged his belly lightly with the fingers of her right hand. She tuned out the noises of the other babies. She tuned out her awareness of Marcy. She let the baby's cries fill her up and crowd out her own cries in her head. When the baby's cries softened and then ceased, the silence was enough to hold her own thoughts and feelings at bay. Her entire being was wrapped up in the baby in her arms, and for this one moment, Catie felt peaceful and content.

Marcy tip-toed over and stood beside Catie, smiling and seemingly admiring both her and the baby. "You, my dear, have a magic touch. What you can do with fussy baby Wallace here is miraculous. Seriously. No one but you can quiet him. How do you do it?" Her voice was a faint whisper.

Catie shook her head. "No," she whispered back, "you saw me. I just walked and sang softly and changed his position. Nothing special. He would have done this for you, too."

Marcy wouldn't let it drop. "Nope. No way. Quit selling yourself short. Out with it. What's your trick?"

Catie frowned. She looked down at the baby in her arms, now sleeping contentedly. In his sleep, he brought his hand to his face and stuck three fingers into his mouth. This little movement brought a smile to Catie's face. She looked at the baby thoughtfully then looked at Marcy. She sighed and furrowed her brows. "I don't know. I really don't think it's anything special. Maybe it comes from much practice. Maybe it comes a little from my grandmother, too." She trailed off and looked wistfully into the distance as her thoughts turned to her beloved grandmother.

"Not your mother?"

Catie looked quickly at Marcy. "No!" She looked down at the baby again and adjusted his position just a tiny bit so his neck looked more comfortable. When she looked back at Marcy, she said, "I mean, I didn't learn from my mother. My mother was fine, but it was my bunică, my grandmother, I adored. I called her Bunicuţă, which is like grandma or granny, because she was so close. My Bunicuţă Mădălina was sun and moon and stars and all of the flowers in the world to me."

Marcy smiled. "Catie, your accent sounds even more exotic when you talk about your past. It's like you're speaking of a distant time and world." Marcy had no idea. "I want to know more about you and what Romania is like. Will you tell me?"

Catie felt her eyes open wide. She quickly looked down at the baby in an attempt to hide her shock and fear. "Uh, tell you what? There really is nothing special about me to tell. Nothing at all." Her words tumbled out quickly. Her heart was pounding hard against her chest, and she hoped that Marcy couldn't hear it. She didn't dare tell anything. Who would want to hear, anyway? She was insignificant, a nobody, and certainly not worth hearing about.

"I bet there is. We all have stories. You're the first person I've met from another country. Humor me and tell me about yourself and your life in Romania."

Maybe Marcy was just curious in general. Catie wasn't accustomed to people taking an interest in her. Sure, sometimes Alexandru did, but that was usually driven by his own anxieties. He wasn't selfish, of course. Catie knew selfish, and her son was not selfish. But he was only a boy. Marcy was an adult, a coworker who seemed to want to know Catie. But why? Was she gathering information to use against her? Her heart pounded against her sternum. Was Dumitru using Marcy to find and punish Catie? Catie blinked rapidly in an attempt to bring her blurry surroundings back into focus. She didn't know what to say now. How could she respond? She had no words, not that words could crowd past the boulder in her throat, anyway. She tried to swallow, but it hurt. Her mouth had gone dry, but she was afraid to get a drink of water and risk throwing it up. Her mouth needed water, but her stomach was queasy and couldn't handle it. Typical of her stupid body. It was always at war with itself. She squeezed her eyes shut and sighed. She flinched when Marcy touched her shoulder.

Marcy abruptly pulled her hand away from Catie, but she remained where she was. Rather than mocking Catie or shunning her, she said gently, "Catie, I'm sorry. I wasn't trying to pry. You don't have to share anything you don't want to."

Catie looked at Marcy. She felt her cheeks burn with shame because of how she instantly overreacted. She hated herself for being this way. No wonder she was alone in the world. Maybe she could make things right by telling Marcy some general things about her life in Romania. Hopefully it wasn't too late. Had she driven Marcy away? Catie knew she wasn't worthy of friendship, but if Marcy was willing to be her work partner, that would be nice. It was nice to come to work and have somebody to talk to, smile with, maybe even laugh with. She hoped she hadn't screwed that up. She shook her head and sighed, "You don't owe me an apology, Marcy. Sometimes I react to things in a stupid way. It's not you. I actually would like to tell you some things about growing up in Romania."

Marcy clapped her hands together once. "Good! Because I want to hear about it."

Catie studied Marcy carefully to make sure the invitation to talk was real. Satisfied, she lowered Wallace into a crib, straightened, and looked, speechless, at Marcy.

"All right. Let's check diapers and bottles, attend to the wide-awake babies and stuff. I'll listen. You talk. Go."

"Go?"

"Go. You know, talk away."

"Where do you want me to start?"

"Hmmm. Maybe tell me about your grandmother."

Catie swallowed. She dried her sweaty hands on her shirt by squeezing the bottom of it, and she kept crunching and wringing and squeezing because she still had a nagging uncertainty despite her decision to talk to Marcy. Was talking to Marcy really safe? Instinctively she looked around, eyes wide and heart thumping again, searching for evidence that she'd be overheard now and punished later. Seeing nothing obvious, she closed her eyes, and after uttering a silent plea asking God to be okay with her talking to Marcy in general and about her life in particular, she searched the depth of her memories.

# Romanian Countryside

## *1975*

# Chapter 3

Needing another rest, Cătălina plopped the heavy wooden bucket down in front of her. Water sloshed out. She watched a little wave of it splat on her bare feet, roll off, and seep down into the hard ground. Squatting, she traced her index finger along the tawny skin revealed when the water took some of the dirt with it, dirt that had been enjoying riding on her feet since she stepped out of the bath basin last week. Mother had been livid that Cătălina had frolicked through the dusty yard before she was completely dry, because her feet had instantly become dirty again. Mother wouldn't let her wash them a second time, though. She told Cătălina that a naughty girl like her didn't deserve to clean herself twice, and that she was selfish and bad for even suggesting such a thing. Mother was right. Others needed to use that water, too. Cătălina had no right to clean off dirt two times in a row.

The wet paths of exposed skin blurred into the remaining dirt around them as Cătălina's eyes filled with tears. She didn't deserve her mother's love; that's why she didn't have it. Cătălina must really be rotten, she believed; otherwise her mother and her father and her sisters and her cousins and her aunts and her uncles would love her as much as they loved each other. Maybe if she got this bucket of water to them right away, they would be pleased with her. She would make them all so happy because she could be faster than the sun, delivering the first bucket of water before the bright yellow ball popped over the mountain top; she had to be speedy because the sky's quiet streaks of purples and pinks and the roosters' noisy *cucurigus* promised everyone that the warm light was on its way again. They'd see that she brought the first of several buckets all by herself without complaining. They'd admire how she did it even though her oldest sister Viorica, who was old enough to be more responsible, had abandoned Cătălina at the water pump. But no matter. Cătălina would show them all what she could do and that she could be counted on.

Picturing the warm reception she'd have when she returned quickly with the water, she smiled broadly, yanked the kerchief off her head, dried her tears, replaced the kerchief, and stood straight and tall. She shook her scrawny arms to prepare them for their task, and then she grasped the bucket's handle with both hands and hefted with a grunt. She staggered backwards a few steps but regained her balance and set out for home. Elated at the thought of making her family happy, she began to sing softly to herself as she wobbled along. She couldn't see the ground in front of her because the bucket of water she was hauling blocked her view, which meant that she also couldn't see the jagged rock smack in the middle of her path. When her foot struck the rock, she tripped and stumbled forward forcefully. She heard the bucket clatter to the ground just before she hit the ground with a thud that shook her body. Then she felt all of the water that she had been carrying in the bucket, water that was supposed to be for everyone's use to cook and to drink, rush underneath her tummy as she lay face-down in the dirt.

"Oh, no!" she leapt to her feet and snatched up the bucket, desperately hoping to save some of the water. But it was no use. The bucket was empty. She tossed it away from her and watched it bounce once, twice, three times, four before it stayed on the ground. She listened to the dirt scratch under the bucket as it rolled as much as the clunky handle would allow. Defeated, she plopped down beside it. She buried her face in her hands and began to cry. When she became aware of fiery pain, she slowly peeled her hands off her face to investigate the source. She cocked her head and studied her foot. She couldn't see the dirt anymore because now her foot was nearly covered in sticky blood. Her big toe was red and raw, and it throbbed painfully. Feeling sore and scraped and very sorry for herself, her sobs came again. A distant voice shocked her out of the despair. She couldn't make out the words, but she recognized the harsh bark. Mother! Cătălina couldn't let mother see her with an empty bucket!

Leaping to her feet and snatching the bucket for a second time, Cătălina sprinted back toward the pump. A family of white ducks quacked their displeasure at her when she charged into their path, but she didn't care. Their displeasure was temporary and couldn't hurt her. Mother's, though, only seemed to get worse and worse and made Cătălina feel hurt and sad. Nor did she care about the stinging pain in her foot. She couldn't let it stop her from filling her bucket before Mother saw it empty.

At last Cătălina reached the pump. She shoved her bucket onto the ground beneath the metal spigot and stepped beside the pump. She stretched herself as tall as she could, grasped what she could reach of the curvy handle that reminded her of a snake, and lifted with all her might. It didn't budge. Come on, pump! Cătălina squeezed her eyes shut and whispered,

"Dear God, I love you very much and thank you for this chance to give water to my family. Please let this pump work for me. Amen." She opened her eyes, shook her arms like she had earlier when she needed strength to lift the bucket, grasped the bottom of the handle, and pushed up. Even when she squatted down to use her legs, though, it didn't move. Cătălina glanced quickly over her shoulder. Seeing no one other than the now-content ducks, she resumed her efforts. She scrambled up the stone base of the water pump. It was almost as tall as she was, covered in places with slippery green moss, and she was very tired, so it wasn't easy. But she absolutely couldn't give up. Once she was near enough to the top, she braced her hands on the flat platform and hoisted. When she pulled herself up onto the surface, her feet scraped across the large stones. She grabbed her bloody foot and cried out in pain. As she rocked back and forth, she caught a glimpse of two figures in the distance. She inhaled sharply. She had to hurry!

Now that she could stand right behind the pump and pull, it was a bit easier to work. It made a horrible squeal that hurt her ears when she lifted the handle, but once she saw the water pour out into her bucket below, she didn't even care.

"Cătălina Gabor!" The growl announced Mother's arrival. "What in the world do you think you are doing? And why do you look like that? You're dress is ruined, and you are covered in mud. Why? You are even dirtier than usual." Mother didn't say anything about Cătălina's bloody foot. "You are no better than a pig, rolling in mud. But a pig knows no better. You should know better, but you are just a stupid little girl. And why are you just now filling the bucket? What have you been doing all this time? Don't just stand there with your mouth hanging open, answer me!"

Which question was she supposed to answer? Mother fired so many at her, and it didn't help that her heart was pounding so loudly in her head that she could barely hear or think.

"Cătălina!"

"Yes, mother." Cătălina swallowed hard, but something was stuck painfully in her throat. It was hard to breath and to talk, and even when Cătălina poked her throat with her fingers, it wouldn't go away.

"Well? I'm waiting."

"Um, well, Viorica filled the bucket earlier, but she left right away and I had to carry it all by myself, and—"

"Are you blaming your sister for your horrible mess? You little brat! Not only are you worthless, but you want to make your problems everyone else's fault!"

"No!" Cătălina shook her head so vigorously that she felt the ties of her kerchief slap against her neck with the back-and-forth motion of her head. "That's not what I meant! I—"

"Now you are contradicting me? Get down here at once."

Cătălina wasn't even firmly on the ground when her mother spat, "You stupid child. You left the pump on. Look at the water being wasted." She nodded sharply toward the bucket. "You are irresponsible. Get back up there and turn off the pump." Cătălina didn't dare to ask her mother to just reach over and shut it off; instead, she turned and obeyed.

As Cătălina worked her way down the stone foundation for the second time, she heard a soft, lilting voice. Despite her fear and pain, she smiled to herself. Bunicuță Mădălina was the other figure that Cătălina had seen, and she was here now.

"Violeta, be gentle. It looks like Cătălina has had a hard time."

"And now so will the rest of us have a hard time because she is late with the cooking water." Violeta gestured at her own mother. "You know as much as I do that we are all hungry. We eat only a little bit in the morning and a little bit at night."

"And that is Cătălina's fault?"

Violeta folded her arms across her chest. "It is her fault that our hunger will stretch out longer, yes." Despite the fact that Cătălina was standing less than two meters away, Violeta raised her voice. "Do you hear that, Cătălina? Now everyone has to wait even longer to eat because of your carelessness."

Cătălina hung her head. "Yes, Mother. I'm very sorry."

Violeta harrumphed. She shook her head and looked at Mădălina. She sighed. "You know how I feel. Cătălina shouldn't even be here."

Mădălina glanced quickly at Cătălina in time to see her wrap her little arms around her middle. Cătălina continued to look at her ground. To Violeta, Mădălina said, "How could you say such a thing? Cătălina is a delight."

"She's nothing but a hassle."

"She's only five years old, for Heaven's sake."

"She's another mouth to feed. Let President Ceaușescu feed her!" Violeta threw her hands up in the air and stomped toward a nearby tree. Looking only at the tree, she continued her rant and gestured animatedly. "He says no birth control, no abortions, says everyone have lots of babies, so many little Romanians to make a big pool of workers for a big, glorious Romania; then he should feed them all. He can raise them. But does he? No. He does nothing for us. Nothing at all! I'm tired of it." She spun toward Mădălina. "And I'm hungry. This child," she pointed sharply at Cătălina, "who was wanted only by Nicolae Ceaușescu and the Communist

Party, doesn't do any more than our government to make life better."

Mădălina rushed toward her grown daughter. She put her hands on her shoulders and ordered, "Violeta! Hush!" She looked around frantically. "What has gotten into you? Do you want the *Securitate* to overhear? Do you? You will be hauled away to prison never to be seen again!"

"Do you see any *Securitate* right now, Mother?"

"No. But that doesn't mean a thing. They are everywhere. All the time. They have eyes and ears. Some stand out in their military uniforms, yes, but some blend in and we don't know who is an ordinary citizen like us and who is secret police. You know that! You must watch what you say at all times!"

Cătălina, still looking down, didn't dare to look up. She didn't know what was worse: the things her mother had said about her or the things Bunicuță had said about the secret police. Cătălina was well aware of the *Securitate*, but she didn't realize that they were watching all the time. Was that right? Had they seen her waste water when she tripped clumsily? Would she go to prison? Would her mother? Would they be together, or would they be separated? She was afraid, and she began to shake. As much as she wanted to run to Bunicuță for comfort, she was rooted to her spot, frozen in fear.

Violeta jerked away from Mădălina. "I don't even care. I just don't care anymore." She looked over at Cătălina and shook her head sadly. "I'm going home. Bring the water, Cătălina." Without looking at her mother or her daughter, Violeta walked away.

Cătălina heard pebbles crunch as her mother departed. More pebbles scraped and slid, and soon the embroidered, frayed hem of Bunicuță's dingy dress appeared in Cătălina's vision. Instantly, Bunicuță's arms embraced Cătălina and pulled her in close. Weary and upset, Cătălina sobbed. It felt so good when Bunicuţă stroked her hair through her kerchief.

"Oh, my precious dear one, my Dragă. Please ignore the things your mother said. She didn't mean it."

Cătălina leaned back and sniffed. She ran her sleeve across her face. When she realized that she just made her sleeve dirtier than it already was, she looked, wide-eyed, at Bunicuţă.

Bunicuţă smiled. "It's okay. I don't think that makes your dress any worse for the wear."

Cătălina smiled back. She frowned. "Bunicuţă, Mother did mean those things she said. I know it. She is not nice to me like she is to my sisters. She is nicer to my cousins than she is to me, too. None of them like me, either." Her chin began to tremble, and Bunicuţă became watery and blurry.

"Dragă. You are a wonderful little girl. Sometimes people don't act nicely because they have big problems they are dealing with. Your mother worries about a lot of things, so she acts unkindly sometimes. It's not good that she does that, but always understand that it's because she has so many other problems. Some people let their problems dictate how they act. Your mother is like that."

"You're not like that, are you, Bunicuţă?"

Mădălina smiled. "I try very hard not to be."

"Well, I wish the rest of the family would be more like you."

Mădălina threw her head back and laughed. "Oh, Cătălina. I love you."

"I love you, too."

"Now, I think we should get this bucket of water back home, don't you?"

Cătălina's eyes grew wide, and her hands flew to her mouth. "Oh no! I forgot. Yes, we must hurry." She grasped the handle with both hands as she had done before, and she hefted. Mădălina reached over and grabbed the handle.

"Let's carry this together, shall we? And once we have it delivered, let's go visit Bunică Rodica so she can fix up that nasty owie on your foot."

Cătălina smiled up at her grandmother. She said a silent prayer to God thanking Him for Bunicuță Mădălina. As they walked quietly toward home, they passed the duck family that Cătălina had disrupted earlier. She studied them with a frown. "Bunicuță, look at those ducks."

"What about them, child?"

"Are they better than people?"

"Mmmm. That's a tricky question, Dragă."

"What do you mean, Bunicuță? How is it tricky? Either they are better than people or they aren't."

"No. Nothing in life is that easy, Dragă. Nothing is one extreme or the other. Why do you ask about the ducks and people?"

Cătălina looked down at her pulpy, bloody toe. "Well, when I was running back to the water pump, I zoomed through that cluster of ducks. I think I scared them. They waddled away speedy quick. I saw them scatter apart." Cătălina let go of the bucket and spread her arms and even her fingers to represent the scattering. Mădălina swiftly adjusted her hold on the water bucket, and with a deftness that comes from having balanced and carried thousands upon thousands of water buckets in her lifetime, kept every single much-needed drop in the bucket. Oblivious, Cătălina continued, "But when I reached the water pump and looked back, there they were in their little bunch again." She pulled her arms in tight against her and hugged her torso to represent coming together. She dropped her arms and sighed. "But I was scared, too. That's why I ran as fast as I could back to the pump. And I was even hurt. See?" She lifted the offended foot a few inches off the dirt and hiked up her dress so her grandmother could see it. While doing this, she hopped on her other foot so she would continue to move forward beside Mădălina.

"I do see. You were very strong and brave to go back to the pump for more water, Cătălina. That was good of you to do."

Cătălina sighed again, the deep sigh that should be reserved for someone who has lived so many more than five years. "But what difference does it make when people are different than ducks, Bunicuţă? Those ducks stayed together. Not like people. People push each other away. Ducks are better."

Gracefully shifting the bucket to her right hand, Mădălina placed her left hand on Cătălina's shoulder. "If you think about it, Dragă, people stick together, too, just like the duck family. Look at how human families live together. We share homes; infants all the way through the elderly live together under one roof. Think about our house. Your mom, dad, sisters, an uncle and aunt, cousin, and you and I are in a bunch." She lifted her hand from Cătălina's shoulder and closed her fist in a gesture similar to Cătălina's earlier one to indicate coming together. "And who lives next to us but more family? Your other grandparents and more uncles and aunts and cousins. We are a family of humans the way our feathered friends are a family of ducks."

Unconvinced, Cătălina shook her head. "No. It's not the same. All of those ducks were gathered together. No one was left out. The mama duck didn't quack angrily at any of her ducklings. People aren't like that. People get angry, and parents play favorites with their children. They love only some. Mamă doesn't love me at all. My sisters hate me and my cousins hate me. Ducks are better than people." Cătălina stopped, crossed her arms over her chest in a huff, tilted her head toward the now-blue sky, and shouted, "I wish I was a duck!"

As if to add another exclamation mark to Cătălina's point, the barking laughter of boys followed Cătălina's shout. She turned and looked down the village street to see a half dozen or so boys playing some sort of game. Two of those boys were her cousins, Filip and Cosmin. "Yeah, we wish you were a duck, too, and then we'd break your neck and roast you. We'd have a decent meal for once!"

Cătălina looked up at her grandma. "See?"

Mădălina put her hand on top of Cătălina's head. "It's okay. Filip is only showing off in front of his friends. It's what boys do. It's best to pay no mind and to just keep quiet. Smile at him, then turn away." Cătălina obeyed. Filip and Cosmin ignored her. Filip called to Mădălina.

"Hello, Mădălina. Is that water for dinner?"

"It is indeed, boys."

"Does that mean we're having something hot and fresh tonight?"

"It does, if Cătălina and I make it home to help cook."

"Yes! It's about time." Both boys were in front of Mădălina and Cătălina in a flash. Their simultaneous offer to carry the bucket degraded into a squabble. Mădălina settled it promptly by assigning the task to Cosmin, the older of the two brothers. Cosmin flashed Filip a smug grin before promptly sauntering toward home.

Filip bent down, swiped up a handful of pebbles and hurled them at Cosmin. Cosmin must have heard them hit the ground, for he called, "Missed me!"

Mădălina stopped Filip before he could repeat his angry gesture and suggested that he run out ahead of Cosmin, beat him home, and help start a cooking fire. His face brightened as he perked up at the idea. He looked at Cătălina and stood up straighter. "I am the one with the important task. You wouldn't know what that is like, would you? Oh, and by the way, you have something on your foot. Let me get it for you." He stomped on Cătălina's injured foot, laughed when she howled, and took off running, surpassing Cosmin in no time, and disappeared around the corner as he headed for home.

When Bunicuță knelt down, Cătălina clung to her. Her foot hurt, her feelings hurt, and her ego hurt. She had tried so hard today, and it all ended in disaster. She appreciated Bunicuță's soothing voice when she began to sing softly. When she stopped singing, Cătălina said, "See? Ducks are better than people."

Bunicuță hugged her tightly. "I'm a person, Dragă, and you're a person, and I'm confident that our love is stronger than duck love. God's love is stronger, too. Now never mind Filip. He's a person, too. God wants us to separate the sinner from the sin. We should always love each other, but that doesn't mean we always love what someone does." Cătălina cocked her head to one side as she thought about that. Bunicuță went on, "I will have a quiet talk with Filip's mother, of course, but the best way for you to handle him is to ignore what he did. Smile and act like it didn't bother you. That's how you should handle everyone when they do hurtful things. Just know that they don't mean to hurt you, and have forgiveness in your soul the way God has forgiveness within His whole being."

Cătălina's heart swelled at this talk of love and forgiveness and God. Her heart thumped in a funny way, though, when she thought of Mamă and Filip and even Cosmin a little, the way he just ignored her rather than standing up to his younger brother when he had said he would break Cătălina's neck and eat her. They clearly didn't love her the way Bunicuţă did. Bunicuţă. Her love was quiet and warm and covered her the way the beautiful tapestries draped themselves over the shiny crosses and sacred altar in their living room. Cătălina glanced over at the ducks pecking away at bugs. They were cute, and they weren't being mean to each other. Yet they didn't have their wings wrapped around each other in hugs and couldn't talk about love and forgiveness and God. Cătălina smiled up at her beloved Bunicuţă. Bunicuţă smiled back as she wiped Cătălina's face, streaked with a mess of dirt and tears, with her apron. More words weren't needed. They simply began to walk, hand in hand, toward home.

After the pair had walked yards, words were needed. Mădălina stopped walking and looked down at Cătălina. "Dragă, you're really limping now."

"Filip made my toe worse."

"Well, you are a brave and good girl to keep on without complaining. You're very strong, do you know that?" Cătălina looked down. "You are, Cătălina. You're only five but are already becoming wise. If you can just keep on without com-plaining, life is easier. Now, I think we should see Bunică Rodica before we help with the meal."

As they approached, Cătălina sensed that something was amiss, and she grew fearful even though she really couldn't pin-point why. Perhaps it was the scowl, more puzzled than angry, that befell Bunicuță's face and pulled her eyebrows down with it, or the way Bunicuță gripped Cătălina's hand just a tiny bit tighter. Was Bunicuță worried about the way the men were clustered and talking animatedly under that gigantic tree, the one that Cătălina loved to sit under and play house when she had a rare break from her chores? Certainly that couldn't be a problem, for the men always clustered and gestured and talked loudly. Was it the absence of laughter erupting in bursts as they talked? But why would that upset Bunicuță? Cătălina watched Bunicuță stare in the direction of the men. "What's wrong, Bunicuță?" Bunicuță didn't answer. She just kept staring and scowling, and it seemed that she was too distracted to have heard Cătălina. "Bunicuță?" No answer. Cătălina's heart began to pound furiously in her chest. She yanked Bunicuță's dress with her free hand. "Bunicuță!"

Cătălina must have shouted loudly enough to make Bunicuță pay attention, for to Cătălina's relief, Bunicuță looked swiftly down to look at her granddaughter. "What's the matter, child?"

"That's what I want to know."

"What do you mean?"

"You're worried. I can tell. Is it the men? But what are they doing wrong?" Cătălina knew her own eyes were open wide because she felt her skin pull under the dried places where the tears had been. Her palms were sweaty, too. Embarrassed, she pulled her hand away from Bunicuță's and wiped it on the front of her dress, which didn't do much good since it was still wet from the big spill she did. That's right! Mamă was so angry. Was this the problem? Was everyone upset with her? Were they going to send her away or give her to the *Securitate*? "Bunicuță! I'm sorry! I'm sorry I spilled and I wasted and I took too much time and I made everyone suffer for having to wait. I'll do anything to make it better. Please don't let them send me away." Cătălina dropped to her knees, folded her hands, and begged, "Please, God. I want to stay with my family. Please forgive me. I'll make it up to you if you let me stay, I promise." Over and over, Cătălina promised until Bunicuță slid her hands underneath Cătălina's arms and tenderly pulled her to her feet.

"What are you talking about, Dragă?"

"You're upset. You were staring at the men and frowning and you held my hand tighter. It's my fault. It's because I was bad already this morning. Now the *Securitate* will take me away forever!"

"Oh, child. You are a sensitive one. You have a special gift, I think, Cătălina. You are much attuned to feelings and emotions. That's why your own emotions are so strong. Everything is fine. Except for your foot, but we're about to take care of that."

Bunicuță's words did nothing to relieve Cătălina's fear and anxiety, but they did remind her of the throbbing pain in her toe. The immediate physical pain was worse than the indefinable fear, so Cătălina gave in and let Grandma Mădălina lead her to see Grandmother Rodica. Cătălina followed her Bunicuță like a duckling. The thought made her smile quietly through her pain.

# Chapter 4

Cătălina blinked and rubbed her eyes as she left the bright sunshine that, to her disappointment in herself, arrived long before she made it home, and stepped into the Bunică Rodica's dim cottage. Her eyes adjusted rapidly, and the dimness was no longer a gloomy sort of dark but was instead just a different kind of brightness than outside light. It was the homemade brightness of windows and lanterns and *kilims* and other decorations, and as such was almost better than the outdoors. Almost. Cătălina thought of the sun and sky as God's homemade light and thus the best. But since, according to Bunicuţă, He had given people the ability to bring His light inside, the cheeriness of their homes was special.

Cătălina stood very still just inside the door. Bunică Rodica was tending to a man whose arm looked crooked and had a big bump. Cătălina looked at her own arm, rubbed it to feel its smooth straightness, looked down and studied her throbbing, stinging toe, and then looked back up at the man sitting on the wooden structure that served as both night-time bed and daytime bench. His arm must hurt a lot, even more than her toe, yet there he sat, still, stiff, and stone-faced. His lips were pinched tight and he gazed straight ahead, not even turning toward the door when Cătălina and Bunicuţă arrived. Maybe that was a special thing to do to take away pain. Cătălina pursed her own lips, stiffened her body, and stared straight ahead of her at the cross on the wall. She tried very hard just to look straight ahead like the man was doing, but she couldn't help it; her eyes roamed the shiny gold cross, rimmed in black and colored inside with blue and red and depicting apostles and saints. She looked at the top bar and wondered for the millionth time what the letters said. She took in the middle bar onto which Christ's open arms were nailed, and her heart swelled as she felt the love that Christ had for people and the pain He was willing to endure because of that love. She looked at the bottom bar where His feet were nailed. That reminded her of her own foot, and somehow that made it hurt even more.

Maybe it was because her feelings were still hurt from Vioricas abandoning her earlier. Maybe it was from carrying the heavy bucket or climbing up and down the base of the pump and working the pump itself. Maybe it was the interaction with Cosmin and Filip. Maybe it was from thinking about the man's crooked arm with that big lump. Maybe it was from empathizing with Christ and his pain as she studied His arms—his body—nailed to the cross. Maybe it was all of it. Suddenly, Cătălina couldn't take it anymore. She was exhausted and her arms now ached and her toe hurt and then it hurt more when she thought of how Filip had stomped on it out of meanness and before that her own mother had been mean again, too, and she was still afraid because of the talk of the *Securitate*, and she began to cry.

Her grandmothers stood, whispering and gesturing animatedly about something, beside the bench, and they didn't seem to notice Cătălina. Occasionally a word would make its way to her, words like "systematization" and *"Securitate"* and "evacuate," but Cătălina didn't have the energy or ability right now to strain to hear more. It seemed like the man didn't either, because he just stared straight ahead. He sat as cold and rigid as the clay jugs and bowls arranged on the shelf above him. No one noticed Cătălina, just like always, but this time even Bunicuţă Mădălina ignored her. "Someone help me!" she wailed. "I think my toe is going to fall off, and it can just come off and go away because I'm tired of it hurting. But I don't know what to do when it comes off!" Still her grandmothers talked among themselves. "Why aren't you helping me?!"

At that earsplitting cry, the grandmothers, but not the man, turned. Cătălina didn't expect the man to pay attention to her any more than she would expect her own father to, but she did know that Rodica and Mădălina would. While neither rushed over, at least they finally addressed her.

Rodica spoke. "Cătălina, your toe will not fall off. Look here." Cătălina turned her head in the direction of Bunică's gesture. Once again, she saw the crooked arm with the unnatural bump. She shuddered. Rodica continued, "Ciprian, a man, is more important than a little girl. And his injury is worse than yours. I will take care of him, and then I will take care of you. You must wait quietly over there," again she gestured, this time to the bench on wall opposite Ciprian, "and not bother us with your shouts and pleas."

"Yes, Bunică. Of course." Cătălina hobbled to the bench, smiled at Bunicuţă as she left the cottage, lay down, and closed her eyes. She woke with a start to the pain of something rubbing her toe. Instinctively, she sat up straight and yanked her leg up close as she uttered a protest.

"Cătălina, be still. If you want the pain to stop, stop making such a fuss and let me fix it."

"Yes, Bunică. Thank you."

"That's better. Now, you really did a number on your toe. Your toe nail is gone, and the skin is all torn. But you're lucky. It's not broken like Ciprian's arm." Rodica worked as she talked. Cătălina dug her fingernails hard into her thighs to keep from crying out when her grandmother rubbed her foot with a stinging paste. Rodica continued, "You and Ciprian both were hurt by working so very hard so early this morning. The sky was light enough to shoo away the stars but not quite light enough to make it easy to work. Ciprian fell off a roof he was preparing to re-thatch and you stumbled on a rock you couldn't see."

Bunică Rodica's tone was chastising, but Cătălina didn't even care. Bunică had called her hard-working! That made the pain more bearable. She dropped her hands to her sides so she could look stoic like Ciprian had. If she was hard-working like him, she could take pain like him too.

She watched with fascination as Bunică washed off the paste, inspected the wounds, and draped the cloth back over Cătălina's foot. Next, her grandmother hefted herself off her stool, wiped her hands on her apron, massaged her lower back, and shuffled to the corner shelf stacked full with color- ful, woven baskets. Cătălina watched her open just a few of the baskets and remove a pinch of this and a couple pinches of that and put the pinches into a stone mortar. Cătălina didn't know exactly what her Bunică was selecting, but she knew that the containers held dried flowers and herbs. She knew this because she liked to sneak peeks into the baskets. She liked the variety of sights and smells. Some contents were earthy, some were sweet, and others were pungent, and there were faded yellows, purples, pinks, and reds; some looked like tiny buttons, some still looked like flowers, but the majority of the mixtures looked like brittle pieces of broken straw. Cătălina wondered what Bunică was going to do to her and if the pokey looking, dried-up plants would hurt, but she didn't want to be more of a bother than she already had been today. She just watched in stiff silence.

Bunică added some sort of liquid to the herbs in the mortar then returned to her stool. She said nothing but held the bowl close to Cătălina and let her watch as she ground the contents with a gray and black flecked stone pestle. Cătălina wrinkled her nose at the astringent smell but watched in fascination as the mixture gradually changed from a dark, soupy mess, resembling the water and leaves and pine needles that collected in deep divots after a storm, into a thick glob that looked a lot like porridge. Cătălina couldn't help it. She broke her silence. "I like that color," she told Bunică. "It's kinda like the red on your wall cross, but different. Not as bright and shiny. I like the cross red better, but this is nice, too."

Without looking up, Rodica informed Cătălina, "This is called red ochre."

"Ochre?"

"Yes."

"Oh."

That was the extent of the conversation about the paste. Cătălina was curious and wanted to know more. How did Rodica know what to use and how to use it? She longed to ask, but Bunică Rodica was not open to questions and chatter like Bunicuţă Mădălina. Cătălina was a little afraid of Rodica, so she never asked about the healing work she did for people near and far. Yet she wanted to know so many things. How did her grandmother know what to do? Why did people from different villages travel to see her when they needed to be healed of something? Didn't every village have someone who knew what to do when people were sick or injured? However, Cătălina knew better than to ask so many questions. She knew that she was already a nuisance, and asking questions only made it worse. Of course she was still very curious, but she kept her thoughts to herself to avoid being scolded.

Eventually, Rodica stopped mashing, and rubbed this new paste into the swollen toe. Still in silence, she wrapped Cătălina's foot in a plain white cloth. Cătălina knew that, for whatever reason, Bunică used plain cloths rather than cloths with woven motifs when she did her healing work. Raising herself to standing again, Rodica worked her way toward a wooden chest. Cătălina heard the familiar sound of the bolt sliding across the lock and the creak of the hinges when Bunică opened the lid. Cătălina wondered what she was up to. She found out soon enough when Bunică returned with an old pair of black boots, laces frayed and seams split. She stared wide-eyed as her grandmother put them on her feet.

"There. Your toe will heal soon enough. In the meantime, you can wear Ion's old shoes. They're far too big, but they'll keep the bandage secure. Walk carefully and take care not to trip while you go about your chores." With that, Rodica stood and began to clean up the aftermath of treating a broken arm and a damaged toe. For a brief moment, Cătălina awaited further instruction, but when Bunică continued to tidy without so much as a glance over her shoulder at Cătălina, she knew she had been dismissed. She must have lingered a moment too long, for Bunică did say one more thing. Without turning, her grandmother reminded her, "Cătălina, you do have chores to do."

Oh no! She didn't want to get hollered at again. Her hands were suddenly sweaty, and her stomach hurt. She jumped off the bed, ignored the pain in her toe, and tried to run toward the door. The gigantic shoes made her stumble.

"Cătălina," Bunică scolded harshly "Did you not listen to me, or are you too stupid to understand? Those shoes are too big. You must walk quickly but carefully."

"Yes, Bunică." Afraid to linger any longer, Cătălina hobbled out of the quiet house and into the lively outdoors. Food preparations were underway for tonight's meal. Cătălina clopped toward the giant kettle suspended over the fire. She stretched herself as tall as she could, but it wasn't enough to allow her to grasp the handle, lift the lid, and peek inside.

"Ha!" A voice taunted, "You can't do it! You can't even look inside a pot because you're not good enough. You're just a short, stupid girl!" Cătălina didn't have to look to know it was Filip, her bully of a cousin who never seemed to leave her alone. Why couldn't he be like the other children and just ignore her?

"Go away, Filip!"

"Don't tell me what to do!" Filip shoved her from behind. Cătălina cried out as she fell forward toward the fire. She squeezed her eyes shut so she didn't have to see the flames attack her. But she didn't feel the flames. Instead she felt the whoosh of air as she was lifted up, up, up by the strong arms of her uncle Eduard.

Eduard adjusted Cătălina on his hip before rebuking Filip, who now stood with his arms crossed tightly over his chest, glaring at Cătălina. "You should know better than that, Filip. You're five years older than Cătălina, and you're a boy. You shouldn't have pushed your cousin when she was so close to the fire." Would it have been okay for Filip to push her if they weren't near the fire, Cătălina wondered. She thought it best to keep her question to herself, though, so she kept her mouth shut. Eduard was still addressing Filip. "...*mămăligă* for lunch, so—"

"Aw, cornmeal porridge again? That's all we ever have! What is this then?" Filip gestured angrily toward the pot. "I thought we were having something better." He kicked one of the rocks rimming the fire.

"Filip! The women are preparing tonight's meal. For lunch, it's *mămăligă*. Oana and Violeta are preparing it, and they need eggs and cheese to top it. That always makes it better, doesn't it?" He smiled broadly at Filip, who brightened and nodded. "Can they count on you to gather eggs?"

Cătălina glanced in the direction of the chickens, bobbing their heads, strutting to and fro, and making noise. *Like boys*, she thought. She bit her cheeks and looked away so she wouldn't laugh. When she looked back, Filip was gone, already sprinting to his important task.

"Now for you, Cătălina. I have a very important task for you." She looked at her uncle with eager anticipation. She had another chance to do something good today, to make up for all of the problems she had caused. Not only that, it was for her uncle Eduard, the man who gave his hugs freely to his wife Oana and his little son Dionisie and still had more left over that he so very often shared with Cătălina. When *Bunicuță* led the prayers or told stories by the fire on cold winter nights, it was Eduard who invited her to sit with him and would snuggle with her beside Oana while she cuddled Dionisie. Eduard was the most patient man she knew. Cătălina didn't even mind that he didn't ask if her toe was up to a task. It didn't matter, because she wouldn't let a toe get in the way of what the rest of her needed to do. She grinned and put her arms around his neck. "Of course. I'll do anything you ask, Eduard."

Eduard jostled Cătălina on his hip. "What a good little girl you are, Cătălina. That's always a proper response. Before I tell you, though, would you like to see inside the pot?"

"Yes, please!"

Eduard pulled the kerchief off of Cătălina's head and used it to protect his hand from the heat of the handle as he lifted the lid. Cătălina leaned forward but kept her arms wrapped around Eduard's neck because the flames still made her heart pound after her cousin-induced near catastrophe. She looked at the contents, inhaled to see what spices she could smell, wrinkled her nose, and looked back at Eduard.

Eduard hooted. It hurt her ears, but she tried not to show it. She didn't want him to put her down because she rather liked being held this way. In a voice as booming as his laughter had been, he said, "Wow. I didn't think someone so little could wear such a disgusted, skeptical expression. What? You don't think this looks scrumptious?" Cătălina shook her head and stuck out her tongue. Another guffaw from Eduard preceded his glancing around as if he were checking his surroundings for spies. Perhaps he was, thought Cătălina. Was he checking for *Securitate*? Was she going to be taken away to prison? She didn't really know what *prison* meant, but from the way Bunicuţă had sounded terrified earlier when she and mother were talking at the pump, Cătălina just knew it was a very bad place. She clutched Eduard tighter. When he looked back at her, he was relaxed. His eyes twinkled; they weren't pinched and tight like Bunicuţă's had been. Eduard whispered, "I don't think it looks good either. Not at all!" He made a face and stuck out his tongue. "That's because it isn't good right now. Know what's in there?"

"It looks like bones."

"It is bones. Pig bones. I helped butcher the pig, thank you very much. Some of the meat will be used to make tonight's *mititei*. These bones need to boil down first to mix with the meat and whatever spices women use in this dish." He replaced the lid and stuffed Cătălina's kerchief into one of the front pockets on her dress.

Sausages! One of Cătălina's favorites, a rare treat for them all. Her mouth began to water at the thought of the savory meat, and her stomach growled in anticipation. Eduard tickled her. "Hungry?"

"Well, no more than usual, I guess, but I'm excited to eat tonight."

"Cătălina, you are a very good girl for never complaining about being hungry. Some of the others should learn from you, especially Filip." Eduard smiled at her, and Cătălina beamed. Her smile faded, though, when it occurred to her that mother and father had made it painfully clear that she wasn't allowed to complain or generally express displeasure. So was she really a good girl on her own, or had mother and father just pounded it into her? She didn't want to think about it. Thankfully, her uncle changed the subject.

"Now I need you to do that special job for me. Are you ready?"

Cătălina didn't know what the special job was, but whatever it was, she would make herself ready. She'd do anything for her Eduard, and for Oana, too. "I'm ready!"

"That's my girl!" Cătălina felt her cheeks get that warm glow that happened when she was happy. Like the *mititei*, it was a rare treat.

"What can I do?"

"Everyone is too busy to take time to watch Dionisie. He's crawling around everywhere getting in the way and could get hurt. I don't want my son to get hurt. Will you watch him today? Play with him and keep him out of trouble?"

Cătălina thought she would burst with glee. Taking care of Dionisie was her favorite thing in the world. Well, it was tied for second. She also loved doing anything with Bunicuţă. She felt proud that Eduard would trust her with his son. Letting go of Eduard, she clapped her hands in excitement. "Oh, yes! Where is he now?" She wriggled out of Eduard's arms and hopped to the ground.

"Last time I saw him he was in the house getting underfoot."

"I'll go get him and keep him out of the way." Without waiting for a response, she took off, probably faster than Filip when he ran off. She forgot that she was wearing Ion's old shoes, and she fell with a thud and an oof as she sprawled across the ground yet another time this morning. But no matter. She had a job to do; she was being allowed to take care of Dionisie. Her injury wasn't important, and she had to just ignore the hurt. Yanking the shoes off her feet and tossing them aside, thinking only of Dionisie rather than the consequences that would surely come from casting off the shoes that her grandmother had put on her feet, she hurried to the house to find her younger cousin.

# Chapter 5

· · · · · · · · · · · · · · · · · ·

    Cătălina felt like a little leaf beetle sitting on one leaf of a humongous oak tree when she sat down on the wooden bench of the massive four poster loom. It was the first time she had been allowed to sit there, and she looked around reverently. She scooted as far forward on the bench as she possibly could without falling down onto the dirt floor beneath her. She felt her toes brush against the wooden pedals, but she couldn't make the pedals move. Maybe if she slid up just a little more, she could position her feet on them better, more solidly. She squeezed the back of the bench with both hands, stretched herself as long as she could—she could feel the tightness of her muscles as her body reached and extended—and pushed with her toes. One of the pedals moved! She had actually made it move! She was becoming a weaver just like Bunicuţă! But Bunicuţă used her hands, too. Cătălina shifted her weight to her left hand while simultaneously whooshing her right hand to the bar in front of her. Quickly, she did the same with her left hand. Now she was hanging, suspended, from the loom. It was an awkward position, and she lost her tentative grip. She slipped off the bench and landed hard on her behind on the floor under the loom.

Cătălina wasn't hurt, but she was alarmed. Panic rose up into her belly, making it hurt, and from there up her throat, making it burn, and then up into her head, making it throb and spin. What if her failure to even sit on the loom made Bunicuţă decide that Cătălina was too stupid and clumsy to learn how to weave the linen that would be made into so many things, like clothing and the cloths that were embroidered intricately and used as stunning *kilims* on alters, over tables, on crosses, and other such things? No! That couldn't happen, could it? Bunicuţă had promised Cătălina when she had turned six during the summer that she would teach her how to weave when autumn came. It was a promise. Bunicuţă always said that a promise is a promise. Worried that she had just done something to break the sacred vow, Cătălina scrambled out from under the loom. She crawled out, popped up to standing, and bent over to brush off her dress. A shrill shout slapped Cătălina to attention. She stood straight, stiff, and still like those *Securitate* men who had been hanging around the village quite a bit lately. Her mouth went dry and her throat seemed to close. She coughed.

"Cătălina! Just what do you think you are doing?"

"I'm waiting for Bunicuţă, Mamă. She's going to teach me how to weave." Cătălina looked at her feet.

"Look at me when I'm talking to you, child." Violeta crossed their home in four stomps. Cătălina pressed her back into the loom, but of course that did nothing to hide her or make her disappear. Her mother placed both hands on Cătălina's cheeks and jerked her head up so Cătălina looked her in the eye. "There. That's better. Stupid girl. Now, tell me what you were doing just now."

"Mamă, I'm going to have a weaving lesson. Bunicuţă said she'd be right back. I'm waiting for her."

"Playing on that loom is not waiting nicely!" Cătălina winced at the intensity of Mamă's voice. Even though her face was up close to Cătălina's, their noses almost touching, she continued to bellow as if she were yelling at her from the other cottage. Cătălina lived here in this bungalow with Bunicuţă, Mamă and Tată, her sisters, her uncle Eduard and aunt Oana, and her baby cousin Dionisie. The rest of her family lived next door. No matter where anyone was at this moment, Cătălina was sure they could hear Mamă screaming at her for naughtily playing on the loom. Her cheeks felt warm at the thought, not a cozy warm but the warmth of ugly gray coals as they turned to ash and died out. Mamă continued her tirade. "You are useless, Cătălina. Useless and irresponsible. What if you had broken it? Huh? What then, you stupid girl? Go." She pointed to the door. "Get out of here. Go find your sisters and tell each of them that you will be doing their chores again today."

Cătălina looked through her welling tears and noticed a blurry and distorted Filip peek into the cottage, stick out his tongue, disappear, promptly reappear, stare at Cătălina, and disappear again. At the moment, Cătălina couldn't care less about her cousin. She cared only about what was happening with her mother. "No! Please, Mamă. Bunicuţă said I could weave now, weave right beside her. I want—"

"Don't. You. Ever. Talk. Back. To. Me." Violeta slapped Cătălina hard across the face in emphasis. She grabbed her shoulders and gave them a hard shake. "Ever! What you want doesn't matter. Now get out." Violeta pointed sharply to the door and held her arm that way.

Cătălina bent her knees so she could slip down and out of Mamă's grasp. She ducked away and ran, sobbing, toward the door. She didn't make it out of the door, for she bumped smack dab into someone. Cătălina gasped and looked up. Bunicuţă! Her heart started to pound, pumping relief and sorrow and shame and fear and hope through her whole body, so many emotions so quickly that she started to tremble.

"Whoa. Dragă. Are you running away before we start our lesson?" When no one answered her question, Mădălina looked at Violeta and frowned. "What's going on here?" Her scowl deepened as she listened to Violeta's litany of tattle-tale-like complaints about Cătălina. When Violeta closed her mouth and rested her tongue, Mădălina spoke firmly yet quietly. "As you well know, I am teaching Cătălina to weave. We will proceed with our lesson now, so please excuse us."

"Mother! Cătălina was being disobedient and naughty by playing on that loom."

"On the contrary, it sounds to me that she was doing as she was told. She sat on the bench and wanted to explore how things work. That shows curiosity and intelligence, not impishness and stupidity as you say. Now, go or stay, but step out of our way so we can work the loom."

"Mother!" Violeta said again. "I have given Cătălina different orders. She is my daughter, and—"

"And you are mine." Mădălina's words were measured and her tone cool, belying the softness of her stance and calmness of her delivery. She said nothing more, nor did she make a move toward the loom. She simply looked at Violeta until Violeta moved.

As Violeta walked toward the door, she paused briefly and glared down at Cătălina. "When you have finished your lesson, you will do all of your sisters' chores. I am on my way to tell them they are done for the day."

"Yes, Mamă," Cătălina whispered. Without another word, Violeta strode out the door.

Cătălina didn't know what to do or where to look. She had displeased Mamă again. She never did anything right, no matter how hard she tried. She should be used to Mamă's tirades by now, but she couldn't get used to her cutting rebukes any more than she could the cutting pangs of hunger that lived in her belly. Maybe Mamă's behavior wouldn't sting as much if she hated her other daughters, too. But it was only Cătălina that she didn't love. Clearly, Cătălina was doing something wrong or had a horrible flaw that made her unlovable. But Bunicuță loved her. Cătălina covered her face with her hands and trembled. What if she kept messing up, and Bunicuță stopped loving her? What would happen then? Eduard and Oana were nice to her, but did they love her? She loved them. She tried so hard to show everyone her love by being obedient and helpful, but she always did something wrong. Now Bunicuță might stop loving her, too, because of her behavior on the loom. She'd never get to learn to weave and finish learning how to embroider. She'd never make nice things to show her love for people and for God. "I'm sorry! Please forgive me," she wailed through a fresh round of sobs.

Bunicuță knelt in front of Cătălina. "Dragă, stop your tears," she crooned. "Please look at me." When Cătălina complied, Bunicuță lifted her apron and wiped Cătălina's tears and nose. Cătălina bit her lip and breathed with short, ragged, uneven breaths, but she didn't cry. She relished in the feel of the fabric, a little scratchy and a little soft all at once, rather like Bunicuță herself. This was one of Cătălina's favorite aprons. She loved the deep blue of it, like the night sky when a million stars give it a heavenly hue. She loved to run her fingers along the white dashes that lived inside the few wide stripes that ran from Bunicuță's waist all the way down to the bottom of the apron. Cătălina did that now, and when she reached the bottom she played with the colorful tassels hanging around the apron's edge. Somehow, making the tassels dance made her feel better, calmer. "There. That's better," Bunicuţă said quietly. She mentioned nothing more about what had happened. Instead, she took Cătălina's hand and led her to the loom, which stood, solid and unbroken, patiently waiting for them. Cătălina smiled at it and up at her Bunicuţă.

Sitting on the loom's bench beside Bunicuţă made Cătălina forget her troubles. She swung her feet as she listened to the wood bang and clack with the loud yet hollow sound of very old, very dry wood. She cherished the rhythmic sound of the parts of the loom working together, the dull, faded wood of the body of the loom that contrasted with the dark, shiny wood of the bench; the bench had been polished with the labor of love as women in her family spent countless hours sitting there, creating the essentials of life and making them beautiful. Too soon, the noise ceased and Bunicuţă folded her hands in her lap. "There. All done!"

Cătălina giggled. "You didn't make anything!"

"What do you mean? I was weaving."

"No you weren't!" Cătălina laughed.

"But why not?" Bunicuţă looked perplexed.

"Bunicuţă! You don't have any thread in the loom! See?" Cătălina scrambled to her knees and pointed forward where the thread was usually strung.

"Ah! I see now. How smart you are, Cătălina. You figured out the first step of the loom before I even told you." Cătălina beamed with pride. "It's a good lesson to remember, Dragă. Never act before you are prepared." Cătălina, sensing some deep importance in that statement, grew solemn and looked into her Bunicuţă's eyes. After a few seconds,

Mădălina swiveled to face the other way and rose from the bench. She beckoned for Cătălina to follow, and together the two of them searched through a large trunk, Mădălina instructing Cătălina on thread selection for various uses. When they returned to the loom, they began the laborious process of threading the heddle and the reed. Cătălina's nimble little fingers took to the task naturally, as did her whole being. Sitting next to Bunicuţă, working in silence, they fell into the same rhythm, and it seemed as though they were working as one. She silently thanked God for giving her the ability to prepare the loom, and she asked him to let her be with Bunicuţă forever and ever. She felt a warm glow deep inside of her, and she hoped it meant that God had granted her wish.

As if she had read her mind, Bunicuţă looked down at Cătălina and smiled a little smile. "You are a natural at this, Dragă. I think God has given you a special gift. We will be thanking him in the perfect way. Do you know what we're making?" Cătălina shook her head. She hadn't asked because asking too many questions was disrespectful; it was better to keep her mouth shut and wait for others to speak when ready. Bunicuţă continued, "We're going to make one more of these." She reached up and pulled a basket off the shelf above them, lifted the lid so Cătălina could peek inside, and then tenderly lifted out the top cloth. She unfolded it to reveal a rectangular cloth, smallish in size but large enough to cover Bunicuţă's arms up to her elbows and hang down off her arms a few inches on both sides. The middle third was white while the ends were embroidered in elaborate patterns in vibrant red, blue, and yellow.

Cătălina bounced up and down. "That's like the ones we have! The ones we drape on the crosses and the altar and the shelves when everyone comes from all around on Sundays when you do church. I love those! They're so beautiful. Are we really making one, Bunicuță?"

"We are indeed. I've been making these for the last week. See?" Again she let Cătălina peer inside. Cătălina stared in. She closed her eyes and breathed in the scent of new cloth: a pure kind of clean that doesn't need soap to chase away odors and dirt, combined with a light scent of the loom itself; old wood mixed with the smooth, mellow, only slightly sour smell of the linseed oil used to keep the loom in good working order. She always delighted in how things came together, mingled and shared themselves and formed something great. She breathed deeply again. This time her nose picked up the new-cloth smells plus the scent of the old basket. She tried to imagine what this combination smelled like and thought maybe it all smelled of sticks that fell from trees during the winter and became buried deep under the snow. When springtime came and the snow melted, there were the sticks, smelling damp and woodsy but bathed in the fresh, clean perfume of spring. Yes, this basket and its contents combined to make something fresh and delightful. Cătălina opened her eyes and beamed up at Bunicuță. "Go ahead, Cătălina. You can touch them. Just don't take them all out and unfold them. Refolding will take time away from our weaving project."

Gently, Cătălina slid her hand into the container. She explored the linen with her fingers, and counted aloud as she determined just how many little tapestries Bunicuță had made recently. "One...two...three...four...five...six... seven...eight." Keeping her hand in the basket, she looked at her Bunicuță and exclaimed, "Wow! That's a lot. And we're making another one. Why?" She put a hand over her mouth.

"Whoops. I'm sorry to ask questions," she muttered through her hand.

Bunicuță smiled at her. "It's okay. We're taking these to the Orthodox Church in the next village. The word is that they have a new priest. I want to give him this gift and ask him for permission to use his church." She looked at nothing in particular and said, almost to herself, "It would be marvelous to worship the Lord in a real church again instead of here."

"Would you still lead the prayers and everything, Bunicuță, or would the new priest?" Cătălina's hand had remained in the basket, fingertips rubbing the textured embroidery, but now she pulled it out and chewed nervously on her thumbnail. She loved the way Bunicuță prayed with everybody, on Sundays when they came to their home and the other days of the week, too, when people came to her for guidance. She was so proud that it was Mădălina, her very own Bunicuță, who brought God so close. She didn't want to give that up.

"Of course I would, Cătălina. The priest we're going to visit is an Orthodox priest, not Greek Catholic like us. I would just like to have a proper sanctuary for worship."

Cătălina wrinkled her forehead and cocked her head to the side. Forgetting that she wasn't supposed to ask questions, she inquired, "Why haven't we used the church before?"

"The old priest wouldn't let us," Mădălina informed her matter-of-factly. Cătălina opened her mouth to ask why, but promptly shut it again. When her pressing question forced her mouth back open, she clamped it shut and pushed her palms against her jaw to hold it in place. Mădălina smiled and rested her hand on Cătălina's head. "You want to ask why we couldn't use the church, don't you?" Cătălina nodded vigorously but kept her hands against her jaw. "It's not a fancy answer, Dragă, and it's not a nice one, either. Our religion was done away with long before you were born, almost thirty years ago. According to President Ceauşescu and those before him, the Greek Catholics aren't supposed to exist."

Cătălina opened her eyes so wide that she felt air on her eyeballs. "You mean we're supposed to be dead? Why?" Her eyes were big; her voice was small.

"I don't know, Cătălina. The communists didn't like Greek Catholics, and they did a lot of very bad things, cruel things, to our priests and bishops and to people that disobeyed by going into churches, too. Many were thrown in prison or executed. But most of us ordinary people were left alone. We just can't have churches of our own, and we're not supposed to worship. Try as they might, though, the government can't control what's in our hearts. They can't keep us from loving God and worshiping him. We just do it in secrecy."

Cătălina's heart was like a goat in her chest, kicking hard against her ribs. "But if the *Securitate* find out, will they kill us? Will we be dead? Is that why they killed grandfather when Mamă was in your tummy? Did he try to go to church? What if they find out that we are having church here? What will happen?" Her questions came out in a rush, and her voice trembled with fear.

Mădălina walked first to one window and then the other. She peered out of each of them, taking care to look in all directions. She did the same at the door before returning to sit on the bench of the loom. She closed her eyes and sighed. After what to Cătălina seemed like an eternity, Mădălina opened her eyes. "Listen carefully, Cătălina. I will only say this once, and then I am done talking about it. Talking can be dangerous. It can make things worse than they already are, so it is much better to remain silent and accepting of what is." Mădălina looked intensely at Cătălina. Cătălina felt compelled to nod, even though Bunicuţă hadn't asked her a question. Mădălina gave a curt nod in return. "Good.

"Your grandfather was killed in the middle of winter in 1947. He didn't like the communists who were taking over Romania after the war. He resisted them, and he was killed for it, as was anyone who tried to stop the communists. When Nicolae Ceauşescu took power in 1965, he was even worse than the leader before him had been. Brutal." Mădălina gazed out the window. Cătălina stretched herself straight and tall and strained her neck in an attempt to see what her grandma was looking at, but she couldn't see anything special. It looked like she was staring at nothing at all. Still, Cătălina looked at that nothing with her. Mădălina shivered.

Finally she looked down at Cătălina. "Dragă, the only thing the people of Romania can do is to go along with what President Ceauşescu and his government order. It's the only way to survive, to live.

"It's why the one single church left is the Orthodox Church. Instead of resisting, they cooperated, so even though Ceauşescu doesn't like God and religion, he allows the Orthodox Churches to exist." Mădălina turned to face Cătălina squarely. Cătălina had long since stopped fingering the cloths that Bunicuţă had carefully woven and embroidered, so her hands were free. Mădălina picked up Cătălina's hands and held them in her own. "Do not be fooled by this, my little Cătălina. The government is everywhere, and they don't trust anyone, including the Orthodox leaders. Ceauşescu uses the Church, but the minute he is angered by them, he will wipe them out as swiftly as he did the Greek Catholic Church." Cătălina felt the bones of her knuckles and fingers crash together painfully when Bunicuţă squeezed them, but she didn't want her to let go.

When Bunicuţă said nothing further, Cătălina asked tentatively, "Is it dangerous to ask the new priest for permission to use his church? Will we be killed?"

Mădălina rubbed her thumbs over Cătălina's hands. "It's disobedient. That's why we will be extremely cautious. Sometimes, if you're careful and not too pushy, it's okay to take a risk. Most of the time, though, risks aren't okay. Înţelegeţi?"

Cătălina nodded solemnly. "Yes, Bunicuţă, I understand."

Mădălina leaned forward and looked at the lidless basket that sat beside Cătălina. "I think we need to get the last cloth in the basket and deliver it, don't you? Are you ready to get to work?"

At last, Cătălina brightened again. "Yes! Of course I am!" Together, Cătălina and her grandma finished threading the loom. Cătălina was too small to work the big parts; Bunicuţă did that, but Cătălina stood by her side the entire time, neither whining nor wavering, happily helping Bunicuţă guide the shuttle from right to left and back through to start over.

Next came the embroidery. Cătălina had been learning how to do that and had practiced on her own little scraps of cloth. To her delight, Bunicuţă let her embroider with her right on this special cloth. Cătălina chose the beautiful yellow thread. "I like all of these colors, Bunicuţă. Blue reminds me of the sky. Red reminds me of some of my favorite flowers. But yellow is best of all because it reminds me of the sun."

Mădălina smiled at her. "What's special about the sun, Dragă?"

"The sun is warm, and it feels nice. It shines down on me and makes me feel good. It makes things grow. And there's enough for everyone and everything. The sun is a lot like God's love, I think. I want to be like the sun."

"I think you are most right, and you are indeed like the sun, Cătălina. You are only six years old, yet you have a lot of love shining out of you."

Cătălina beamed, then turned her attention to her embroidery. She watched her Bunicuţă deftly weave intricate patterns of religious symbols and geometric shapes. Cătălina added touches of yellow here and there as she was instructed. Cătălina was enjoying herself so much that she was disappointed when Bunicuţă put down their creation and announced, "There. We're done. Nice work, Cătălina. You are learning well, and you have quite a talent for this." Cătălina felt a flush of joy and pride at Bunicuţă's words. She smiled happily even though she was still disappointed that they were done.

Her smile faded. "Thank you, Bunicuţă. Now I must go. I have my sisters' chores to do." Cătălina felt herself droop. Even her toes dipped more toward the ground. She didn't do it on purpose, and she knew she was supposed to sit up straight, but her sadness was too heavy. It wasn't too heavy for Bunicuţă, though. Nothing seemed to be. She felt her Bunicuţă's hands slide under her arms and gently pull her erect.

"Yes you do, Dragă, but first I'd like you to accompany me to the next village and help me offer our gift." She handed Cătălina the basket of sacred cloths. Cătălina reached out and slowly wrapped her fingers around the smooth handle— such a contrast to the knobby basket itself— and then she pulled it toward her slowly, reverently. She slipped her arm under the handle and let the basket hang from the crook in her elbow. She slid her other hand into Bunicuţă's. Bunicuţă's hand was rough like the basket, while her own was smooth like the handle. Cătălina liked the feel of both the basket and Bunicuţă's hand, and she hoped her own hands would become course like that someday.

Cătălina was so excited to be going on this important outing that she didn't even care when Mamă, after talking to Bunicuţă, looked down at her and grumped, "Go, Cătălina, but you will pay for this. Tomorrow you will do all of your sisters' work plus your own, and you'll do this for a very long time." Nor did she care when she was ignored by most of her relatives when she left with Bunicuţă. Filip didn't ignore her; he called out that she was a stupid, worthless girl. No one corrected him, so he must be right. Still, she was going on an outing with Bunicuţă, so she was content.

They walked in silence for a long time on the dusty road. Golden fields of wheat waved at her, and gorgeous sunflowers, rows upon rows of them that seemed to stretch into forever, looked at her with happy faces. Cătălina felt warm inside, and welcomed. Goats and cows and sheep and wooden windmills looked like big polka-dots on fields that were turning brown under the autumn sun. Ducks and geese shared the road with granddaughter and grandmother, waddling by to a destination unknown to Cătălina. Occasionally, a horse pulling a cart with a person or two plus goods clip-clopped by them. What a great way to get around, Cătălina thought. Her own family didn't have horses; they didn't have enough land. That's why she and Bunicuţă were walking to the next village. Cătălina's legs ached, but she didn't complain because Bunicuţă seemed fine. To distract herself from the aches, she fixed her gaze on the trees dotting the countryside and made a game out of seeing how many different colorful hues she could spot in a single tree. She noticed with disappointment that most trees were green plus just yellow or just orange or just red. She wanted to see a tree that had leaves of all these colors together. When occasional gusts of wind blew some leaves off the trees, the leaves swirled together and landed in a colorful heap. She loved seeing the bright mix, but she hoped that the trees weren't sad to be losing their leaves.

At long last, they reached the village. It wasn't difficult to find the Orthodox Church. It was the most magnificent building Cătălina had ever seen in her entire six years of life. Her village had nothing this glorious. It was made not of wood but of stacks upon stacks of stone, a little similar to the water pump in her village, but different, too. The stones that made up the base of the water pump were ordinary round rocks. These were square and fit perfectly together. Some of the square stones were small, but most were big. Basket of linens clutched in one hand, Cătălina reached out tentatively with her other hand and touched one. She spread her fingers wide across its cool surface. The stone was bigger than her whole hand! Like the rocks that formed the base of the water pump in her village, these square stones had moss growing on them. Fingers still splayed, she rubbed her hand back and forth across these stones that were part of the towering old church. She closed her eyes and wiggled her fingers; now they brushed against the spongy moss, now they rubbed the rough, hard stone. This was like her family, she mused. Some were like the moss, soft and yielding and able to curl around some-one. Most though, were like the stones, hard and un-giving, hurtful if you rubbed them the wrong way. She shivered and jerked her hand away.

Her hand hit the building again immediately because she didn't know that Bunicuţă was going to open the door, and as it swept toward her, its low groan startled her and made her jump. She dropped the basket, scampered to Bunicuța's side, wrapped her arms as far around her as she could—her hands couldn't touch each other, but they didn't need to for they had Bunicuța's apron to hold on to—and looked up at her Bunicuța. Mădălina held the door so it no longer moved. "What's the matter, Dragă? You're not afraid, are you?"

Cătălina looked down. She couldn't lie to her Bunicuța, but how could she tell her the truth, that she was suddenly terrified by what might be waiting behind this ominous door? Instead of answering, she asked a question of her own. "Why did the door make that awful sound, Bunicuța?"

Mădălina looked down at Cătălina and placed a hand on her head. "Because it's very old, Cătălina. It's been here much longer than either of us has. It's been here for hundreds of years, and it will be here hundreds more. You wouldn't stop loving somebody just because they were old and a little noisy, would you?"

"No!"

Mădălina smiled a smile that was bigger in her eyes than it was on her lips. Her eyes roamed from Cătălina's eyes to her kerchief. She ran her fingers gently down along the sides to the knot under Cătălina's chin. She adjusted the knot and rubbed the ends of the ties between her fingers.

"Is there something wrong with me, Bunicuța?" Cătălina put her hands on her cheeks because they felt hot. Her stomach felt squishy, too.

"Of course not. We're about to enter into a house of God, so we want to make sure we look proper and crisp."

"Would God be angry and make us go away if we didn't look proper and crisp?"

"Oh, no. Not at all, Dragă. God sees what's on the inside. It's who we are that God pays attention to, not how we look.

We just want to look as nice as we can to show respect to God and this new priest we are about to meet. And speaking of that, we need to go in. Ready?"

Cătălina nodded as she stooped down, picked up the basket, and handed it to Bunicuța. Mădălina opened the door once again—Cătălina only jumped a little bit this time—and together they entered the church. Once her eyes adjusted to the dimmer light inside, Cătălina gasped. How could a building look even bigger on the inside than it did on the outside? She tilted her head back and looked up. It seemed like the parts of the ceiling went all the way up to heaven. Was this place a part of heaven? She and Bunicuța walked past a font filled with water. She raised her hand to poke a finger into it, but Bunicuța stopped her with a sharp shake of her head. Cătălina jerked her hand back to her side and rubbed the fabric of her dress.

They continued walking down a long aisle with benches on both sides. When she whispered about how big the benches were and how many were there, Bunicuța told her they were called pews. They walked toward what seemed to Cătălina to be a much larger and more ornate version of the altar that Bunicuța set up on Sundays when people came to pray and worship God. She stopped short and gazed at the treasure at the front of the church. Despite her aching fatigue from the long, dusty walk, she perked up. She stood on her tiptoes and strained to see everything that was on the altar, but she was too short and the altar too far away. She wanted to go to it, to examine it, to take in everything that was around it. Bunicuța, though, had stopped and was now in one of the rows of pews. She sat with eyes closed, hands together, and head bowed so that her chin almost touched her chest. Cătălina knew that Bunicuța was silently talking to God. She knew that she shouldn't bother people when they were praying; however, what she didn't know was what she should do. As usual, she looked to Bunicuță for guidance. Cătălina slipped in beside Bunicuță, bringing her hands together and bowing her head. She appreciated the rest. Her feet, legs, back, and all of the rest of her body welcomed the relief. She breathed deeply and inhaled a sweet, smoky scent. It reminded her a little of the Bunicuță's candles, but somehow different, too.

Cătălina was lost in the smells of the church and her own thoughts, so when a man spoke beside her, she jumped. "Good afternoon. I certainly don't wish to disrupt your prayer, but I am wondering if there is something I can help you with." Cătălina's eyes flew open, and she leaped to her feet. In front of her stood a man so tall she had to tilt her head back to see him. Cătălina didn't know what to say, but that was okay because she wouldn't have been able to talk anyway. Her heart was pounding and her throat was squeezed so tightly closed it hurt. She felt a gentle nudge from behind. With great effort, Cătălina forced her legs, nearly para-lyzed with fright, to move. She inched ahead, just enough to allow Bunicuță to squeeze past her but not far enough to get too close to this man. When she had talked about him, her Bunicuță had referred to him as *preot*, a priest. His bushy eyebrows pointed down at his small eyes in a way that she had never seen eyebrows settle, not even Tată's when he was angry—but of course, while her father did grow angry easily, he wasn't exactly mean, not compared to Mamă anyway. The *preot* looked mean. Were priests mean? Or what if he was one of those *Securitate* men? They sounded mean and scary. What if he took her and Bunicuță away because they came here? Cătălina hid her hands under her apron so no one would see them shaking. She focused on Bunicuță and tried not to look at the man.

Mădălina bowed her head humbly. "Greetings, *Pater.*" *Father*, Cătălina thought to herself. *He doesn't look like much of a father, not like Eduard is to Dionisie.* She wanted to hear what Bunicuță was saying, so she leaned in slightly to make herself focus. Bunicuță was telling the *preot* about their village. "Word has spread to my village that there is a wonderful and gentle new *preot* here at St. Hypatius. Am I correct in assuming that this is you?"

"Indeed. I am Pater Claudiu Lungu. Welcome. What brings you to St. Hypatius?"

Cătălina didn't quite relax, but she started to breathe normally again instead of in quick, shallow bursts that made her dizzy. This man didn't act or talk in an unusual way, which was good, but that didn't mean bad things wouldn't happen. She inched ever closer to Bunicuță then became very still again as she listened.

"Our village is very small. Our single church was destroyed over two decades ago, and even if we had access to resources, we couldn't afford to build a new one. We still worship God, but we do so in a home." Mădălina paused and gazed around. She gave a small sigh. "We would love to worship properly in a real church. I came in hopes of making arrangements with you. Perhaps you would allow us to use your church to worship on Sundays when your own services are over. In exchange, we can offer you handmade items, food, carpentry and repairs, and cleaning." Mădălina said nothing further.

Pater Lungu sighed deeply. "Why did your village send a woman?"

"Because in the absence of a priest, I am the spiritual leader. There is no one else to do it."

"Hmmmph." The *preot* looked down and scrutinized Mădălina as if really seeing her for the first time. His comment about Bunicuță being a woman puzzled Cătălina, and she wondered if he was only looking at Bunicuță closely now because he didn't want to pay attention to her very much before. He was scrutinizing her, and his eyes fell on her necklace. The V of his eyebrows sharpened. "You are Greek Catholic?"

"We are."

"I'm sorry, but I have nothing to offer you. This church is for those of the Eastern Orthodox faith. You have no place here." He turned and strode up the aisle toward the back of the church.

"*Pater*! Please wait." He stopped, but he didn't turn around. "Some churches like yours open their hearts and their doors to Greek Catholics. Won't you consider sharing your holy space?"

Pater Lungu spun around. He spoke loudly and articulated his words with his arms. Cătălina wanted to crawl under a pew when he began to speak. When she watched his face redden, she wanted to bolt out the door. Because she couldn't leave Bunicuță's side, she stayed put and wished with all of her might that they could leave. She squeezed her eyes shut.

"Share this church with Greek Catholics? Are you mad?" The bark of a laugh that escaped his throat made little bumps appear on Cătălina's arms, and she shivered. The *preot's* laugh became words once again. "Looking at you, it's clear that you have lived enough years to know our history and to know what happened during the Communist take-over."

In a reasonable volume that contrasted with Pater Lungu's voice, Mădălina squared her shoulders and stated, "I have first-hand experience, *Pater*. I know the Romanian government very well." Her words were level and matter-of-fact. They invited neither argument nor scorn. Pater Lungu continued his tirade anyway.

"Yet you show up at my doorstep and beg to use my church! How dare you! Do you mean to endanger my life and the lives of the people of this church? Are you merely ignorant and selfish, or are you sent by the *Securitate* to test me?" He stomped past Mădălina and Cătălina, proceeded all the way to the altar where he stopped and bowed his head. Cătălina looked up at her Bunicuţă and watched her wait patiently, as if no angry words had been hurled. Bunicuţă placed her hand on Cătălina's shoulder but otherwise remained still and silent. Cătălina didn't know how Bunicuţă kept from running away.

The preot slowly turned to face the pair. He approached. His shoes sounded like Uncle Ion's blacksmith tools, metal striking metal in rhythmic staccato, as he walked back up the aisle. He stopped directly in front of them. "Madam," he addressed Mădălina at a normal volume and a tone that seemed sad to Cătălina. "I do regret the way things are. It's not that I don't want to share my holy space with you and other Greek Catholics. I simply cannot do so." He paused and shook his head slowly. "I cannot risk the lives of the members of this church. When word reached President Ceauşescu, and you and I both know that it would, this building would be destroyed, and the people who use it hunted down and executed. I will not take that risk. And now, I must bid you good-bye."

Mădălina studied him. Cătălina wondered if her Bunicuţă could see the agony in the preot's eyes. Perhaps she did, for she responded kindly, with quiet dignity. "Pater Lungu, thank you for listening. You clearly care about your people, and they are lucky. Sadly, it seems like caring people are hard to come by anymore." She held out the basket she had been clutching the entire time. "Please accept this gift. My granddaughter and I made these cloths. They are embroidered in the Eastern Orthodox fashion." She extended the basket toward Pater Lungu.

He fingered the ornate gold cross hanging from his neck. "Given that I can't offer you use of my church, I couldn't possibly accept such a lavish gift."

"These come with no strings attached. This is a gift, not a bribe. We worked hard to make them, and they are full of faith and Godly love." Mădălina touched Pater Lungu's hands with the basket. Tentatively he took hold of it, then he slowly pulled it toward him.

"Thank you. Thank you both." He looked down at Cătălina. She looked at him only briefly before averting her eyes.

There was nothing left to say. Mădălina took Cătălina's hand, and they walked silently up the aisle, through the gigantic wooden doors, and began their journey home.

# Chapter 6

Cătălina felt the smooth dirt path under her bare feet. It was still cold and hard, but much of the winter snow had melted down into the ground and had already started nourishing new blossoms. The big rug draped over her arms, preventing her from seeing her feet, but she didn't want to look down anyway. She wanted to look up, up at the clear blue sky and the swollen buds on the trees, up to feel the sun's warmth that felt so good against the chill of the air. She took a deep breath and smiled at the way the world felt in her nose. The chilly air rushed in, and so did the sun's warmth. The sensation made her nose tingle, and she sneezed. She sniffed. The smell of muddy snow combined with clean, bright pine needles and made her feel energized—energized enough to beat all these rugs.

She let go of the rug she was carrying. It dropped with a dull thud and puff of dust beside the others. Cătălina tenderly touched her *mărțișor* to ensure that it was still pinned to her dress right over her heart. Her lips formed a little smile as her fingers brushed against the red and white thread, thin like broom bristles but so much softer. The threads were braided together and tied into a bow, and dangling from each end was a wonderful, tiny, doll made of red and white yarn. The girl doll had a yellow flower with a light blue center on both her apron and kerchief, while the boy doll had a light blue flower with a yellow center on his hat. They complimented each other perfectly because they were in love. Cătălina knew they were in love because she liked to fiddle with them when she could, telling little tales about their lives. The dolls always wanted to be in love in her stories, and they were in love dangling from the *mărţişor*. It was wonderful.

It was also wonderful that her own father had given her this splendid talisman. True, he gave them to her mother and her sisters, too, and did so every *Mărţişor*, March first. This year, Tată had given her this very special *mărţişor* to wear. He had asked Bunică Rodica to make them all for him, as he always did because his large hands, coarse from all of his labors, couldn't make these fine trinkets, but he chose what they would look like. For Mamă, Viorica, Flavia, and Daciana, Tată had selected round wooden disks, each with a different symbol etched into it. In past years, Cătălina's *mărţişor* from Tată had also been wooden discs, and she had always loved them. This year, however, Tată had asked Bunică Rodica to make these yarn dolls. After he had pinned the talisman for health and strength onto her dress, Cătălina had asked him why she deserved such an honor. Tată had smiled at her, leaned closer to her, and whispered, "Because I love you." Even now her heart thumped in happiness at the thought. Mamă would never say such a thing, and Tată and Mamă always agreed with each other, but here he had given her a very special *mărţişor* and said that he loved her. Just knowing that was enough to endure Mamă.

Cătălina could endure Mamă, but still she feared her wrath. She glanced around furtively to see if Mamă was nearby. As she did so, she saw Filip peeking out from behind a giant tree, staring at her. Immediately, he ducked back behind the tree. Cătălina shook her head. This wasn't the first time she had caught him watching her; he added this new level of obnoxiousness to his behavior this winter. Whether he'd show up at her house or she was at his, he'd either pick on her—bully her, really—or just stare at her with a look on his face she couldn't interpret. He was a boy and she only a girl, so no one seemed to stop him no matter how he was treating her. She just tried to ignore it, to smile and turn away the way Bunicuță had taught her.

None of that mattered right now, of course. She had been assigned the big task of beating all of the rugs from both homes, rugs that were dirty and stale from the long, bitter winter. She wouldn't beat life back into them by standing around. To avoid the rebuking that would come if Mamă caught her standing there doing nothing, she hurried back home for the remaining rug. Cătălina was relieved that no one was inside. She didn't want to have to shoo anyone away in order to take the rug. This one was the biggest rug they had. It stretched out in front of the table that on Sundays became Bunicuță's altar. Family and visitors crowed in and sat on benches, chairs, and the rugs on the floor. This blue rug with all of its colorful, woven flowers, birds, and patterns was hand made by Bunicuță's mother and grandmother before Bunicuță was even born. The colors had faded slightly with time, but generations of care had kept the quality good. Cătălina felt proud to be part of that care.

She dropped to her knees and rolled up the rug. Hopping to her feet, she jumped to the middle of it, straddling the now log-like object. She stepped so both feet were on the same side of it, bent down, and lifted with a grunt. It hardly budged. She tried again and still got nowhere. She stood straight, dusted off her hands, and frowned at the rug. Perhaps she could drag it. She hopped back to the end of the rug, grasped it, and pulled. It moved! Continuing in this way, she slowly shuffled and slid and backed out of her door. Now that she was outside in open space, she could unroll it. Maybe it would pull easier that way. She gave it a try. This way was a little better; she could move meters instead of centimeters at a time. Still, this wouldn't efficiently get her where she needed to go. She took a deep breath, grasped the rug as tightly as she could, and ran backwards. The rug moved with her, until a small, fast-moving streak tore across the yard and half dove, half plopped onto the rug with a squeal. The rug came to a halt and fell out of Cătălina's grasp. Cătălina stumbled backward and landed smack on her behind. The figure on the rug squealed.

"Dionisie! Your cousin is trying to work, just like your mother is." Oana's voice was stern yet kind. "Cătălina, I'm so sorry," she said as she approached. Cătălina noticed that she looked haggard. Her hair was sticking every which way out of her kerchief, and her apron was streaked with mud below her knees. The reason for her appearance was now crawling around on the rug. Oana bent down and used part of her apron to attempt to wipe dirt off his face. Thwarted, she grunted and stood. "He's in such a playful mood, and I'm getting nothing done. I have to go out to the pasture, but Dionisie in the pasture will be disastrous." Oana sighed. "Sometimes I miss the days before he could walk," she confessed.

"Would you like me to watch him, Oana? I can beat the rugs and play with him, too." Cătălina jumped to her feet and brushed the dirt off the back of her dress.

"Cătălina, you are a lifesaver!" Oana leaned down and embraced Cătălina swiftly. Then, hands on hips, she looked at the rug and frowned. "If you drag this all the way to the clearing and back, not only will it remain dirty, it will be ruined. How about if I help you carry it now, and I'll send someone later to help get it back?"

Cătălina sighed with relief. "Thank you, Oana." No sooner had they moved Dionisie and picked up the rug, though, a voice called, "Oana! Are you coming?" Cătălina saw Eduard in the distance, arms folded across his chest. Oana let go of the rug, which made Cătălina lose her own grip. When it hit the ground, Dionisie jumped back on.

"I'm on my way," Oana called to her husband. To Cătălina, she said, "Well, our plan isn't going to work. Do you think you can push the rug in a wheelbarrow?"

Cătălina shrugged and nodded. "I think so."

"Good. I bet you can. Go grab that wheelbarrow," Oana pointed to the cart leaning against their cottage. Cătălina trotted over and returned promptly. She and Oana worked the rug into the wheelbarrow, plopped Dionisie precariously on top, and then Oana rushed off.

"Are you ready for a ride, Dionisie? Hang on." Cătălina tried to talk to her young cousin, but found that it was hard to talk and bite her lip in concentration at the same time. Her load was heavy, and squirmy, and she nearly tipped over the whole works on her way to the clearing. Arriving at last, she let go of the wheelbarrow's handles and shook out her hands. Dionisie giggled and shook his own hands. Cătălina hid her hands behind her back. Dionisie lost interest and made a move for the edge of the wheelbarrow. "No! Don't go to the edge, or you could fall." Cătălina wasn't ready to set him on the ground and wrestle with the rug, so she decided to stall. "Look, Dionisie. Watch this." Cătălina hid her hands behind her back and began to sing, "Where is Thumper?" When she brought her arms out, she wiggled her thumbs in front of the toddler, letting him grab them and play with them. Gently, she pulled them back as she began to sing again. She and Dionisie had gotten all the way to "Where is ring man?" when one of her sisters appeared in the clearing. "Flavia!" Cătălina exclaimed.

"Cătălina, what are you doing?"

"I'm cleaning the rugs like Mamă asked, and I'm taking care of Dionisie for Oana. Do you want to do these things with me?" Cătălina asked eagerly. It would be fun to do chores with a partner. Flavia sighed and folded her arms across her chest. This stance that resembled Mamă drained the joy out of Cătălina. She dropped her hands, smoothed her apron, turned and plucked Dionisie out of the wagon, and looked at her sister.

"Give him to me." Flavia held out her arms for Dionisie. Reluctantly, Cătălina handed him over. "Now, you'd best get to the rugs. They won't clean themselves. Mamă sent me to check on you, and it's good that she did. Honestly, Cătălina, you are so irresponsible. You play when you're supposed to be working and expect everyone else to do your chores. These rugs need to be back in place before dinner, so you'd better hurry." Flavia turned and marched off with Dionisie.

"Wait! Flavia, no! Oana asked me to babysit Dionisie. She said I could look after him while I did the rugs."

Flavia turned around but didn't return to Cătălina. She said coldly, "But you weren't doing either, Cătălina. You were playing with Dionisie like he was a toy, and you haven't even taken that big rug out of the wheelbarrow. It seems to me that you were just avoiding work. You're lazy and naughty. Good-bye, Cătălina. See to it that you get these done quickly and properly." She spun and strode away, Dionisie squirming in her arms.

Cătălina felt her cheeks burn. She placed her hands over them to see if they were hot. They were. The fingers that had just been playing with Dionisie were now warm from the heat in her cheeks and wet with tears. Was Flavia right? Was she naughty? And lazy? She had needed a break because her whole body was sore from pushing the wheelbarrow, heavy with cargo. So she did want to pause and rest for a minute. Did that make her bad? If it did, she was sorry. She truly didn't mean to avoid work. She thought she was help-ing Oana by playing with Dionisie. Yet Flavia had taken him away and accused her of mistreating him. What would Oana think? The thought instantly cooled her cheeks as dread filled her. She didn't want Oana to stop trusting her, to stop liking her. Oana and Eduard were her very favorite aunt and uncle. She couldn't let them down. It was with great urgency that Cătălina returned to the rugs. She took tremendous care to beat them swiftly yet thoroughly; one by one, she attended to them, beating, shaking, and returning them to their homes. When the time came to deal with the big, heavy rug, she went to the village square in search of someone to assist her.

Filip and his brother Cosmin were at the market. Darn. She could have asked any of these nice people to help her with the rug, but because she had family here, she would be expected to ask them first. She didn't want to interrupt Oana or Eduard in the pasture, especially since she'd already let them down with Dionisie, but she couldn't go there and look for others without them seeing her. She couldn't just leave the rug in the clearing. She couldn't drag it back. It was too heavy for her to even lift into the wheelbarrow. She failed with Dionisie, and now she was failing at this. Her stomach began to ache terribly, and she was afraid she would be sick. The entire market blurred as her eyes filled with tears. Suddenly, something hard landed nearby. Cackling laughter followed. No. Filip and Cosmin had evidently spotted her. Cătălina lifted her apron and wiped her eyes and nose. She spun on her heels and marched away, away from the boys more so than toward the clearing, but it was to the clearing that she headed.

She had nearly reached the clearing when she heard footsteps behind her, so she started to run. At age six and a half, Cătălina hadn't yet learned that running often brought more trouble than standing still. "Hey, girl!" Cătălina recognized Cosmin's voice because it cracked as it shed its childhood timbre and made room for the low sound of manhood. She felt a hand grab her upper arm. Her body jerked backward, and she stumbled to her knees. She twisted around to see Filip gripping her arm. His face snaked its way into an oily sneer.

"We were talking to you, *girl*," The word "girl" oozed from Filip's mouth and sounded ugly and dirty. Cătălina's heart pounded in her throat, and words couldn't get around it.

Cosmin leaned down and slapped her hard across her face. Filip laughed. He grabbed Cătălina's other arm, and then he pulled both arms back as hard as he could. Cătălina cried out in pain. Cosmin slapped her again. He hooted. "This is fun. Hey, Filip, this is what beating the rugs must be like. Come try this." The boys traded places, and Filip took his turn slapping and hitting Cătălina until Cosmin wanted his turn again. He shoved Filip out of the way and struck Cătălina's face with one hand and punched her stomach with the other. Cătălina folded forward and howled, and then fell silent. Her body shook, and she couldn't make it stop. Her cousins' voices sounded muffled under the roaring in her ears.

"Hey, Cosmin, that's enough. You've gone too far."

"You've got to be kidding me."

"Look. We wanted to have some fun. We did. Now let her be for now."

Cosmin snorted. "What are you, a girl? Why don't you go get our sisters and all of our *girl* cousins, too? You can help them with laundry and cleaning, and then you can play with dolls with them. You're pathetic." Cosmin kicked the toe of his boot into the dirt, causing tiny bits of rocks and twigs to pelt Cătălina. He shoved Filip hard as he marched back to the village.

Cătălina waited to hear the sound of Filip's footsteps retreating after Cosmin. She waited longer. She could smell and taste the dirt as her breath rushed in and out in bursts. The inside of her mouth was gritty and so dry she couldn't spit out the dust. Filip placed both hands on her shoulders and pulled up. Cătălina whimpered. Filip straddled her, adjusted his grip, and yanked harder. "Come on, Cătălina. It's not that bad. Get up."

Slowly, Cătălina crawled forward and out of Filip's grasp. She rose. She didn't know what to do next. Should she turn to face him? Say something? Say nothing? Run away? She sniffed and ran her sleeve across her face. The indecision was paralyzing. She wanted Filip to go away. Instead, he approached her. "We, uh, we were just playing with you, Cătălina. We wanted to play, but you wouldn't listen. You ran away. You made us chase you. We made the effort to run after you but when we reached you, you still wouldn't play our game. You resisted, and look what happened." Cătălina looked at her cousin. His words were coming out faster, and his cheeks were flushed. She met his eyes, and he raised his voice. "Yeah, that's right. This is your fault, Cătălina! Your fault. So don't even think about running and tattling unless you want to get in big trouble."

Cătălina couldn't make sense of what Filip was telling her. Her own fault? For them beating her like a rug? Her nose started to run more again, and her arms couldn't keep up with it. "Leave me alone, Filip!" she spit out between sobs.

"Don't tell me what to do!" His shout made Cătălina cover her ears and squeeze her eyes shut. Her breath caught when she felt Filip grasp her wrists. To her relief, he simply lowered Cătălina's arms down. "We need to get that rug back, Cătălina. Let's go."

Cătălina forced herself to smile at Filip. Her mouth had a hard time pushing her cheeks up, but she managed to shape her lips into a small smile. She was unable to form meaningful words, and she wouldn't have been able to work them past the big egg in her throat anyway, so she said nothing. In silence, Cătălina, Filip, and the wheelbarrow hauled the huge rug home.

Cătălina worried over what Mamă would say about her dress and her face, which must be filthy because she could feel caked dirt crack when she opened her mouth wide. Would Mamă understand if she told her what Filip and Cosmin had done? Whose side would she take? Cătălina's head pounded and her stomach churned and burned. She decided to just hope that she would see Bunicuţă before she saw Mamă. As it turned out, she didn't have to deal with it at all, because when she and Filip arrived, pandemonium had broken loose.

# Chapter 7

......................

Filip dropped the wheelbarrow and bolted toward the cottages. He weaved through a crowd of people and disappeared from Cătălina's vision just as the rug spilled out of the overturned handcart. Cătălina called after him, "Filip! Wait!" Of course there was no answer. Her words simply mingled with all of the shouts and cries around her and disappeared.

What was happening? Where was her family? She stood on her toes and stretched tall. She couldn't see anyone among all of the people, villagers and soldiers alike. She needed to get home, but unlike Filip, she couldn't just run off. Mamă had warned her sternly about her responsibility to get all of the rugs, even this big one—especially this big one—back in place in better condition than when she removed them for cleaning. A pack of shouting men rushed past her. Frantically, she righted the barrow and yanked the rug. Shouts, screams, mayhem accosted her. She grunted and heaved and begged and pleaded and prayed, and it barely budged. "Come on, rug. Hurry. Please." Where was her family? Suddenly, something rammed into her shoulder, jolting her and pitching her forward. Startled, she straightened and inhaled sharply. She found herself staring at a large man wearing a dark blue uniform with emblems on the sleeves and chest, a matching hat, and shiny black boots. He had a very big gun, and he was poking it into her arm. A *Securitate*!

"What are you doing, girl?" Cătălina couldn't move— not even her mouth, because it had dried up even more and seemed to be stuck shut. The secret policeman pushed her with his gun. She stumbled and landed on the ground. Again the man pushed his gun into her, this time against her chest. "I asked you a question."

At that moment, a gun shot rang out somewhere in the village. Cătălina threw her hands over her ears and screamed. She shouted, "I'm going home! I had to beat this rug, and I have to get it back home but it's too heavy and I don't know where my family is!" She began to sob.

"Are you completely stupid, girl?" Cătălina just stared at the gun against her chest. "Look over there." She turned her head very slightly in the direction the man pointed. She saw only chaos: people moving quickly, others standing in bunches before being forced apart by *Securitate*, people moving in and out of homes, carrying things, dropping things, having things ripped out of their arms by the police, some people being struck by the police. She heard a gunshot again. Cătălina cried harder. "Your home doesn't exist anymore. Your possessions are meaningless. Including this stupid rug." He kicked it hard before swinging his gun over and filling it with bullet holes. He fired bullets into all of the little birds perched on cherry tree branches.

"No! Stop!" Cătălina loved those birds, embroidered so beautifully by women who lived long before her. She would sit on the rug and pretend they were her special pets. Now this man was shooting them. She scrambled to her feet and lunged toward him.

The man stopped. He glared down, stone-faced, at Cătălina. "You really are stupid, girl. Let's go. We're finding your parents, although I should shoot you right here and leave you with your precious carpet." He leaned over and with one arm swooped her up. He flung her over his shoulder like she was a sack of flour and walked further into the village. He bellowed, "Who recognizes this child?"

A woman called out, "That is Cătălina Gabor. She... she lives over there." From her position dangling down the *Securitate* man's back, Cătălina recognized Iolanda Albu, the woman who used to be a healer alongside Bunică Rodica until her daughter died when they were doing surgery on her stomach. Now the only time she saw Iolanda was on Sundays at church. It was so sad. Iolanda always slipped in a little late, sat as alone as she could, and slipped right back out at the very end. She didn't speak much, but now here she was bravely talking to the Securitate man to help Cătălina get home. Cătălina gave her a small wave in frightened acknowledgement. Iolanda waved back, the same type of wave. Suddenly, Cătălina felt herself spinning as the *Securitate* man pivoted toward Iolanda. She felt his body jerk as she heard a deafening noise. All at once, she could smell and taste something sharp, acrid. Her eyes began to sting, and everything was quiet other than a high-pitched ringing in her ears. She saw a flash of metal as the man shoved something into a holster. It was the gun he had poked her with just a little bit ago. When he swung back around to march toward her cottage, Cătălina saw Iolanda Albu slumped on the ground. Blood flowed from somewhere underneath her and soaked into the ground beside her. Cătălina began to shriek.

Her shrieks came to an abrupt end when she hit the ground with a hard thud. She found herself on her back, the wind knocked out of her. She gasped and gasped but couldn't get enough air. It didn't help that every breath she took caused sharp pain to shoot through her chest, shoulders, and back. Suddenly, hands slid under her. Cătălina's eyes flew open. "Bunicuță!" Grandma and granddaughter hugged each other tightly. "Oh, Bunicuță! He shot Iolanda! That horrible man shot Iolanda dead in the street, and I don't know why. Maybe because she helped me by pointing to where I live. Bunicuță, why? What's happening? Why?" Cătălina sobbed her questions.

To her shocked surprise, rather than answering her questions or even continuing to hold her, Bunicuță let go and hushed her. "Cătălina, please. Not now."

"Why? What's happening?" Cătălina asked again, again through tears.

"The systematization we've been hearing about. It's happening. We're being forced out, they haven't told us where. They just stormed into the village and ordered us to prepare to evacuate. You must get up now and help me. I want just a few things from the altar. But we must move swiftly and be careful to hide what we take with us." Together, they scrambled into the house. "Cătălina, be swift. Take the small candle holders and put them in your pockets. Good." Cătălina watched in silence as Bunicuță grabbed her favorite cross and shoved it under her dress then pulled and twisted and adjusted her clothes around it. She bunched the fabric of her apron around the top bar of the cross because it stuck out at an angle. Next, Bunicuță instructed, "Now, let's shove everything else off and onto the floor."

"Bunicuță!"

"Do it, Child. We must make it look like the *Securitate* ransacked it." Her arms felt like lead, but she did as she was told.

When everything had clattered to the floor but was still rolling about, Bunicuţă whipped off the altar cloth and beckoned to Cătălina. "Come here, Dragă. I'm going to tie this around you to make it look like another layer of your apron." As she was doing so, gunfire rang out nearby. Cătălina screamed and covered her ears. She felt a hard yank as her grandma tied the final knot. Cătălina spun to face her.

"Bunicuţă, I'm scared!"

"Yes. So am I. We all are, Dragă. The best thing to do right now is to hurry and to fully obey the *Securitate*."

"Aren't we disobeying by taking these things?"

Mădălina sighed. "Cătălina, please don't ask questions right now. Come on. We must go outside."

As they stepped out of the house, Cătălina saw her aunt Adelina run by, herding her children. They were all crying. Where was Uncle Neculai? Her question was answered when she heard Adelina shout, panicked, to Cătălina's father, "Grigor! The *Securitate* took Neculai!"

Then Tată went running past. Cătălina watched in horror as he ran right up to a *Securitate* and shouted, "Where did you take my brother?" The *Securitate* answered him with the butt of his gun. Cătălina watched the man hit Tată so hard in the head that Tată fell to his knees.

"*Tăctic!*" Cătălina shrieked. "Daddy!" Her throat felt sore from all of the shrieking and screaming, but she didn't care. She couldn't help it. She watched in horror as the *Securitate* man straddled her tată, bent down, and hit him again and again. Oddly, it was another *Securitate* man who made the brutal one stop. Cătălina discovered immediately, though, that it wasn't because the second *Securitate* man wanted to help her *tăctic*.

The second *Securitate* man nudged the first and barked, "Stand up and let's go. It's time to round up these worthless peasants and get them out of here."

The first man stopped beating Grigor and stood to face the other. "If they're so worthless, let me finish this one off first."

"No. We're leaving now. Come." And with that, they were gone.

Cătălina dashed to her father. "*Tăctic*! Are you okay? Please, *Tăctic*, get up."

Grigor groaned. "Cătălina, I'm fine. Back up so I can stand."

As he staggered to his feet, gun fire sounded from every-where, all around them. *Securitate* on horseback cantered through, using cattle prods to herd people to the village square. The more people screamed, the harder the *Securitate* prodded. Cătălina cried out when the group stomped over the beautiful, heirloom rug that she had just cleaned. To think that she had avoided dragging it! Now it was full of bullet holes and trampled flat by hundreds of muddy feet. She yanked on Bunicuţă's hand. "Our rug! Our wonderful rug that your own Mamă and Bunică made. We must get it!"

Bunicuţă resisted and pulled Cătălina's hand back. "No, Dragă. It's gone now. There's no saving it. But we aren't gone, and we can save each other. People are more important than things, Cătălina." Cătălina began to cry again, but she nod-ded her assent.

Once in the square, one of the *Securitate* men stood on top of the water pump's stone base and bellowed, "You are being relocated to Bucharest." When people collectively gasped and protested, he pointed his gun into the crowd and shot. Screams and loud sobs told Cătălina that the bullet had hit someone, but she was too short to see above the crowd to learn who it was. The *Securitate* man continued, "Our revered President Ceauşescu has great plans for Romania. We will become a great industrial nation, and our agricultural industry will be efficient and a model for the rest of the world to admire. Your farming methods are backwards. They are obsolete. You are obsolete. Your village will be razed and the land incorporated into the government's agricultural industry. You will live in special apartments erected in Bucharest for your kind. You will contribute to making Romania great by working in our factories and having babies as President Ceauşescu has already ordered." He said nothing further. He jumped of, mounted his horse, and blew his whistle to signal the rest of the *Securitate* to cattle-prod everyone on their way.

Cătălina felt numb. She couldn't move. The only reason she began to move was because Bunicuţă, who was holding her hand, started to walk. Cătălina's arm stretched until it couldn't, and her legs had no choice but to stumble along with her Bunicuţă. As they left the village and started down the muddy road, Cătălina smelled smoke. She turned her head. Surrounded by people, the only thing she could see was plumes of black smoke rising into the air. Were they burning homes? When she heard many different voices cry out, saying various things about fire and the *Securitate* torching the village, her heart sank. "Our loom! Bunicuţă, our loom!"

Bunicuţă nodded. "I know, Dragă. I know." Cătălina waited for more, but Bunicuţă didn't speak again. She watched tears roll quietly down her grandma's face. When she heard the sounds of people being beaten, likely the people who spoke about the fires, she knew that it would be best if she, too, kept silent.

As the sun worked its way toward the distant horizon and the shadows grew longer and longer, the sound of hundreds of feet walking changed from clomps to shuffles. Cătălina heard a lot of sniffling and throat clearing and coughing, but she heard no talking. Occasionally, she heard sounds of the *Securitate* brutalizing people. By then, though, everyone had learned not to protest. Cătălina didn't understand how people could stand silently by while friends and loved ones were poked with a cattle prod or kicked or punched or struck with a gun.

Long after it became pitch black and bitterly cold, the *Securitate* herded everyone into an open field and ordered them to sleep. Without blankets or a fire or, especially, without the comfort of her cozy cottage, Cătălina couldn't sleep. She was happy her family was around her, but everyone was too frightened to talk. Dionisie, who like other little ones, had been crying for a very long time, was finally quiet. She curled up and lay on the frozen ground in the dark of night. She began to shiver uncontrollably. She jumped, startled, when she felt someone scoot up against her. An arm went across the top of her, and another slid underneath her. She felt herself pulled backward. Her heart began to pound. Who was this? What did he want? She was astonished when she recognized the voice that whispered, "Come here, Cătălina. I'll keep you warm, and you can keep me warm."

She didn't move but instead remained curled into a tight ball. "What are you doing, Filip?" Like Filip, she whispered very quietly.

"Trying to get warm. I thought you would want to get warm, too." Cătălina said nothing. "Well, do you?"

"I guess."

"Then let's lie here together. Loosen up so I can get my arms around you better."

"Are you going to beat me up? Or take off running and leave me alone?"

"No. I'm sorry about those things."

"Well, okay." Cătălina was too worn down to argue. She jumped again, but didn't dare speak more for fear of attracting the *Securitate* and their brutality, when Filip began to stroke her arms, legs, and stomach. Eventually, mercifully, his arms went limp and his breathing became heavy. He had fallen asleep. Cătălina was distressed to such a high degree that she couldn't sleep. Horrific images swirled in her head: Iolanda, secret police, fire, Tată being beaten, so very much brutality everywhere, and then Filip's hands all over her. These all rushed through her mind over and over and over again, and sleep eluded her. The sky had grown a half shade lighter, from pitch-black to black when the *Securitate* started to shout and wade through the puddle of human beings huddled on the ground. Boot kicks, hand slaps, and cattle prods quickly brought people to their feet. The march to Bucharest resumed.

Cătălina watched with envy whenever she saw the *Securitate* men pull food or drink out of their satchels. Her mouth was too dry to water. She hoped they would get to Bucharest soon so she could have something to eat and drink. Better yet, she hoped they would all turn around and return home. She remembered the plumes of smoke and the smell that accompanied them, and it made her whole body sad and achy.

The sky was once again sunless—moonless and starless, too, as gloomy as the cellar at home; oh, how she wished they could all go back home—when she saw an ominous glow ahead. Murmurs in the crowd told her that it was Bucharest, and she shuddered. As they entered the city, she saw that the glow was from lights that weren't kerosene lamps. The pathway was lined with poles that were topped with fancy lanterns that made light without fire. Most of the lanterns were dark and lifeless, but the few that had light cast eerie, glowing circles onto the ground below. Rather than dancing and flickering, the light held still, not going anywhere or doing much to brighten the world around it. She shuddered again. What was this place? Without warning, she was bumped from behind and found herself on the ground with a thud. Almost instantly, someone lifted her from behind and plopped her back on her feet. "Don't stop like that again, Cătălina. Do you want to attract the attention of the *Securitate*? Do you?" She glanced over her shoulder to see the source of the gruff voice. It was Tată, and she could barely recognize him because of his swollen, dirty, and discolored face. She gasped. "Go, Cătălina." He shoved her. Terrified, she went.

The throng of defeated villagers surrounding her coupled with the oppressive darkness made it nearly impossible to see much of the city around her. She couldn't see it, but she could smell it and hear it. It didn't smell at all like grass and mud and flowers and hay and animals. It smelled disgusting. She didn't quite know what it smelled like, but she knew she didn't like it. She gagged. Looking at the expressions on the faces around her, she guessed that others shared her opinion. As they followed the *Securitate* through the streets, she heard dogs, so many loud, snarling, creatures that didn't sound anything like the animals she was accustomed to. She strained to see them and was horrified by what she glimpsed: a large pack dug viciously through bags and bins, barking and snarling and squabbling. One broke away and ran in her direction, and she screamed. Bunicuţă squeezed her hand but said nothing.

At last they arrived at a large, rectangular building. Cătălina was exhausted and didn't have it in her to be curious. One of the *Securitate* men shouted from atop his horse, "Welcome home, peasants! The first and the second floors are occupied by vulgar plebeians from other backwards villages, but the third and fourth floors are available. *Securitate* forces guard the building at all times, so I wouldn't try anything if I were you. Work orders will arrive in a few days." When no one moved, he lifted his head and shouted, "These bumpkins apparently need help getting into the building," and the cattle-prodding and hitting resumed.

People began shouting and protesting and crying. Cătălina heard gunshots again. Screams. A woman's voice shrieked, "Flavia! No!" That was Mamă's voice! Did something happen to Flavia?

"Bunicuţă!" Cătălina tugged at her grandma's dress. They tried to push through the crowd, but they were caught up in the momentum of the group as the *Securitate* forced everyone into the building.

# Sacramento, California
## *2018*

# Chapter 8

Catie had been looking over at Marcy as she talked, but suddenly she found that her throat had closed around her words, trapping them inside. The image of the *Securitate* soldier high on his horse, bellowing orders, superimposed on Marcy. Catie blinked rapidly and looked down at the baby whose diaper she had been changing. Catie's heart thumped against her chest, and she could hear her own labored breathing. She felt the temperature in her cheeks rise with her embarrassment. Why did she feel scared after all of these years, decades? And why had she told Marcy about her childhood? Would she use it against her? It was so personal. She shouldn't have shared.

Catie deftly completed the diaper change, slid one hand under the baby's upper back to support her neck and head and slid the other under her bottom with the clean, dry diaper, and swooped her up to hold her against her shoulder. She retreated to the other side of the room where she swayed and softly sang a Romanian lullaby she used to sing to Dionisie to soothe him. This served several purposes: it helped the baby remain content, it helped Catie calm herself, and it allowed her to avoid Marcy.

The baby did remain content; however, Cătălina's other intentions failed. She still felt shaky and agitated, and she could hear her heart pounding in her head. She wondered if Marcy, who was walking her way, would be able to see the veins throb in her temples. Dumitru always said that he could see it when she was scared or anxious, and he said it was gross and a sign that she had no control. The temperature in her neck and head increased even more, and she turned to the wall. She removed one hand from the baby, just briefly so as not to hurt her, and brushed her hair forward so it covered her temples and hid part of her face. When she looked out of the corner of her eye to peek between the wavy brown strands, she saw Marcy standing beside her. Marcy touched Catie's arm, causing Catie to jump and her embarrassment to deepen.

Catie couldn't, wouldn't, speak. Marcy filled the silence. "Wow, Catie. I can't imagine how terrible it would be to live through any of that."

"It wasn't all bad," Catie felt an urgent need to defend herself and her old way of life. She shook her head and rushed on, "Maybe I didn't say it right. No matter how bad things were, Bunicuţă was loving and kind and brought me and everyone else closer to God. And Eduard and Oana and Dionisie were good...." She shook her head again and looked down at the baby sleeping contently on her shoulder. She should put her in her crib and change another baby's diaper. Hastily, she skirted Marcy and lowered the baby into her crib then hustled to a little one who had been fed but not changed. Without making eye contact with Marcy, she carried the baby to the changing table and went to work. Unfortunately, Marcy was at her side again.

"Catie, I didn't mean that everything was hard to live through, and I'm sorry. I wish I would have had a relationship with a grandmother like you had with yours."

Catie glanced at Marcy for the first time since she stopped telling her story. "You didn't have a good relationship with a grandparent?"

Marcy shook her head. She plucked an 11-month old boy out of a playpen, balanced him on an arm, and gracefully lowered herself onto the floor. She shifted into a cross-legged position and with her fingers helped the budding walker stand and balance. She glanced up at Catie. "No. My family was too rich and busy to bother with me. My parents had high-powered careers and spent any bit of time off they had at their country club rubbing elbows with important people." Catie looked quizzically at Marcy. She couldn't tell if Marcy sounded bitter. Marcy smiled with half of her mouth and shrugged her shoulders. "It used to make me really angry, but now I'm all grown up and far away from their pretentious lives, so I figure, whatever. My grandparents were far too important to deal with a child, too. One set has always lived the snobbish life in Boston. The other, my father's parents, lived in New York City like we did, but our penthouse over-looked a different side of Central Park than theirs, too far away for regular visits." At that, Marcy did sound sarcastic.

Catie was taken aback. She tried to keep the incredulity out of her voice when she asked, "But who stayed with you at home? Who raised you? Certainly you had relatives living with you or at least close by to come and go every single day." She thought of her own apartments in Bucharest. While tiny, families shared them as they had shared their cottages in the country. And doors were always open to others, especially to family.

Again, Marcy shook her head. She bounced the baby as she answered, "No. I had a nanny until I was seven and went to boarding school."

Cătălina furrowed her brow. "What is boarding school?"

"A private school—that means parents pay for it instead of sending their kids to a public school that is free to them— where kids stay for the whole school year. There are boarding houses, buildings with rooms where kids live for the year with one or more roommates." Marcy made a disgusted noise and stuck out her tongue. The baby laughed. Surprised, Marcy looked at him and did it again. He squealed. After a few rounds of this, Marcy looked back at Cătălina, who was across the room tending to someone. She returned and joined Marcy on the floor. "Boarding schools suck." Marcy made a face.

Cătălina hated to keep asking for clarification, but there were so many English words and phrases that didn't make sense to her. She picked up a colorful rubber block with Eeyore on it, and squeezed it gently, watching it yield and spring back rather than looking at Marcy when she asked, "Suck? Like a baby drinking from a bottle?" Cătălina felt her cheeks burn again.

"No. Suck like it's horrible. Like it sucks ass, because sucking a butt would be disgusting and awful." After a brief pause, she said, "Actually, I'd rather suck a butt than go to boarding school."

Cătălina couldn't think of anything to say other than, "Oh. I think that boarding school must have been very terrible. I'm sorry you had to go, Marcy."

Marcy smiled and shrugged again. "Yeah, well, that's all in the past. And we're in the present. Living right here, right now. And I for one want to live fully." She stood and twirled with the baby. Cătălina maneuvered painstakingly so she was on all fours before slowly rising to stand. She grimaced. She opened her eyes to see Marcy studying her. "Are you all right,

Catie? You look like you're in pain. I've noticed it before but wasn't sure if I should mention it. Are you always in pain?"

"Almost always, yes." Catie closed her eyes and sighed. The words had escaped before she had a chance to check them.

"Have you seen a doctor?"

"Once." Catie turned and walked away. She was happy that a baby had begun to wail because it gave her an excuse to leave and not appear rude. She felt guilty for being happy that the baby was upset and said a silent prayer for forgiveness.

"Well, what happened?" Marcy didn't let the baby's loud discontent stop her from badgering Catie. Catie suddenly felt her silence grow loud in the room as the infant stopped his yowling. She made a show of putting him into the crib and settling him in in order to gather her thoughts. In her lifetime, she had come to hate direct, personal questions because whether she answered them or not, her choice—her silence or any of her words—was almost always wrong, and there were always painful repercussions. Her choices to talk or to remain silent had only been safe with two people in her life: Bunicuță and Pater Vasile Cojocaru in Bucharest, but neither one of them was part of her life anymore. A deep sorrow weaved itself around and through the pain in her muscles and bones, deepening her melancholy. She looked at Marcy and made a decision. She'd talk to her more and see what happened. After all, so far Marcy had been safe, and Catie hadn't read anything malicious in her body language after she told her about some of her childhood in Romania. If Marcy turned out to be vicious and spiteful, well, Catie was certainly used to that and would endure it like she endured everything else, and she'd be silent again.

"Unfortunately, not much happened."

"Ooooh! It burns me when doctors don't help. I've had some great doctors, and I've had some awful ones. One time, I went in to this jerk for....Whoops! I'm sorry, Catie. I asked about you because I care. Sometimes I get lit up about stuff, and I talk too much. Please go on with your story." Marcy smiled.

Cătălina smiled back, an uncertain smile, just a little turn of her lips. She had lost her nerve, but she forced herself to talk. She didn't really want or need to talk about this, but she didn't want to displease or upset Marcy. She took a deep breath in attempt to center herself and calm her agitated heart. "There's really not much to tell. I've had so much pain in my body for so many years. Dumitru, my ex-husband, would never let me see doctors. After I had lived here for about a year, I realized that I could see a doctor if I wanted to. But it was just a waste of time and money." Cătălina shrugged.

"What do you mean? Couldn't they figure out what was wrong? Did they even really try? Did they do tests? Send you to specialists? The morons shouldn't have just given up!" The baby Marcy was holding fussed when she raised her voice. She rubbed the fuzzy little head and whispered, "Sorry, Lilly." To Catie, she stage-whispered, "Sorry, Catie. Again. Go on."

Catie froze. Her throat ached making it difficult for air to move in and out. What had she been thinking, talking to Marcy freely like this? She'd already revealed too much about herself. Now that she was in America, was she already forgetting Dumitru's lessons?

*They had been married a few years when they decided to throw their first dinner party. During the party, Cătălina had enjoyed talking to Réka, the wife of Dumitru's friend Sebastian. Like Cătălina, Réka too was from a small village that had fallen to Ceaușescu's system-atization program and was relocated to Bucharest. Exchanging stories with someone who had experienced similar horrors, while difficult, had been comforting somehow. That they even found some things to laugh about was refreshing and had added just a touch of light to a very dark memory. Réka and Sebastian were the last to leave, and when Cătălina closed the door behind them, she turned to Dumitru with a grin. "Wasn't that a wonderful party, Dumitru? I'm so happy that I got to meet many of your friends' wives, especially Réka." She lost her smile and fell silent when she noticed Dumitru's demeanor. He stood rigid in front of her, hands balled into tight fists, breath coming in short, shallow bursts. "Dumitru, what's wrong?" She hated that her voice trembled, but it trembled because she was beginning to learn exactly what was wrong when he looked like this. She had also known that he would both tell her and show her.*

*"Don't play dumb with me, you stupid cunt." He shoved her against the door and pinned her shoulders hard against it with his hands. He pressed his face to hers so closely that she felt the tip of his nose on her nose and smelled the remnants of their dinner: pork and cabbage and onions and parsley and dill (they had had sarmale and cheftele and potatoes and gogosi aromate for dessert. She couldn't smell the warm, sugary, homemade doughnuts on his breath. There was no sweetness on Dumitru's breath. Instead, she could smell only the sour, acrid smell of meat, vegetables, beer, and cruelty. The smell made her gag as he screamed at her, but she couldn't wriggle free. She stopped trying after he pulled her toward him and slammed her back against the door once again.*

*"Why were you talking to my friends? Why were you talking to their wives?" Cătălina could only stare. What did he mean, why was she talking? It was a party. "Answer me, woman!" His bellow made her eardrums quiver.*

*"Dumitru, I—"*

*"Shut up! Just shut up! You are nothing but a whore who doesn't deserve a voice. Is that want you wanted? To be everyone's whore tonight?*

*Is that why you flirted with them all, men and women?" Cătălina was stunned. That she could formulate no response didn't matter, for Dumitru's tirade continued without pause. "And why did you talk about yourself? No one cares about you. You made me feel embarrassed for you, and then when you wouldn't stop, I had to feel embarrassed because of you. You humiliated me at my own party, you cunt. You ruined the night, my night and everyone else's." He had begun slamming her against the door in time with his words, making her bite her tongue. Metallic-tasting fluid pooled in her mouth. She swallowed it to avoid further provoking Dumitru. She had less control over the fluid pooling in her eyes. "You cry now, you weak little whore? How will this feel?" Dumitru pulled his arm back and made a fist. Cătălina flinched hard in anticipation of the punch. Instead of striking her, Dumitru laughed. He returned his hand to her shoulder, breathed into her face, and then once again jerked his arm back. Once again Cătălina flinched. Once again he laughed. Again he replaced his hand, again he pulled back, again she flinched, and again he laughed. On the fourth time, Dumitru pulled his fist back and immediately smashed it forward into Cătălina's face, knocking her head hard against the door. Dumitru at last let go of her shoulders, and she slumped to the floor. She remained crumpled in a heap, her face against the floor in a puddle of blood, snot, and tears. She waited for Dumitru to leave, to go off somewhere for a long time, but she knew he hadn't retreated. He ordered her to rise, and she tried but was too slow. "You like the floor, you cunt? Is that what you were hoping, to get Réka on the floor with you? She wouldn't want you, Cătălina, not after what you told her about your life. But if you like the floor so much, you can clean up tonight's mess from down there." Because she had pulled herself into a kneeling position, she saw Dumitru stride toward their dining table, grab hold of the table cloth, and yank it hard. Plates, dishes, silverware, drinks, food, candles, everything from the evening cascaded and crashed onto the floor. A scream escaped her lips. Dumitru charged over, and she feared for what would come next. To her surprise, but not quite relief, he*

*merely lifted her to her feet and shoved her hard toward the table. "Clean*
*it up." He walked away, and she began to clean.*

Yes, Dumitru had taught her well over the years that she
was worthless, a nobody, and that people didn't want to hear
the things she had to say. She knew, too, that revealing things
about herself was a very dangerous thing to do. She neither
could nor should talk to Marcy about her doctor visit. How
could she admit that the general doctor thought that the best
way to help her was to send her to a psychiatrist? How could
she use the words he used: depression, complex post-trau-
matic stress disorder, anxiety disorders? Warning her that
their conversation wasn't enough to diagnose her, he gave her
the name and number of a psychiatrist and leaflets about
these conditions he thought would be important to investigate. Later when she read them at home in bed, she grew hot
with embarrassment. How could she tell Marcy about these?
How could she tell her that he, more familiar with depression
and anxiety than C-PTSD, had prescribed some medication
he said would help, that she could use while she waited to see
the psychiatrist? How could she tell Marcy that she didn't
have enough money for the medication or the psychiatrist but
that she didn't want these things anyway? These flaws of hers
would be far more shameful to disclose than the simple stories
of the Romanian countryside that she had now told two people: Réka and Marcy. She sighed. Marcy was looking at her
expectantly. To avoid ruining the nice relationship they were
forming, she'd tell her a partial truth to appease her.

"Well, he talked to me about different conditions that
involve pain like this. One is fibromyalgia."

"My landlady has fibromyalgia. I always feel so bad for
her because she seems so miserable. What are you going
to do? Are you going to have tests or whatever they do to

diagnose you? And of course get the medication you need. My landlady takes some stuff. She was telling me about it once. It seems like it's at least a little helpful. You should go back to the doctor, Catie."

Catie shrugged. Again, what should she say? What could she say? Again, an incomplete truth: "The doctor only said that it might be fibromyalgia. It could be something else. For now, he told me to eat healthy, exercise more, and stop focusing on my pain."

"What?! Are you kidding me? That's it?!" This exclamation made Lilly, awake in Marcy's arms, bellow.

"Here, give her to me." Catie reached out and took Lilly, held her close, spoke softly to her, and played with her hands and feet. Soon, she quieted and stuck her thumb in her mouth. Catie lowered her gently into a crib.

Marcy spoke. "I've said it before, and I'll say it again. You've got a special touch, Catie. Do you have lots of experience with babies?"

Yes, she thought, but she wasn't ready to go off on yet another topic about herself. She was suddenly exhausted and anxious about all that she had said. She glanced at the clock and noticed with relief that parents would be picking up their babies very soon.

Marcy didn't wait for an answer but returned to her other topic. "So back to this doctor. Are you going to go back to him or see someone better?"

Catie shook her head. "Neither. I don't have the time or the money. I learned that insurance only pays for part of a doctor visit. Florina and Alexandru are teenagers and have things come up that they need a doctor for. I want to save the money for them for when they need it."

"But Catie, you're in pain. There are things that can be done to help you so you can enjoy your life more."

Enjoy life? That was an odd concept, as strange as some of the new words and phrases she was picking up. Life wasn't for enjoyment. Life was labor. Life was suffering. Life was coming closer and closer to God in order to live with Him in heaven after you died. That's when enjoyment happened. Sure, Catie enjoyed moments in her life, like learning to use the loom with Bunicuță, like going regularly to a real church here in Sacramento, like first meeting Dumitru, like her children. But life itself, the main parts of living that existed all around the nice moments, wasn't meant to be enjoyed. She smiled at Marcy then. "Marcy, you made me feel better."

"So you'll change your mind and go see a different doctor?" Her voice was enthusiastic.

"No. Because you made me think. And remember. All of my pain and my feelings and hardships are just because that's life. My life here on this earth is about suffering and learning and loving God and preparing for Heaven. Going to the doctor again is a selfish thing to do for many, many reasons, including for trying to reduce my suffering. I needed to have that reminder. Thank you, Marcy." She smiled and fell silent.

"Oh my God, Catie, that's not what I meant! At all!"

"It's okay, Marcy. That's very much what I needed, and I'm grateful."

Marcy raised her arms as she exclaimed, "Catie!"

Involuntarily, Catie flinched. She raised her arms toward her face as if to shield it but quickly lowered them. She reached up and made sure her hair was covering her temples because they were throbbing again. They matched her heart rate. She saw Marcy's eyes widen and her jaw drop then close again. Shoot. She suddenly regretted everything, every single word she had uttered today. She was so stupid; she never learned this lesson, that she must keep her mouth shut. And she should avoid people and conversations altogether. What must Marcy think of her? Would work be awkward from now on?

Neither woman had the chance to speak, for parents began to arrive for their babies. Marcy and Catie each talked to the parents, telling them what went on that day, how their child did, and providing written documentation of how much was eaten, how many diapers changed, bowel movements, how much spitting up happened, interaction and demeanor, and more. Marcy had told Catie on more than one occasion that these parents were over-the-top obsessive; after all, the number of poops plopped or toys chewed on probably wouldn't be on their Harvard applications. Catie thought the parental concern was delightful. She shuddered and was saddened every time she thought of the abandoned babies she cared for in Romania. These babies at Hey Little Diddles had people who cared about them so much they were even interested in what went into their diapers. That was nice.

After the last baby left, Marcy walked over to where Catie was sanitizing the changing tables. "Catie, I really enjoyed talking with you today. I like getting to know you more."

Catie stared at the table she was wiping down. "Please don't feel you have to lie, Marcy. I understand why you would be angry or disgusted." Catie knew her voice sounded sincere, because she was very sincere. She understood very well that who she was and what she did angered and disgusted those around her.

"What? Why would I feel those awful things? How about we go out for a drink before heading home? I won't ask you any more questions, I promise."

Catie felt the blood drain from her face. She wondered briefly where it went when it did that. She shouldn't go out with Marcy before going home. Dumitru had always let her know in no uncertain terms that spending time with a friend when she was supposed to be at home taking care of him, the kids, and the house, was selfish, wrong, dirty, and disgusting. She didn't want to be any of those things anymore. But she liked Marcy. She already said things she shouldn't have today that just might make Marcy loathe her. How would Marcy feel about her when she didn't go get a drink with her? She'd find out very soon. "I...I shouldn't...I can't, Marcy. I just... well, I have to get home to prepare dinner."

"Relax, Catie. It's perfectly fine. I don't have kids, and I forget that other people do have kids that need them. Maybe we could plan something sometime."

"I'd like that." Catie was surprised that she did like the idea even though it was intimidating and she didn't know if she could ever do it.

# Chapter 9

As usual, Catie got off the bus at a stop that was several
blocks away from the stop closest to her house. She filed civilly
up the aisle of the bus and down its stairs and stepped onto the
pavement. She didn't think she'd ever take for granted these
American busses that were so easy to ride compared to the
chaotic, overcrowded, every-man-for-himself-and-look-out-
everybody-else-because-you'll-be-pushed-and-shoved-and-
trampled-if-you're-in-the-way busses of Bucharest. Around
her, bus riders dispersed. Shoes clicked in staccato bursts or
clunked heavily or traipsed languidly. She pretended that her
own shuffle was an important part of the symphony of shoes
going places, doing important things, and when most of the
people strode away in various directions, Catie felt alone.

It took less than five minutes to get where she was going.
When she arrived, she stopped and gazed up at St. Theocharis
Greek Catholic Church. The very symmetry of the cathe-
dral—or mini-cathedral if she compared it to those medieval
wonders in Romania—inspired awe and gave her pause. It
was a representation of God's perfection. The gigantic double wooden doors both welcomed people and humbled them.
The doors were so tall that Catie felt tiny whenever she passed
through them, and she liked the feeling because it reminded

her that yes, she was small, but God was bigger than every-thing and watching over her, protecting her like no one in this world did. Catie's gaze left the main doors, took in the double pointed lancet arches that framed them, the elaborate stone relief of Jesus and His apostles that filled the space between the top of the doors and the point of the arches, and her gaze rose up, up, up the center tower with its stained glass, lan-cet-arch windows and rested on the three-bar cross that had comforted her since she was very young.

Catie looked at her watch. Good. She had just enough time to go inside for a few minutes.

She grabbed the black iron ring on one of the doors and pulled. Because of deep aches in her fingers and hot nee-dles of pain searing her shoulder, she couldn't swing it wide. She wedged herself in the space she had made between the door and the inside of the church and inched her way in. When she stepped forward, the door shut behind her with a bang that echoed through the cavernous great hall. Startled, she jumped. She wished loud noises would stop upsetting her so much. She paused, closed her eyes, and tried to breathe slowly and deeply so she didn't feel in such a state of arousal. As she did, the smells of St. Theocharis wafted into her nose and infused her with peace. Wood oil, incense, candles, old books—the smells of sacredness and sanctuary and divinity—soothed her. She opened her eyes and made her way down the long aisle to the first pew. Placing a hand on the pew for support, she genuflected toward the Tabernacle, shuffled to the middle of the pew, and lowered herself onto the kneeler.

Rigid and still, she bowed her head, closed her eyes, and silently prayed. Her mind wandered a little, and she chastised herself. Yet her mind kept wandering where it wanted to go. She needed to keep so many things to herself, stuffed way down yet always close to the surface. It was tiring and very heavy. She was so grateful to God for being there to listen, for saving her, and for paving the way to a place far better than anywhere on this planet. She could talk to Him and to the saints, especially her own St. Basil, like she could talk to no living person on Earth. Thoughts of all that she had said to Marcy rushed into her mind, and her body didn't feel as still anymore. Her heart pounded, her chest constricted, and she suddenly felt sweaty. She needed to cough but held it in painfully. A tiny cough escaped, but she kept the rest in check. Dumitru's lessons in self-control had paid off, Catie thought wryly, but oh, what a price she had paid.

Without warning, someone knelt beside her. Her eyes flew open and she leapt to her feet, whacking her left foot hard against the kneeler and nearly losing her balance. "Oh my, Catie. Please forgive me. I didn't mean to startle you." The *preot*—priest, Catie corrected herself because she needed to think fully in English now—sat on the pew and smiled warmly. He gestured beside him. "Will you sit beside me for a moment?"

Furtively, Catie glanced around to see who might be watching. She silently berated herself. Of course no one was watching. She was tired of acting instinctively on old habits, but she couldn't seem to be able to stop. It was frustrating. Catie stole a glance at the priest beside her, still smiling warmly. He didn't seem to notice what was going through her mind. She forced a smile in return. "Father Stasiuk. You have done nothing that requires my forgiveness. I'm very sorry I jumped. It is my fault, not yours." She sat down beside the priest. She blushed and looked away because it seemed it was more painful for her to sit than it was for this man who was several decades older than she. She forced herself to hide her shame and look at him.

Again Father Stasiuk smiled kindly, a genuine smile that reached his eyes and deepened all of his many wrinkles. He leaned in toward Catie and whispered, "You know what I think? I think that the Lord might just think that we can both be forgiven." He winked at her. Catie's smile was more genuine this time. She liked Father Stasiuk. She found his Ukrainian accent charming and slightly reminiscent of home, and he was gentle and caring yet a commanding presence at the altar. He continued, "I won't keep you, Catie. I just wanted to say hello and see how you are. Are you and your children doing well?"

Not really, thought Catie. But she couldn't say that, couldn't impose her burdens on someone else, couldn't bear the disdain that she was sure she'd receive as a response. She swallowed, smiled, and replied, "Yes. Everything is fine. Thank you, Father, for asking." She felt nauseated and dizzy. How could she lie to a priest? That was like lying to God Himself. Her throat tightened, and she felt the pressure of tears. She willed herself not to cry. She succeeded; however, her nose began to run. She rummaged through her purse for a tissue.

"Catie?"

"Truly, we're fine. I appreciate you asking."

"If you'd ever like to talk, other than confession, I mean, you know where to find me." He smiled again.

"Thank you." She didn't trust herself to say more, so she simply smiled back. Surreptitiously, she glanced at her watch. Oh no! She was late. The kids must be starving, and Catie wasn't home to start dinner. What should she do? She couldn't keep her children waiting, but she couldn't be rude and cut off Father Stasiuk. The blood flowing through her head sounded like a roaring ocean. It felt like one, too, as she grew dizzier. Her problem was solved when the priest stood.

"Catie, I must be headed home. Lesya is making kruchenyky, and my mouth has been watering all day just thinking of it. Will I see you again on Sunday?"

"Of course. We will be here as always." The thought warmed Catie. Dumitru had forbidden Catie to go to church, and it had been devastating. She did what her beloved Bunicuţă had done when she was growing up. She worshipped at home. The difference was that no one else came as they had when Bunicuţă provided spiritual services, but Catie was glad about that. Dumitru wouldn't have allowed people to come anyway, so this way there was no conflict. But now that she was living in Sacramento, far, far away from Bucharest, she could go to church.

"Fantastic," Father Stasiuk said. "Now, I must be getting home. Stay as long as you wish. The door will lock behind you."

As the priest walked up the aisle, Catie thought again how odd it was to hear him refer to his wife. While she knew that Greek Catholic priests were allowed to marry, she also knew that most didn't. She was happy for him and for his wife. God is about love, so wouldn't he want his priests to experience love? And all people, too. The difference between God's love and people's love, she mused, was that God's love is pure and unconditional. Often, human love was contingent upon something else or was a lie or a trick. Catie much preferred God's love. And speaking of love, Catie needed to get home to Florina and Alexandru. She loved her children deeply, and she felt very guilty for dragging them across the globe to live somewhere unfamiliar and unknown. She needed to be there for them always, letting them know they were loved and helping them adjust. Catie hurried through the rest of her prayers, said an additional prayer for forgiveness in being so rushed, and headed out the door to shuffle the rest of the way home.

Twenty minutes later, she stepped into her house, pulled the door shut behind her, and called, "Florina! Alexandru! I'm home. I'm so sorry I'm late. You must be starving." She stopped talking and stood listening, waiting for a response. She felt the muscles in her face bunch up in confusion and concern. She had expected to be greeted with an outburst of ire from Florina, a frenzy of cantankerous behavior between Florina and Alexandru, or both. But neither occurred. The house was quiet. "Kids?" She called again.

Her heart suddenly beat rapidly, painfully, against her chest and in her temples as a thought struck her. Dumitru! Somehow he had found them, and he had stolen Florina and Alexandru. But how? She pressed the heels of her hands against her temples and dug her fingers into the top of her head. Finding her was supposed to be impossible. Unless... No. It just wasn't possible. Or was it? Frantically, she tore through the house in search of children or notes or evidence, anything. The fear super-charged her. Everything looked brighter, and she heard sounds she didn't normally hear: curtains brushing noisily against the wall as they billowed in the breeze; floorboards creaking more loudly than usual. Wait! What was that? Was someone in her bedroom closet, waiting to ambush her? Wasn't that one of Dumitru's fun games? Hiding, lying in wait for her to inadvertently come near, and then pouncing on her, knocking her to the ground, and beating her for "allowing someone to break in and hide in order to hurt her." Was he in her closet now? The room blurred, and she blinked it back into focus. *Not this time, Dumitru.*

Catie glanced around the room for something to protect her. She spotted the empty vase on her dresser. It was small, but she knew from experience how painful a vase or similar object could be when it was broken over the head. Subconsciously, she rubbed the top of her head as she moved to grab the vase. She licked her dry lips, tried to swallow—it took two attempts—and charged at the closet, tossed it open, and shouted, "What did you do with the children?" Silence. When she swung the vase down, it swept through clothing. She brought the vase up to her chest and watched it shake in her hand. She gasped for breath, gathered herself to check Florina's and Alexandru's rooms. Nothing there, either. No people. No evidence of clothing or other things removed. But that didn't mean much. Dumitru could have forced them out in a hurry without bothering to pack.

Still frantic, Catie returned to the kitchen. She had flown through it before but could determine nothing because of the disgusting mess still waiting to be cleaned. She felt her energy drain completely out of her body as she surveyed the kitchen. What should she do? She had no idea how to go about figuring out where Dumitru had taken her children. She had no one to call. She was starting to like Marcy, but she couldn't call her for something like this. Father Stasiuk was home now, and she had no way of reaching him; she knew neither his address nor his private number. The police? Absolutely not. They wouldn't help. If anything, she'd be taken away and locked up for being a neglectful parent and disobedient wife for running away. Without her children, she had nothing to live for. Catie bit her lip to still her trembling chin, but it didn't work. She began to sob.

"Mamă! What's wrong?"

Catie jumped at the sound of her son's voice, dropped the vase she had continued to hold, jumped again at the sound of it crashing to the floor and shattering, twisted around to face Alexandru, and threw her arms around him. "Alexandru! You're here!" She pulled back and held him at arm's length as she surveyed him from head to toe and back again. "And you're okay!"

"Of course I'm here and okay, Mamă. Why wouldn't I be?" His voice was soft, his tone confused.

Catie closed her eyes and sighed deeply. "I know it's silly, but I thought your father had come here and taken you and Florina." She stepped back, crunching ceramic pieces into even smaller bits. She sighed again. One more thing to clean up. As if he read her mind, Alexandru stepped toward the little closet where they kept cleaning supplies, grabbed the broom and dustpan, and began to sweep up the shards of vase. Catie tried to grab the broom. "No! I've got this. I broke the vase, and I must clean it up." Her voice was tight and had risen in pitch.

Alexandru put his hand over hers. "I've got it, Mamă. It's okay. I'm not Dad. I can clean up, and I won't beat you for not doing it." Catie bowed her head. Hearing those words come out of her son's mouth made her ill. She hated that her children knew so much, had seen so much. Did it harm them, seeing their mother treated that way? And they saw the truth so there was no hiding the fact that she was someone who was flawed and incompetent and fully unworthy of love. She thought of the bloodroot flower. *I love me not. And I don't deserve it, anyway.* Alexandru broke into her thoughts. "Hey, and didn't you see the note I left you?"

Cătălina looked at him. "You left a note?"

"Yeah. The counters were too full, so I stuck it on the fridge. See?" He pointed to the refrigerator. Almost the entire surface was plastered with papers. Report cards, Florina's beautiful drawings, Alexandru's ribbons and certificates from events, mostly sports-related, at school, prayer cards, and fliers reminding them of important events either decorated or cluttered the fridge, depending on what they were. There was her son's note, stuck on top of one of his sister's pencil drawings of a busy street in Bucharest. Catie recognized the buildings on either side of the drawing. The way her daughter captured the movement and energy of the throng of people on the sidewalks amazed Catie. It saddened her, too. Florina clearly loved Bucharest and was homesick. She didn't consider Sacramento with her mother and brother to be home.

Catie pulled Alexandru's note off of Florina's drawing. "Alexandru, if your sister had seen this, she would have been livid, and you would have received an earful."

Alexandru grinned. "I know." He laughed.

Catie shook her head and looked at the note, tiny, messy words scribbled onto a little Post-It note. Even if she hadn't been frantic when running through the kitchen, she probably wouldn't have spotted this. Still, her son had made a genuine effort to tell her where he was and when he'd be back, so she didn't chastise him. She looked at the note again. "So you were playing soccer?"

"Yeah. My friends all play. We play mini games during lunch at school. They say I'm a natural." He grinned. "They think it's because I'm from Eastern Europe so I must be good. Anyway, they invited me to come to practice with them after school today so I did." Catie watched him begin to walk around the small area. He had always carried his enthusiasm with him in his body, and when he was excited, he was animated. She smiled but then quickly returned to a neutral expression. A lifetime of being punished for showing emotion when no one wanted to see her feelings worn on the outside had made her conscious of every twitch of her face. Wearing a neutral expression was a habit drilled into her by hand. She continued to pay attention to Alexandru.

"The coach talked to me after practice. He was impressed with my playing! He wants me to be on the team, Mamă. I really want to. What do you think? Can I?"

He came to a stop in front of her and leaned back against the counter. Dishes clanked when he did so, which made Catie sigh. "But what about running track? I thought you liked it." Catie had been happy that Alexandru wanted to be on his school's track team. It meant that he was adjusting well to America and participating in activities with people his age. Also, because it was a school sport, it was free. Catie didn't know how soccer worked since it wasn't affiliated with the school.

Alexandru shrugged a shoulder. "Eh," he grunted. "I like running, but not really in an oval. I much prefer the speed and type of skill needed in soccer. Plus more of my friends play soccer. It'd be fun. They all want me to play, and the coach says I should start tomorrow." He bounced on the balls of his feet, looked down, and made a swooping motion with a foot, mimicking kicking a soccer ball. He looked back up and swiped his hair off of his face. Catie studied the sparkle in his eyes, the flush of his cheeks. She loved how her son loved life. Despite her childhood, she used to feel that way sometimes, too.

*One sunny Sunday afternoon in the late summer of 1990, shortly after she and Dumitru had begun married life, they were enjoying the day in Herăstrău Park. Stretched on a blanket near other couples doing the same, they kissed passionately and enjoyed the feel of each other, both still needing each other's comfort from the trauma of Mineriad earlier in the summer. The sound of Dumitru's rumbling stomach suddenly interrupted the sound of the pontoon boats on the nearby lake. Cătălina laughed and placed a hand on her husband's stomach. "Hungry?"*

*"Starving." Dumitru leaned forward and kissed her passionately again. He rubbed his hand along Cătălina's bare leg and up under her skirt. "But this is what I'm hungry for," he muttered. Moments later, his stomach rumbled again. This time Dumitru laughed. "Okay. Maybe we should eat."*

*"I think that's a good idea." Cătălina kissed him once more and then wriggled to her knees to unpack the picnic basket. As they were enjoying their lunch, relaxed and content on the blanket, a young woman approached on the path. Cătălina waved enthusiastically and jumped to her feet as the woman approached. "Adriana!" They kissed each other's cheeks, and Catie invited her to sit.*

*Adriana lowered herself onto the blanket. "I can only stay for a second. Daniel is waiting for me over there." She gestured in a direction farther up the path and off to the side. Before speaking again, she selected a sărățele from the plate that Cătălina extended in her direction. She took a bite, closed her eyes, chewed, and swallowed before proclaiming, "Cătălina, l love your cheese sticks. Anyway, I'm so glad I ran into you two here. Daniel and I and a bunch of couples are going clubbing tonight. Want to come?"*

*Cătălina smiled broadly. "Yes! That sounds like fun. Of course we'll come, won't we Dumitru?" She turned to look at her husband. Her smile faded when she saw his face, hard and pinched. His eyes looked like they had receded deeper into his face, and they had a cold look to them. Could eyeballs look cold, Cătălina wondered to herself. She tried to picture the eyes of her family members but couldn't. Dumitru's intense glare chased away all of her thoughts. She swallowed. He had looked like this a couple times before, so she had a guess as to what was going to follow. She shuddered.*

*"Actually, no. We won't be joining you tonight, Adriana." Catie was surprised at his kind, jovial tone. She hadn't expected that. Maybe she had been wrong about the meaning of his expression. "But we'd love to join you next time. Perhaps soon?"*

*"Of course. We might go again this weekend. I'll let you know. Now, I must get back to Daniel."*

*After she had gone, Dumitru talked to her in a low growl, "Pack up our things. We're going home." He stood, stomped on the plate of sărățele, breaking the plate and squishing cheesy bread into the blanket. Cătălina stared at him, mouth agape in confusion. "Now!" he bellowed.*

*Ignoring the looks of the people who had turned to the sound of Dumitru, Cătălina scrambled to clean up and pack the basket. In her haste, she cut her finger on a shard of broken plate. She simply wrapped a napkin around it to absorb the blood, and then she followed Dumitru home. She remained a few steps behind him because whenever she trotted and caught up with him, he shoved her backward and walked faster. Eventually, Cătălina gave up and just stayed behind him.*

*When they reached their apartment, Dumitru stomped in ahead of her and slammed the door in her face.*

The memory of the slamming door echoed loudly in Catie's head, jarring her out of the recollection. She felt dizzy, so she placed her hands against the edge of the counter to brace herself. Instantly, sharp needles of pain shot from her wrists to her shoulders. She stood straight. Absentmindedly, she lifted her right hand to her left shoulder and let her fingers find the thick scar. She traced the outline of it, ran a finger up and down the length of it, and pushed down on it to flatten the ridge that rose up over the surrounding skin. It was the first scar Dumitru gave her, and he had done it with the jagged edge of the plate he had stomped on in the park.

He had blamed her for breaking it, and then he had thrown it at her. She was grateful that it had hit her shoulder; it could have hit her neck or her face. At the time, she wasn't grateful that he had thrown it, and she had made the mistake of letting Dumitru know it.

"Mamă, breathe into this." Cătălina looked in the direction of the voice. Why was Dumitru calling her Mamă? Was this another of his mind games? What was he handing to her? She couldn't breathe. She clawed at her throat in an attempt to make it open. When she did, she could feel her heart beating in the soft hollow just above the V of her collarbones. It was beating too fast! "Mamă!" She heard the voice again and blinked several times to bring the face into focus. It was Alexandru, and he had a paper lunch bag. With shaking hands, she took the proffered bag and put it over her mouth with the expertise that comes from years of repetition.

Alexandru helped her sit at the table. Once her breathing had returned to normal, Catie rubbed her forehead and stared at the messy kitchen. The sight still exhausted her, but it was easier to look at that than at her son. Alexandru popped his head into her vision. To her chagrin, he said, "I'm sorry I asked about soccer. I don't have to do it."

"A mother's ears hear more than words. You are a very thoughtful young man, but I know how much it would disappoint you not to play soccer with your friends. I'm proud of you that they asked you to play, Alexandru, and play you will!" Catie forced enthusiasm into her voice. She would not take away her son's zest for life the way her family and, later, Dumitru had robbed Catie of hers. She'd figure out a way to pay. In fact, last week's church bulletin announced that embroiderers were needed to make new adornments for the altar, pews, crosses, and walls. She'd look into that.

Catie took her son's face in her hands. "I mean it. You deserve to play, and I don't want you to worry about it. I was thinking about something different that made me anxious. It wasn't you." Catie's gut twisted and tumbled over itself. She was sick at the thought that Alexandru might blame himself for her reaction. She had been blamed and beaten for things her whole life, but in her case, it was justified. Alexandru, on the other hand, had never done anything to warrant blame and hatred, and she would make sure he never felt as though he had.

Alexandru beamed. He hugged her. "Thanks, Mamă."

"You can thank me by having fun and enjoying soccer. Now, do you have homework tonight?"

"Ugh. Yes. Math and social studies."

"You have a lot of social studies homework. Is it a hard class?"

Alexandru shrugged. "Not really. It's just that there's a lot of reading. Many people finish in class, but it takes me longer because the readings aren't the same as normal talking English so I don't know some of the words. But I'm getting better at it."

Catie scooted to the edge of her chair, posture stiff. She gasped, and when she tried to talk the words just croaked in her throat. She cleared her throat and tried again. "Alexandru! You speak English so well. I didn't know that you were having trouble understanding in school." She shook her head. How did she not know that language was a problem for her son? What about Florina? She shook her head again to focus on her son. "What about your other classes? Science and English and—"

Alexandru laughed and put his hand on Catie's shoulder. "Relax, Mamă. It's okay. You've seen my grades. I'm doing well! He straightened to his full height and looked proud. Catie smiled in spite of her worry. "Mr. Lewis does a great job of giving notes so the vocabulary words in the textbook make sense. And the books we're reading in English class happen to be available in Romanian too. Mr. Chancelor ordered copies for me, and I read both. My ability to read specific things in English is catching up to my speaking and listening." He moved his feet as if he were maneuvering a soccer ball again. "It's pretty cool, actually." He grinned and wiggled his eyebrows. "And what's really cool is having chicks dig my accent and me speaking Romanian!"

Catie furrowed her brows and tilted her head to the side. "Chicks? Like baby chickens?" That didn't make a whole lot of sense, but then neither did teenage boys.

Her son laughed. "No! It's slang. Chicks. You know, girls."

Catie frowned. Derogatory terms weren't funny. "That doesn't sound very respectful, Alexandru. I don't want you calling people belittling names."

"It's not derogatory. They like it." Catie sighed. She wasn't sure about that, but now wasn't the time to get into it. Maybe she'd ask Marcy about the word, and if it was bad she'd figure out a way to take it up with her son.

For now, she said, "Well, okay. You have a lot of homework. You should get started, and I'll make dinner." She watched her son swoop up his backpack, sling it over one shoulder, and head to his room. The door shut, and a few short moments later, loud noise reached the kitchen despite Alexandru's closed door. While technically it was music, to Catie it seemed like nothing other than noise pollution. She stuck out her tongue in disgust. With a sigh, she placed the palms of her hands on her thighs and slowly stood. As she rummaged through the cupboards in search of something to prepare, a thought struck her. She chastised herself for not thinking of it before. How horrible she was. She quickly shuffled to Alexandru's door and knocked. At the invitation to enter, she poked her head into his room and inquired, "Do you have any idea where your sister is and when she's coming home?"

"Nope."

"Great. I haven't found a note from her."

Alexandru snorted. "Of course she wouldn't leave a note. She's selfish and inconsiderate." An impish grin exposed white teeth. "She's the devil child. I'm the perfect one."

"Your sister isn't the devil. But I will say that you are wonderful." To spare him the pressure of a response, she swiftly shut the door and returned to the Sisyphean challenge that was her kitchen.

* * *

Catie awoke with a start. She bolted upright. The first thing that came to her awareness was the kink in her neck. She massaged her neck with her hands. Why did it feel this way? Disoriented, she looked around. This wasn't her bedroom. Not again. Where was she? Where had he taken her to punish her this time? She blinked rapidly. Objects began to take shape. A chair over there, a round side table, a lamp that she knew was brightly colored and patterned during the day but now hid itself in the dark. This was her living room. She looked down. She had been sleeping on the couch. No pillows. That would explain the kink in her neck. Next, she became aware that she was covered in a sweat that was growing colder by the moment. She must have had another nightmare. She shivered herself into her room. She had one knee already on the bed and was about to swing her other leg up and under the covers when she remembered what she had been doing in the living room in the first place. Florina! She hadn't come home yet.

Yanking her quilt off the bed and wrapping it around her, she hustled down the hallway to Florina's room. She didn't have to knock because it was wide open. Everything remained undisturbed because there was no Florina there to disturb it.

Frantic, Catie, rushed to the kitchen to look at the clock on the microwave. The glowing blue numbers, brighter than the blue emergency lights on a police car at night, screamed the time. Three forty-eight. Almost four o'clock and no Florina! What had happened to her baby girl? Well, not a baby anymore, but still her baby girl in her heart. Not for the first time, Catie cursed the fact that she couldn't afford to buy cell phones; all three of them had them from Bucharest, but they were useless here. She had a basic phone now but could only afford a single line. After she paid for Alexandru's soccer, the next thing would be cell phones.

Catie returned to the living room. She tried to look out the window, but with the darkness beyond it, it was just a mirror and all she saw was a scraggly, ugly, pathetic hag looking back at her. Dumitru's description of her, one he gave her when Florina was young, was spot-on. The hag in front of her blurred as tears filled her eyes. Oh, Florina.

As images splattered in her mind of what might have happened to Florina, the knot in her stomach grew so big and so heavy that it pushed against her legs until they threatened to give out. She staggered back to sit on the couch. As she sat, she chewed her nails with electrified energy. Finally, she could sit no longer, and she sprang to her feet. She had paced the room many times when she heard a key jam into the door's lock. Her heart stopped, then quickened. She held her breath and sat very still because she wasn't sure how she should react to Florina. Yell? Question her? Hug her? All of these? None of these?

The door swung open, and Catie watched her teenage daughter stride in without hesitation. She kicked the door shut with her heel as she casually looked around. "Oh. Hey Mother."

Catie stood, approached Florina, opened her mouth to talk, shut it again, and rubbed her eyebrows with her thumb and finger as if that would shake her thoughts loose. Florina wasn't the least bit apologetic. She acted as though this behavior was okay! She acted like her father. Catie's throat closed at the thought. Her hand moved from her forehead to her throat.

Florina sighed impatiently and nudged Catie aside. "If you're just going to stand there opening and closing your mouth like a stupid fish, I'm going to bed."

Catie found her voice and followed Florina to her room. "Florina Grigorescu! I have been very worried about you. Not coming home for dinner, not leaving a note, not asking my permission, not coming home until four in the morning," Catie ran her hands through her hair before folding them across her chest, "all of that behavior is unacceptable, and—"

"And *what?*" Florina yanked off her spiked pumps and threw them on top of a pile of her other shoes. She pulled down lacy tights, a leather miniskirt that barely stretched over her butt, wriggled out of a shirt that looked three sizes too small, and reached her arms behind her to unfasten her bra. She stopped. "God, mother, turn around. Can I have a little privacy? I know how fond you are of women, but watching your own daughter? That's gross. God."

Cătălina turned around and took a few deep breaths. She rubbed her temples. She would not get pulled into this fight. She needed to focus on Florina's late night. When she heard Florina slip on her nightgown, she turned back around. "Where were you?" she demanded.

"Out with Jeff."

"Who is Jeff?"

"My boyfriend. Duh. I mentioned him last week before school. Keep up." Florina flopped onto her bed then sat up, cross-legged, and began to brush her hair.

Catie narrowed her eyes. "Your hair is quite disheveled, Florina." Her daughter shrugged and kept brushing and smoothing. "Who did you and Jeff go out with?"

"No one. It was just us."

Catie felt her eyes widen. "Just the two of you? Not other couples?" She heard her own voice rise in pitch.

Florina made a dismissive noise. "No, not with other couples. It was a *date*. Ugh. Don't look at me like that. We're in America, not Romania. People don't always go out in big groups here."

Catie nodded sharply to the pile of shed clothes on the floor. "I see you dressed like you are in Romania. People dress differently there, Florina. Female clothes are often skimpy, but their behavior doesn't match. Here, when people dress skimpy, their behavior matches. Your hair is all over the place, your makeup is smudged, and it's four in the morning on a school night. What have you been doing?"

"Mother, settle down. You're going to wake Alexandru. I've been with my boyfriend doing American things." She huffed and dropped the brush, watching it bounce on the mattress.

"American things?"

Florina leapt to her feet and stood face to face with Catie. Catie noticed the smell of alcohol on her daughter's breath.

She opened her mouth to say something about it, but Florina talked over her. "Yes, American things. *A-mer-i-can*! You should be glad, Mother. You ripped us away from our home, you took us away from Dad, sneaking so he couldn't stop you or keep us. You brought us all the way to this stupid country. I don't even want to be here! I hate it! Jeff is the only person I like, and I'm going to be with him whenever I want to and to hell with you and Alexandru and school and everything else. Dad was so right about you. I hate you! Get out of my room!"

Catie felt herself sag as all of the anger left her body. Florina's behavior and words were unacceptable, but her daughter was hurting. Catie put her hands on Florina's shoulders and attempted to kiss her cheek. "Flor——"

Florina ripped herself away from Catie's touch, plopped down onto the bed, and rolled over to face the wall.

Catie sighed. "I expect to see you in the kitchen in three hours. You have school." She turned and left the room, pulling the door shut behind her. She paused at Florina's door, rested her forehead against the smooth wood, and whispered, "I'm so sorry, my daughter."

Too burdened with guilt and sorrow to hurry to bed, Catie returned to the living room to retrieve her quilt. She sat for a moment in the dark room. Everything was still and silent, but Catie felt an electric charge all around her. It happened that way frequently; when her anxiety was so great, it rose to the surface, spilled out of her body, and filled the spaces around her.

As she sat, she heard the clomp of footsteps nearing her door. The paper woman was delivering the daily newspaper. Catie hoped the woman wouldn't get an electric shock from the anxiety in the air. Catie stood and walked closer to the window so she could see out. She watched as the woman, about her own age, laid the paper gently in front of the door then turned to walk back down the sidewalk. She didn't so much as glance into the window. Why not, Catie wondered. Was it the rule of her job not to look in windows? Probably. But was it more than that, too? Did she, like Catie herself, avoid looking in things, at things, around things because she had been punished harshly for doing so? Was it easier just not to look, not to connect? Was the woman happy that way? Or was she lonely? Maybe she was someone that couldn't talk to Catie, but who could be a silent window-friend. The newspaper was her way of saying, "Here, I'm connecting with you the only way I can." Catie went to the door, opened it, picked up the paper, and put it on the dining table before going to her room. *I accept your offering, my special window friend.*

Finally, she crawled into bed and curled up much like Florina had. As she pulled her heavenly quilt around her, her fingertips traced the image of St. Basil. She thought of one of his quotes: "A tree is known by its fruit, a man by his deeds." She closed her eyes and prayed to her saint and to Jesus Christ Himself, "How, oh Lord, do you know me when none of my deeds are right?" Catie made the sign of the cross and drifted to sleep on her river of tears.

# Chapter 10

On her way out the door, Catie paused at a patch of flowers in her yard. Alexandru had bounded happily out the door early, headed to play soccer with his friends before school. Getting Florina up had been a nightmare. Catie withstood the brutal name-calling and other harsh accusations for the sake of getting her daughter awake and away to school. Not wanting to make things worse than they already were, Catie ignored Florina's treatment of her. Miraculously, both children left the house in plenty of time for Catie to get to work on time. That didn't mean she was thrilled with how the morning had been with Florina, though. Catie reached down, plucked a flower, and as she walked to the bus stop she played the same game she had yesterday. She started with *"I love me"* on the first petal and progressed to *"I love me not"* for the rest of them.

She reached work as Marcy did, and Marcy greeted her enthusiastically with, "Bună dimineaţa!"

Catie grinned broadly. ""Bună dimineaţa to you, too, Marcy. How do you know that Romanian greeting?"

Marcy shrugged. "I looked it up online. I thought it would be fun to learn some Romanian. But I didn't know about all of those little symbols on letters. I have no idea how to pronounce the words. I used the sound button for that one. I don't know if I've told you this, but I love how beautiful Romanian sounds."

Without meaning to, Catie thought of Dumitru's gruff voice barking at her. Of her mother. Of the *Securitate*. She shuddered. "No. I don't think it's beautiful at all. Not when it's striking out in a snarl. It's ugly."

"Well, I suppose anything would sound ugly if it were snarled. Do Romanians snarl everything at each other?"

Catie tilted her head to one side as she contemplated this. She wasn't sure what she wanted to say, and she definitely didn't know how she could explain the things she could say. Catie focused her attention back on Marcy because Marcy resumed without giving her a chance to think. Or maybe Marcy had given her a chance, but Catie had been too slow. She sighed and silently cursed her brain. It seemed to be filled with goo, slowing everything down and making thinking of even the simplest things feel nearly impossible.

"Catie! You're not listening. What's up?"

Catie felt her cheeks burn. She patted them and moved a hand up to wipe beads of sweat from her brow. Clearly, she couldn't even pay attention to one person, a person she could have become friends with if she weren't so inept. She looked down and mumbled, "I'm sorry, Marcy, I, um, well..." Catie trailed off. She was spared from further comment by parents arriving with babies.

As the two women settled in to their morning routine, a process Marcy always referred to as "wee-one wrangling," Marcy asked, "So how was your night?"

Catie shrugged, and then winced at the pain that shot through her shoulders and up her neck as she did so. She let her frown deepen because she didn't have the strength to hold up a smile.

"Wow, that bad, huh?"

"What? No. I didn't even say anything." Catie placed a hand to her chest and pressed slightly in an attempt to stop her heart from pounding. She was usually so skilled at masking how she truly felt. What had she done to make Marcy know that things were bad last night? She turned ever so slightly sideways, busying herself by organizing supplies on the changing station yet allowing herself to glance surreptitiously at Marcy. As she watched for clues that would give away Marcy's thoughts, she didn't see anything disapproving or hostile. And when Marcy spoke, her voice sounded light.

"You didn't have to say anything, silly. You just look drained. I have a good friend with triplets and a husband who travels a lot. She often looks weary, so I recognized your look. You two make me glad I'm single, childless, and carefree."

Catie seized the opportunity to shift the conversation. "You don't have a boyfriend?"

"Nah. I mean, I did. I dated a guy, Nate, for a couple of years. He was all right. We got along and had fun and stuff, but it wasn't a permanent thing."

Catie's curiosity was piqued. In spite of herself, she blurted, "Why not? Was there something bad that caused you to break up?" As soon as the sentence was out of her mouth, she realized in horror that she had asked someone a direct personal question; no, actually three total. Dumitru had grown tired of her questions and had taught her not to do that. Had she forgotten that lesson so soon? She backpedaled, "Marcy, I'm sorry for asking something so personal. Please don't answer that."

"Catie, we're friends. That's not too personal. And no, nothing bad happened. Nate got transferred for his job. His company moved him to Maine. We talked about my going with him, but I like living here. I care about him, but I discovered that I didn't love him enough to go with him, especially someplace only a few states away from my family." Marcy stuck out her tongue.

"You had a choice? And you chose not to go? With your man?" Catie was incredulous. She forgot about not asking personal questions.

"Well, yeah." She bent down to dig through a few of the colorful bins that lined a wall, selected a few toys, some squishy and textured, some smooth and jangly. She popped back up and jostled them in her hands. She shrugged nonchalantly and continued, "I thought of a future with him and one without him. He was nice and all, but not happily-ever-after-riding-into-the-sunset-on-horseback. Not that I want to ride horses with someone. I had enough of that growing up, and frankly, if I never see another horse in my life that's fine with me. I much prefer my chinchillas, thank you very much."

"Chinchillas? What are chinchillas?

"Oh my gosh! You work with the crazy chinchilla lady, and you don't know what chinchillas are? Here hold these. I'll be right back." Marcy thrust the handful of toys into Catie's arms. Catie promptly placed them on a blanket and grabbed baby Gus who was becoming frustrated with his tummy time. As Catie bounced Gus gently in her arms, she watch Marcy rummage through her oversized bag and stride back to Catie with her phone. She tapped the screen a few times, then swapped phone and baby with Catie so Catie could look at the pictures.

Catie broke into a grin as she swiped the screen. Fuzzy balls of gray fluff that had tails like squirrels, round ears like mice only bigger, and bodies of bunnies were caught jumping or nibbling on toes, presumably Marcy's, or emerging from tunnels. "These are adorable! Do they just run free in your house like this?"

Marcy shook her head. "No. They'd get into too much trouble and leave little poops everywhere. They're like Pez dispensers. I have a room that I let them out in, and we play. They jump high." She raised Gus over her head as she did it. He laughed. "They hop down." She swooped him down, which elicited more giggles. "They bounce all over the place." Marcy bounced him up and down. He spit up all over himself and the floor.

Catie gasped. "Oh no. I'm so sorry. I'm sorry about the mess, Marcy. If I wouldn't have asked about your chinchillas, this wouldn't have happened. Here, let me take care of this." Her words came out in a rush. In a swift motion, she swiped a cloth from the changing table, stepped to Marcy, took the little guy out of her arms, comforted him, and bent to blot the carpet. Her face burned, and she refused to look at Marcy when she spoke.

"What the heck, Catie? This isn't your fault. It's not anyone's fault. It just happened. Babies spit up."

"Of course they do, but he wouldn't have done so just now if I hadn't asked you about the chinchillas. I do such stupid things all the time. I'll take care of this."

"Catie—"

"Please." She continued to dab furiously at the floor. She still refused to look at Marcy, and she didn't look up again until she heard Marcy cross the room to answer a cry. As she cleaned and changed Gus, Marcy returned to her side.

Softly, Marcy asked, "Why did you react that way, Catie?"

Catie focused on Gus, counting the snaps of his sleeper out loud to him as she fastened him back up. She scooped him up and cradled him, rocking him slightly. "There you go, little guy. Now you're all ready for play time." She lowered him onto a large blanket with two other babies, ensured that they each had a nice assortment of soft toys and noise makers, and then before standing, she said a silent prayer that Marcy had forgotten about her question.

When her prayer was answered, Catie offered up another silent prayer, this one of gratitude. Rather than pressing her about her reaction to Gus's spit-up, she looked at Catie with admiration and stated, "I love watching you with the babies, Catie. You seem so natural. I suppose being a mother helps."

"It does. But I've always cared for babies and children, so I've had a lot of practice."

"Did you babysit? I always wanted to babysit when I was home from school in the summers, but my parents forbade it. They said it was beneath me, and they made me work for one of their friends, a congresswoman. Oh my god it was awful. I would have been happier babysitting." Suddenly, Marcy's eyes widened and her mouth dropped open. "Oh! I bet that sounded awful. I don't think babysitting is beneath me or anyone. That was my pretentious, self-important, selfish parents. I wasn't trying to insult you!"

Marcy looked so troubled by her perceived offense that Catie couldn't help but smile. "I don't think you were insulting. Besides, it's true that I'm beneath you." She saw that Marcy opened her mouth, presumably to protest or ask another question, so Catie rushed on without giving her the chance to do so. "Anyway, I always took care of younger members of my family, and I worked in an orphanage for more than three decades."

"Three *decades*? A decade in English means 10 years."

"Yes, that's correct. I started when I was seven, and I worked there until I left Romania to come here."

"What? How did you work at an orphanage when you were seven? How was that even legal?"

Catie smiled. "Romania isn't like the United States, especially not when it was under Communist rule."

"Fair enough." She shook her head. Rather than looking Marcy in the eye, Catie watched Marcy's ponytail jiggle back and forth with the motion. "But what about school? Don't children in Romania go to school?"

Catie felt an urge to defend her home country. "Of course they do. I went to school. Only sometimes, though." Her face and hands felt like they warmed up several degrees, so she looked down at the floor and hid her hands in the pockets of her pants. Mortified, she noticed a spot on her thigh and brushed furiously at it. When it didn't fade, she sighed and looked back up but didn't look directly at Marcy. She continued, "I attended school when I could, but it wasn't always possible." Catie shrugged. Silently, she asked God to let Marcy change the subject. Her prayer was at least partially answered, for Marcy didn't mention school again.

"So how did you come to work at an orphanage when you were seven?"

Catie's chest tightened, and her heart protested the sudden confinement by beating rapidly. After she swallowed twice to clear away gooey paste, *lipici*, that had lodged there, she was able to speak. "I was searching for my little cousin, Dionisie. He was taken away from our family when the *Securitate* killed his parents, my favorite uncle and aunt."

# Bucharest, Romania
## *March 4, 1977*

# Chapter 11

· · · · · · · · · · · · · · · · · · · ·

Picking her way through the dark and around obstacles littering the tiny apartment, carrying small tin cups filled with primrose tea to her grandparents, Cătălina stumbled when something—or rather, someone—grabbed her ankle. She fell flat onto her stomach, arms outstretched, and hands empty because the three cups now lay on their sides several inches in front of her. Liquid pooled around them.

"Filip! Look what you made me do." Cătălina twisted around and was now on all fours, glaring at her cousin.

"Cătălina!" Cătălina squeezed her eyes shut and sighed. Her mother was on her in an instant. "How dare you blame Filip for your clumsiness! You are a horrible, wasteful child who cannot even take responsibility for her own misdeeds. You are a disgrace, Cătălina. A hurtful one at that. That was the last of our ration of tea. We won't have more for quite a while, but you don't seem to care about that." Mamă was now screeching, hands gesturing furiously at Cătălina. Cătălina knew no one would come to her rescue, so she merely looked down and endured the tirade. "You careless, selfish, *răsfățata!*" She slapped Cătălina hard across her cheek. Cătălina raised her hand to rub her stinging skin, but her mother grabbed her wrist and yanked her hand away as she continued. "We are all nearly starving. We don't have enough to eat. We don't have enough to drink. No one in Bucharest does. And you just spilled the last of our tea on the floor. I'm ashamed to call you my daughter." Mamă stomped away, but there wasn't far for her to go. She stood against a wall and glared at Cătălina. Cătălina looked at Filip. He stuck his tongue out at her and went back to carving an image on a chunk of wood. He stooped over it so his face was close to the wood, presumably to make it easier to see in the dark. The electricity had been out for days now, not that it mattered. They didn't have much to use anyway thanks to President Ceauşescu's rationing program. Cătălina watched Filip for a few seconds. She hoped he cut off the tip of his nose.

Her eyes filled with tears. Mamă was right. She was a horrible person, a disgrace. Bunicuţă called to her, "Cătălina, come here after you wipe up the mess." Cătălina nodded, cleaned the mess with a towel, returned the cups to the bucket, dunked them in the water, shook them off, and put them away. She still missed cleaning the way they had in the country. It had been a difficult chore to pump water and haul it home, but at least they had a regular supply of fresh water. And they could make soap. Here, there often was no running water, and soap and other supplies were hard to come by even if they had rationing coupons. She felt very guilty and ungrateful for thinking these things. Mamă was right about her. Head bowed and steering clear of Filip, she approached Bunicuţă and crawled onto her lap. It was noisy in the apartment as people shuffled about, talked loudly, or prepared for bed. However, when Bunicuţă whispered to her, Cătălina heard her loud and clear in her head and in her heart.

Bunicuţă's rough fingers brushed against Cătălina's forehead and against her cheek. With knobby fingers that were never fully straight, Bunicuță tucked a loose tendril of Cătălina's hair back under her kerchief. "Tell me what's on your mind, Dragă."

"Oh, Bunicuță, you heard Mamă. I'm a horrible disgrace. I'm a disgrace to everyone, even God!" Cătălina shook with sobs, and she leaned into her grandma.

"Now why would you say that you're a disgrace to God, Dragă?"

"Because I secretly hoped that Filip would cut off his nose." Cătălina whispered this into her grandma's ear even as she continued to cry, which made her words choppy. Cătălina's heart swelled when Bunicuță understood her anyway. Bunicuță always understood.

Bunicuță gently pushed Cătălina upright so they were face to face. "Dragă, you're not a disgrace to God. And you're not a disgrace to me, either." She winked at Cătălina. "Now, God does want us to live a certain way. He wants us to be patient with each other. And kind. And loving and forgiving, too. Remember what you just told me about what you wanted to happen to Filip?"

Cătălina felt heat creep up her neck and face and under her kerchief. She looked down and muttered, "Yes. I'm very sorry."

"I'm glad you're sorry, Dragă. That's why you're not a disgrace to God. You are kind, and you feel bad when you do something wrong. Filip was wrong to grab your ankle."

Cătălina sniffed. "He didn't even admit that he did it, and he didn't say sorry, either. He just stuck his tongue out at me. But I bet I know what he's going to do." She didn't wait for her grandma to ask what it was Filip was going to do. "He's going to say sorry tonight when everyone is asleep. He's going to crawl under my blanket the way he does sometimes, and he's going to touch me everywhere and want to show me he's sorry." Cătălina shuddered. She leaned forward to whisper close to Bunicuţă's ear. "I hate Filip. I hate him."

"Cătălina, I know you've said before that he does these things. No one ever sees it, and his mom and dad don't think he'd do that."

"But he does! Do you believe me, Bunicuţă?"

She sighed softly. "Yes. I do. But you aren't going to change anyone's mind. Filip is a boy. What I'm going to tell you is very important, for your life and your relationship with God. Are you listening with your full attention?" Cătălina nodded solemnly. "Good. You were worried that you're a disgrace to God. I meant it when I said that you are not a disgrace to Him. To stay in God's good graces, it's very important that you have the right attitude about people and their sins. You must separate the person from the sin. The sin is wrong. Filip's behavior toward you is wrong, a sin. It's this behavior that is sinful and that needs to be rejected. Filip himself is a person, a soul, and he needs to be forgiven."

Cătălina tilted her head to the side and wrinkled her nose as she looked at Bunicuţă. She was listening, and she was try-ing her best to understand, but she didn't fully understand. Because a person did the actions, committed the sins, didn't that make the person sinful? She wasn't sure how to ask this without sounding disrespectful.

Bunicuţă laughed despite the seriousness of the topic. "You look baffled, Dragă. I don't blame you. It has taken me a lifetime to understand, and there are many answers I don't have. I keep seeking them, though. We'll leave this lesson as it is for now. The big thing I want you to remember, Dragă, is that the person and the sin are separate."

Cătălina nodded. "Thank you, Bunicuță." She slid off her grandma's lap and straightened her dress. "I need to go help put the little ones to bed now." Cătălina headed next door to start with Dionisie. Before fifteen full minutes passed, disaster would strike.

Wrestling an overtired toddler, one nearly old enough to be out of diapers, into a fresh diaper was a challenge Cătălina enjoyed. Dionisie was so good-natured that it was fun. She could turn it into a game with him, and eventually she'd have the diaper securely fastened. A few pokes of the pin into her fingers weren't a big deal. She almost had the second pin in place when the entire apartment rumbled. The floor shook, and the ceiling above her swayed. The diaper pin pierced deep into her finger and tore its way back out. Blood gushed. Her finger throbbed. Dionisie howled. From somewhere in the vicinity, her father's voice bellowed, "It's an earthquake!"

Cătălina snatched up Dionisie and held him tight against her. Her Uncle Eduard and Aunt Oana were suddenly beside her. Oana reached for her son, who dove into her arms. Eduard put his arms around both Cătălina and Oana and began to usher them all to the hallway. The rumbling, though, was too powerful. They were knocked to the ground. Cătălina heard the apartment groan and creak; she heard objects crashing, smashing to the floor; she heard shouts and screams; she felt pieces of the ceiling pelt her back, head; and then she heard nothing. Silence. In less than a minute, the earthquake stopped as abruptly as it started. With horror, she realized that her underclothes were wet, but as she slowly worked herself into an upright position, she realized that that was the least of her problems.

Beside her, Dionisie howled. Strangely, his howl was muffled and distant behind the ringing in her ears. Cătălina watched as Oana comforted Dionisie. Eduard was surveying the damage around him as he brushed plaster off his sleeves. He made eye contact with Cătălina. He swallowed hard and cleared his throat. "Come on, Cătălina. Let's go find the rest of our family." He spoke loudly, and she heard him clearly. He whispered something softly to Oana and kissed her cheek. Still clutching Dionisie, Oana stood and joined Eduard and Cătălina.

Cătălina recognized nothing as she picked her way through what used to be her apartment. Well, that wasn't exactly accurate. Brightly colored fragments of stuff—knick-knacks, religious icons, things that were once useful but were now broken and bent—poked out of chunks of plaster and wood. She stumbled on twisted wire but had nothing to grab onto for support, so she fell into a pile of jagged glass that used to be a light. She turned her head to the side as she fell, and the glass missed her eyes. It found her cheek, though. Cătălina inhaled sharply and brought her hand to her face. She felt sticky wetness. She stared numbly at her hands. One still bled from the cut and tear of the diaper pin. The other was now painted in blood from her cheek. She started to shake, and she didn't know if her body was doing it on its own or if another earthquake had begun. She glanced around. Others were stumbling because the ground was shaking yet again. It stopped.

Abruptly, the ringing in her ears was replaced with shouts, yells, shrieks, cries. Eduard was now across the room talking with the men in her family. They gestured animatedly. A few ran out the door. Oana and Dionisie were with some of her aunts. Her mother and sisters weren't with them. Cousins moved or stood still, cried or appeared to be in a daze. A chunk of ceiling crashed beside her. She began to cry. Suddenly, her father's strong arms swooped her up and carried her swiftly into the hallway. "Hush, Cătălina. You'll be okay. We don't have time for crying now. The building isn't stable. Everyone is leaving, and so must we." Her tată put her down, but when a herd of people barreled past her down the hallway toward the stairs, she clung to his leg, put her feet on his, and buried her face against him. It made her cheek sting. She did it anyway. Tată pushed her away. "Cătălina, please. We must go."

"Is everyone okay? Where are Mamă and Viorica and Daciana? And Bunicuţă! Where is Bunicuţă?" Stepping over mountains of rubble, Cătălina moved back toward the apartment where she had sat on her Bunicuţă's lap only a short while ago. It was where she had left her. Cătălina ignored her father's shouts to come back.

Her father was right behind her. His voice was loud and gruff. "Cătălina! Are you stupid? Get outside *now*. Everyone else, you, too. She's already dead. There's nothing we can do other than make sure we're not killed, too. Now go! Everyone."

At that, Cătălina pushed and stumbled into the destroyed apartment. There she was. Her Bunicuţă, the person she loved more than anyone and who loved her back even when others didn't. Blood, already drying, caked her face. Her head sat at an odd angle. Something had struck her head. A chair that wasn't theirs lay on its side beside Bunicuţă. Cătălina looked up at the gaping hole in the ceiling. She jumped onto Bunicuţă's lap and started to scream. When arms tried to pull her away, she wrapped her arms around Bunicuţă's crooked neck and clung tight.

"Cătălina, stop this nonsense." Her father's voice was gruff, but Cătălina didn't care. She shouted her prayers over the top of her father's words and all of the commotion around them. Over and over, she implored her Bunicuţă to get up, and over and over she begged God to help her. She wiggled and jerked against her father's grasp, and she wiggled and jerked harder when another set of hands, large and strong, grasped her wrists and pulled her arms apart.

Cătălina lifted her face away from Bunicuță's neck and looked up to see who was helping her father pull her away from Bunicuță. "Uncle Neculai, no! Stop! Tată, leave me alone! I want to stay here with Bunicuță. Go away!"

"Cătălina, obey your father. Mădălina is dead. We—" As he spoke, a thunderous noise reverberated throughout the apartment. "Enough, Cătălina!" With that, Neculai yanked her arms apart hard, pulled her off Bunicuță, threw her over his shoulder, and waded his way through the debris littering the floor. Cătălina screamed and pounded on his back with balled fists.

Outside, she felt Uncle Neculai's shoulders sag. She didn't stop crying, but she stopped pounding in order to arch herself up and look around her. Fires scattered here and there illuminated the spaces immediately around them. There was nothing whole left to illuminate. Bits of this, chunks of that were strewn about, piled on top of each other. Cars and homes were in pieces. Glass, bricks, clay, ceramic, metal, wood all mingled together in twisted heaps. Several yards away, a section of road had split apart and tried to swallow entire cars. People stood in clusters or moved around as quickly as they could. Names were called. Sometimes answers came; other times only silence. Two buildings suddenly collapsed in two great booms; hers was one of them. A fight had broken out near the split in the road. Men with guns were upon them. The *Securitate*. They ended the fight by shooting the fighters. Screams. People running to the fallen fighters. Gunshots fired in the air. Cătălina screamed and threw her hands over her ears to block out all of the horrific noise, and she buried her face in her uncle's back.

Her sudden movement must have spurred her uncle into action, for suddenly she found herself roughly bouncing as he stomped over debris. Cătălina hoped his boots would protect his feet and legs. They reached a group of people. Their family! Were they all here? Not Bunicuţa. Cătălina began to sob. She felt hands reach under her arms and pull her off of Uncle Neculai. "Oh, Tată! What's happening? I'm scared. I—"

"Not now, Cătălina!" Her father's voice was loud and harsh. She threw her hands over her ears again.

"But Tată —"

"Silence! You disobeyed us and nearly got us killed. Look around you, at all of the people who have just lost their homes and their loved ones. Stop feeling sorry for yourself and find a way to help." He looked at Viorica and Daciana, nodded sharply at them, and shoved Cătălina in their direction. She stumbled over debris but didn't fall. "Stay with your sisters, Cătălina, and obey what they tell you to do. Do not disobey them the way you disobeyed Neculi and me."

"Yes, Tată."

Ignoring Cătălina, he asked Viorica, "Where is your mother?"

"Over there." Viorica pointed down a narrow alley. A woman sat on a pile of rubble with her arms folded on her knees and her head resting on her arms. "She muttered something about Bunicuţa and Flavia and how they're dead and she just wandered over there."

Cătălina heard her father sigh, saw his chest rise and fall. "All right. You girls stay together, and stick with the family.

Women and children, everyone stay together. Men, come with me. Let's try to figure out a plan."

"I'm coming with you." Cătălina turned her head at the sound of Filip's voice.

"No you are not." Her uncle Ion, Filip's father's, voice was stern.

"I'm twelve years old, and I'm not staying here with a bunch of women and children."

Ion strode forward and struck him hard across the face. "You will do as I say, boy."

Filip scowled as he watched the men go. He spat blood at Cătălina's feet then raised the back of one hand to his mouth, dragged it across his lips, and looked at it. Even in the dark, Cătălina could see the red blood.

"What are you looking at, *girl?*"

Cătălina was shaken and frightened and devastated and didn't want to deal with Filip. She just shook her head. Filip looked at her. When Viorica and Daciana told them to go find a place for them all to take shelter, Cătălina didn't budge. Filip gently tugged on her sleeve and said, "C'mon, Cătălina. Let's go."

Their own silence lost among the chaos and noise that assaulted them from all directions, they wandered, skirting fires and people, turning away from members of the *Securitate* who fired their guns seemingly at random, scampering up piles of rubble and waiting for stray dogs to tire of barking at them and go somewhere else, and attempting to remain steady during rumbling aftershocks. Filip kicked at pieces of rubble. Cătălina stepped over or around them. More than once, her dress caught on sharp objects, a nail here, a jagged metal bar there, and by the time they stopped, the bottoms of both her dress and apron were shredded rags. Cătălina looked over and saw that the bottom of Filip's pants looked the same. She looked at him with a frown. "Bunicuţă would have made our clothes into rag dolls." Filip blurred as Cătălina's eyes filled with tears. Her nose began to run. She wiped it on her apron and sniffed.

"I'm tired. Let's sit down for a while, Cătălina."

She looked around her and saw no suitable place to sit. Judging by all of the people wandering and hollering and searching, there were no suitable places for anyone to sit. "Where?"

Filip shrugged. "I don't know. Maybe let's go into one of these buildings."

"That's dangerous! The buildings could collapse at any time, just like ours did. And besides, look," she pointed down the street. "The *Securitate* are starting to guard the buildings. I'd rather stay out here."

"But we could sit and rest inside. And maybe we could find something to eat or some things we might need since our stuff is gone. We could help our family that way."

"No, Filip."

"Aw, c'mon. Think of it as an adventure. We could play treasure hunters. Or maybe we could be actual rescue people! Who knows how many people are trapped inside these buildings. We could get them out and be heroes! And we might even see some dead bodies, too. How cool would that be?"

"You mean a dead body like Bunicuţă's, Filip? How could you say such a thing?" Cătălina buried her face in her hands and started to cry. When she felt Filip's hand on her shoulder, she jerked away. "Don't touch me."

"I'm sorry, Cătălina. I didn't mean that. I loved Mădălina, too. She was just like my own grandma."

Cătălina ignored him. She felt him tug on her arm. "I see a place where we can rest. Not a building," he added quickly. "Look up, and I'll show you." When she did, he pointed to a car. A light pole had crashed across the front, but the main part was okay.

Cătălina followed him to the car and crawled into the back seat beside him. It felt like a lot of time passed. Cătălina's eyelids grew heavy, but Filip's voice jerked her back to awareness. "*Mărţişor.*"

"What?"

"*Mărţişor.*"

"What about it?"

"We didn't celebrate it this year." He reached over and rubbed the front of her dress. First with one hand, then he shifted slightly and rubbed her dress with both hands. Cătălina scooted away. Filip sat back against his seat and said simply, "None of us has a *mărţişor*. March first was just a few days ago. I miss that celebration. I miss so many things about the country, Cătălina."

"I do, too. Everything is horrible here. And now we have nothing. Even Bunicuţă is gone!" Cătălina couldn't help it. She began to cry again.

Filip put his arm around her and pulled her close. He removed her kerchief and stroked her hair. He hunched over slightly, lifted her chin, and kissed her lips. Cătălina gasped and tried to wriggle away, but Filip was quicker and stronger and older and easily pinned her against the seat. When he eventually took one hand off her shoulders so he could hike up her dress with it, she had just enough leverage to squirm away, open the car door, and escape.

She stopped abruptly. What was she escaping to? Nothing but devastation and destruction. Bunicuţă couldn't help her this time. When Filip appeared at her side, she didn't try to run. She just looked straight ahead. Her only movement was the blinking of her eyes and the slight rise and fall of her chest. Filip elbowed her. "C'mon Cătălina. We need to go back and report that we didn't find any place to be safe."

# Sacramento, California

## *2018*

# Chapter 12

She and Filip hadn't found anyplace to be safe that night. All these years and a lifetime later, it felt like she were still searching, fruitlessly, for a place to be safe. She was searching when she met Dumitru, she searched all the while she was with him, and she was searching when she came to this new country. And she still felt like she hadn't found one.

She had been sitting in a rocking chair and feeding an infant—she couldn't remember her name at the moment—as she talked to Marcy. Now the baby wriggled and fussed, and Catie became aware that she was agitated, rocking the chair too fast and bouncing her leg up and down. She dropped the bottle because her hand wouldn't grasp it tightly enough. Marcy spoke to her, but Catie didn't know what she said. She didn't want to know. Marcy reached down and tenderly lifted the baby off of Catie's lap.

"No! Don't take her away from me. I can take care of her. I can love her properly. Let me show you." She reached for the baby, but Marcy was already placing the baby in a crib.

"Of course you can, Catie. I meant it when I said that you are have a special touch. Right now you seem very distressed. Are you okay? I think you need to go take a break."

"No!" Catie sat up straight and scooted to the edge of her chair so quickly that she was surprised that she stayed on the chair. "I am fine. I love these children, and I want to care for them." She leapt to her feet and tried to move around Marcy, but she had stood so quickly that she experienced head rush. She saw dark spots and bursts of lights floating in front of her eyes. Between those spots and bursts she could see Bunicuţă sitting in her chair with her neck at a horrible angle and blood pouring forth from her head; she saw fires and rubble and panicked people; she saw her mother, despondent and away from her family on a pile of crumpled apartment; she saw Filip with her in that car. She blinked rapidly. Where was she right now? She heard the cries of a baby, or was that the wailing of thousands of Romanians after the great earthquake? Catie shook her head. She was confused. When someone touched her elbow, she jumped away and stumbled on something on the ground. What was it? Debris and rubble? Bodies? There had been so very many bodies in the days, weeks, following the earthquake. Was it something of Dumitru's that she just crushed? She dropped to her knees to see what damage she had done. This was a blanket. A baby blanket. Oh no! Had she stepped on a baby? No! Where was the baby? Frantically, she looked around but saw only toys. She was confused. From a distance, she heard her name.

"Catie." When Catie looked in the direction of the sound, she heard her name again. "Catie." Catie blinked to pull her surroundings into focus. She realized she was at work. She inhaled sharply and tried to stand. Her attempt to gracefully spring to her feet was a lame one. She stood up in stages, placing one foot flat on the floor in front of her, then bracing both hands on that bent leg, and then rising up just enough to place the other foot flat on the floor; hands now on both thighs, she slowly, carefully, straightened. She squeezed her eyes shut and winced at the fiery pain that shot through all of her joints. As usual, she felt like she had been struck by Thor's Hammer. When her children were little, she and Dumitru would sometimes take them for walks through the city. Dumitru especially loved a huge stone sculpture known as Thor's Hammer. He would pretend that he was Thor and, as Thor, he was the one who had slammed it into the ground causing the concrete all around it to break into chunks. The kids would climb and play on those chunks, and Catie would act so grateful to have her big hero "Thor" in her life. She had to act loving and grateful to stave off the blows that would come from Dumitru's hammer if he thought she was an ingrate. Catie shuddered as she stood in front of Marcy, finally fully straight.

"Catie, I don't think you are okay. Would you like to go home for the day? I can call Irene, and she'll just have one of the floaters fill in here."

Catie shook her head. "No!" she exclaimed vehemently. "I'm fine. Really. It's just sometimes I get caught up in a memory when I'm thinking of something that I feel strongly about."

"Yeah, so maybe you need to just chill out for the rest of the day. Go home. Your kids are in school, right? So you could have the house to yourself. Or stop by the pet store and pick up a chinchilla." Marcy grinned.

Catie put her hands up, palms out, and made a tiny pushing motion. "No, Marcy. Please don't call Irene. She already thinks very little of me, and this will only make it worse. I can't lose my job."

"You won't lose your job just for taking the rest of the day off."

"I might, and I can't risk it. I..." she decided against telling Marcy that she didn't deserve to take a day off, anyway, so she simply trailed off. She could think of nothing else to say at the moment. She sighed.

"Okay. I won't keep pushing you. But you really should at least take your break now. Take your lunch with you."

"Actually, I don't have a lunch, so I'll just stay here. I like being in here."

Marcy crossed the room to her bag and rummaged through it until she found what she was looking for. She returned to Catie and jiggled a sandwich bag containing two oddly shaped tan clusters with various pieces of things protruding in multiple directions. "Look! Homemade peanut butter granola bars. I made them last night." Marcy looked at the bag and jiggled it again. "It was my first attempt at this particular recipe, plus I had problems cutting them. They look a little strange, but trust me, they taste good. Here." Marcy thrust the bag into Catie's hand and led her out the door. "Take these with you on your break and enjoy them. They'll give you an energy boost. Have a relaxing break, and I'll see you in a bit." Marcy disappeared back into the room, and the door clicked shut behind her.

A group of four- and five-year-olds marched past Catie in a crooked line. They were all singing a song, and Catie smiled. Her smile faded into nothingness when she thought of why she was out in the hallway. She sighed and surreptitiously surveyed her surroundings. She didn't want to be caught standing here. She didn't want to go into the breakroom and face people there. She couldn't go back to the infant room yet. With the hallway now empty, but only temporarily, she headed for a side door and stepped outside. Before letting the door shut, she bent down and wedged a stick between the door and the frame so it wouldn't shut fully and lock her out. She leaned back against the side of the building, looked up toward the bright sun, and closed her eyes. Her throat suddenly felt painfully tight. She looked at the tree a few yards in front of her and watched it blur. The pain, both physical and emotional, of the morning and all the way back through her past overwhelmed her, and she cried silently as she stood against the building and clutched Marcy's bag of homemade peanut butter granola bars.

Catie wiped furiously at her eyes. She didn't have time for this, and she couldn't afford it. What if Irene or any other employee of Hey Little Diddles saw her out here, avoiding work and wallowing in her emotions? Catie was absolutely not her mother, and she wouldn't act like it. What would Bunicuţă have said about her being out here, floundering? What would Dumitru have done to her? She imagined the consequences, and lived them in her mind because she so clearly deserved them.

She started back inside but remembered the bag of granola bars she was carrying. She opened the sandwich bag, lifted it to her nose, and smelled it. Definitely peanut butter. She closed it again. Did Marcy's kitchen look like Catie's too often did, with the peanut butter jar open on her counter surrounded by a mess of other food and utensils, Catie wondered. Catie couldn't imagine Marcy being such a slovenly woman. Dumitru had repeatedly pointed out Catie's slovenly ways and disciplined her for them. At first, she was baffled by Dumitru's low opinion of her cleaning habits, because from the time she was very little, she had done housework and chores and helped Bunicuţă with preparations for church services. After Bunicuţă had died, Catie wanted to continue to be someone who made her proud, and she strived for that every day. She honestly couldn't see why Dumitru thought she was untidy and disgusting. As he continued to point out her oversights and shortcomings, though, she could see his point, and she was ashamed. The harder she had tried to please her husband, the more she failed. Even with his brutal instruction, she could never get things quite right. And now, look at how messy her home was sometimes—just occasionally, but still it happened. Maybe she really had needed Dumitru's lessons and punishments. She sighed.

The deep sigh caused her to catch a whiff of Marcy's granola bars, and her thoughts came tumbling back to the present. She needed to get back inside, but she couldn't go back in with these bars and risk hurting Marcy's feelings or angering her. Despite a complete lack of hunger—her gut was too full of stress and memories—she smelled the contents again. The granola bars did smell good. Maybe she could eat them. She leaned back against the building, closed her eyes and let the sun's warm rays wash over her, and ate the bars as quickly as she could. They tasted fabulous, but her stomach twisted in protest with every bite. Nonetheless, for Marcy's sake, she ate them both. Feeling uncomfortably full yet happy because Marcy had seemed to genuinely care enough to share her food, Catie headed back inside.

She kicked the stick away from the door and allowed the door to click shut. When she turned to walk back to the infant room, she saw Irene emerge from a room across the hallway. She wanted to hide, but there was nowhere to go. She thought about praying for the ground to open up and swallow her, but that was too much like an earthquake, and she never wanted to experience one of those again. The only thing she could do was grit her teeth, ball her fists, walk slowly forward, and say a silent prayer to St. Basil for protection.

Irene was upon her in an instant. "Catie, what are you doing?"

"I..." she began. She had to clear her throat before she could meekly respond, "I stepped outside for a short break." She looked at her little Timex watch. "I only took a short break. I was outside for seven minutes, and I'm going back to the room now."

Irene waved a hand impatiently. "Yes. That's fine. I'm wondering what you are doing coming in that door. All doors other than the front are locked from the outside. Did you prop it open?"

Catie's stomach lurched, nearly forcing the granola bars up her throat. She swallowed. "Yes. But I was standing beside the door the whole time. I didn't walk away and leave it propped."

Irene made a noise that sounded like a hissing tortoise, a rushed breath of air meant to be fierce and intimidating. "At least you had enough common sense not to leave an open door unattended in a daycare center. If our doors are propped, the environment is unsafe. Kids can wander out and strangers can wander in. If our parents think our building isn't safe, they will take their business elsewhere. I hate to lose business." Irene glared at Catie.

Catie felt the heat of shame creep through her veins and return to her heart, making it constrict painfully. She looked down. "Yes, ma'am. I'm sorry. It won't happen again." Catie felt as though she were a child again, facing yet another chastising by her mother. She felt a longing for Bunicuţă and an unexpected desire to go home, not her apartment, not home to Dumitru, but home to Romania, to the rural countryside. If Irene fired her now, perhaps she should. It would please Florina immensely. But it would likely devastate Alexandru.

Irene ended Catie's dilemma. "Good. I do trust you that you won't do it again. Now go care for those infants." Irene smiled stiffly. Catie summoned the energy and the courage to smile back at Irene, and then she hustled back to Marcy.

Marcy welcomed her cheerfully. Catie felt guilty for it. Here she had shirked her duties, leaving everything to Marcy, yet Marcy still was nice. When Marcy asked her how her break was, Catie said what she knew Marcy wanted to hear: It was helpful and relaxing and she was glad for the granola bars. She fell silent, saying nothing more, especially nothing about Irene, and smiled at Marcy.

"I'm glad you feel better, Catie." She paused and shook her head. "Man, I can't imagine living through such a devastating earthquake, going through everything that you did with that, and losing someone I loved." Again Marcy paused. Catie was surprised to see Marcy's cheeks redden. Marcy must have been surprised or embarrassed, for she pivoted, walked away, and sat down on a blanket to interact with the three babies lying there.

Catie joined her. "What's wrong?"

"Well, I suddenly feel really awful about a thought I had a lot when I was growing up. I actually wouldn't have been sad to lose my grandma or anyone else. I used to wish that something bad would happen to my family. I'd fantasize that they were killed somehow when I was away at school and I wouldn't have to go to boarding school anymore." Marcy scrunched up her face. "Isn't that awful? Did you ever wish anyone in your family was dead?"

Catie cocked her head to the side and debated whether or not to make a confession to Marcy. She decided that since she had been talking so freely to her, something that surprised her, she might as well participate in this topic that Marcy started.

"Well, no, I didn't wish my family members were dead. I did wish that I was dead, though. Especially after the earth-quake. I prayed and prayed that God would send Bunicuţă back and take me instead, but he didn't seem to want to do that. However..." She looked at Marcy thoughtfully as she continued, "Sometimes I do still wish I was dead, except I don't want my children to be sent back to their father." Catie noticed that she was wringing her hands. She yanked them apart, but like magnets they slammed back together of their own volition. Catie watched their anxious wringing motions and said, "I often found myself wishing that Dumitru were dead. I'd fantasize all the time about him having a gruesome accident. He works for the subway, and the subway system in Bucharest is disorganized and dangerous. I mean, it's getting better now, but it was very bad in the 1990s when he started there. The meaner he became, the more I hoped that there would be a subway accident that killed only him. But then he'd have nice streaks where he was kind and loving and fun, and I felt like the worst person in the world for wishing him dead." Catie scooped up baby Wallace, settled him on her shoulder, and cuddled him.

"Well, neither one of us actually killed anyone, so I'd say that we're actually pretty darned awesome. No. Even better. Superheroes. Wonder Women!" Marcy grinned.

Still feeling guilty over her desire to see Dumitru die, thoughts of Florina suddenly popped into her head. "My daughter wouldn't agree with you," Catie said flatly. "Kicking and screaming is how she left Romania and her father, and she's still doing it. You see, she shares her father's opinion of me. She wanted me to let her stay in Romania with her dad, but she doesn't know him like I do. I know that if I left her there alone with him, he would turn the rage he had against me and my son toward her." She closed her eyes and shuddered. "I couldn't let that happen."

"You're even more of a Wonder Woman, then." When Catie snorted in disbelieving dismissal, Marcy leaned over slightly to grab the phone out of her pocket, tapped some buttons, laughed, and then instructed Catie to go check her phone. Reluctantly, Catie lifted herself off the floor, went to her purse, and took out her phone. The text message was a cartoon image of Marcy dressed as Wonder Woman and looking fiercely triumphant. Catie couldn't help but smile.

"How did you make this?"

Marcy shrugged. She showed Catie her phone. "It's just an app. It's called Bitmoji." She tapped through it to show Catie how to use it. "You should get it, Catie, and make yourself. It's fun! And don't delete the Wonder Woman I just sent you. Use it as a reminder of who you really are."

# Chapter 13

Catie eased herself onto the hard bus seat. Before settling fully in for the ride, she reached into her purse and hefted out *The Count of Monte Cristo*. It had been her favorite book for as long as she could remember, and she had long since lost track of the number of times she'd read this wonderful story. She ran her hand over the cover. Her fingers, cracked and callused, caught on some of the frayed threads of the cloth cover. Her fingers were quite likely the cause of the frayed threads. Her touch seemed to have that effect on everything, she mused. Well, not everything. Not the actual story inside the cover. That was one of the reasons Catie loved to read. She enjoyed the perfection of each and every story for what it was, a story about people who weren't perfect. Yet the protagonists were usually so likeable despite what life threw at them. They were fictional characters in fictional worlds and likeable despite their flaws. Catie was a real person in a nonfiction world and was unlikable because of her flaws.

She pushed that depressing thought aside as she opened the book. No sooner had she begun to read when her phone dinged. She closed her book, shifted in her seat to dig in her purse for her phone, muttered an apology to the woman glaring beside her, and looked at the screen. It was a text from

Alexandru from a friend's phone. He must have decided not to risk leaving a note for her at home again. Apparently he'd be home a little late again because he and some buddies were staying after soccer practice to work on drills. She smiled. He seemed so happy to be here. And why wouldn't he be? He didn't have his father to badger, belittle, and beat him. *"Du-te dracu*, Dumitru," she muttered. Go to hell.

"Great. I'm sitting next to a crazy who talks nonsense out loud." The lady next to her harrumphed and scooted closer to the window. Catie closed her eyes and sighed. She opened her eyes again so she could escape into her book and away from her thoughts and feelings. She glanced at her phone again and saw Marcy in her extremely short list of texts received. She tapped the message to see the Wonder Woman picture again. Seeing the picture was upsetting. Marcy had what it took to be a superhero, but Catie never would. Ever. Impulsively, she deleted the message and returned to her book.

By the time the bus dumped her out at her stop, she wasn't quite so tense. She still felt the omnipresent veil of sadness pressing down upon her, though. She knew from a lifetime of experience that being in the presence of God would help soothe her and give her the ability to get through another evening and another night, so she headed for St. Theocharis.

After she dipped her fingers in holy water and made the sign of the cross, she moved silently down the aisle. Father Stasiuk was busy doing something at the altar. Catie didn't want to disturb him, so she genuflected and slid into a pew about half way down the aisle. She watched him for a while. He was bent over the altar, but not just because he was reading something. His frame seemed more stooped than before, even since yesterday. When he turned to walk up the aisle, his feet stayed so close to the floor with each step that he nearly shuffled. Still, when he looked in Catie's direction, he smiled jovially, and when he reached her, Catie noticed that his smile reached his eyes and made them sparkle with vitality.

"Catie! I was hoping I would see you before I left for home. I need your help. It's for the church."

Catie's breath caught in her throat. She loved being able to help. "Of course, Father. What do you need?"

He gestured around him with a sweeping motion. "Our tapestries are like I am. They're getting old and need to be replaced. Maybe you noticed the call for embroiders in the bulletin recently. You have embroidered such beautiful cloths for us before, and I'm hoping we can hire you for more. I'm wondering, too, have you ever created something on a larger scale, such as tapestries for the walls and altar?"

"I have, Father. My grandmother taught me how to weave and embroider when I was very young, and I have made things most of my life. But I'm afraid I can no longer make something on such a grand scale. I don't own a loom." She bowed her head and whispered, "I'm sorry. Can you forgive me?" She was furious with herself, and terrified that she had upset Father Stasiuk, St. Basil, and God himself. When the Church needed something, it was unforgivable to refuse. But she would have said yes if she could have. She tasted bile. Maybe Marcy's granola bars would make their way out of her after all. She swallowed hard. She had to swallow several times before the bile receded and the lump in her throat became smaller. She was so caught up in her self-hatred and worry that she had almost forgotten that Father Stasiuk was still sitting beside her, so when he placed his hand on her shoulder, she jumped. If he noticed, he didn't say anything.

"Catie, that's quite all right. Looms aren't exactly a common household item anymore. You can use the one here.

We'll figure out a schedule that doesn't burden you. There's no hurry to complete them. It's just time to start working on replacing these old tapestries so our walls look like a proper tribute to God." He squeezed her shoulder. "So what do you say? Will you help?"

Catie smiled on both the outside and the inside. Father Stasiuk had actually come to her for this incredibly important task. In doing this, she would be like Bunicuţă, and she'd be doing more for this priest who had played a role in her escape from Dumitru and taken her in when she and her children arrived. "Yes, Father. I'd love to."

"Wonderful. Thank you, Catie." He made a small grunting noise. "Oh, I shouldn't have sat down. I'm afraid I'm a lot like the tapestries. My age is showing, and I will soon need to be replaced. I think it might be time to think about retiring."

Catie felt dizzy, and she felt her temples begin to throb. No. Father Stasiuk couldn't leave. He was one of the two people who helped her escape. Although he was Ukrainian rather than Romanian, he reminded her of home. And, even though they couldn't risk communicating, he represented her one connection to Vasile. Sure, there were some church members here who were Eastern European, but she didn't know them and she wasn't good at getting to know people. His leaving would be a great loss. Her life seemed like nothing but loss: of people, of places, of love. She turned her head to the side so he didn't see the tears brimming in her eyes.

"You seem upset. My ego is grateful to you for wanting me to stay, but the more humble part of me knows that you will be quite fine without me."

She shook her head. "No. You are my only connection to home, and I think you are a wonderful priest."

"Don't worry. I have a feeling that it will be quite some time before I do retire. There's not exactly a surplus of Greek Catholic priests around here. Now, how about we pray together before going to our homes?"

* * *

The moment Catie stepped in her door, she saw an explosion of evidence that her son had come home after school before heading back to soccer practice. His backpack lay on its side in front of the couch. The sweatshirt he had left the house in this morning, despite Catie's providing him with the day's forecast of warm weather, was hanging inside out over the back of a rocking chair. His Nikes, a gift from Father Stasiuk when they had arrived from Romania, made themselves comfortable in two different locations on the floor. A cluster of tiny black particles, what Alexandru called turf rocks, gave away where he had sat to put on the soccer cleats a friend had lent him.

Catie sighed as she bent to pick up first one shoe and then the other across the room. She placed them neatly beside the front door. She returned and grabbed his sweatshirt, draping it over her arm. Ignoring the little black turf rocks for now, she picked up his backpack, but immediately dropped it. The noise it made when it hit the floor sounded a bit like the wrecking ball President Ceauşescu's work crews used to raze buildings and homes when he wanted something different in their place. She could barely lift the backpack, yet Alexandru carried that around on his back all day. She frowned. Was this so heavy that it could damage his back? He was so young; he couldn't afford to hurt his back and deal with a lifetime of problems. What if it made it hard for him to work? What would he do then? She pictured people in Bucharest, dirty and beaten down, begging for just a bite to eat. Was this her son's destiny because of his heavy school books? She squeezed her eyes shut and rubbed her temples. Her anxiety was exhausting. She needed it to stop.

She didn't necessarily forget about her latest worry, but she pushed it to the back of her mind so she could be more productive. She didn't want Dumitru to come home and catch her lollygagging and punish her for it. She grabbed the handle of the backpack and dragged it as quickly as she could toward Alexandru's room. Then it hit her. Dumitru wouldn't be coming home to this house because she was living across the world from him, and he didn't know where she was. The thought made her feel lighter. Her fear of him was just an old habit that was dying hard. She looked forward to the day when she would stop thinking that he was going to keep beating her and yelling at her, to the day when she would no longer be afraid that he would find her and come, to the nights when she could sleep peacefully. Then, she would finally be fully free. Then, she might be worthy of having people in her life again. Then, she wouldn't be lonely anymore.

The anxiety, fear, relief, exhaustion, loneliness and despair swirling through her made her so dizzy that she had to sit down on a chair in the kitchen. She put her head in her hands, and the emotions came out in her tears. She didn't want to sit here and cry, but all these emotions made her head throb relentlessly and her heart pound painfully so she needed them to get out of her body. Her tears could wash away the emotions.

Crying helped a little. She had a headache and was so weary, but her throat wasn't painfully tight and her chest didn't seem to hurt. She took a slow, deep breath as a test and was glad to discover that pain didn't shoot through her chest and shoulder. Catie leaned back in her chair and surveyed the kitchen. Alexandru had made himself a snack. The clean kitchen had given him plenty of space to use, and it seemed as though he had used all of it. How could one person make such a mess by having a simple bowl of cereal? She rose to her feet to put away the milk and the box of cereal and tidy up the rest of the kitchen.

Catie shook her head. Alexandru was a good boy, but it simply never occurred to him to pick up after himself or help her clean up. Sometimes he helped if she asked, and if he didn't, it was because he had a legitimate excuse like studying or writing a paper, but he didn't ever seem to think about pitching in on his own. She hated to nag him about it, though. As a woman, it was primarily her duty anyway. Also, she wanted him to be able to adjust well to his new home rather than slaving over housework. Aside from his mess-making, he really didn't give her any other problems at all. Unlike his sister. Catie looked up at the ceiling and raked her fingers through her hair. What was she to do about Florina?

She knew that part of Florina's problem was that she was homesick. She had a lot of her father in her—Catie frequently marveled at how her daughter, a girl, could be so much like Dumitru while her son, a boy, could be so much like her. One trait Florina and Dumitru shared was a diminished ability to directly express any emotion other than anger. They both also acted out their feelings instead of sitting down and talking about what they were thinking and feeling. Therefore, it was Florina's behavior rather than her words that reflected her longing for Bucharest.

Maybe Florina's homesickness was Catie's fault. "Maybe?" Catie snorted sarcastically to the empty kitchen. It was completely her fault for running not just away but far, far away.

Maybe she wasn't providing enough reminders of home to make her feel cozy. Catie shook her head. She was such a horrible, rotten mother. How could she have been so selfish? But living with Dumitru, she feared not just for herself but for her children. Their move had been for them even more than it had been for her. Would Florina ever understand? Ever forgive her? Catie closed her eyes as she remembered the day they had fled Romania.

# Bucharest, Romania
## *November, 2017*

# Chapter 14

It was a blustery, steel-gray day, and the wind cracked against people and objects. Cătălina's hair whipped into her eyes and mouth. Her attempts to shake it out were unsuccessful, so she was forced to stop, drop her bags, and pull her hair away from her face. It proved to be an impossible task; her fingers were white with cold and prickly with pain. She found herself longing for the kerchiefs she had worn as a child. She gave up trying to push her hair back, grasped the handles of the bags despite agonizing throbbing, and trotted after her children, who hadn't noticed—or hadn't cared—that she had stopped. "Children! Wait!" Cătălina hollered as she watched them disappear around a corner. She heard her heartbeat drumming warnings in her head: catch them! Catch them! Catch them! If they thought they had lost her, they would head home. The meticulous plans would be ruined. Everything would fall apart. She couldn't allow that to happen. She broke into a run in the direction they had turned. As she hurried, she smacked into someone and dropped her bags. "I'm sorry," she muttered as she ran forward. People shouted after her, but she couldn't take the time to look back or answer. At last, she caught up with them.

"Mamă, what's wrong? What happened?" Alexandru sounded concerned.

"Where are the bags?" Florina sounded impatient.

"I...I dropped them." Cătălina worried that she sounded anxious. Her words squeaked by the lump in her throat. She was panting, though, so maybe she just sounded tired and out of shape. She looked around her. They were near the meeting point. She glanced at her watch. Vasile was likely already there. "Come on, children, let's keep walking."

"What about our bread and vegetables?"

Cătălina's panic rose. They couldn't go back for them. There wasn't time.

"It's okay, son. We need to keep moving. I can shop again tomorrow." Her stomach flip-flopped with the realization that she wouldn't be here tomorrow to shop. She walked faster.

"But Mamă, you know that Tată will be upset. Very upset. Please, let's go back. I'll help you shop again." Alexandru tugged on Cătălina's arm.

Florina slapped Alexandru's hand away. "Shut up, Alexandru. I'm cold. Why should we suffer because of her mistake?" Florina trotted ahead.

"Your sister is right. It's my mistake. I'll deal with it. Right now I want to get you two out of the cold." She wondered if he noticed that she didn't say "home."

The three of them pushed and shoved their way through the dense crowd. All the while, Cătălina scanned for Vasile. Finally, she spotted him, standing tall and also scanning the crowd.

His gaze met hers. She wanted to run, to him and away from him all at once. She was nauseated and dizzy with both terror and relief. It was happening. Now. She and Florina and Alexandru were getting away from Dumitru. Was she ready?

Yes. But was she doing the right thing? She pulled on the hem of her jacket rhythmically, counting the tugs in a fruitless attempt to calm her mind and body.

Vasile reached them. "Well hello there, Cătălina." He smiled at Florina and Alexandru. "You all look freezing. I'm ready to leave. Are you? If so, I'll gladly give you a ride."

"Yes! I am so tired of being out here. Yes, we'll take a ride. How far do we have to walk to get to your car?"

"Florina, that is rude. Perhaps you should warm up by having a brisk walk home."

Vasile nudged Cătălina gently. "This bitter cold is making people bitter. I'd like to give all of you a ride." He pointed. "I'm parked very close. Let's go."

As Catie and her children followed him, she said a silent prayer of gratitude that neither of them had questioned the coincidence of Vasile's appearance. Florina didn't even bat an eye at the fact that he was a stranger to her. She just wanted a ride and evidently didn't care from whom. It took less than two minutes to reach Vasile's car. He had been fortunate to find a spot right up on the sidewalk, nestled among other fortunate drivers.

Vasile ushered them all into his car, maneuvered away from the market, then sped away in the wrong direction, toward the airport. Florina was at first confused and then livid. "Livid" actually didn't quite describe it. When they told Florina and Alexandru that they were fleeing Dumitru, Florina had become enraged, shaking Vasile's seat roughly, unbuckling and flinging her seatbelt so violently that the metal end piece hit the window with a loud crack, and pulling fiercely at the door handle in an attempt at escape. Thankfully, Vasile had locked out the controls on the doors, or she would have tumbled out of the car that was speeding along the highway at over 130 kilometers per hour, dodging speeding vehicles carrying honking and gesturing drivers.

Oh how Cătălina longed for the peace of the country-side she had known for only six years of her life but remembered forever. Would her new home be peaceful? She had no idea, and she was terrified, yet resolved. For the sake of their survival, she had to get all of them out of here. Now that she was finally escaping, so many things were hard about all of this. Was she doing the right thing? They had loved each other once, she and Dumitru. Had she really stopped loving him now? When Cătălina had been just a little girl and tormented by her cousin Filip, Bunicuţă had taught her that God wants people to separate the sin from the sinner, to dislike the sin but not the person. Here she was running far away from that advice, from Bunicuţă, from God. Didn't that advice apply now as it did before? Was Dumitru really any worse than Filip? Filip. Her eyes welled as she thought of him. She shook her head and pressed her hands over her face. Vasile was right. They had to go. And besides, he was a priest, a representative of God here on Earth. He was the one who encouraged her, who had made all of these arrangements in order to keep Dumitru from catching her. So maybe this was not just necessary but okay. She sighed. She was confused and scared and anxious for her children.

Cătălina was knocked back to the present moment when Florina struck her on the side of her head with her purse. Father Vasile slammed on the brakes in the middle of the highway, not bothering to pull over. They all pitched roughly forward and back. Loud honking, squealing tires, and a stream of cars—most with arms stuck far out of their windows making rude and hostile gestures—streaked past. Father Vasile was calm and undaunted and didn't seem to be bothered by the fact that they were parked on a busy highway. With a trembling hand, Cătălina reached over and poked the button to turn on the hazard lights.

"What the fuck are you doing?" Florina picked herself up off the floor—she hadn't bothered to refasten her seat belt—rubbed the red welt on her forehead with one hand and shoved Father Vasile's seat with the other.

Cătălina spun in her seat. "Florina Grigorescu! You will not treat Father Vasile with such disrespect. I—"

"Or what, Mother? What will you do?" Without giving her mother a chance to answer, she sneered, "Yeah. That's right. Nothing. Not a damn thing. I'm not letting you or this asshole," she shook his seat again, "take me away from my home! Fuck both of you."

Alexandru, who until now had been stupefied, still, and silent, looked at his sister. "Shut up, Florina. Just shut up. Do you even realize how you sound? You sound like a spoiled, self-centered brat with no sense of respect or class. Father Vasile is kind and doesn't deserve to be talked to like that, especially when he's just trying to help us."

"What..." Florina began but trailed off. For a brief moment, the car was calm. Cătălina heard nothing but honking horns and zooming cars. She glanced at Vasile. He either didn't notice the other cars or didn't care that they were whizzing around them while they were stopped right there on the highway. He had been watching Florina and Alexandru but must have sensed that she was looking at him, for he looked at her. He smiled sadly and squeezed her hand. "Oh my God. You two know him." She spat her accusation.

"Yeah. So what?"

At the same time as Alexandru answered, Cătălina said, "Yes, we do."

Florina shook her head. "What? Why? I mean, how?" For once, she seemed to be at a loss for words.

Cătălina wanted to answer her daughter, to explain, to reassure her that she and Vasile had become very good friends over the years but nothing more than that. She wanted to describe this wonderful man so her daughter trusted him and his plan to help them escape. But, like Florina, she found herself at a loss for words. This all was becoming crushingly overwhelming. The fear and hope and relief and regret and physical and emotional pain rendered her speechless, useless to Vasile, Florina, and Alexandru. She should be calming Florina, encouraging Alexandru, and talking with Vasile for the last time. This last thought sent shockwaves through her body causing what felt like all of her being, body and soul, to tremble. He was her best friend, more so than Dumitru had ever been, and as guilty as she felt about it, their friendship made her happy. Now, in the ultimate act of friendship, he was sending her to a far-away part of the world and she was losing him. She wanted to capture him in her memory, so when he spoke to Florina, she held on to his words and the very sound of his voice.

"Your mother and I met at Hospital Number Three, the orphanage where she has worked for a very long time."

"Yeah. I know where she works." *Worked*, Catie thought, *past tense. This life is over.* Florina crossed her arms over her chest and challenged, "But you're a priest. Aren't you supposed to be in a church?"

Vasile nodded. "Yes. My duties to God and His people take me out of the church every day. My focus is on all of the orphanages in Romania, to help get children out of them and placed with loving families. Your mother is the one who gave me a tour of Hospital Three and helped me learn the system so I could do my job well."

"And it was love at first sight. How romantic." Florina's voice was high and exaggerated, and she folded her hands, placed them over her chest, and fluttered her eyelashes. She then shoved her hands down, balled fists whacking the seat, and in her normal tone growled, "Dad was right not to trust you, Mother. All along he knew you were no good, and I've known it too." She spat toward the front seat, hitting only the console. Vasile glanced at the wet spot but otherwise let it go.

Alexandru chimed in. "Get over yourself, Florina. And Tată. Tată is cruel, yet you don't see it. Father Vasile and mother are kind, and you won't see that. I go to Hospital Three most days after school because I don't want to be home if Tată comes home. When Father Vasile is there," Alexandru looked at him and smiled, "he's nice. He doesn't attack me or belittle me or call me names, and he listens to me, really listens. And he's a priest. He's good."

Florina glared at him. "Did you know about this stupid escape plan, asshole?"

Alexandru shook his head firmly. "No. I did not. But if I had, I would have gone along with it. I want to get far away from Tată." He leaned back against the seat and blinked rapidly. "I don't want to be near him ever again. I'm scared of what's ahead but more scared of what's behind." He crossed his arms over his face and muttered, "I'm not going to cry. No matter what you say, Tată, I am a man. I don't cry." He stopped, then began to sob. He lowered his arms when he felt Father Vasile's hand on his knee.

"It's okay, Alexandru. It's okay."

Alexandru nodded. He nodded again when Cătălina turned in her seat and reached back to pat his leg. "We're going to make it okay, Alexandru."

Everyone jumped when Florina resumed her yelling. "This is all just fucking great. You three go off and do what you want. I don't care where you go, but let me out of this car and leave me out of it!" She went back to yanking on the door handle and pounding on the window, which made Cătălina return her attention to the swerving cars roaring around them.

"Vasile, I think we'd better start moving again before someone runs into us."

He shrugged and grinned. "This isn't exactly the first time someone has done something like this. And Romanians drive like maniacs whether or not there is an obstacle in the road." He glanced at Cătălina before turning his attention back to the road. "Maybe the drivers in California will be better."

At last they passed under the sign for the *Henri Canada Aeroportul Internaţional*. As Vasile parked the car, Florina continued to voice her displeasure. Vasile turned off the engine and twisted back to look directly at Florina.

"We don't have time for any more of this." His tone was firm yet gentle, something that Cătălina loved about him. She admired how he commanded attention without being brutal. "We need to get you out of here now. Your father's temper and violent behavior has worsened, and it is too dangerous for you to stay here."

"It's only dangerous for them." Florina gestured angrily at her mother and brother. "They don't have Tătic's love because they don't deserve it. Tătic loves me, and I'm not leaving! Take me back to him!" As tired as she was of Florina's tirades, Florina's cries for her *tătic*, her daddy, suddenly lashed at Catie's soul, but because she loved her daughter, she couldn't let her stay. She knew Dumitru well. It was too dangerous.

"I won't go!" Florina screamed.

"You will go because you must," Vasile stated.

"You go." She gestured angrily at her mother and brother. "Both of you cowards fly away and never come back. You're hated here. But I'm staying."

"Impossible." Father's word was clipped. "Your father's threats to kill have increased, and his blows have become more severe. He is unpredictable and violent." He paused and glanced at Cătălina. Their eyes locked. Her chin quivered. He twisted in his seat again to turn back to Florina. "Your father has now turned violent toward your brother, and I can guarantee you that he will come after you."

"You don't know that." Florina's tone was pure scorn.

"I am certain of it. He is capable of more than you even realize." The priest twisted again to face forward. He shot a sideways glance toward Cătălina, who blanched and nodded. Looking at Florina in the rearview mirror, he declared, "You cannot stay with him any longer."

"You're wrong. Wrong!" She grabbed his seat and shook it again. "Wrong!" Vasile looked at Florina. He shook his head. Florina made a noise and crossed her arms over her chest. No one spoke for several seconds. "Okay, fine. Maybe he has been a bit more intense lately. But I love him. I love it here. I love my friends. I don't want to leave." She shoved the driver's seat again. Father Cojocaru rocked with it but otherwise remained still. Florina continued, "I don't see why we can't just go stay with Bunicuț. Oh, wait, we can't. Because just like Tătic, Grandpa hates you. Everyone does, Mamă. You're hated by your own family, but your family loves Tătic. What does that say about you?"

Cătălina knew what it said about her. She had known it her whole life. And she had silently accepted all of her well-deserved castigations throughout her life. But it wasn't just about her anymore. Dumitru had turned on Alexandru, and it was only a matter of time before he abused Florina, too. Cătălina was certain of it. And Dumitru's violence was becoming more intense and smacked of death. Cătălina hated that fleeing the country was their only choice, but it was indeed their only choice. He would be able to find them anywhere in Romania, so she and her children had to vanish without a trace. She wiped her eyes with the tissue that was balled in her fist and tried to steel herself for the very long journey that was about to begin. She looked around. Alexandru was sitting quietly, and Florina was still arguing with Father Cojocaru.

"Listen to me carefully, Florina. Your only choice is to leave this country. You are not to have contact with your father, your grandfather, your aunts or anyone else. It would be best if you had contact with no one here. Your mother and brother won't either." He looked at Alexandru, who nodded his agreement.

"That's a load of shit!"

"Florina!" Why was that the only thing Cătălina could say to chastise her daughter?

"It's a load of safety, is what it is. If your father discovers where you three are, he will hunt you down, and he will kill you. All of you. His rage will be so great that you will be in danger if you stay here. And you are right about your grandfather and aunts, your mother's father and sisters. Dumitru has convinced them to love him, and over the years he turned them more and more against your mother. If they hear from you, they will tell your father, and he will hunt you down and kill you. This is not a safe situation."

"Whatever."

"It's the truth."

This time, Florina only shrugged. "I don't care about Mother and Alexandru."

"Fine. Then don't. But you seem to care an awful lot about yourself, and leaving now is the only way to protect yourself."

Florina spat at the priest who had driven her part of the way to safety. The car was silent. With one hand, Cătălina swiped at the tears cascading down her cheeks, and she dabbed at her nose with the wet lump of tissue in the other hand.

Vasile turned away from Florina and shifted to face Cătălina. He reached out to take both of her hands in his. He squeezed. Cătălina squeezed back, and her tears flowed faster and harder. She tried unsuccessfully to stifle a sob.

"It will be okay, Cătălina," the priest assured softly. To Florina and Alexandru, he repeated, "It will be okay. You will be safe." He looked pointedly at Florina, "Unless you screw this up by contacting someone here."

Subdued, Florina said, "I won't. I promise."

Father Cojocaru said, "It's time to go. He touched the bag he had brought for Cătălina. Everything you need is here. Passports and other documentation for all of you. Instructions for customs when you land in San Francisco. Remember, Father Stasiuk will be there waiting for you when you're through customs and past the security check area."

Catie could only nod. She looked back at her children, one stunned and one angry. "This is for you, children, for your lives. Come with me now."

Before he unlocked the car doors, Father Cojocaru looked out of the front window and nodded. Four armed men in uniforms approached the car. Catie hadn't noticed them before. She knew that the days of the *Securitate* were long past, but still the sight of armed officers caused sharp pain in her chest and made her temples pound. Vasile was still holding her hands, and he squeezed them again. "Airport security. I asked them to help you get all the way to your gate."

"Why? To keep me from bolting?" Florina's words were sharp, accusatory.

"Yes." Father Cojocaru informed her. "And just in case somehow, impossibly, Dumitru got wind of this. We were very careful, but that man is sneaky."

Alexandru had been staring at the security guards. He smiled. "Cool!" He waved his phone, the one that would be nearly useless in Sacramento. "Can I take pictures?"

"As long as you don't send them to anyone back here." Father Cojocaru's tone toward Alexandru was warm, but his words carried weight.

"Definitely not," Alexandru assured him.

Father Cojocaru unlocked the doors and stepped out of the car. Catie and her children stepped out, too. Immediately, Alexandru and Florina each had a security guard beside them. Cătălina ran around the front of the car and threw her arms around Father Cojocaru. "Vasile Cojocaru, thank you for all you have done. You are a good man." She looked into his eyes. "I will miss you, Vasile." She buried her face in his shoulder "I'm getting your shirt wet. I'm sorry."

Vasile must have understood her muffled mumbles, for he said, "That's quite all right. Don't tell God, but I like it even better than holy water." Although hugging wasn't a common occurrence in Romania, he hugged her tightly. They clung to each other until a security guard tapped him on the shoulder.

"We need to go, Father. You can come along if you want."

He nodded and stepped back so they could walk forward. He grabbed Cătălina's bag for her. Alexandru and Florina didn't have bags because when they went to the market, they had no idea that they wouldn't be returning home.

Catie's emotions were roiling. She was overwhelmed, and the enormous, loud, bustling airport made everything worse. She was grateful for Vasile and the security guards, because she knew that without them, she never would have been able to figure out how to get to her gate or even get her children onto the plane. She wanted to thank Vasile, but there was such a big lump in her throat that she couldn't force words out around it. Instead, she took his hands and kissed him once on each cheek. She nodded her gratitude to the security guards, and she looped her arms around her children's waists. Florina jerked away, but she walked onto the plane nonetheless. As Catie approached the walkway and handed her ticket over to be scanned, she looked back to see Vasile watching her. He raised his hand. She raised hers. Saying a silent prayer that Dumitru would never find them and that God would be with Father Vasile Cojocaru, she boarded the plane and joined her children in their own row of seats.

# Sacramento, California
## *2018*

# Chapter 15

Catie propped her elbow on the kitchen table and pressed the heels of her hands into her eyes. She held them there until she thought she could safely take them away without tears resuming their flow. She let up gently as a test. Discovering it was okay to drop her arms, she did so. She sat up straight and looked around. Had she done the right thing by uprooting them all and coming here, she wondered. Resolve stirred deep within. Yes. She had done the right thing. She knew it with every fiber of her being.

But maybe Catie wasn't doing enough here to help Florina adjust and to provide reminders of home. Maybe Florina would appreciate a Romanian meal. Something that both of her children loved was American stuff: food, clothing, television, movies, and more. Not that these things were new to them; on the contrary, the city of Bucharest was obsessed with all things Western, especially American. Ironically, to Florina, American materialism was a reminder of home. To Alexandru, it was a sign that he was right smack in America, experiencing America first- rather than secondhand. His new city wasn't stranded in the aftereffects of harsh communist rule.

Catie stood and rummaged through the kitchen. It was pretty barren. Of course it was. She was incompetent and couldn't seem to balance her work and her home. Dumitru was cruel, but some of his negative opinions of her were accurate. She pictured a flower and its petals, and thought, *I love me not.* She sighed. She still wanted to make a nice Romanian meal that they all would enjoy, and she thought it would be nice to make Florina's favorite. She scribbled a note to Florina and Alexandru telling them that she had gone to the store, and she hurried out door.

* * *

Two hours later, Alexandru shoveled the last forkful of his last cabbage roll into his mouth. A bit of rice fell out on the way, and he used his fingers to grasp the grains, rub them in the buttery, creamy remnants of his mashed potatoes, and stuffed it into his mouth along with the bite of cabbage roll.

"Alexandru!" Catie chastised. "That is very impolite."

He grinned sheepishly then shut his mouth after Catie shot him a disapproving look. He chewed, swallowed, and grinned again. "I'm sorry, Mamă. I couldn't help it. Your *sărmăluțe* is delicious, and I'm starving." He paused and glanced at the glass dish holding more cabbage rolls and the bowl of potatoes beside it. He pointed. "Can I have the rest?"

Catie's mouth turned up in a small smile. When Roxana, one of her coworkers at Hospital Three, learned that Catie had given birth to a boy, she said matter-of-factly, "Good luck. When my sons became teenagers, all the money I made went to feed them. My daughters weren't like that. You and your husband should save money now so you don't wind up on the streets like we nearly did." Now Catie was starting to understand what Roxana had meant.

"You can have some of the rest. We need to save some for your sister." When Alexandru reached forward to refill his plate, Catie put her hand on his arm. "But first you must eat your salad." She nodded to the bowl of untouched vegetables beside him.

He laughed. "Oh. Right." As he attacked the salad, probably to get it over with so he could get back to the main dish, Catie's thoughts returned to Florina. She was at once furious and frightened. The strong emotions roiling in her stomach explained why there was enough food for Alexandru to have seconds. She felt too nauseated to eat. She had made this meal especially for her daughter, to reach out to her and help her feel a connection to her home country, but that daughter hadn't even bothered to come home. Again.

At the sound of a loud knock at the door, Catie sprang to her feet, toppling her chair and bumping the table hard enough to tip the three glasses of water that had accompanied the meal. Alexandru's was empty, but hers and Florina's were full and thus soaked the table cloth. Catie didn't notice. One hand flew to her chest in response to the pain of her pounding heart, and the other grabbed a fistful of hair. "He's here. He found us." Her voice constricted in a scratchy whisper. "You must hide, Alexandru. Under your bed." Catie's mouth was dry. She reached for her glass, and it was then that she noticed the mess she had made. She tried to pick up the glass, but her hand shook so hard that she dropped it. She saw a crack splinter the glass, and she knew in that instant that she'd pay dearly. She felt a hand on hers, and she jumped.

"Mamă," her son said, "It's not him. He can't find us, and besides, his pounding would be a lot louder than that." At the second knock, he said, "I'm going to answer the door."

"Alexandru, no."

"Yes, Mamă. What if it's Florina? Maybe she forgot her keys."

"Oh. Well, maybe." Catie couldn't think straight. She knew she didn't want Florina to be locked out, though. As she hesitated, Alexandru went to the door. What kind of a rotten mother was she? How could she let him go to the door? If it was Dumitru, he would likely attack Alexandru in an instant. The sound of a woman's voice broke through her fear. Instantly feeling foolish, she patted her hair to tame the spot she had grabbed, straightened her shirt, plastered on a very fake smile, and joined her son in the living room.

"Marcy! What are you doing here?"

"Look what she brought, Mamă!" Alexandru reached toward a smallish blue duffel bag. It was stiffer, sturdier, than a duffel bag, but it had the same general look. But where a duffel bag would be solid, this one had black mesh on each side. Alexandru stopped and pulled his arms back just before touching it. "May I hold this?" he asked Marcy.

"Of course you can," Marcy answered brightly as she handed Alexandru the little duffle.

He took it from her, peered in the window, and, smiling broadly, held it in front of Catie who was now standing beside him. Little eyes and a nose made an appearance behind what Catie saw was a black mesh window. "Oh! Is this one of your chinchillas?"

"It is." To Alexandru, she said, "I was telling your mom about my chinchillas today, but she didn't know what they were so I decided to come show her. And you."

"Awesome!" As Marcy and Alexandru talked about chinchillas, Catie felt ignorant. Dumb. Marcy had indeed told her about her chinchillas, and she was right—Catie hadn't known what they were. Everyone should know what animals are. Why didn't she know about chinchillas? Was it because her schooling in Bucharest had been minimal at best? Was it because as their marriage progressed, Dumitru had progressively kept her locked away from the world, other than work of course? No. It was just due to her own inherent stupidity.

Up until the day she committed suicide, her mother had hated her, and part of the reason, her mother always told her, was because she lacked intelligence and common sense. To this day, Catie sometimes wondered that if she had been smarter, prettier, better her mother wouldn't have taken her own life to get away from her. But at those thoughts she'd hear her mother's cackling voice—or her sisters' or her aunts' or uncles' or cousins' or husband's—telling her that she was being stupid once again for thinking such a thing. She'd hear them scoff. She'd hear their disdain as they sneered at her, reminding her that she was far too insignificant to have prevented her mother's death. These sadistic voices in her head were right, of course. Really, how could she have prevented it? How could anyone? Her mother had been miserably unhappy and didn't handle loss well. That's a problem when one's life is filled with casualties in the form of lost lives, lost homes, lost ways of living, lost dignity, lost relationships, lost health, and lost wellbeing. Her mother had been one of those people who loses part of herself with every new hardship. Catie had always thought that her mother was like a tree slowly dying; leaves would drop and drop but because the tree was sick, no new buds formed to take their place in the spring. Not that spring ever came, anyway. It didn't. So the tree—her mother—perpetually lost bits and pieces of herself that were never replaced. Without those parts of herself, she had become increasingly depressed, barren, and brittle until she had nothing more of herself to live. One day, she had stepped onto subway tracks just as a train was speeding their way. That was the end. But despite what everyone said, Catie felt guilty for not being a better daughter, a more competent human being. Sadly, her mother had been gone for a long time and Catie was still her unworthy self.

One of her biggest anxieties was that she was even worse as a mother than she had been as a daughter. Look at what she was doing to her own precious daughter. Florina's behavior was wild and dangerous, but Catie couldn't seem to do anything to stop her, to help her. And what about Alexandru? Would she be able to continue to take care of him in the many ways a young teenager needed support? The room suddenly grew brighter and blurrier. When she squeezed her eyes shut to keep the tears in, her head spun. She opened her eyes and blinked rapidly.

She snapped back to attention when Marcy asked, "Catie? Are you okay?" She felt the color red come to life and slither from her chest to the top of her head. She had seen a book in Florina's backpack called *The Red Badge of Courage*. Courage? Ha. For her the book would be called *The Red Badge of Shame*. The image of another book came to mind: *The Scarlet Letter*. That one didn't fit her. Regardless of Dumitru's paranoid accusations, Catie had never been an adulteress.

"Yes. I'm fine." She forced a smile. "I can't believe I've never seen one of these before. He's so adorable!" She startled then as Alexandru thrust the fuzzy gray thing in her face.

"Look! His name is Banana."

"Banana?" Catie looked at Marcy, who laughed.

"Bananas amuse me. So do chinchillas. Perfect fit." She shrugged.

"Okay." Catie wondered if it was a good thing or a bad thing that Marcy laughed at her response. When Alexandru almost dropped the wriggling Banana, Catie stopped analyzing and started to pay attention to what was going on in her living room.

Marcy swiftly stepped up to Alexandru and supported the chinchilla. Alexandru tried to step back, but Marcy said, "It's okay, Alexandru. Chinchillas are really squirmy. Try like this." Marcy helped Alexandru cup his hands under Banana and hold him against his chest. "There. Perfect! But he won't stay still very long. They don't like to be held a lot because they get too hot. They have so much fur. They do love to run, jump, and play, though. Would you guys like to play with me and Banana?"

"Yes!"

Alexandru was more enthusiastic than Catie. It wasn't that Catie was against it. It's just that she hadn't felt excitement for anything in so very many years. It was like she had forgotten how. She didn't want to ruin it for Alexandru, Marcy, or Banana, though, so she smiled and agreed.

Marcy placed Banana into his little carrier, and after getting the go-ahead from Catie, worked with Alexandru to arrange the furniture in such a way that Banana could run free without getting loose and lost in the house. Marcy warned that he could get up and over the back of the couch and put Alexandru on guard duty, a job he happily accepted. Catie completely lost track of time as they played with and laughed at the energetic Banana as he climbed on top of them, hopped from one pillow to the next on the floor, jumped up onto the couch—almost escaping over the back more than once but getting thwarted by Alexandru every time—and scurried through tunnels Marcy had brought along. Catie felt lighter than she had in a very long time, and she cherished the feeling.

She was so absorbed in the moment that she didn't realize that it had grown dark outside. She was so caught up in her enjoyment that she didn't hear the key in the lock or the click of the deadbolt or the squeak of the door on its hinges as it opened. She did notice the sound of the slamming door followed immediately by a loud shout. "What the fuck is all this?"

Catie jumped to her feet and winced at the pain. Hands massaging her lower back, she exclaimed, "Florina! Where—"

"Oh my God. Seriously. What is this?" She gestured angrily, sweeping the room with her arm. When Banana bounded across his play space, Florina screeched. "Eeeew! Is that a fucking rat?" She shuddered but continued, "And who did the rat bring with it? Dad was right all along. You like women as much as you like men. You're so gross." She gestured at Marcy, "What do you see in my mother, you disgusting tramp?"

"Florina! You have crossed the line. That is enough." Catie tried not to shout because she didn't want to be the kind of person who yelled at people, but in this case it was difficult not to scream at her daughter. "You will apologize to Marcy this instant."

"Or what? Huh? What will you do to me?" When Catie was quiet, Florina laughed. "Yeah, that's right. You won't do a thing because you're a weak coward, just like Dad always said." She turned to Alexandru. "And what about you, loser? Are you playing house with your two mommies?

Alexandru braced one hand on the back of the couch and sprang himself over the top. He approached his sister. "No."

"That's all you have to say?"

"Yep." He looked at Catie and Marcy. "I've got some homework, so I'd better go do it. I'll help put the furniture back after my homework. This was fun, and I hope you and Banana come again, Marcy." He took a few steps toward the kitchen and stopped. "Mamă, can I have the rest of the *sărmăluţe?*"

"You made *sărmăluţe?*" Florina looked at Catie. "That's one of my favorites."

"I know it is. That's why I made it. I thought you might be missing Romanian food. We haven't had much of it lately." Catie swallowed and cursed herself for how quivery her voice sounded. Even to her own ears she was weak and worthless.

"It was awesome. Too bad you weren't here for it, you nasty tool."

"Alexandru," Catie sighed. "Florina, there's some left for you. I'd love to warm it up for you."

Florina stood still, staring intently at her mother. She looked toward the kitchen. Catie was sure she was going to accept her offer, and she was stunned when Florina made a disgusted noise, like an angry tortoise hissing, and righteously proclaimed, "No, forget it. I don't want fake Romanian food," and stomped out the door, slamming it behind her.

Catie was at a complete loss for words or actions. She looked at Marcy, who sat still with Banana. She looked at Alexandru, still standing in the same spot. She managed to say, "Well, it seems like the rest of the *sărmăluţe* is yours, Alexandru. I'll warm it up and bring it to your room." To avoid making Alexandru or Marcy speak, she shuffled away to heat up the food that Florina rejected.

Marcy popped into the kitchen. Catie avoided eye contact by concentrating on warming the leftovers for Alexandru. Finally, she turned to Marcy. "I'm very sorry about Florina. She's...well, she's troubled. I'm sorry about the things she said. Tomorrow I'll talk to Irene about transferring to another room." She turned away and began to clean up the disastrous supper table. Everything blurred as her eyes filled. Her nose dripped. She sniffed and wiped her face with a napkin. Why was she always so unworthy of friendship? Why did she always, always drive people away? Or, if they did stay, why did she make them angry, so angry that they beat her? Catie had dared, *dared*, to let herself hope that she could have a fresh start in America. Clearly, though, she was a failure here, too. She blew her nose into the napkin, snatched another off the table, and turned away from Marcy who now stood beside her.

"What? Why would you transfer out of our room?" Marcy's confusion was evident in her words and her tone.

"What do you mean 'why,' Marcy? Florina was awful. She was horrible to you, and she accused you and me of being lesbians."

"First, I'm more concerned about how she treated her mother and her brother. I almost said something but thought it best to hold my tongue so I didn't undermine your authority. Second, it doesn't bother me if she thinks we're just co-workers or friends or lovers."

"Really?"

"Really."

After a pause, Marcy asked, "So, do you want to talk about it? Florina, I mean?" Catie shook her head and wiped the back of her hand across her eyes. "No. I'm fine."

"Okay, but if you change your mind, I'm here to listen. There's one thing I do want you to talk about now, though. It's something you were going to tell me but didn't get around to it."

Catie felt the worry lines in her forehead deepen. She resisted the urge to massage them. Not that it would help the headache behind those lines, anyway. "What?"

"You were going to tell me how you came to work at an orphanage when you were only seven years old."

Catie stared at Marcy. Finally, she nodded. "Let me deliver this food to Alexandru, and then we can sit at the table." When she returned, Catie busied herself making tea. She didn't want to look at Marcy. The stories she wanted to hear were unspeakable. Literally. Catie had absolutely no idea how to begin. Worse, she didn't really want to begin. She had revealed too much of herself already. Why had she done that? And why was Marcy here despite all that she had learned about Catie's incompetence, her un-lovability?

Catie lifted her artificially cheery yellow tea kettle but promptly thunked it down again. She blinked and stared at it. It felt just like the irons the women in her family used to press clothing when they lived in the countryside. She used to love running her fingers over the bumps and ridges, especially the decorative scrollwork under the handle. Absent-mindedly she examined her fingertip and ran her thumb over the skin. Once, and only once, she had poked her finger into one of the holes in the case and was punished with a searing burn from the hot coals inside. Catie shook her head and blinked her tea kettle back into focus. Why did it feel leaden like old-fashioned irons? Desperate to avoid questioning from Marcy, she carried it to the sink, filled it, and returned to the stove, silently praying the entire time that her gargantuan effort was inconspicuous. The simple act of turning the knob to start the burner caused the feeling of thousands of needles pricking her wrists and fingers. She reached for teacups. Her hands shook, and she dropped one. It hit the counter and shattered; colorful shards of ceramic shot across the counter and onto the floor. The sudden drop, the noise, the debris, the sliver in her hand from which ran a trickle of blood, reminded her of life with Dumitru. She cringed and heard herself utter an apology. Simultaneously, images of the earthquake in Bucharest jostled loose from their storage places in her mind. Bunicuţă! Dionisie! She dropped to her knees to protect herself, to find those she loved. Everything was blurry and she couldn't see. Her chest constricted painfully. She was unable to breathe. Had she been struck by something? Someone? Was Dumitru here? Was he punishing her for the mess? Suddenly, she felt hands on her, under her arms, trying to pull her up. She squeezed her eyes shut. Despite being weak, her muscles began to tremble; she felt them shake against the arms that grasped her firmly. She knew better than to resist. A lifetime of experience had taught her that resistance would make everything worse. She had no say, no power. The only control she had was her decision to give in to whatever would happen next. Eyes still closed, she went limp and let herself be dragged away.

"It's okay, Mamă. A cup fell. It's no big deal. Really. We're away from Dad so it's okay. We're okay. You're okay. Really, Mamă." Catie was confused. Why was Dumitru calling her Mamă? At the continued sound of the voice, she finally realized the source. Alexandru. Her son. She opened her eyes but quickly closed them again because the light above her was so bright it hurt all the way through to the back of her skull and back again to the front. "Mamă?" Alexandru sounded so concerned that she opened her eyes again. She looked at him and scooted herself to a sitting position. Someone handed her a wad of tissues. Hands shaking, Catie took the tissues and wiped her face, blew her nose. She looked around. She was sitting on her bed, Alexandru standing on one side, Marcy on the other. As she reoriented herself, she remembered why she was there and was ashamed. Ashamed that she broke the cup. Ashamed that she had a panic attack with Marcy and Alexandru as witnesses. Ashamed that it was caused by memories that were so strong that they seemed to be happening now, not back then, not in her past. Ashamed of herself and who she was. She closed her eyes and leaned her head back against the wall that served as her bed's headboard.

In hopes of diverting attention away from herself, Catie looked at her son. "How's your homework coming?" She hated that her voice was creaky.

"Fine. I'm pretty much done."

"Pretty much?"

"Yeah. I have a reading packet for social studies. I started it, but I need a break." He looked from his mother to Marcy. "Um, could we maybe play with Banana again? Then I'll finish my homework. I promise."

Catie studied him. She must have done so for too long, for Alexandru frowned, worry lines making the corners of his mouth and his eyes all point down to the floor. Catie's heart dropped. She hated seeing him worry, especially about her. A boy shouldn't worry about his mother, she chastised herself. She faked a little smile. "I'm glad you like Marcy and Banana. Maybe they can come back another time. I am very tired and just need to go to sleep." She allowed her eyes to close once again.

She opened them when Marcy spoke. "If you want to, Catie, you can come sit with us. I'll make you some tea." Catie felt sick. How could she turn down this request, especially after Marcy had been so nice? But she didn't think she could do it. Her exhaustion was the deep, achy, dizzying sort that wouldn't allow her to move. The thought of having to tell Marcy stories made it all worse; she tasted bile at the back of her throat at the mere thought of it. Yet what right did she have to refuse? She smiled and quietly acquiesced. She bit her lip to try to stop her chin from quivering.

She sent Marcy and Alexandru ahead of her because she didn't want them to have to watch her creak and crawl her way off the bed. She didn't want them to know the intensity of her pain. It felt like her thoughts and feelings had exploded and shattered like the cup she so stupidly broke. All of the shards of those thoughts and feelings peppered every part of her body like shrapnel, wedging into her joints and twisting, stabbing, into her organs. This was part of her private pain, though, a pain she bore in silence so she didn't bother anyone or make them so angry they would punish her and make it all worse.

By the time she made it to the living room, Marcy and Alexandru had modified the fortress so that Catie could sit on the couch and sip the tea that Marcy had made her. She eased herself down and enjoyed the sight of her son and friend crawling around chasing the jumping chinchilla. It looked like a miniature kangaroo, only much fuzzier.

Suddenly, a door slammed loudly. Catie's heart slammed against her chest and her body froze. What was happening? She opened her eyes just a crack, but everything was dark and she couldn't tell. Something hit the ground with a thud. Catie startled but otherwise remained motionless. A light came on in the near distance. Someone shouted then exclaimed, "The fuck are you still doing here?" Florina! Her daughter was back home. What time was it? Catie didn't know because she couldn't see the clock.

"I'm hanging out here to make sure you came home safely. If you didn't, I was going to help your mom find you." Marcy!

She was still here? Hadn't she told her goodbye? And told Alexandru goodnight? She tried to remember. She watched them playing in the living room, and that's all she remembered. She must have fallen asleep. She should get up now, but she was interested in the conversation coming from the kitchen. She stayed put and tuned back in.

"Really? How the hell do you know what it's like for me," Florina spat.

"Because I recognize all that hatred in you. I hated my life and my entire family when I was your age."

"That doesn't mean you know anything about me! And you don't know as much as you think. I don't hate my entire family."

"Oh. That's great!" Catie thought Marcy sounded too enthusiastic, and she cringed. Florina wouldn't stand for that.

"*Great?* What's your fucking problem? I hate everyone in my family except a few people, and you think it's *great*? You think it's *great* that I have to be here in this fucking place with fucking people that I fucking despise? Fuck you."

"I stand corrected." Catie couldn't believe it. Marcy didn't sound upset. Her tone wasn't angry. Her voice didn't waver. It was like she was talking about ordinary things at work. Catie wished she could be as calm. She never felt calm. Ever. Even if something was fine in one moment, she knew that something bad could happen out of the blue and cause things to be far from fine in the very next moment. She admired Marcy for her unflappability. Curious about whether Marcy's demeanor would crack, she continued to listen. "I shouldn't have assumed."

Florina snorted. "Whatever. Like I care."

"So who in your family do you care about?"

"What difference does it make?" Catie didn't know if Marcy made any kind of response. She didn't hear anything. After a brief pause, Florina said, "Not that it's any of your business, but I care about my dad and my other family back in Romania. I hate my mother and my brother. It's all their fault that we're here, and I'm pissed off that they dragged me here with them. I fucking hate them!"

"Fine. But do you really think this attitude and behavior are going to help you in any way? Actually, you probably do. I did. But it won't."

"I don't give a shit about your opinion about my behavior. You're just some lesbian whore my mother is spreading her legs for."

At that, Catie bolted upright and struggled to her feet. Florina got that lovely line straight from her father. It was something Dumitru once said to a woman who had the misfortune of giving Catie a ride home from work one day. The bus Catie needed had been in a terrible accident, and Dumitru long ago had forbidden her to ride the subway. Because he worked for the subway, she couldn't disobey him and get away with it. She was walking the four miles home when a horn blared beside her. Well, horns blared from every direction. Catie always thought that the fact that everyone used his horn for everything, constantly, rendered the horns rather pointless. But the day of the bus accident, her work friend Marilena pulled up and offered her a ride. Catie had been excited. Marilena had her own car, a blue Dacia, the car designed and made right in Romania. Catie had hopped in knowing that Dumitru wouldn't like it if it took two hours for her to get home by walking. Like always, he'd want his dinner ready and waiting when he arrived home. It would have been fine if Marilena had just dropped her off and left, but she had come into the house with Catie and was still there when Dumitru came home. Dumitru was furious, and one of the scathing remarks he used was the one Florina had just said to Marcy. Dumitru never waited until the children were out of sight or earshot before dealing with his wife.

Catie believed that Florina had the right to feel the way she did about leaving her home, but that did not give her the right to talk abusively to Marcy. She hustled into the kitchen as quickly as her body would allow. "Florina Grigorescu! That is enough. Apologize to Marcy, get into your room and go to sleep."

Florina sneered. "I don't have to listen to you. I can't even go to my room, anyway. My room is in Bucharest." She stomped to her room anyway and slammed her door. Catie jumped but otherwise didn't react. She rubbed her temples. What could she possibly say to Marcy? She was too tired, too upset, to think. She startled when Marcy put a hand on her shoulder.

Marcy said, "It's late, Catie. Don't worry about Florina. I was a little shit when I was a teenager, and look how awesome I am now." She grinned. Catie couldn't help but smile back. "I'll see you tomorrow." She hugged Catie, then slipped out the door.

Catie locked the door behind Marcy then went to bed. Although she fell asleep almost instantly, her sleep wasn't a good one. All through the night, she dreamed of Romania. She dreamed of what happened to her favorite uncle, aunt, and little cousin. She dreamed of her least favorite cousin. She dreamed of horrible things. All night Catie dreamed and woke, sweating, panting, nauseated, crying; dreamed and woke; dreamed and woke. She dreamed of what Marcy wanted to know but Catie couldn't talk about.

# Bucharest, Romania

## *1977*

# Chapter 16

Cătălina stood and watched the group of men trudge her way. Just by studying their stooped shoulders, their scowls, the way they stomped on and kicked at the rubble that still paved streets and sidewalks, she knew. "No luck, Tată?"

Cătălina heard her mother call, "Grigor? Did you find us a place to live?" Her mother's voice sounded distant. She wasn't all that far away from Cătălina, but she was hidden, shrunk. Her mother hunkered between Viorica and Daciana against the crumpled wall of an old building. They were her guardians and protectors. Cătălina noticed that her mother had become the child, her two older sisters a joint mother, and she just a rat making problems and getting in the way.

Before Grigor or her uncles Ion, Neculi, and Eduard could answer, Cătălina heard a man down the street begin to shout. His voice was so loud that Cătălina heard him as though he were close. The large pile of debris on which he stood probably helped his voice carry over everyone.

"We still have no place to live! We are on the streets like all of these mangy dogs." He kicked at one and was punished when the dog snarled and chomped on his leg. He cried out, bent sideways to scoop up a chunk of jagged concrete, and started to beat the dog with it. Cătălina watched, wide-eyed, as the man struck the dog again and again, even after the dog let go, until the dog was completely still. He threw his rubble weaponry into the pack of dogs that hovered on the edge of the mass of humanity on the streets. "Go away! Get out!"

By this time, a crowd had gathered around this man and those around him. Cătălina tried to balance on some debris so she could see the man better, but she kept slipping on the uneven pile. She caught movement and saw Filip snake his way through the crowd. She was going to move away, but he reached her too quickly. Immediately, he lifted her onto his shoulders. "Filip!"

"What's the matter?"

"Put me down!"

"Why? Doesn't this help you see?"

Cătălina wasn't about to admit to him that she could see much better. "Well. That doesn't matter. You're not an adult, you know. You can't just act like one."

"I'm older than you. By five whole years. That's a lot."

"You're twelve. That hardly makes you grown-up enough to put me on your shoulders. Besides, I'm not a baby, Filip."

"Do you want to see what's going on, or not?"

"Yes."

"Then hold still and shut up."

Cătălina returned her attention to the man, who was ranting about the dogs. "Wild, mangy beasts, traveling in packs, sleeping where they fall, scuffling for food in garbage cans. That's what we have become, thanks to President Ceauşescu." Catie was shocked to realize that he was talking not about dogs but about people—about her family and neighbors and her. Listening to him, she knew he was right.

"Why? Why do we have to do this? Why do we have to live like animals? We don't choose this lifestyle!" Catie looked around her. Everyone stood stiffly, looking at the man but neither nodding in agreement nor shaking their heads in denial. No one spoke. The man shouted, "Look! Look all around you." He moved his arms in a sweeping gesture. "On this street and on countless others, there's nothing but ruins. You've seen it. As you scout, day after day after day for shelter, for a place to live that is off the streets, you find nothing but destruction. Yes, we had an earthquake. But that was four months ago. Where are we now? In the same place we were on that horrible night. And why? Because of Ceauşescu!"

"Shut up! Are you insane? You'll get us all killed!" Cătălina strained to see if she knew who spoke that warning, but the person had already stopped talking.

"Aren't we already dead now? What is so great about this," he gesticulated sharply toward the shambles around him, "that we are afraid to speak up? Huh? Our wretched president has chosen to let tens of thousands of Romanians here in Bucharest live on the streets as he causes more and more destruction by razing apartment buildings to make room for his glorious Civic Center." He spat on the ground. "That's right. I have been moving about, talking to people, and I've learned of Ceauşescu's plans and the sheer number of people he is killing or forcing onto the streets. Yet he turns around and orders more and more babies. Babies to help build a grand Romania. How can we feed these babies when we can't feed ourselves? Where do we put these babies to sleep when we don't have sleeping places for ourselves? Our leaders are fucking insane. Irresponsible. I say enough." The man spat again.

"Oh, do you now?" A bitter, vile laugh rang out. Catie watched the crowd across from her part as a man in a military uniform pushed his way forward. The crowd moved aside in several places as uniformed men shoved through. The *Securitate*!

She bent forward and whispered in Filip's ear. "I want to get down! I want to go. C'mon Filip." She squirmed and wiggled.

"Hold still," Filip hissed at her. Don't draw attention to us. Just hold on. I'll get us out of here when I can. Reluctantly, Catie returned her attention to what was happening in front of her.

"You think you're an expert in President Ceauşescu's plans." One of the *Securitate*, tall and broad, stepped up to the now-silent man and chopped his hands down hard on the man's shoulders. The man fell to his knees. When he tried to stand, the *Securitate* officer pulled one of his guns out of its holster, cocked it, and pressed it against the citizen's forehead. "Ceauşescu's plans aren't for you, peasant." He struck the man in the face with the butt of his gun. "Ceauşescu's plans are for a great Romania, and you're...not...part...of... it." The pause between each word was filled in by a swift strike with the gun. Cătălina watched as the *Securitate* man stepped away from the man, letting him fall face first the ground. For a moment, Cătălina worried that he was dead, but he slid his hands under his shoulders, pressed himself part way up, raised his hands to his bloody face for a moment, and once again tried to stand.

"Well, well. Coming back for more, are we? Let's see what you have energy for in prison." He yanked the man to a full standing position and punched him hard in the stomach and again in the face before throwing him over his shoulder. He swung around, surveying the crowd and looking at his *Securitate* comrades. "Disperse this crowd, and let's go," he ordered. Gunshots, screams, and shouts rang through the air.

Cătălina felt herself falling down off Filip's shoulders. She hit the ground with a thud, but Filip immediately helped her up.

"Come on, Cătălina! Let's get out of here." He grabbed her hand, and together, they started to run. They ran and ran, scrambling up, over, and around debris as if they had somehow grown accustomed to its presence over the last four months. Broken buildings whizzed by in a blur. They ran through a pack of dogs so quickly that they escaped without so much as a scratch. They ran until they found a bulldozer, shut down for the day, surrounded by other big trucks that were also shut down. No one was around, so they scrambled behind the blade and hid behind the rollers. They panted and gagged and coughed.

"Shhh," ordered Filip.

"You shush."

Other than their efforts to control their breathing, they were silent for several minutes after that exchange. Filip broke the silence. "Wow. That was intense."

"Intense? Filip, it was horrific. It..." Cătălina stopped abruptly and stared, open-mouthed, at her older cousin. He was crying! She watched as he doubled over and sobbed into his lap. She watched his shoulders and back move, jarred by the force of his tears. She tried to talk, but she couldn't get words out. No, she thought, she didn't actually have any words. She had never seen any man or older boy cry. Shout enthusiastically, yes. Yell joyously, sure. Bellow angrily, of course. The men in her life were expressive in their words and actions. But they didn't cry. They were too strong, too dominant, for that kind of weakness. Therefore, Cătălina was at a loss for what to say or do. As she watched, Filip continued to bawl. She hated it when he touched her, fondled her, hugged her, held her too close for too long, and she didn't think she'd ever be one to touch him first. But her heart went out to him. Her heart and head and all of the soft stuff inside of her actually ached for him; she could feel his pain, and it made her cry, too. Her repulsion at the idea of physically touching Filip became less important than her desire to comfort him. She reached for him and gently pulled him up, and held him tight and they cried together.

Cătălina felt Filip's sobs decrease in intensity until he was silent and still. Cătălina's own tears abruptly stopped; fear pushed despair out of the way and held her in its grip. What was Filip going to do now? She bit her lip to keep from saying something to make this situation harder to get out of. She squeezed her eyes shut when Filip shuffled his knees forward so he was even closer to her than he had been. He held her tightly with one hand and caressed her shoulder, neck, and hair with the other. Cătălina still didn't know what to do, but she knew she didn't want to stay like this and let Filip keep touching her in this awful way. She wriggled loose and stood up. Filip jumped up and stood next to her. He towered over her, and when he glowered down at her, Cătălina felt like one of the mangy rats cornered by a wild dog, cowering because it know it was about to be devoured.

"What's your problem, Cătălina?" When Filip followed his bark by wiping the back of his hand across his eyes and sniffing, Cătălina wondered the same thing. What was her problem? Why would she still feel such love and concern for this person who tormented her so? Maybe she didn't have a problem at all, actually. She was, after all, living the way Bunicuţă had taught her to live: with love and forgiveness in her heart. That thought brought her peace, and she smiled.

Filip smacked the smile off her face. "Don't smirk at me. I asked you what your problem is."

Cătălina's cheek stung, and she rubbed it as she spoke. "I don't have a problem, Filip. I was moving so I could see you better and ask if you are okay."

His eyes narrowed. "Why would you ask that?"

"Well, you were very upset and crying and I wanted to make sure you were feeling better."

"Lies!" Filip smacked her again, harder this time, so that Cătălina stumbled back a few steps. Filip closed in on her before she fully regained her balance. "I was not crying!" He shoved her. "I do not cry. Do you understand? I don't cry!" He shoved her down and swooped down to hover above her, one knee on each side of her chest and his hands gripping her neck. He pulled up and let her head fall back to the ground with a thud.

"Filip! I—"

"Shut up! Just shut up, Cătălina! Listen to me carefully. I don't cry, and I didn't cry just now. If you try to tell anyone I did, I will tell them what a liar you are, and I will tell them that you touched me and tried to kiss me. You know what will happen to you then, Cătălina? You'll be beaten and punished, and when that's over, I will hunt you down and beat you more and then I'll turn you over to the *Securitate*. When that happens, you'll wish you were back with me. Do you understand me?"

Cătălina nodded.

"Say it, Cătălina! Say you understand me and tell me what I didn't do."

"I understand you, Filip. You didn't cry now because you never cry." Because her cousin still held her by the neck, her words were meek and bruised.

"Say it like you mean it, Cătălina, or I swear to God I will kill you now. No one would even miss you, and you know it."

He stood, lifting Cătălina up by her neck as he did so. He glowered at her menacingly.

Cătălina placed her hands on top of Filip's, slid her small fingers under his larger ones, and pried them loose. She wasn't strong enough to pull his hands off her neck, but she had room now to breathe in enough air to get behind her false words and push them out and straight into Filip's face.

"I understand you. You didn't cry now because you never cry."

"That's right. Don't you forget it. Ever. Because if you do, I'll do everything I said I would do." Both hands still around Cătălina's neck, Filip shoved her and let go. She stumbled backward, tripped over a short block of concrete, and landed on her back. The fall knocked the wind out of her, but that really wasn't hard to do because she just didn't have much left inside. She lay on the dusty, rocky ground and closed her eyes while she tried to breathe right again. Little pains shot through her chest when she inhaled, but she didn't care. Clunky boots slid over pebbles, and she felt a shadow settle over her body. She shivered, hopefully imperceptibly, because the person it belonged to was icy and scary. Cătălina felt Filip's boot poke her in the side. She remained as she was: still, eyes closed. He poked again. She stayed still, eyes closed. Again came a nudge, a bit stronger this time, but not painful. "Come on, Cătălina. Open your eyes." She didn't. "Cătălina!" She ignored him. "Fine. Just lie there, then. I'm going back under the bulldozer. Go ahead and just stay here in the open. It's not my fault if you get spotted and arrested by the *Securitate*." Cătălina could still feel his boot against her ribs so she knew he was still there. She waited patiently. Finally, she heard his shuffled retreat. She sighed.

Cătălina knew Filip was right. If she kept lying here and the wrong person noticed, she would be hauled away. But what difference did it make, really? Filip had been right about something else, too. If he had decided to kill her, no one would care. On a good day, she was tolerated. On a bad day, everyone found fault with everything she did. On those days, she wouldn't get any food. It wasn't food she wanted, though. She just wanted her family's love and didn't understand why she could never seem to be good enough to earn it. She knew that Bunicuţă would tell her to be patient and understanding and remember that everyone was doing their best trying to survive and take care of each other. She did try to remember that, but it didn't erase the hurt that came every time her family pushed her aside.

Her back ached, so she rolled to her side and pushed herself up so she could sit on the ground, her back against the concrete block she had stumbled over. She moved as quietly as she could so Filip wouldn't hear her and come investigate. Lifting her feet off the ground so they didn't drag noisily, she pulled her knees up to her chest and lay her head down on them. Filip. What was wrong with him to make him try to do bad things with her sometimes, treat her roughly and cruelly other times, and nicely still other times? There wasn't a single person she could talk to about this. Mamă was lost somewhere inside herself. Her sisters had always been too busy, too important for her. Her bunică Rodica was intimidating; Cătălina avoided her as much as she could. Filip's parents, Tată's brother and his wife, had become very angry and yelled at her when, last winter, Cătălina told them that she didn't want Filip to get naked during the night and put his whole body against hers. They had even pulled Tată into it, causing him to be angry at her, too. He told her they had enough real problems without her trying to get attention by making even more trouble with her exaggerated lies. "But Tată, they aren't lies," Cătălina had begged. "Surely you see him during the day, how he's mean to me?" But Tată didn't admit to seeing anything of the sort, dismissing it as nothing more than the typical behavior of men and boys. This wasn't the first time she heard such a thing.

*One day, about a month after the earthquake, Cătălina tried once again to discuss Filip's behavior with Tată. When she approached him with this, he had been striking earthquake debris with a sledgehammer to clear safe paths for movement; every day he and other men did this because they had learned that if they wanted passable and safe paths, they would have to do it themselves. The government was busy and couldn't be bothered with such mundane tasks for such banal people; the government was concerned with building up the already-grand areas of Bucharest and thus didn't care about the peasants' areas. When Cătălina approached her father, he slung the sledgehammer over his shoulder to listen to her, but as she talked about Filip and the things he did, Tată let the hammer come to rest on the ground. He rested his hand on the butt of the handle and sighed. "Cătălina, look. You need to stop this nonsense. Making up stories about Filip just pushes people away from you and causes them not to like you."*

*"No, I'm not—"*

*Tată held up his hand, and Cătălina knew to stop. She shut her mouth and waited for Tată to either continue talking or dismiss her. He continued to talk. "Don't interrupt a man, Cătălina. And speaking of men, Filip is a boy. He'll soon be a teenager, a young man. He's just being male. Boys and men are like that sometimes, and as a girl you need to understand that." Tată sighed again and placed his large hand on Cătălina's head. She loved the way his pinky touched one of her temples and his thumb touched the other. It made her feel grounded and secure, and she knew that Tată could protect her. She was grateful for him for that. Tată was a grownup. He was strong. He could make her safe. He could make everyone safe by cleaning up the debris from that horrible earthquake. She should stop bothering so he could do his job. She should believe him about Filip, even if she didn't like it.*

*"Okay, Tată. Thank you."*

*"You're welcome. Now go on. These big chunks of rubble aren't going to break themselves apart."*

*Over the next weeks, however, Filip's behavior had worsened. He touched her more often, and he bullied her with increased intensity. One day, when she was watching Dionisie, she had witnessed an exchange between Oana and Eduard.*

*"Eduard, please listen to me. Don't go off trying to trade for better rationing coupons. We're fine."*

*"Fine, Oana? We don't have enough food. Very little supplies. We have no rations at all to buy any power. We can't——"*

*"Power, Eduard? What would we do with rations for power? We're living on the streets! Please. It's dangerous to go out trying to get better rations."*

*To Cătălina's shock, Eduard had strode toward Oana and grabbed her shoulders. "Do not tell me what to do, woman. I make the decisions."*

*Oana had looked down, contrite. "Of course you do. I know that Eduard, I do. I just want you to be safe."*

*Eduard dropped his arms. He looked at Oana right in her eyes. Cătălina began to count after a few seconds. She was at nine when Eduard stepped back and turned away. That seemed like a long time to look into someone's eyes, she thought. No one said anything as Eduard began to walk away.*

*Cătălina busied herself with Dionisie until she couldn't hold in her questions any longer. She put Dionisie on her back and looked around for Oana. She found her picking at a loaf of bread. Oana shook her head and dropped the bread into her lap. "We just got this bread yesterday, and look." She held it up. Fuzzy green circles polka-dotted the bread.*

Cătălina stuck out her tongue. "*My sentiments exactly,*" agreed Oana. "*I'm trying to pick these out so we can at least eat part of it, but I'm not really getting anywhere. This mold has completely invaded the loaf. It's the Securitate of food.*" She exhaled sharply and set the loaf down again. "*So what can I do for you? Is Dionisie being a problem?*"

Dionisie squirmed off of Cătălina's back and ran to his mother. She moved the bread out of the way just in time to catch him as he jumped toward her. Oana kissed him, smoothed his hair, and rocked him. Cătălina smiled. "*Dionisie is never a problem. We were just taking a walk around and, well, I...*" She trailed off. She knew people hated it when she brought up Filip.

"*What is it, Cătălina?*"

Cătălina watched Oana rock Dionisie and Dionisie snuggle into his mother. They had so much love. Cătălina always felt warm and good around them, and around Eduard, too. She bunched her eyebrows together as she thought about Eduard. She just didn't understand. She had to ask. She shook her head to clear her throat because a lump formed there. She thought of it as her worry lump because it appeared in various places whenever she was worried about something. She took a deep breath before asking, "*Why did Eduard get gruff with you earlier and why did he grab you like that? But then he looked into your eyes. Why? That didn't seem mean? Is he mean to you? And is it okay if he his? I know the other men act like this, but now Eduard.*" She took another deep breath and looked down. She saw that her hands were grasping her dress and squeezing it. She relaxed her grip, smoothed her dress, and let go. She started to smooth it again to avoid looking at Oana. Cătălina would be devastated if Oana were angry.

"*Those are some pretty big questions.*" She paused to help Dionisie balance when he slid off her lap. He plopped down about a meter away and began to stack and topple rocks. Oana smiled, but her expression turned serious again when she looked at Cătălina. "*Men are, well, men. Sometimes they do get gruff. These are stressful times. But we also still have each other. Eduard and I love each other, and that is stronger than anything else."*

*Since Bunicuță died on March 4, Oana was the only person who took the time to talk to Cătălina. Bunicuță probably would have said similar things. Cătălina squeezed her eyes shut and thought of the conversations she had had with Bunicuță about Filip. Bunicuță had actually told her things that weren't all that different from what Oana was saying. Cătălina opened her eyes again and looked at Oana through brimming tears.*

*"Cătălina, are you okay?"*

*She nodded. "Yes, I am."*

*"Do you have anything else you want to talk about?"*

*Cătălina hesitated. She was going to ask about Filip's behavior and what she should do about it, but she realized that she would never get an answer beyond the fact that Filip is a boy. And if that was good enough for Oana, and had been good enough for Bunicuță, then it was good enough for her.*

As she huddled into herself on that concrete block, Filip just yards away hiding in the bulldozer, Cătălina recalled the conversation she had had with Oana just a few months ago. That talk had changed nothing: not Filip, not her, not her attitude about Filip's behavior. Would a conversation with Bunicuță have changed anything? Maybe. Maybe not. She would never know because she had lost Bunicuță. She started to cry. She tried to be quiet about it, but she must not have been good enough at silence, for abruptly, there was Filip. She was going to tell him to leave her alone, but she didn't feel like incurring his wrath, so she remained silent. When she felt him tugging at her, she cried harder.

"Come on, Cătălina. It's getting dark. Too dark to find our way back to our family. But we can't stay out here exposed like this. Let's go back to the bulldozer." Cătălina limply did what he suggested. The minute they crawled under the blade, Cătălina curled up against it and gave in to her utter exhaustion. The next thing she knew, Filip was shaking her awake. "Come on, Cătălina. It's morning. Let's work our way back home." He said nothing more. When he set out, she followed him. She stayed behind him until she grew tired of trailing him. She hustled up to join him, and side by side they worked their way home.

\* \* \*

Cătălina pulled her thin cotton dress around her and shivered in the blustery wind. The apartment Uncle Ion had found for them this past autumn was dark and shabby and small, but it held the whole family and because so many people lived there, it was warm. In fact, it was so warm that the cold air blowing in from outside actually felt refreshing. Out here, though, in the food line, the air was not at all refreshing. Her face stung and her fingers and toes were numb. She bounced up and down to warm herself up. Dionisie thought it was a game. He grabbed her hands and jumped with her.

"Goddammit, hold still."

Cătălina stopped abruptly. She turned to see who said it, so she could apologize, but she couldn't tell. She muttered a vague apology into the crowd. Eduard scooped up Dionisie and plopped him on his shoulders. Cătălina tried to stand still, but she kept getting nudged this way and that by the throng of hungry, thirsty, impatient people. People were agitated, but the line itself wasn't moving at all—she was still standing beside the same pothole she had been standing beside for what seemed like hours. She imagined that it was a magic, food-bearing hole. All she needed to do was get on her knees and say a magic spell and food would rise up out of it. Good food. Real food. Meats and potatoes and vegetables and gravies and bread and butter and dumplings, all the good things from her life in the countryside that was but a distant memory. She clutched her stomach to quiet its painful rumblings. Oh, how she wished she could whisper that spell. She would give everyone in this line so much food that they could feed their families for days, weeks, months, forever. She'd send so much home with Oana and Eduard and Dionisie that they would hardly to be able to carry it. She would stay here for as long as it took to feed everyone in Bucharest until they grew plump. She smiled at the thought of everyone having enough good food to eat. Maybe then everyone would feel better and be happier and nicer. Unfortunately, though, that pothole was really just an ordinary pothole with its cracks and fissures and pools of rank water and debris. She poked at it with her toe.

She snapped her head up and forgot about the pothole when she heard commotion ahead of her. Voices rose and people grew antsier, more agitated. She noticed some people around her straining to see what was happening. She most definitely did not want to know. All of her experiences told her that commotion meant nothing but trouble, often big, big trouble. Cătălina squeezed her eyes shut and covered her ears, but she felt exposed so, eyes still closed, she threw her arms around her uncle Eduard.

Abruptly, everyone except very young children grew silent and still. Cătălina knew then that the *Securitate* had made another appearance. Only they had the power to quiet an unquiet crowd in an instant.

"Wow. I just love the sound of obedience," one shouted. "Don't you, Toma?"

"Why yes, Sergiu, yes I do," the one presumably named Toma answered. "Should we reward them?"

"Hmmm. Good question. How?"

Toma shrugged. "Perhaps we could allow them access to today's food without using their ration coupons." Cătălina heard some people inhale sharply, but no one uttered a word.

The one called Sergiu walked slowly through the crowd, seeming to ponder Toma's suggestion. Cătălina's heartbeat quickened. Was he really considering giving them free access to food today? That would be a gift that most of them would relish with humble gratitude.

Sergiu had returned to stand by Toma. "It is quite impressive that these peasants show proper awe and respect for us, isn't it Toma?"

"Indeed, Sergiu. Perhaps—"

Sergiu's arm shot into the air, palm flat and fingers stiff. "Silence, Toma. Listen. I hear the sound of children. Do you hear it?"

Toma stretched forward and made an exaggerated show of listening. "Now that you mention it, Sergiu, I do hear children."

"But why did I have to mention it, Toma? Children are noisy, especially when there are many." He began to move through the crowd, shoving people out of his way as he went. Still, no one made a sound. "But I don't see a great number of children, do you?" He shouted over the crowd to Toma, who was also pushing his way through the crowd in the opposite direction of Sergiu.

"No, Sergiu, I do not. Not nearly enough as there should be, anyway."

"Get over here, now." Sergiu's voice was now a low growl, but still loud enough for Cătălina to hear clearly. Worry lumps popped up and throbbed in her temples, her chest, and her stomach. When Toma reached Sergiu's side, Sergiu asked him, "Why aren't there more children here? Are these plebeians disobeying President Ceauşescu's orders?" Without waiting for a response from Toma, Sergiu addressed a woman in the crowd. Cătălina couldn't see the woman, but she heard the exchange. "You! How many children do you have?"

"I have six, sir."

"I only see three pathetically clinging to you. Where are the others?"

"They are older sir, boys, and they are with their father."

Sergiu moved on to another random person. Cătălina missed much of this exchange because the crowd was no longer silent and still. Panicked voices blended together so Cătălina couldn't hear anything specific. She heard only the sound of fear and terror growing louder. She did hear Eduard's voice. "Come. Let's go while we have a chance to sneak away." Gently, he ushered them through the crowd. Others were attempting to leave as well, and Cătălina thought they could escape undetected. She screamed, the noise escaping involuntarily, when the one called Toma appeared in front of them.

"Halt!" He shoved Eduard hard in the chest with the butt of his gun. "Where do you think you're off to?"

"We—"

"Shut up!" Are these your children?

"Yes, sir. My daughter and son." Cătălina stepped close to Eduard, and he put his arm around her.

Toma reached out and snatched Dionisie from Oana's arms. She gasped, uttered, "Dionisie!" and reached for him. Toma stepped out of her reach.

"Dionisie. Is that your name?" Cătălina watched Dionisie nod. "What a big, strong name. I bet you're a big, strong boy." Dionisie nodded again, this time more vigorously. Toma held his free hand out and extended his finger. "Show me how strong you are. Try squeezing my finger." Dionisie grabbed it and squeezed. "Ouch!" Toma pulled his hand away. "You are very strong." Dionisie giggled. "I bet you're very smart, too." Dionisie nodded. "So tell me, smart man, is this your sister?" Cătălina's breath caught in her throat. She couldn't exhale past her worry lump.

"No."

"Oh, really?" Toma exclaimed. His voice was light, but the look he shot Eduard was stone. "So who is it?"

"That's Cătălina."

"Well, hello, Cătălina." Toma made her name sound like a sin. He turned back to Dionisie. "Do you have brothers and sisters, Dionisie?"

He shook his head. "No."

Toma addressed both Eduard and Oana. "Why doesn't Dionisie have any brothers or sisters? Do you know the law? Or are you too stupid to count? Dionisie here makes one child. That means you are four short of the requirement. Why aren't you doing your part to create a great, powerful Romania?" Dionisie began to squirm in Toma's grasp. Toma grumped at him, "Hold still." To Oana, he grumped, "Why have you not produced more babies?"

"Sir, we're trying." Oana's voice shook as she cried. "Please. Please understand. I've carried two babies and lost them before they were born. Please give us Dionisie and let us go home. We are trying to have children for a great Romania. I promise."

"Is this true?" Toma addressed Eduard.

Eduard nodded. "Yes, sir. It is." Eduard's voice was tight, and Cătălina thought that he must be very scared but trying to hide it.

"Liar!" shouted Toma. Cătălina jumped. "You lied about Cătălina being your daughter. How can I trust you now?"

"I swear, I'm telling the truth."

"Sorry. Can't trust you. This is what I do to liars." Cătălina saw a streak of silver just before she heard an enormous boom that ended in a high-pitch whine reverberating in her head. Eduard slumped to the ground, taking Cătălina with him because her arms were still around him. Blood ran from a hole in his forehead and poured out from the back of his head. She screamed. She heard Oana scream. She heard Dionisie scream. She heard Toma say to Oana, "You are no good to Romania if all you do is produce dead babies." Cătălina saw the same silver streak, heard the same enormous boom, and saw Oana join Eduard on the ground.

"No!" Unthinking, Cătălina sprang up, stumbled just slightly, and charged at Toma. Toma swooped her up with his free arm. She kicked and struggled. She heard Dionisie screaming and screaming. Dionisie! She had to get him away from Toma. She wriggled and kicked and grabbed at Dionisie.

"Settle down." He shoved her off, and she landed on the ground with a hard thud. She tried to jump up to lunge at Dionisie, but Toma stepped on her. He bent down and leered at her, still grasping Dionisie. Dionisie reached out for Cătălina as he wailed, but Toma held him just out of Cătălina's grasp. "This child belongs to the state now, and he'll be placed in an orphanage to receive excellent care until he's old enough to serve President Ceauşescu. When you wake up, I want you to go home, wherever that is, and tell everyone what happens to liars and people who don't give Ceauşescu babies." Cătălina tried to lunge for Dionisie. The last thing she saw was the butt of Toma's gun.

# Sacramento, California
## *2018*

# Chapter 17

Catie stood in the hallway beside the door to the infant room. She heard Marcy in there, moving things around, and she heard a crash as Marcy dropped something heavy. Catie jumped. Her body fought with itself, some muscles twitching to move and others squeezing them painfully to hold them in place, as two strong instincts clashed. She had an almost overpowering urge to run in and pick up whatever mess was on the ground, but it wasn't quite strong enough to overpower her urge to hide out here and avoid Marcy. She hated herself. She was a truly awful human being. Dumitru had always been right. She was a worthless person, undeserving of love. Yes, Catie was completely unlovable. So why was Marcy being so kind? After last night, Marcy must surely realize that Catie is simply someone who won't make a good friend. She sighed and rubbed the bottom of her shirt between her fingers. Absently, she watched her fingers toy with the hem. Disgusted with herself for standing out here avoiding Marcy, she tugged at her shirt, smoothed it out, and resolved to avoid Marcy from inside the room instead.

Catie slunk inside and quietly busied herself with things that didn't need to be done.

"Catie! How'd things go with Florina this morning? And how's Alexandru? He was so fun last night. Banana loved him."

Catie kept her gaze fixed on Marcy's feet. She liked her sandals, with their swirls of orange and purple and teal. They accentuated her toenails, painted with teal polish. Her toe ring made of braided silver bands was cute. Catie would wear jewelry on her toes if she could. The pain she felt in her feet, though, made jewelry-wearing impossible. Catie looked at her own feet, took in the clunky, plain, black shoes that fully covered her feet. Even her socks were black. Marcy's feet matched the season, the fresh, cheerful spring. Catie's looked like tired winter leftovers. Fitting for the wearer, Catie mused.

"Catie. Look at me."

Catie sighed. She didn't want to see the disgust that undoubtedly clouded Marcy's face. She didn't want to talk about last night, either. She noticed more feet in the room, which meant the parents were trickling in with their babies. Later, when all of the drop-offs had been made, she'd give Marcy a small token of appreciation by answering the question she'd avoided twice. Then, she'd go back to being just an employee of Hey Little Diddles, doing her job in silence and going home to Alexandru and, hopefully, Florina. She distanced herself from Marcy to begin work. For more than an hour, she managed to be anywhere in the room other than where Marcy was, but then she had to change a diaper. She couldn't leave a baby unattended on the changing table, so she was stuck when Marcy cornered her.

"Catie, what's with you? I—"

"You've asked me why I worked at an orphanage from when I was a child until I left Romania. I will tell you." Catie rubbed the baby's feet with lotion and power before tucking his legs back into his sleeper. She counted the snaps aloud to him as she fastened them, scooped him up, and settled him in the swing before returning to Marcy. Without looking directly at her, Catie took a deep breath and told her, "My little cousin Dionisie, no more than a toddler, was taken away by the state police right before my eyes. The police shot and killed his parents, my uncle and aunt, and took Dionisie away. One of the police officers told me that Dionisie belonged to the government of Romania and would be placed in an orphanage until he was all grown up. I wasn't able to stop them from taking Dionisie. The police officer hit me with his gun. When I woke up, I was lying on my aunt's body. She was dead underneath me. My uncle was dead beside me. Dionisie was gone. Before I ran home, I knelt before Oana and Eduard—that's my aunt and uncle—and promised them that I would find Dionisie and take care of him."

Catie looked out the window and wrapped her arms around her waist. She shook her head. "Every day I left home before sunrise and didn't return until dark. Because there was so much destruction all over the city, it took time to find orphanages, which were referred to as hospitals for irrecoverable children. The only place that was being built up was the Civic Center. That was essentially a lavish palace for President Ceauşescu and his government. I had heard rumors about this monstrosity, but when I saw it with my own eyes, I was shocked. It was so enormous, already so fancy, yet everywhere else was destruction. People, things, all were neglected for the sake of building this extravagant palace. Many people became homeless when Ceauşescu ordered apartments buildings razed. He even flattened a museum, stadium, hospital, and churches—churches!—to make room for his shrine." Catie's eyes filled with tears. "He should have been repairing damage, not making more. He should have been helping his people." Catie turned away from the window and looked at Marcy. Seeing her face reminded her of how ashamed she was, how she didn't actually deserve to look at Marcy. She shook her head again and stepped away.

She busied herself with caregiving as she finished her account of working in the orphanages. "Anyway, when I found the first orphanage, hospital for irrecoverable children, I was so happy to finally be able to get Dionisie. Only he wasn't there. And I was relieved. It was terrible! The building itself looked so cold, impersonal. It was just stark gray, cold-looking. With rows of rectangular glass window all the same size and spaced apart perfectly. It looked neat and orderly, but very uninviting. Inside was far, far worse. It was complete chaos. Babies and children were crammed two, three, four to a crib. Even older children were stuffed into cribs. But they weren't cribs like this, Marcy." Catie gestured around the room. "No. They were metal cages, with very high bars and rods for a ceiling. The older children had their hands wrapped around the bars and would shake and shake the bars." Catie made her hands into fists and moved her arms like she was shaking an old-fashioned jail door. "There wasn't always material for diapers, so babies and children sat in their own messes. These poor things wailed or moaned. Some banged their heads on the bars or walls. I cried out for Dionisie and started to look for him until I was stopped. Some of the women were very cruel to me, and one tried to throw me outside. But one was nice. She rescued me and asked how she could help me. Together, we searched all through that orphanage for Dionisie, and she looked through her records for a boy who had just been brought in by the *Securitate*, but she found nothing. Dionisie wasn't there. I was devastated. I thought for sure I would find him there.

"I learned that there were many more places just like this one. I searched four more." Catie stopped and swallowed hard. She put her hand to her throat to try to ease the worry lump away. She looked around the warm, cheery, safe room before looking right into Marcy's eyes. "Those 'hospitals' weren't hospitals at all, Marcy. They didn't heal or nurture. They made little children—and bigger ones, like Alexandru but very scrawny, stuffed into cages and all twisted up just staring into space—extremely ill. I searched and searched and became more determined and more frantic at the thought of my little Dionisie, who was so loved by Oana and Eduard, all caged up and neglected." Catie swiped at her eyes and didn't even care that Marcy was right there to see her do it. In fact, she saw Marcy do the same thing!

"Catie, I can't imagine the horror of that. Please tell me you found him and got to take him home."

Catie shook her head slowly and sadly. Her voice thick and melancholy, she went on. "When I was arrived at Bucharest Hospital for Irrecoverable Children, Number Three, I was told that it would be impossible to find Dionisie. They told me that sometimes the *Securitate* decide to keep babies they take for themselves. Sometimes they wait awhile before taking a child to a hospital so no one comes looking. They convinced me that my best chance of finding Dionisie would be to stay there and work. Then he might be dropped off someday, or maybe I would get word from another hospital that Dionisie had arrived." She shuffled to the window and gazed out at the bright blue sky. She mused that in her earliest memories of the countryside and Bunicuţă, the sky always looked blue and sunny, but her memories of Bucharest and the rest of her life were gray and gloomy. She hadn't thought of that before. Marcy's approach prompted her to stop thinking about the sky and just finish the story.

She shrugged and continued to stare blankly outside. "So I stayed. I worked at Hospital Three from that point on. I asked about Dionisie whenever I could. Over the years I called or visited all of the other orphanages so many times. But I never had any luck. I know that Bunicuță, Oana, and Eduard wouldn't want me to stop looking, so I never did. I know, too, that they would want me to take very good care of the babies and older children in the orphanage, even the ones older than me. So that's what I did. Even though it often made my husband very, very angry. He didn't like that I was caring for someone other than him or his children. He didn't like that I wouldn't let Dionisie go. I paid a very high price for staying at the orphanage, but I didn't give in to him. That is the one area where I defied my husband." She paused. "Well, that, and leaving him.

"By the time I left Romania, the hospitals for irrecoverable children were called centers for disabled children and were better than the orphanages of the 1980s and 90s. I'd like to think that I did my part alongside other hardworking, caring people to make things better. But I never found Dionisie. To this day, I wonder what happened to him. I think of him every single day. I will never stop thinking of him. It's the least I can do."

Catie fell silent, and neither woman spoke. Catie walked across the room, comforted a crying child, sat down with her, and gave her a bottle. She watched the baby drink contentedly, eyes closed and chubby fingers touching the bottle. Catie smiled. Her smile faded when Marcy approached.

"Catie. I can't imagine how traumatic that would have been. I'm so sorry." She paused. When Catie said nothing, Marcy resumed, "So maybe we could talk more tonight. Alexandru wants to play with Banana again. What do you think? Your place or mine?"

Catie blew out a breath of air and looked at Marcy. "I don't think either place, Marcy." She averted gaze and stared at the baby in her arms.

"Why not?"

"Look. I'm not feeling well and just want to go home. I never feel well, but nothing can be done about it. That's just how I am. I'm not a good person to be around. I'm not a good mother, so my daughter behaved unacceptably last night. You aren't going to want to hang around me. I'm just not good enough. I like to be alone. Please."

"Catie, that makes no sense."

"Marcy. Seriously. Just stop, okay. We work together in this room, and I don't want it to be awkward."

Marcy held up her hands, palms facing out. She shook her head. "You know what? Fine. Fine, Catie. You just have your pity party and wallow in misery. Enjoy that." Marcy walked away to feed another hungry baby.

All day, Catie maneuvered around Marcy. They talked as necessary for work, but otherwise focused exclusively on their charges. *As it should be*, thought Catie. Still, Catie already missed conversations with Marcy. She knew, though, that this was for the best. Marcy's behavior, too, was proof that nothing Catie did was ever good enough and that she deserved to be alone and unloved. As she rode the bus home, she fished *The Count of Montecristo* out of her bag. She opened it up very carefully so as not to further loosen the brittle pages and removed the bookmark. She smiled sadly at the picture of St.

Basil. She turned it over and read the names she had written years ago: Bunicuță. Dionisie. Oana. Eduard. *Te iubesc.* I love you. She tried to read the book, but the pages blurred and became wet as tears splashed down. She closed her eyes, leaned her head back, and rubbed the bookmark between her fingers.

When the bus jolted to a stop, her heart quickened in that pleasant way that it did when she was about to give the offering of her labor to her church. She kissed her bookmark before closing it into the book, swiftly tucked her book into her bag, and worked her way up the aisle and off the bus. Today she had to wrap both of her hands around the handle of St. Theocharis's gigantic wooden door, a door so heavy that the handle was more of pole; a door so heavy that even with both hands and arms Catie could barely open it today. Whether her body was weak and hurting because she had something wrong with her like a disease or from years of enduring Dumitru's increasingly harsh abuse, she didn't know. It didn't matter, anyway. It just was what it was. Her physical condition receded into the back of her consciousness as she breathed in the scent of incense and holiness. It was how she imagined Heaven to smell. She breathed in deeply several times before making her way into the sanctuary to find Father Stasiuk.

He was busy at the altar, so Catie knelt in silent prayer to wait. She did need to get home for her children, but interrupting someone was never an option. She would wait. Her patience paid off, for when he did join her, Catie felt calmer inside than she had all day. She wouldn't go so far as to say she felt spritely, but she did feel a little lighter and looked forward to creating a schedule for making the tapestries. Once Father Stasiuk had spoken, Catie returned his greeting.

"Hello, Father. I am glad to see you, too. I'm wondering if I can talk to you about coming in to use the loom."

"Of course. Do you have something in mind?"

"Well, yes, I do." She paused and averted her gaze. Who was she to suggest a time?

"What is your idea?" Father sounded impatient. She needed to get on with it.

"I was wondering if I could come in on Saturdays? I would come here to work during the week, but my schedule at Hey—"

"Catie. You don't have to explain. The church is open seven days a week, and it will be fine for you to come in on Saturdays. Now I must excuse myself." He stood and walked back toward the altar but paused and turned back. "Thank you, Catie." He made the sign of the cross toward her before continuing the short trek to the altar and disappearing through the door behind it.

Catie watched him go. He had been so curt. She wasn't sure if she had done something wrong. Probably. The men in her life had always been gruff. Part of it was just men being men. Men here in America acted differently than men in Romania. It still struck her as odd that the men here weren't very, well, masculine. Father Stasiuk wasn't American. He was Ukrainian and very likely more like Romanian men than weaker, softer American men. Yet no matter their heritage and inherently brusque disposition, Catie somehow seemed to make men not just surly but angry and mean. She desperately hoped that Father Stasiuk hadn't turned against her. Catie closed her eyes and sighed. Inside her head, for God and St. Basil and Bunicuță, she prayed a prayer of gratitude for the tapestry job. Then she stood, genuflected as she left, and headed home.

# Chapter 18

· · · · · · · · · · · · · · · · · · · · · ·

Catie caressed the loom nestled into a corner of the large storage shed behind the Church of St. Theocharis that Saturday morning. It was much smaller than the loom that had been in her family for generations until the *Securitate*'s fire destroyed it. However, it was most definitely a traditional loom that she knew how to use. She moved around the loom, assessing its condition. The faded, dry wood felt brittle under her calloused fingers. As she ran her hand up and down one of the upright posts, she pricked her finger on a splinter of wood. She jerked her hand back and studied her finger. A little piece of the loom pierced her skin. She bit it with her front teeth and extracted it then sucked on her finger to stop the bleeding. She pulled her finger out of her mouth, studied it, and satisfied that the bleeding had stopped and she wouldn't smear blood on the loom, she continued her inspection. "Poor loom," she crooned. "You have been neglected and now you are brittle. I'm sorry if I was too rough with you and caused you to lose a piece of yourself in my finger. I promise I'll be gentler with you. I'm going to take care of you and bring you back to life. How would you like to be able to make beautiful cloths and *kilims* and tapestries again? That would be nice, wouldn't it?"

Catie crawled under the machine on hands and knees, and she stood on the bench—after removing her shoes, of course, so her shoes didn't damage the bench. After her thorough inspection, she sat down and informed the loom matter-of-factly, "You need some tender loving care, and I am going to give it to you. I'll help you feel well so you want to create beauty for the world once again. To do that, I must go find some supplies to clean you up."

Catie maneuvered around freestanding cabinets and sets of drawers. It felt strange, wrong somehow, to be here alone. She felt like an intruder, a violator of this sacred space. Granted, this was simply the church's storage shed and therefore not exactly sacred, at least not in the same way as the church itself. Suddenly, another thought hit her. What if she wasn't alone? What if someone had seen her come into the shed and was lurking outside, waiting for the opportunity to creep in and attack her? She squeezed her eyes shut and huffed out a breath. Muttering through clenched teeth, she proclaimed, "No. I'm not going to do this. I'm not going to be scared. I'm not going to worry because I'm not going to get punished. It's okay for me to be here. Father Stasiuk asked me to do this and gave me permission to use the loom and find anything I needed anywhere in this shed." In fact, Father Stasiuk had walked her out the back of the church and over to the shed earlier that morning. He seemed to be back to himself, kind and patient—a contrast to his snippiness the other day.

Not wishing to upset him again, Catie forced herself to get on with her tasks. She pawed around in search of items that she needed to clean and repair the neglected loom. As she foraged, God seemed to be sending her reminders of how she had ruined her budding friendship with Marcy. She opened a drawer to find a fuzzy dust cloth that reminded her of Marcy's chinchillas. She promptly slammed the drawer shut. She needed a dust cloth, but not one that would look like Banana hopping about as she moved the cloth around the loom. Besides, the chinchilla cloth was too downy, anyway. She didn't want to use something that would put fuzz in places that shouldn't be fuzzy, so she moved on.

She located a plastic sack filled to the top with white cloths. She removed the top one and shook it out to inspect it. It was perfect. Clean and plain, thin enough to be practical yet not threadbare. She began to fold the cloth to return it to the bag when she found herself reminiscing about babies. She wondered how many diapers she had changed in her lifetime. Between her cousins and babies and children at the orphanage and her own precious babies and now at Hey Little Diddles, Catie wondered if the number could be in the millions. It seemed like it, anyway. The diapers at Hey Little Diddles were weird, though. She had to use these puffy, plastic-y, things that seemed to chafe the babies' tender skin. The first time she changed one of these diapers, she had had to ask Marcy where the pins were and how to best pin one so the material didn't tear. Marcy had been incredulous that Catie had never seen a disposable diaper before, but she was also nice about it. Marcy hadn't belittled her by calling her a stupid moron for not knowing about modern American diapers, nor had she laughed at her. She didn't make a big deal out of it at all. She simply explained and demonstrated.

Catie sniffed. She had to use the cloth to wipe her nose and dab at her eyes. Marcy had always been so kind to her, and recently she even had tried to become a true friend. What had Catie done? As always, she ruined her chances of friendship and made Marcy hate her. Work had been almost unbearable the remainder of the week; Catie had survived so much pain and hardship in her life that she knew that while the pain never truly left, nothing was literally unbearable, either. So yes, she had been able to get through the work week alongside Marcy, but it was awful. Marcy's silence roared in Catie's head and heart and reverberated through her bones. In her mind, she shouted Marcy's unspoken judgements over and over again. *"You're a worthless piece of garbage! You ruined your daughter! You are unlovable! You're a terrible friend and awful to be near! I hate you!"* Catie dropped the sack of cloths and threw her hands over her ears. When she squeezed her eyes shut, she pictured her garden blooming with bloodroot flowers. She imagined herself scooping them all up in one big huge bouquet and then shouting at them, *"I love me not!"* In her mind she saw all of the dozens and dozens of petals take off into flight like birds flying away from her. Catie opened her eyes and shuddered. Suddenly the shed felt cold and empty. She was alone.

She hated that she had destroyed her new friendship with Marcy because she really liked her. Marcy was the type of person who didn't punish everyone else just because Catie was horrible. While Catie was here at St. Theocharis today, Alexandru was at Marcy's house. Marcy had offered to be his reading tutor, and in exchange, Alexandru would help Marcy with chinchilla tasks like cleaning their cages every week. Marcy was definitely the kind of person Catie would have wanted to have as a friend.

She had to use the cloth to wipe her face again. "I'm sorry, cloth. I'm pretty sure you didn't want to be used in such a disgusting way." She didn't want to put this cloth in the bag with the clean ones, so she tied it on her head like the kerchiefs she wore a lifetime ago in a distant part of the world.

She patted it and adjusted the knot and then allowed herself a little smile. It felt good, like she was back in the countryside working with Bunicuță. She glanced down at the sack of cloths. They were just what she needed for dusting and oiling, so she snatched up the whole bag. The other day, Marcy had accused her of throwing herself a pity party. Bunicuță didn't tolerate brooding and would warn Catie that she should take great care to participate in life no matter how hard it became so she didn't become like her mother. No, Catie did not want to be like the woman she had to call her mother. Touching her kerchief and invoking the spirit of Bunicuță, she continued her search for supplies.

Half an hour later, Catie was back at the loom. In front of her lay her findings: a bag of cloths for dusting and oiling, sewing machine oil, lemon oil—which wasn't as good for treating wood as boiled linseed oil but that she was pleased to find nonetheless—screwdrivers, and wrenches. After some basic care and maintenance, this sturdy loom would be ready to create beautiful pieces once again. She unscrewed the cap of the bottle of lemon oil and inhaled deeply several times. She loved that smell. It was the smell of freshness. Although there had been no lemon trees that she knew of when she was a child in the Romanian countryside, lemon oil always reminded her of her first home, clean and fresh and surrounded by trees and flowers and ducks and animals and people giving each other *mărțișors* in the spring. She breathed in the scent once more then replaced the cap. The lemon oil would have to wait a while. First she needed to dust and tighten all of the screws and bolts. Catie pushed up her sleeves and began to work. She fell into a pleasant rhythm, but, unbidden, her thoughts turned to her past.

# Bucharest, Romania
## *2017*

# Chapter 19

Cătălina shifted on the faded and frayed rug. It was too threadbare and ratty to provide a cushion between her body and the concrete floor. She winced at the electrified pain that shot from her left foot all the way up her leg to strike her hip with a fiery jolt. She gave up searching for a comfortable position. It was a fruitless effort anyway, as no matter how she arranged herself, she was stiff and sore everywhere. Holding very still, she continued to read to the group of children circled around her.

Nine boys and girls, aged six to ten, listened to Cătălina read from a large book of *Basme Românești*, her favorite collection of Romanian fairy tales. She used to read them with Florina and Alexandru when they were this age. This was the book she had had since the earthquake had destroyed so much when she was seven.

*She and Filip were out scouting for food and shelter when they found this book among the debris in a large pile of rubble. She scraped her fingers trying to extract it, but it was worth it. What a treasure! She was so upset at Filip when he yanked it out of her hands, but quickly her feelings turned to terror and then gratitude. While she was admiring the book, two dogs charged at them. Filip ripped the book out of Cătălina's hands and used it as both a weapon and a shield as he fought off the dogs. As her attention switched from stories to survival, she sprang into action, grabbed a jagged and splintered remnant of someone's furniture from the heap of rubble, and joined Filip in fending off the wild dogs. She swung and struck one of them hard on its side which made it yelp and whine off into the distance. Filip sent the other one limping behind the first, and he and Cătălina stood panting and staring at each other on top of the debris.*

*"I hate all these wild dogs! Is the book okay?"*

*Filip inspected it. "Pretty much. There are bite marks and scratches on the back, but the pages are fine. See?" He shrugged and handed it to Cătălina. She turned it over and over and rubbed her hand on the back cover. She studied it thoughtfully.*

*"These marks will remind us that we are able to fight off even the wildest dogs and also that something doesn't have to be perfect to be wonderful. I think that Bunicuță would have told us something like that." She looked at Filip, and her eyes filled with tears. "I can't believe she's gone." She looked down and watched tears splash between her feet.*

*Filip put his arm around her. "I know." He sighed. "Why don't we go find somewhere to read this?"*

They had gone off to read some of the book, temporarily abandoning their adult assignments. Now here she was, a lifetime later, reading it to orphans who were in the same general age range as she and Filip had been when they found this book. The book had been a temporary distraction from misery back then, including offering her that day a temporary reprieve from Filip's horrible advances, and she read it to children at the orphanage to offer them a break from their reality as well. Most seemed to enjoy their reading sessions with Cătălina. Now, though, today's session was almost at an end because it was chore time for the children. As she wrapped up, she saw a man dressed in black slip into the circle. She smiled slightly but didn't stop reading until she finished the segment of *Pasărea Măiastră*.

Once the children had scattered to begin their labors, Cătălina smiled at the man who sat cross-legged on the tattered rug. "Vasile!" She cringed inwardly. It felt disrespectful to call a priest by his first name. It had taken a great deal of convincing on his part, but eventually Father Cojocaru got her to call him Vasile. She hated it, though, and only did it to please him. Not wanting to linger in the uncomfortable feeling inside caused by her being so causal with a priest, she rushed on. "It's Tuesday, and you usually come on Thursdays. I'm happy to see you of course, but why are you here?"

"I received a message today from someone in America. There is another couple interested in adopting a child or maybe two, and I'm visiting the orphanages to assess the children and collect files so I can send profiles and reports." He uncrossed his legs and nimbly hopped to his feet.

Cătălina maneuvered onto her hands and knees, rose to a kneeling position, worked one leg out in front of her, placed one hand on the floor—fingertips only because she couldn't put too much pressure on her wrist—and one hand on her bent knee, and, very slowly, began to stand. She felt a hand grasp her arm, and she recoiled. "Cătălina, let me help you up." The voice belonged not to Dumitru but to Vasile. She felt her face and neck grow hot with embarrassment. She relaxed and let him help her up.

Father Vasile was by far her favorite priest among all who visited the orphanage, which was why she was ashamed to her core for who she was and for letting him see her struggle to rise. She desperately wanted to avoid talking about her pain and the reason behind its intensity today, so she thanked him quickly then rushed on. "You are kind to be so thorough when you investigate adoptions. Not everyone is." She sighed and glanced around. "There are so many adoptions from America and other places, but still not enough. Even though conditions are much better now than they were when I came here almost four decades ago, this is still an institution." She shook her head. "These places aren't homes with families. They're not filled with hate because there are good people here doing the best they can, but they're certainly not filled with the love that children desire and deserve."

Vasile stared at Cătălina. She shifted uncomfortably. He narrowed his eyes. Her heart pounded. Was he going to ask about her movement struggle? "All homes aren't loving, are they Cătălina?"

"What do you mean?"

Vasile took a deep breath. He stuck his hands in his pockets. Cătălina averted her gaze because she couldn't bear his scrutiny. "Cătălina, will you come sit by me on a bench outside?"

Instantly, sweat seeped from Cătălina's pores. The wetness of it combined with her thundering heart and dizzying thoughts and emotions created a tempest within. She wished it would form a tsunami that would overtake her, drowning her, relieving her of her misery. Unfortunately, she heard the call of a lifeguard.

"Cătălina? Cătălina! Can you hear me? Are you all right? Shall I call for a doctor?"

The threat of a doctor grounded her. "No!" She shook her head. "I mean yes, I am fine. No, I don't need a doctor. Please. I don't want a doctor." She rubbed her palms together to dry them. No, she would not, could not, see a doctor. Twice she had incurred Dumitru's wrath by seeing doctors early in their marriage.

The first time was for a grotesquely swollen ankle that turned out to be badly sprained, the result of Dumitru's shoving her into a large pothole in the street after a man looked at her. The second was for the headache, nausea, vomiting, and long-lasting nosebleed that happened when she stupidly forgot to put Dumitru's morning juice in the freezer early enough for it to form the ice crystals he loved. He was angry that she let him down and started his day off poorly. To remind her of the importance of the freezer for the juice, he had grabbed her by her hair, dragged her to the appliance, shoved her head just far enough inside that it was in the door's path, and proceeded to slam the door on her head again and again and again. When it was all over and he realized what he had done, he had cried. He sobbed into her disheveled hair and told her how much it meant to him that she took such good care of him and made him feel loved when she did things like freeze his juice the way he liked it. When she hadn't made the ice crystals, he told her, he thought that she no longer loved him or cared about him, and he went crazy. She had forgiven him. What else could she have done? After all, she had a brand-new baby girl who needed a loving, peaceful home; as her mother, the responsibility to provide that was Cătălina's.

She shook her head to clear the horrible memory. She just couldn't go see a doctor. She looked at her friend imploringly. "Please, Vasile, no doctor. I am doing well now."

Vasile held up his hands, palms out. Cătălina flinched, but otherwise didn't move. Vasile harrumphed. "Okay. No doctor. But will you at least come sit with me on that bench?" Cătălina nodded and followed the priest outside. Noises from the street made a valiant effort to drown out the anxious noises in her head. Horns blared. Drivers punctuated their yells with gestures. Vasile placed his hand on Cătălina's shoulder to steer her toward the side of the building as a car screeched up and parked on the sidewalk. His hand lingered several seconds longer than necessary, and when he slid it off and away, it felt to her that a cloud settled in its place because the electric warmth was suddenly gone.

They reached the back of the building and climbed a few stairs to a small, grassy park. The park was populated with several benches which were in turn populated by people smoking cigarettes. They found an empty bench and settled in. Cătălina closed her eyes and turned her face to the warm sunshine. To her, the sun was God himself blessing the earth and all living things in it. "It seems that you enjoy the sun as much as I do." Cătălina opened her eyes and looked at Vasile. He was smiling at her.

She smiled back. "Yes. My *Bunicuță* used to say that it was the light of Heaven, and maybe even God himself, helping us grow and love each other warmly."

"Your grandma sounds wise indeed. I think of the sun the same way. Let's pray together in this sunshine." At that, Cătălina almost whooped with glee. In her life with Dumitru, her prayers were always said in silent isolation. He didn't like religion and forbade her to attend church. But just as the communist regimes of the past could take away the Greek Catholic churches but not the faith of the people, Dumitru could prevent her from attending church, but he couldn't take away her faith or her prayers. She had ways. She was surprised when Vasile asked about one of her methods. "Do you have a prayer rope, Cătălina?"

She smiled. "I do. I have two, actually." She bent over and removed the lace from one of her shoes. She sat up straight, wrapped it around her wrist and hand, and held it out for Vasile to inspect. She was usually proud of her method of sneaking around her prayer ropes; disguising them as shoe laces had tricked Dumitru for years. However, showing Vasile now made her anxious and ashamed. Would he condemn her for using such a sacred object as a shoelace? She withdrew her hand, rested it on her lap, and fiddled with it while she stared down at her lap. "Um, please forgive me, Father. I respect prayer ropes as sacred. I only store them in my shoes so I can have them with me to use. Dumitru forbids anything religious, and if he found a prayer rope in the house his punishment would be brutal. I could take it, but I couldn't stand to lose my prayer ropes. He pays no attention to my shoes, and if he did I doubt he'd realize that ordinary shoelaces aren't knotted like these." In spite of herself, her mouth turned up slightly in a small, sly smile.

"Creating a prayer rope and disguising it as a shoelace is creative and brave, Cătălina. You don't need forgiveness, but you do have my admiration." If he noticed her gasp slightly in surprise, Vasile didn't mention it. Instead, he removed his own prayer rope from around his neck and said, "Let's say the Invocation of the Holy Name together, shall we?" In unison, Vasile and Cătălina quietly chanted, "Lord Jesus Christ, Son of God, have mercy on me, a sinner" repeatedly as they moved from knot to knot on their respective prayer ropes. Catie was soothed by the rhythm and the sound of the chant and found herself feeling not just calm but content, both emotions that were only occasional visitors to her life. Her insides jolted with joy when Vasile rested his ring and pinky fingers on his palm, touched his thumb, first, and second fingers together and then placed them gently on her forehead. She felt alive as he touched first her forehead, then her chest, then her right shoulder, and finally her left and said in turn, "In the name of the Father, the Son, and the Holy Spirit." She allowed herself to look at him, not just at him but into him. When he looked her in the eyes, she didn't look away. The jolt she felt was a new kind of jolt. At once, she saw him as both a priest and a man, and she knew that thinking of a priest's masculinity was very wrong, a carnal sin. She looked away.

Vasile began to speak, cleared his throat, shifted on the bench, and began again. "I'm not quite sure how to discuss this with you, Cătălina, so I'm just going to say it. I'm very concerned about you. I think that Dumitru abuses you, and—"

"No! He is not. Dumitru is loving and caring. Why would you think that?" Cătălina heard her voice rise in pitch, something it did when she was stressed or anxious. She prayed that Vasile wouldn't know this about her voice. Her muscles twitched with the desire to run way, but she couldn't leave. It was not her place to walk away from a man, and not just a man but a priest. She clenched her teeth and forced herself to remain here with Vasile.

"I see new bruises on you every week when I come, and you are very hard on yourself when we talk. I'm afraid that Dumitru is abusing you not just physically but emotionally and verbally, as well. Today you can only move with great difficulty. And did you not just say that you would incur his wrath if he found your prayer beads?" He softened his tone. "Is Dumitru hurting you, Cătălina?"

"No!" She looked at Vasile's face but couldn't quite look him in the eye. How could she be blatantly lying to a priest? "I mean, what he does isn't really abuse. Yes, he says things and does things that hurt, but it's only because I've done something wrong to deserve it."

Vasile shifted toward Cătălina. "*Deserve* it? Cătălina, what would possibly make you deserve to be abused in any way?"

"Vasile, I have been nothing but a bother my whole life. Dumitru is just continuing lessons that I didn't learn properly when I was a child."

"We're all sinners, Cătălina. No one is perfect. I am far from perfect. Do I need abuse to learn lessons?"

"Of course not, Vasile!"

"Neither do you."

She shook her head. "It's not abuse. It's discipline. And I do deserve it. But whether or not I deserve it is beside the point. I take his cruelty so the children don't have to. Also, God wants us to forgive. I have forgiveness in my heart, Vasile. But to truly forgive, I must show it by accepting Dumitru and his actions. I must separate the sin from the sinner, another lesson my wise *Bunicuţă* taught me. "

"Cătălina, that's not what forgiveness—"

Again Cătălina shook her head. "Besides, I don't believe that Dumitru chooses to behave the way he does. He's a good person who has experienced great trauma. He lashes out sometimes without even meaning to."

This time Vasile shook his head. "I know from the conversations we've had over the years that you have experienced a great deal of trauma of your own."

"It's not the same."

"Really?" When Cătălina only shrugged, Vasile continued, "You mentioned just a little while ago that I am kind in the adoption process, thoroughly investigating families and children for the best placements. I was glad that you said that. It means a lot to me. Do you know why?"

Cătălina looked at Vasile. "I don't." It was a mere whisper.

"Because like so many of us Romanians during and after Ceauşescu's rule, I experienced a lot of losses. I was orphaned in the big earthquake of 1977." He looked down and toyed with the prayer rope he still held. "More than orphaned, I guess. I lost every single person in my family. We had a decent sized house, one that held the whole extended family. We were kind of squished, but not miserable. Anyway, the house just collapsed, crumbled to the ground." He moved his hands together as if he were crushing some object between them. "And the roof landed on top of it all." He clapped one hand onto the other. Cătălina jumped slightly with the noise. "I wasn't home when it happened. I had been out trying to get our rations. On my way home, I stopped at this marsh and was goofing around with frogs even though it was dark outside. Then the ground shook and shifted and rumbled and roared. I lost my footing and landed in the marsh." He shivered. "It was cold and stagnant. And suddenly empty and very eerie. All of the birds took flight and the frogs went wherever they go to hide. Even the bugs were gone. It was just me, cold and wet. Once the ground stopped quaking, I hightailed it home. I couldn't believe the destruction around me. I ran toward my house only to find it flattened. My entire family was inside. They all died. I know they died because I spent the whole night and the next morning removing bits of roof and digging through the rubble. I located all of their bodies. They were pretty much in groups in three different areas of the house. Given that I was only eight years old at the time, I was exhausted and sad and scared. My hands were bloody and full of splinters so I tried to wriggle myself into my crushed house for comfort but got stuck. I gave up and fell asleep. I woke up when a neighbor pulled me out. He said I could live with him and his family. But it didn't work out. There wasn't enough food for his own children, so he certainly couldn't take on another person. He dropped me off at an orphanage. I existed there, barely, for eight years. I escaped when I was sixteen."

He turned so that he could look at Cătălina without turning his head. "I know that you've been working at orphanages since you were a child, so you know what they were like back then. Maybe you even visited my orphanage and saw me. I hated the metal crib I was in, hated that they suck me in diapers when I was eight years old so they didn't have to let me out to go to the bathroom, hated that I was trapped in that cage with four other boys my age or even older, two of them in straitjackets who just moaned and banged their heads on the bars. I hated that no one did anything to help. I hated that most people were mean and cold and uncaring. Most of all, I hated that my family was gone. I..." Vasile trailed off. He continued to fiddle with the prayer rope. Finally, after long moments of silence, he blinked rapidly and swallowed hard. He stared at Cătălina. Tentatively, she touched his shoulder. She resisted the sinful urge to embrace him. He smiled weakly and sighed. "Anyway, the reason I told you all this is to help you see that trauma and loss don't turn someone abusive. It didn't turn you sour and cruel, nor did it make me that way. I want to bring God's love and peace to others, and I want to connect children and adults in the best way possible to make loving families. You and I, we use what we have gone through for good. Does Dumitru do good, Cătălina?"

His tone was so sincere, without a hint of judgement, that she didn't know how to respond. Her instinct was to make excuses for her husband, to defend his actions. She had always believed that he was the way he was because of his background. Bunicuţă had taught her that people had reasons for behaving the way they did. She had taught her that forgiveness was important and to see past the behavior to the person himself. So that's how she approached Dumitru. She understood him, forgave him for the things he said and did, and knew in her heart that he was better than his actions. He loved her. He needed her. She needed to be there for him. Didn't she? She rubbed her temples before answering Vasile's question. "Dumitru...Dumitru loves his children. He loves me, too. And I do have a purpose with him. I think maybe God united us so I could receive his physical and emotional blows. If I'm taking them, no one else has to. Especially not his children. By opening myself up to the bad, I'm freeing up the good to come out." It wasn't all that different than her relationship with Filip, she realized. "Things like this happened in my own family, Vasile. It's just the way things are."

"Cătălina. That's wrong."

She was confused. On top of that, she was disappointed in herself. Vasile believed she was doing wrong when the only thing she had ever tried to do from the time she was small was to do right. Bile rose into the back of her throat. She swallowed. "I'm sorry. I'm so sorry. I'm not trying to be wrong. Do you believe me?" She bit her lip to keep it from trembling, but all that did was push the tremors down into her chin. Vasile hadn't answered her. He didn't believe her, and he knew that she was just plain wrong. She turned away from him because she didn't want him to see the tears cascading down her cheeks.

"Cătălina." Vasile moved off the bench to squat in front of her. He gently tugged at her arms to remove her hands from her face. He lowered her arms so he could hold her hands, and he squeezed them gently. "Cătălina, look at me." He waited. When she complied, he said simply, "You are not wrong. That is not what I meant. I meant that your idea that Dumitru is just this way because of a difficult past and that you exist to take his abuse is wrong. His abuse is wrong. That's what I meant. Okay?"

Cătălina nodded. "Okay."

"Do you think I'm wrong?"

"About what?"

"About my strong opinion that you don't deserve to be abused."

She shrugged, then winced at the pain. She heaved a ragged sigh. "Honestly, I don't know. I've never thought if it this way before, and it's confusing. Plus whether or not I deserve it isn't the issue. The issue is keeping him from harassing my children."

"Okay. Fair enough. How about this: will you just keep thinking about what I've said? And he clearly hurt you badly recently. If the abuse, not just the physical but the verbal stuff too, worsens, will you please come to me? I'm safe, and I'll help you." Cătălina tried to speak, but only managed a nod. "May I pray over you, Cătălina?" She nodded again, more vigorously this time. Vasile sat beside her and placed a hand on her head. Quietly, just for her, he uttered a prayer. "Lord God, watch over this dear woman, Cătălina Grigorescu, who is a loving, kind, and nurturing human being who is a blessing to those who know her." Amen.

Vasile helped Cătălina to her feet, and together they walked back inside. For the rest of the day and into the night, Cătălina thought of all of the things that Vasile had said. She had to force herself to act normally with Dumitru, and she was terrified that he'd see through her façade. Now, as Dumitru snored beside her in bed, she continued to wonder. Were Dumitru's cruel actions and cutting words simply a product of his past? Did he really love her, or did he just tell her that every now and then as part of his controlling behavior? She had always believed that he loved her but just couldn't control his emotions. He hadn't been this way when they met.

# Bucharest, Romania
## *1989*

# Chapter 20

Cătălina bounced off a big, burly man, ran into a young woman about her own age or perhaps a bit younger, and stumbled forward. She caught herself and mumbled an apology over her shoulder to the two people she had just crashed into. She steadied herself and stretched as tall as she could in an attempt to locate *Tată*, or anyone else in her family. They were all here, but she became separated from them in this undulating mass of humanity. There! Up ahead and to her right stood her uncle Neculai. She was unable to tell if he was with anyone else, for the crowd blended together, vague shapes and colors indistinguishable from each other because there were so many people smashed so closely together. She pressed herself through the crowd and more than once found herself sandwiched uncomfortably between people. A collective shout of anger and renewed chants of "Down with Ceauşescu!" roared around her, the force of it nearly crushing her. She resisted the urge to throw her hands over her ears. "Hey! You! Woman!" Was someone talking to her? She looked around. Beside her, a man shook his fist in the air in unison with the crowd but stared at Cătălina as he did. "What's your problem? Are you here for the revolution, or are you here to walk around and get in the way?" His eyes grew wide, then narrowed. He stopped shaking his fist. "Or are you connected to the *Securitate*, sent by your husband to spy on us? Maybe I should take care of you for the sake of the Romanian people." He unsheathed a knife that Cătălina hadn't noticed hanging at his side. She threw her hands up, palms out.

"No! Please, sir," she shouted at him. "I'm only looking for my family. We came because we are tired of Ceaușescu and his *Securitate*. We are tired of the lack of food and fuel and power. We are sick of the destruction around us while he pours money and resources into the Civic Center." Cătălina had to stop and catch her breath, clear her throat. Shouting that much just to be heard by someone right across from her made her throat hurt. She looked at the man. Did he believe her? She held her breath. Finally, he holstered his knife, turned away, and resumed his chant. She exhaled. She tried to reach Neculai, but found it impossible to move. The crowd pressed in on her from every direction. She was stuck. Angry shouts rose into the air. People called for more food, better living conditions, and, mostly, an end to Ceaușescu and the *Securitate*. Despite the density of the crowd, the cold December wind wove its way between people. She pulled her threadbare coat tight around herself and joined in the chanting. After all, she had come with her family to protest and to do her part in affecting change. "Down with Ceaușescu!" she shouted over and over to the rhythm of the crowd.

She watched people in the crowd. Was she the only one who was uneasy about this? Of course she wanted a new leader, change for the better. She both feared and loathed the *Securitate* and wanted them out of Romanian life. Yet she had seen the unstoppable ruthlessness of Ceaușescu's regime over and over again, from the time she, her family, and the entire

village were evacuated from the countryside. She had witnessed too many brutal murders and violent deaths to think
that the president and his military police wouldn't crush this
protest. She pulled her coat even tighter and looked around.
Oh, how she wanted to be with her family. "Down with
Ceaușescu!"

Dakka dakka dakka dakka ratatatat ratatatat dakka dakka!
Shots were being fired! Dakka dakka dakka! Screaming. From
every direction, screaming. From every direction chaos.
From every direction, "Down with Ceaușescu!" Between the
screams and as they scrambled, people still yelled for the
fall of the president. Ratatatat ratatatat dakka dakka dakka!
Now Cătălina did throw her hands over her ears. The crowd
surged forward, one angry mob on the move. Members of
the crowd around her dropped as they were hit by police fire.
Living people stepped on the fallen as they marched forward,
shouting, dissenting, voicing decades of complaints. Hands
still covering her ears, Cătălina looked around frantically. In
the spaces between the moving mob, something caught her
attention. About thirty meters away on her left, a man knelt
on the ground calling to people rushing past. Stretched in
front of the man was another man. She sprang into action,
her healing instincts inherited from Bunică Rodica kicking in.
As she pushed and shoved her way over, Cătălina could tell
that the man on the ground was dying; she had seen enough
scenes like this in her nineteen years to recognize it.

When she finally reached the men, she dropped down
and began to assess the bleeding man. The other one spoke,
"Please. Can you help my brother? He's been shot. Help
him!" He cradled his wounded brother's head in his hands.

Cătălina glanced at him. "I'll try." She turned her attention to the wounded man. His shirt was covered with a red

circle of blood, and blood trickled out from under him. The bullet had sliced right through him. She shuddered slightly as she thought of Oana and Eduard and the images of them after each was shot in the head. A groan returned her to the moment; it came not from the man bleeding out but from his brother. Cătălina glanced at him. His lips were pinched tightly together, and deep worry lines cut through his forehead. She returned her attention to the wounded man. She attempted to peel back his shirt, but some of it stuck to the wound. The area that she could see was darkened and swollen. She put her ear to the man's chest and heard a sucking sound when he inhaled. She knew that there was nothing she could do. She had some knowledge from her childhood with her grandmother and from her first aid at the orphanage, but her skills were limited. She closed her eyes and sighed. It was unlikely that even Bunică Rodica would have been able to help this man.

"Please. Stay with me, Andrei." The man sounded scared and desperate. She had to at least try, even if the effort would be futile. Quickly but carefully, she worked the man's shirt away from the wound. Next, she used the wounded man's hand to cover his wound. She applied pressure to his hand with both of hers. She felt his chest rise once, twice, then stop. She kept her hands in place. After a pause, he inhaled once more. He exhaled. After another pause, Cătălina knew that that breath had been his last. Slowly, she let her hands slide off of the body.

She looked at the other man. He began to shake his head rapidly. "I'm sorry," Cătălina whispered. Her heart went out to him. She had lost so many loved ones, had lost homes and ways of life, so she could imagine the crushing hurt he was feeling. She made a silent promise to this stranger that she would help him. She couldn't explain it in words, but she had an overpowering urge to take away his pain, to be something good in a life that could be so horrible. She studied him. He was still shaking his head as he stared at his brother, the man he had called Andrei. He was breathing rapidly, his chest beginning to heave. Cătălina maneuvered so she sat beside him. It wasn't difficult to do, for, aside from others like them who had stayed with the wounded and dying, the crowd had surged on. She wondered briefly where her family was and if they were okay, but her primary concern was for this grieving man. She put her hand on his arm.

"No." He looked at Cătălina. "My last brother. He can't be gone. He...he just can't. I..." He pitched forward and sobbed, his forehead on Andrei's. Cătălina knew that it was only under extreme circumstances that a man would cry in public. Men were stoic, strong, and dominant. For a man to show weakness like this, especially in front of a woman, meant that the depth of his pain was unfathomable. Her heart swelled. She wanted to make things better for him. She didn't want to make him feel weak by talking to him while he was in this state, so she knelt quietly beside him and rubbed his back.

When he sat up, Cătălina dropped her hand. She said nothing but instead waited to see what he would do. She felt agitated inside, torn between wanting to stay here and help and needing to go find her own family. Was someone she loved lying in the street, shot to death by the *Securitate*? It was possible. She risked a glance at the man beside her. Tightly clenched teeth made his jaw muscles bunch and twitch. He looked at her. "I really am very sorry," she told him.

He nodded. "So am I." After a long minute of silence, he added, "Thank you."

Cătălina wasn't entirely sure what he was thanking her for, but she didn't know him enough—or at all—to ask, so she just nodded. He turned away and stared into space. After a few more minutes, she asked, "What's your name?"

He looked at his brother as though wanting him to answer the question. His brother didn't answer, of course. Eventually, he said, "Dumitru. Dumitru Grigorescu." He nodded at the still body on the ground in front of him. "This is...was... Andrei Grigorescu."

Dumitru fell silent once again. Distant shouts and shots punctuated the air. Icy wind pelted them with bits of debris. Cătălina shrank inside her coat as much as she could and waited. Dumitru hadn't asked her for her name, so she couldn't just tell him. That would be disrespectful and out of line. He didn't seem interested in her presence, so she wanted to leave to continue her search for her family. But did she have the right to just dismiss herself? Women deferred to men. But again, she didn't know this man. Ugh. Being nineteen was proving to be a hassle. She was now expected to act like a woman, which wasn't that much different from being a girl. The difference was that people were even less patient and tolerant of her mistakes now than they had been when she was a child. She closed her eyes, conjured images of her favorite women, now long gone, Bunicuță and Oana. She thought of what they might do. Both would probably be understanding of this man's plight and thus still and patient; she had witnessed Oana being still and patient and loving with Eduard no matter what his moods were. That's how she would be as a woman—still and patient and loving and caring and understanding. That should be easy, for she had a wellspring of love and care bubbling deep within her. Eyes still closed, she folded her hands in her lap and said a silent prayer to her intercessor

St. Basil that she would be strong enough to be the type of woman that people needed and capable enough to meet any need. As she concluded her prayer, she felt electrified inside, as if her soul were glowing brightly. This vision of herself felt right and good. Really, she mused, it's the same mission and purpose she had felt for as long as she could remember. It was why she had always worked so hard to help her family and why she tolerated Filip. She couldn't take credit for her deep empathy and desire to help others, though. It came from God and Bunicuţă. Now that she was old enough to recognize it, she was ready to fully manifest it in her role as an adult woman. As a child, she had been awkward in her role because she was still developing the skills she needed to love and care for other people. As a result, she often incurred the wrath of both men and women, her sisters, her cousins. Now, though, she was grown. Joy surged through her, and a sense of peace, too. She was no longer conflicted over whether to remain here or go. She was needed here, and this is where she would be until she wasn't. Then she would locate her family and do what needed to be done for them. In this moment, she waited quietly beside the man named Dumitru.

After some time had passed—Cătălina didn't know how much, and it didn't matter—Dumitru looked at her. "Will you help me take his body somewhere?"

Cătălina nodded. "Of course. Where would you like to take him?"

He shrugged. His entire forehead wrinkled as he contemplated the situation. Finally, he suggested, "Ah, I know this isn't legal, but maybe we could get him out of the city somehow and bury him in the country. I don't want him to have to rest forever in this hellhole." He looked at his brother's body, smoothed his hair, and then studied Cătălina. "I know it's risky. We could be thrown in prison or shot on the spot if we're caught. I don't give a damn if they kill me. They'd be doing me a favor. But I don't want to drag you into danger."

"It's okay. I don't mind."

"Are you afraid?"

"Yes. But it's a feeling I'm accustomed to. I've lived in fear my whole life, and I go on anyway. This is no different."

Dumitru studied her, seemed to appraise her. Finally, he nodded once. "Okay." He stood. When Cătălina was also on her feet, he said, I'll carry him by his arms and shoulders. You take his ankles." When they were each in position, he instructed, "One, two, three, lift." They heaved the body up off the ground. Dumitru grunted with the weight of his dead brother. Cătălina stumbled slightly as she found the best way to hold a heavy body.

"Which way do you want to go?" she asked.

"Um, probably that way." He nodded his head in a vague direction. They staggered north, but after less than ten minutes, both were sweating and panting. Cătălina's arms already ached. They hadn't even gone two blocks. Her arms began to shake, and she lost her grip. Andrei's feet hit the ground with a thud.

Dumitru set down his end of the body and stomped toward Cătălina. "Klutz! You dropped my brother!" He gestured angrily at Andrei. "Are you completely inept? He doesn't deserve to be thrown on the ground." He glared at Cătălina, his face almost touching hers.

She took a step back. "I'm sorry, Dumitru." Her heart pounded about a dozen times in her chest before he broke his gaze.

He scrubbed at his face with his hand and pulled down slowly on his beard. "No. I'm the one who is sorry. That outburst was uncalled for." He ran his hands through his hair. "I lashed out at you, but the real issue is that my brother is gone."

Cătălina was shocked. She had to blink a few times to fix her eyeballs; they were dry because she held them wide open too long. She had never heard a grown man apologize before. She wasn't quite sure how to respond, but because Dumitru wasn't saying anything, she felt that she should say something. "I understand, Dumitru. This is horrible. I wish that the *Securitate* hadn't shot your brother, and I hope this uprising is successful. That way, Ceauşescu's reign will be over and Andrei will have contributed to the fall."

Dumitru's face softened, and he gave her a small smile. "Yeah. Let's hope for that. Now we face the issue of taking care of Andrei. I really, really want him out of Bucharest, but we can't carry him into the countryside. So..." He looked around. "Ah ha! Stay here with Andrei. I'll be right back." Cătălina watched him stride away. Despite the fact that he was fairly thin, probably courtesy of the food shortages, his shoulders were broad. His dark hair was disheveled. His clothes were dirty and wrinkled. She wondered, what was his story? Not that he looked all that different from everyone else; there was just something haunting about Dumitru that made her want to learn more. He disappeared around a corner. Cătălina sat on the ground, a dry patch with no snow, by Andrei to wait.

Soon, Dumitru returned. He pushed a wheelbarrow. "Look what I found," he said, triumphant. "There's a stockpile of equipment that the workers use for the endless construction of the Civic Center," he turned his head and spat on the ground. "What a fucking waste that is. Assholes. Anyway, I liberated this wheelbarrow from its slavery to the state. It's a fitting ride for Andrei. He would have loved the idea of riding in a liberated wheelbarrow." He finished the cigarette he had been smoking and crushed it into the ground. "Come on. Let's get him in here. He's already getting stiff, so it will be hard to settle him in if we don't hurry."

"Are you sure it's wise to use this? If we get caught, this will make it even worse."

"Are you questioning me?"

"Of course not. It's—"

"Really? Because it sounds like you're questioning me. If you don't want to do this, forget it. I'll do it myself. Get out of here."

"No. I want to help. I'm sorry I said anything. Let's get him in the wheelbarrow."

"Fine." He searched his jacket pocket for a cigarette, lit it, and let it dangle from his mouth. Belatedly, only after they had hefted Andrei up into the wheelbarrow and arranged him so he wasn't likely to fall out, he reached back into his jacket pocket and offered one to Cătălina. She hesitated. She craved one, but should she take one from this man? "Well, do you want one or not?"

"Yes, thank you. I just hate to take one from you. It's not like they're easy to get." Dumitru took one out of the pack, stepped close to Cătălina, and held it out. "Here. I'll light it for you." She watched his hands as he lit her cigarette. They were large, strong, and steady yet gentle and nimble with the cigarette. She wondered what those hands would feel like on her body. Her face suddenly burned, and she looked away as soon as the cigarette was lit. Where had that thought come from? What kind of terrible person was she? Silently, she said an urgent prayer for forgiveness. She was so busy berating herself for being an awful person that she didn't realize Dumitru had spoken until he nudged her.

"Hey. I asked you if you're ready to take Andrei's body out of here. So are you?"

"Oh. Yes, of course. Let's go." As they walked, Dumitru pushing the wheelbarrow and Cătălina steadying it, she grew increasingly anxious. Clusters of people milled about, some civilians and some *Securitate*. They seemed to be leaving each other alone, but Cătălina could sense the tension with all of her being. She saw it in the way people scurried stiffly to steer clear of the soldiers. She heard it in the whistling wind that filled the empty spaces where words should have been. She felt it in her aching muscles, muscles that were attempting to bear the weight of the struggles of her fellow citizens of Bucharest. She could smell it, taste it, in the death and the blood and the filth and the dogs. She gagged involuntarily and almost lost her cigarette. She pinched her lips around it. Ever vigilant, she continued to scan her surroundings. Tanks rumbled past. Gunshots sounded in the distance. A military truck sputtered by, the open back crammed full with soldiers, guns pointing upward as if they planned to shoot God himself. She heard the thumpa thump of the wheelbarrow over the bricks in the road. Everything was painfully loud and eerily silent at once, and that was disconcerting. She had to fight the overpowering urge to run far, far away. Dumitru seemed to need her still, so she kept going. Was she stabilizing the wheelbarrow, she wondered, or was it steadying her? Maybe both. Shouts and the sound of boots clacking on the bricks captured her attention.

"Hey, you two. Stop!" Her heart started to pound so hard and fast that she both heard and felt it inside her head. They had been caught by the *Securitate*! She thought she might vomit. She gagged but swallowed it down. She glanced at Dumitru. He had paled, but otherwise he seemed calm. When they reached them and began to talk to Dumitru, she saw flashes of Eduard and Oana and Dionisie. She couldn't breathe. Images of their bodies on the ground, of Dionisie being ripped away, played in her mind, bright and loud. She gasped for breath. The cigarette fell to the ground. She began to cough and shake. She heard people talking, but their voices were distorted and she couldn't make out the words. Pain ripped through her chest. A heart attack? Was she dying? She felt a hand on her shoulder, and she jumped, startled. *Securitate? Securitate!* This was it. The end.

"Hey. It's okay. Seriously. It's good. You can stop now. Go ahead. Breathe right." Cătălina could understand these words, and she thought she recognize the voice. It sounded like the man, Dumitru, who had just lost his brother and was so distraught. He spoke again. "There. It seems like you're breathing better. Keep it up." Cătălina fingered her necklace, a silver cross. The texture and shape of it were soothing. Slowly, her heart rate and breathing returned to normal. The images were still there, however. She looked at Dumitru to try to superimpose his face on the awful images running through her mind. She wiped her eyes.

"I am very sorry. This happens to me from time to time. I think of horrible things that have happened, and I feel very upset. I just react that way, I guess." She looked down. "I'm sorry," she repeated. Her teeth began to chatter from the cold, but she didn't know if it was the cold winter weather or the frigid temperature of her fear as it slid around inside of her. The reason didn't really matter that much because it just was the way it was. She clenched her jaw shut in hopes that

Dumitru wouldn't notice. She balled her fists tightly to hide her shaking. When he touched her shoulder, she jumped.

"Hey. Don't apologize. The police are gone. Let's go sit somewhere for a while, okay?"

She nodded and looked around at the rubble and garbage and destruction. "Where?"

Dumitru looked slowly around, as if carefully surveying every possibility for the best seating. Finally he nodded toward a building. "There. That recessed doorway will hide us at least for a little while. Come on." When he draped his arm across her shoulders, Cătălina let him lead her toward the doorway. He ducked into the little alcove, kicked rocks out of their way, and helped Cătălina sit down, propping her against the wooden door. The cold from the concrete seeped up into her body, making her shake harder. She felt Dumitru move around beside her. She turned to look at him, and she watched him wriggle out of his heavy canvas jacket and drape it around her shoulders. He adjusted it carefully before letting his arm rest around her shoulder. Her chest contracted again, squeezing her heart and making it pound in a bizarre rhythm. She didn't like this. Not at all. Images of Filip and his advances flashed through her mind. Involuntarily, her body shrunk in on itself. The arm around her shoulders flexed, and she felt herself pulled closer against this man's body. She squeezed her eyes shut. "Hey." His voice was deep and resonated in this small space, but it was gentle. She opened her eyes and looked at him. "Relax," he told her. "It's okay."

For some reason, perhaps because she needed to, Cătălina believed him. She nodded. Neither spoke. For several minutes, they stared at the nothingness in the street. Nothingness. She sat up straight and looked at Dumitru. "Where is Andrei? The wheelbarrow is gone. What happened?

"He's gone." His voice was a low growl. He cleared his throat and spat on the ground beside him. "They took him away from me." Then he shouted, "Those sons of bitches took the only brother I had left!" He slammed his fists into the concrete and began to hit his head against the door behind him. "Who do they think they are?" He screamed, "Who the fuck do you think you are?" He hit his head harder against the door, over and over again.

Cătălina scrambled to her knees and scooped him into her chest. She cupped her hand over the back of his head to cushion the blows. When he continued, she held him tighter. Her heart absorbed some of his grief, and she ached for him. She wanted to cushion him, protect him from the world and from his own strong sorrow and rage. Finally, he stopped. He thunked his head against the door one last time and let it rest there. Cătălina loosened her grip on him and watched him. His eyes were closed, and his breath came in pants. She remained as she was, completely still and kneeling before him, until he opened his eyes. Jolts of fire ran through her when he looked into her eyes. Her cheeks burned, so she looked down to hide them. She had no idea what to say to him. She knew she wanted to help and care for him, but she wasn't quite sure how to go about it. She decided to remain quiet and wait for a signal.

A few more seconds passed before Dumitru moved. He shifted slightly, gently turned Cătălina around, and said, "Come sit beside me again." As she did, he readjusted his jacket around her and pulled her against him once more. When he spied her hand, he gasped. The skin across her knuckles was split open, and blood smeared her fingers and back of her hand. "What is this?"

Cătălina studied her hand. Her knuckles were swollen, and she could already see some bruising under the drying blood. It throbbed. She shrugged. "It's nothing. It looks worse than it is." She was determined not to be a problem the way she always had been with her family.

"It doesn't look like nothing. How did it..." Dumitru trailed off, and his eyes widened. "Oh my God. I did this to you, didn't I? When I was hitting my head." He shook his head. "I'm sorry, Cătălina. I can't believe I hurt you like this. Please...please forgive me."

He sounded distraught. She rushed to comfort him. "No, Dumitru. It was my choice to put my hand there to protect your head. You didn't even realize it was there. I could have moved it, but I didn't want to. I wanted to do what little I could to help you."

Dumitru looked at her for a long time. Cătălina pictured Bunicuţă and Oana and how they used to be with the men in the family, and she became still. She was surprised to discover that she felt comfortable, natural, being silent with Dumitru. She settled in and waited for him to speak. Eventually, he said, "Thank you. I really am sorry that I hurt you, but I appreciate what you did. I guess I was pretty upset."

"The *Securitate* took your brother away. Of course you were upset."

He sighed. "I had three older brothers. Andrei was the last one alive."

"That must be terrible for you. And your parents."

Dumitru shook his head. "Our parents are long dead. My father was killed in a mine accident when I was a kid. My mother fell ill less than a year later. She was sick for a while. Got sicker. Died. It was just me and my brothers after that. We all did the only thing we knew what to do. We worked in the mines. You know the most recent round of strikes a couple years ago? And how they were brutally crushed? Both my brothers were among the hundreds who were massacred. It was a violent mess, and they fell. Andrei and I escaped and came to Bucharest. The conditions here are as abysmal as they are in any mining district. Our survival has been nothing but a struggle. Things need to change, so we participated in this uprising today, just like you did. You know how that ended." He stopped and leaned his head against the door, but this time he didn't bang it. He just rested it there and closed his eyes.

Cătălina was a bit stunned at how quickly and dispassionately he told that story. The monotone delivery was a sharp contrast to the emotional outburst that had preceded the story. Yet his pain and his turmoil must be completely overwhelming, so much so that putting it in words might be nearly impossible. Instead of asking him to talk about it more, she simply snaked her hand through his. She held her breath. She didn't know if he would like her holding his hand, but she needed him to know that she was there for him. When he squeezed her hand and held it tightly, she released the breath she was holding and smiled. Because it was her injured hand, pain shot through her fingers and up her arm, but it was okay. It was more than okay. It was unlike the pain inflicted on her by Filip because Dumitru was expressing approval and because Dumitru needed her. It was wonderful to finally be needed. All of the ugliness around her faded into the background in this moment. It didn't disappear, exactly, but she felt good sitting here with Dumitru, temporarily away from the chaos.

Too soon, Dumitru sat up straight. By default, because she had been resting against him, Cătălina was now sitting up, too. "What's wrong?" she asked.

"The world is wrong. Don't you wonder what is happening right now?"

"Yes, I do. I am also concerned about my family."

"You were here with family? Why didn't you stay with them?" He threw his arms out to the sides, as if he were incredulous that she left them.

"I tried. We became separated." Cătălina's frown deepened. "I really should go now and try to find them before dark."

"It is too dangerous for you to go out there alone. I will go with you." Dumitru brushed past her and started to walk back in the direction from which they had come. Cătălina watched his long purposeful strides as he moved further away from her. People were clustered about, and she didn't want to lose sight of Dumitru. Clutching his jacket tightly so it didn't fall off, Cătălina ran to catch up with Dumitru.

\* \* \*

It felt like hours had passed. In reality, Cătălina didn't know how much time had gone by since she and Dumitru set out to search for her family. Uf! Someone nudged her hard in the side, causing her to stumble sideways. She scrambled to regain her balance and keep pace with Dumitru. The crowd was so dense. How would they ever find someone from her family? Were they even alive to be found? Cătălina caught snippets of conversations as she and Dumitru pushed and shoved and fought their way through the throng.

"Blood flows ankle deep at the foot of the Civic Center."

"So many dead."

"The dead ones are the lucky ones."

"President Ceauşescu is finally where he belongs, in Hell with the devil himself."

"Nonsense. Ceauşescu himself is the devil, and he's alive. We've accomplished nothing today other than making more misery. He will crush anyone who comes out alive."

Cătălina believed this last comment. If he were dead, this would be over. But chants and cries and sporadic gunshots and tank motors and treads grinding on the surface of the street continued. Overhead, a helicopter chopped by. The sky was darkening, giving bright color to the gunfire. As the light left, deeper cold rushed in to fill in the spaces. Her fingers and toes were already painful and prickly. She rubbed her gloveless hands together, squeezed her fingers, and stuck her hands under her armpits. Dumitru was doing the same. She tugged on his shirt. "Let's go to my apartment. We ran out of fuel rations long ago so we don't have heat, but at least we'll be out of the wind. Maybe someone will be home. Or maybe they'll work their way later. Even if not, I think we should stop looking for the night." She hated herself for the words she just said. She wanted to take them back, but Dumitru spoke first.

"Your family has an apartment?"

"Yes. We all share one, and it's crowded. But at least it's shelter."

"Why didn't you say that before? We could have gone there right away to get out of the cold." He sounded irritated.

"Because I wanted to find my family, and I know that they're not going to just abandon the uprising, desert the revolution, while it's still happening. Would you have?" She cringed inwardly. It wasn't her place to challenge a man. She fully expected him to leave. She was surprised when he didn't.

"No. I wouldn't have. Nor would Andrei." He smiled crookedly. "Hell, he probably would have been livid that I stopped to try to help him and to spend all that time trying to cart his body out of the city. So I believe you that your family wouldn't retreat to their apartment, either." He began to bounce on the balls of his feet and blow on his hands. Cătălina watched the vapor from his breath rise into the air like cigarette smoke. "Right now, I don't think we'd be abandoning the cause if we went inside, do you?"

She shook her head. "Not at all. Besides, look at how thin the crowd has become. I wonder what has happened."

"There's another reason we should go to your apartment. Maybe someone will have word. As in the truth, not street gossip." He put his arm around Cătălina's shoulders. "So where do you live?"

She looked at his hand flung over her left shoulder. What a day. She didn't know what to do about his arm this time, nor did she care. She was too tired. "It's this way," she told him and began to walk. He remained by her side with his arm on her the entire walk home. When they reached her neighborhood, one gigantic cluster of gray concrete tenement buildings pocketed with tiny windows in long rows, she picked her way through the dark to her building. "Step carefully," she warned him. "There are potholes and debris, and as you can tell there are no streetlights to illuminate the paths. There are no hallway lights inside either, so stay close to me." She pointed up. "My apartment is dark. Everyone must be out. Let's go in."

She led him through the dark, up six flights of stairs, and into the apartment she shared with her extended family. She had been right. No one was home. She rummaged for food, rounded up some bits of this and scraps of that for the two of them and saved the rest for the others. She let Dumitru have some of her portion because men were generally bigger and needed more food than women.

They ate in silence. As they finished, Dumitru looked at Cătălina and said quietly, "Thank you for letting me eat with you. Now that I'm alone, I won't always have someone to eat with." He looked down at his shoes. Cătălina heard him sniff. After an agonizingly long pause, he sat back and once again looked at her. "So, yeah, it's was nice to not have to eat alone tonight."

Cătălina's heart fluttered in a strange way. Strange, but pleasant. She felt as though this man was why she had been put on this earth, why she had endured so much. She had always had so much love to give, and Dumitru was who she was meant to love and care for. If he would let her, she would make sure that he would never have to eat alone. She couldn't say that, of course, but she made a silent promise to God that if He would let Dumitru be in her life, she would love and care for him forever. As she ended her prayer, Dumitru took her injured hand in his and tenderly kissed each knuckle, each fingertip. He dropped her hand and they both quickly stood when the door burst open. "Tată! You're safe!" Cătălina rushed to greet her father. As she was introducing Dumitru, a few others returned, too.

Many things happened that night. In small groups, members of her family returned until everyone was finally home safely. Romania was now free from the rule of Nicolae Ceaușescu and his brutal police force. Cătălina fell in love with Dumitru. He seemed to feel the same, and after that night they didn't part ways until Cătălina boarded the plane for America twenty-eight years later. Her family and Dumitru fell in love with each other. Her family was so smitten with him, in fact, that when the abuse began in earnest about a year later, they wouldn't believe her. They reminded her of the lies she had told about Filip just to get attention, and they chastised her for doing the same to Dumitru now. She never could convince them, no matter how bad she looked or what she said or did, which was why she had needed to take such a drastic measure as escaping the country in order to be safe from Dumitru.

Dumitru and Filip bonded almost instantly. The same age, they seemed more like twin brothers than mere friends. Initially, Cătălina wasn't wild about Dumitru being so close to Filip. Both were volatile and unpredictable, which could be bad for Cătălina. When it became obvious that Filip's interest in her had changed and they weren't going to gang up on her, she stopped worrying about it.

Over the years, Filip—and the rest of her family— remained part of their lives. Dumitru's family was gone. He would have been alone if it weren't for Cătălina and her family. He had nightmares about the deaths of his three brothers. He told her about these events while she was comforting him every time he had a nightmare, which was often. She didn't know anything about his extended family, and he would never talk about them. Her family was his family now.

Dumitru had always been closer to Filip than anyone else, until Filip was no longer a part of their lives. Cătălina felt nauseated every time she thought of it.

# Bucharest, Romania
## *November, 2017*

# Chapter 21

"Stop!" Cătălina slammed the door and charged at Dumitru. "Get away from him!" Dumitru turned and swatted Cătălina away, like she was nothing more than a fly. She hit the wall hard, regained her balance, and tried again. She wasn't strong enough to pull or push Dumitru away from Alexandru, so she did the next best thing. She flung herself onto the floor between Alexandru and Dumitru's foot, so when he kicked again, he kicked her rather than their son. She saw his thick boot swinging at her, and she closed her eyes and covered her face. Swiftly, sharply, he kicked her in the ribs once, twice, three times, four. When no more strikes came, she opened her eyes and saw him walk toward the kitchen. She shifted and put her arm around Alexandru, who was curled into a ball crying softly. She rubbed his back and stroked his hair. Searing pain shot through her with every movement, but that wasn't important. Her son's pain mattered more than her own. She lifted her head up and looked into the kitchen when she heard Florina's voice. Florina! She had been here watching this?

"Here, Tătic. Have an apple." She tossed her father an apple. She was leaning on the counter, propped up on her elbows, eating one of her own.

"Thank you, sweetheart." Dumitru kissed his daughter on the head. "I'm sorry you had to see that. That wouldn't have to happen if your mother and brother were more like you."

"I know, Tătic. I don't understand them." Without pause, she switched the subject. "My friends are meeting to see a movie. May I join them?"

"How many will be there? Is it a group or just a few?"

Florina hugged him. "Don't worry. It's a group of us."

"Boys?"

"Yes. But more girls. Like always. The same people you already know."

"That's my wonderful girl." Dumitru hugged Florina back. "Go have fun."

Cătălina sighed. She squeezed Alexandru's shoulder lovingly as she struggled to her feet. Alexandru remained rolled into himself like an armadillo. Florina stepped over him and walked out the door. Cătălina focused on her husband. "You have gone too far, Dumitru."

He leaned toward her, cupped his mouth around her ear, and bellowed, "Do not judge the way I discipline my own son, woman!" Cătălina recoiled and threw her hand over her ear. The pain was intense, and her ear rang. "And don't move away from me when I'm talking to you!" Dumitru grabbed Cătălina and roared, "Do you understand? Or are you too stupid? You're brainless, Cătălina." He made a noise and shoved her away in disgust. "You're retarded, that's what you are. That's where Alexandru gets it. He's a moron, Cătălina. He will be good for nothing. Look at this letter that arrived today." He waved it in Cătălina's face but didn't give her a chance to read it. "Our brilliant son earned second place in the city science competition. Second place. Second! Only second!" Cătălina cringed at the new round of shouting that threatened to break her eardrums.

"Dumitru! Second place is—"

"Is losing, Cătălina. Alexandru is nothing but a loser. He's a failure." Dumitru grabbed Cătălina's jaw and jerked her head in Alexandru's direction. "And look at him now. He's not only an idiot, he's a worthless coward." Dumitru shoved Cătălina out of his way and clomped to where Alexandru still lay curled into a ball. He bent over and yanked Alexandru to his feet, shaking him hard as if to straighten him out. As he shook him, he shouted, *"Retardat mintal! Retardat mintal!"*

"Stop it, Dumitru! He is not mentally retarded, and I want you to leave him alone! You've gone too far this time. Back away from him, or—"

Dumitru barked a harsh laugh. "Or what? You think you can stop me? You are grotesquely scrawny and weak. And this *retardat mintal rahat* certainly can't help you."

"Do *not* call him that!" Cătălina slapped Dumitru hard across the face. It was the first time she had ever struck him. She inhaled sharply, and then she did it again. He grabbed her wrists and squeezed. He lifted her up off the ground. She lashed out with her legs to kick him, but he positioned her so she couldn't do it. He pressed his fingers hard into the soft part of her wrists. She cried out in pain.

"Yeah, that's what I thought. You're powerless against me, woman."

Cătălina attempted to free herself. Dumitru gripped harder in response. He could physically overpower her, but she held one bit of knowledge that could bring him down. Early in their relationship, she had vowed never to mention it. Later, she realized that she might use it as a weapon against him if she needed it. Now was the time. She had to distract him, get him away from Alexandru. She took a deep breath, sent up a silent prayer to St. Basil for help, and blurted out, "You're not the first person to think that I am powerless, Dumitru. You're not the only one who pushed me around and had his way with me."

"What?" Cătălina watched his face twist in confusion then his eyes narrow in suspicion. "What do you mean, Cătălina?" it was a low growl.

Cătălina felt a surge of adrenaline. She wanted to hurt Dumitru. Interfering in his relationship with Filip would be such a pleasing way to do it. "Filip was interested in me long before you were, Dumitru," she taunted. "He was hot for me, Dumitru, and sometimes he couldn't keep his hands to himself. He bullied me just like you do, too. No wonder you and he are best friends, as close as brothers." Her arms were numb, but she wouldn't give him the satisfaction of knowing that. "So am I powerless, Dumitru, or am I so used to it that I don't even care?"

He let go of Cătălina and started pacing around the kitchen. "Fuck! He touched you? What did you do with him? Did you lead him on, you whore?" He grabbed her by the throat and squeezed. He let her go. "No. You are weak and powerless and always have been. This was on Filip. His actions. His fault. I'll kill that son of a bitch!" He ran his hands through his hair.

Cătălina's blood ran cold. She shook her head rapidly. "No. Dumitru. It wasn't as bad as you think. I didn't mean—"

"Shut up!" Dumitru stomped toward the door, shoved Alexandru out of the way, and slammed out the door.

Cătălina stood rooted to her spot, hands over her mouth. "Măicuţă?" Alexandru called. Mommy. He only called her mommy now when he was very sick or hurting or scared.

Right now he was probably all three. She was too. She rushed to him and embraced him.

"I'm so sorry, Alexandru. I'm sorry he did this to you again and I'm sorry you had to hear all of that and I'm sorry he left this house in a blind rage." Arms still around him, she rocked him. Her mind spun. This couldn't keep happening. Dumitru was completely out of control, worse than ever before. She would take Alexandru and sneak away right now, but she had no idea where Florina had gone. She was daddy's girl at the moment, but if Cătălina and Alexandru left without her, Dumitru would turn on her and she would receive the entirety of his fury. She couldn't do that to her daughter. She was trying to think about what to do, but she couldn't concentrate. What was Dumitru doing right now? Was Filip safe? Yes, he had been bothersome when they were children and yes, he molested her, but that was in the distant past. What had she done by mentioning it? She let go of Alexandru to wipe away tears.

Alexandru looked at her. "Come on, Măicuţă. Let's make supper together."

She stroked his hair. "My wonderful son. You are an amazing person, and I don't want you to ever think otherwise."

The night passed slowly. Alexandru went to bed. Florina came home and went to bed. Dumitru was still absent. Cătălina waited for him on the couch. She was wide awake when he came home at 2:45. "Cătălina! How nice of you to wait up for me. I'm famished. Would you make me a couple of sandwiches?" He walked to the couch and helped her up. He pulled her close. She gasped. Her eyes frantically roamed his face, his hands, his clothes. Blood spattered his forehead and streaked his hands. His clothes were smeared with dark, sticky streaks. Cătălina gagged and covered her mouth with her hands.

"Dumitru! What…what happened? What did you do?"

He shrugged. "Oh, nothing of your concern. Filip and I just hung out. Had a meaningful conversation. It's fine now." He inspected his hands. "I'm going to get cleaned up a bit while you make me those sandwiches." He pulled out his shirt and looked down at it. "Yeah, I think I ruined my clothes. Don't worry about washing these. I'll take care of them." He whistled as he strutted toward their bedroom. He stopped. "Cătălina dear, you don't ever have to worry about Filip again." He turned and continued into their bedroom.

Cătălina suddenly felt frigid, and she started to shake uncontrollably. She managed to walk to the kitchen. She must have made food, for she suddenly realized that Dumitru was sitting at the table eating sandwiches. He was just sitting there, chewing away, reading the newspaper, like he hadn't beaten his son less than twelve hours ago, like he hadn't abused his wife, like he hadn't just murdered his best friend. Cătălina's mouth went dry. She tried to take a drink, but her hands were shaking too hard and she spilled water down the front of her shirt. She was vaguely aware that Dumitru stood up and, saying nothing, went to bed. In a veritable trance, she cleaned up after Dumitru then shuffled to the table where she sat, motionless, waiting for sunrise.

Once she was showered and changed and everyone was out of the house, she rushed to work. It was Wednesday, so she didn't expect to see Vasile. He had told her repeatedly, though, to call him if she needed help. She extracted her phone, dialed his number, and asked him to come. He arrived in less than half an hour. She had been carrying a large stack of diapers that she had just folded, but when she saw him, she dropped them to the floor and stepped on them as she rushed to him.

"Oh, Vasile! He has turned on Alexandru, and I think he did something very terrible last night. It's enough. He has become more dangerous than ever. We can't stay with him any longer."

Vasile embraced her. "Slow down, Cătălina. Please, tell me everything." They sat on their bench outside the orphanage. When she had finished, she noticed that Vasile was pale. "Okay. I've been ready for this day, and I have a plan already in place to help you escape. Before I tell you, I need you to trust me completely. Cătălina, do you trust me?"

"Of course. I trust you fully, and I will do as you say."

He nodded. "Good. We're going to get you and your children out of here."

# Sacramento, California
## *2018*

# Chapter 22

. . . . . . . . . . . . . . . . . . . . .

"Ouch!" Catie yanked her hand away from the loom's cloth roller and massaged her fingertips with her other hand. That pinch was punishment for being careless and allowing the cloth to bunch up. She shouldn't have had to place her hand on the roller to smooth out the piece of material she was weaving. She sighed and resumed the process. She wanted to add just a few more inches so she had a properly sized cloth to embroider tonight, one that, if good enough, could be draped over one of the gold crosses that stood tall in the church. To distract herself from her throbbing fingers, she hummed to herself. She resurrected the songs of the Romanian country-side, the music of Bunicuţă, the essence of Vasile, because he would hum these very tunes to infants he held and rocked. She felt her cheeks grow warm at these thoughts, and somehow all of her pain was more bearable. She weaved and hummed rhythmically until she had created a suitable piece of fabric. She gently and lovingly removed the piece from the loom and folded it to take home with her.

"Catie! You are still working?" Father Stasiuk's voice boomed through the storage building, suddenly and loudly. Catie jumped to her feet in alarm, toppling the bench as she did. She cried out. As she stepped away from the loom, she tripped over her pile of cleaners and oil and rags.

"Oh! Please! I am so sorry I left these supplies out because I was using them to tweak the loom as I worked; I was planning on putting them away. Please don't hurt me." Catie's words ran together as she dropped to the floor and scrambled to gather her maintenance supplies. She kept her head down and made herself as small as she could. For the millionth time in her life she found herself envying tortoises. She wanted to retreat into a hard, protective shell and never emerge.

"Catie. Catie!" She heard her name called and couldn't avoid it any longer. She stopped scooping up items and looked up to face Dumitru. To both her relief and horror, she saw that it wasn't Dumitru at all, but Father Stasiuk. She was at St. Theocharis in Sacramento, California in the United States. Father Vasile Cojocaru had rescued her and sent her far, far away from Dumitru. Thinking about Dumitru so much today must have put him in her head and under her skin. She didn't want him there, and she shuddered. "Catie?" Father Stasiuk called down to her again. She struggled to her feet. The old priest helped her the best he could. When she was on her feet, he chuckled. "We make quite a pair, don't we? Catie smiled sadly. Over two decades of Dumitru's lessons and punishments would be with her for life, it seemed. "What's with your silence, Catie? Did everything go okay down here today?"

She tugged on her shirt and smoothed out any wrinkles she might have made by diving on the ground. "Yes, Father. Today has been very good. Take a look at this." Catie reached toward the loom and gently presented Father Stasiuk the cloth she had woven.

He rubbed it between his finger and thumb, and he gripped it with both hands and tenderly but firmly stretched the cloth horizontally, vertically, and diagonally. As he studied the fabric, a smile spread slowly across his face. "This is amazing. Are you sure you made this on this loom?" He tapped the old machine with his knuckles. "I was concerned that it either wouldn't work at all or wouldn't produce cloths of high quality. I think God has worked a true miracle through you, Catie."

She flushed with pride and stood straighter. She smiled. "Thank you, Father. At first, the loom was lifeless, but I found the right supplies to revive it. I made adjustments as I worked." She bent over and picked up some scraps of fabric. "The loom needed some coaxing and some reminders of how great it can be. As you can see," she gestured to the long cloth the priest still held, "it seems to have remembered. This cloth just might be suitable for draping on a cross if it will hold embroidery properly. Would it be acceptable for me to take this home? I will return it to the church."

"Of course it's okay." He fiddled with the cloth, studying it as he folded it. When it was a small rectangle, he held it in one palm, ran his hand over the top of it, and presented it to Catie, who took it cautiously. She smiled in thanks but said nothing. Father seemed very solemn, and she wasn't sure what would be appropriate to say. She waited. Eventually, he said, "I will enjoy returning to St. Theocharis to see all of your tapestries and cloths, Catie." She tilted her head and knotted her brows. She knew he was considering retirement, but he had told her that it would be some time before he actually did. What had he meant just now?

"What...what do you mean, Father? I thought it would be a long while before you retired."

"Catie, it's..." He trailed off as he grasped the loom, seemingly to steady himself.

"Father, are you okay?" Without thinking, Catie reached out and put one hand on Father Stasiuk's arm and one on his back. "Maybe we should go back into the church. This shed is rather stuffy." Catie fought to keep her voice steady and neither too loud nor too soft.

Father Stasiuk straightened and released his grip on the loom. His smile settled the butterflies in Catie's stomach. "I think that's a good idea, Catie." He looked around the shed and ran a finger under his collar. "How did you stay in here for nine hours?"

Catie had been escorting Father Stasiuk to the door but paused at his words. "Has it really been nine hours?" She had gone into the church to use the facilities twice, but she hadn't paid attention to the time. It certainly didn't seem that such a big portion of the day had passed. When he nodded, she simply said, "Wow," and continued with Father Stasiuk out of the shed, across the lawn, and into the church. The fresh air outside and the spaciousness inside the church were revitalizing. Catie led Father Stasiuk to a pew, and the two sat side by side.

"I think I should get right to the point. You've been here all day and your family would probably like to have you home." *Not likely*, Catie thought, but she didn't speak that depressing sentiment. "Also, my wife will have dinner ready soon." He shifted slightly so he was looking more at Catie than he was the altar at the front of the church. Even that small movement was labored and seemed to cause him difficulty. "You have probably noticed that I haven't been well lately. I'm becoming tired and weak, and it is only with great difficulty that I can move. I've been to the doctor, and he's in the process of determining what's wrong. I do know that whatever it is, it is time for me to retire. It's becoming very difficult for me to do my job well. I was hoping to wait longer, but I can't. The bishop has accelerated the process of finding a priest who will be a good fit for this congregation"

Catie nodded. She wanted to say something nice, to express her concern for this wonderful man who had helped her escape Dumitru, but she found herself speechless. Not only did she not have words, but it seemed as though she had nothing inside of her at all. She felt hollow, devoid of absolutely everything. She had experienced so much pain and so many losses. The loss of this connection, this reminder of Vasile and Romania, felt like one loss too many. She dug in her bag for a tissue. She dabbed her eyes, but it did no good. She began to twist it in her hands. Bit by bit, it began to tear apart, just like her life from the moment she had been born.

"Are you okay, Catie?"

She nodded. "I'm fine." She tried to smile, but her muscles just couldn't fake it this time. She buried her face in the mess of torn tissue and sobbed. She felt the priest's hand on her head and heard him chanting in prayer. It was something Vasile would have done, had done with her many times over the years they had known each other. The thought was at once both dismaying and comforting. She summoned strength from the memories of Vasile and the words of Father Stasiuk now. Oh, how she didn't want to go on any longer. But was the choice really hers? No, it wasn't. Maybe someday, but not now. She had two children to love and support. As the priest prayed over her, she prayed her own words to St. Basil and God himself that she could keep going. When she felt Father Stasiuk's thumb and first two fingers on her forehead to make the sign of the cross, she opened her eyes. When he had completed the cross, he leaned back against the pew. Catie turned to look at him.

"I'm sorry, Father. I didn't mean to be so demonstrative. I am just sad to see you go, and I'm worried about you."

"Thank you, Catie. It's nice that you aren't rejoicing that I'm leaving."

"Of course not!"

"I do wonder, though, why you are so very upset."

"Well, I…" She stopped and toyed with the soggy wad of tissue bits in her hands. How could she begin to explain the depths of her sorrow and anxiety about this? "There are so many reasons, Father. One is that I am lonely here. You are the only adult in my life."

"Catie, is that really true?"

"Yes."

"Not all that long ago, you told me about your work at the daycare and how you were glad to have a coworker you like."

Marcy. He was referring to Marcy. But Catie had ruined that relationship. She shrugged. "It's just a work partner."

"Really? It didn't seem that way when you told me about your work and your partner. I thought that it seemed that maybe you were becoming friends." His tone was neutral, emotionless. Catie couldn't interpret him at all. What did he mean? What was he trying to say? Catie swallowed and cleared her throat.

"Well, um, we're not friends."

"Oh." He raised his eyebrows. To Catie, they looked like big, furry chinchilla tails lifting into the air. She shook her head and rubbed her temples.

"Okay. Fine. My coworker's name is Marcy, and I like her. I thought that we could be friends, but I was wrong. I'm ashamed of who I am. I've deserved all of the bad treatment I've ever had, from my family and from my husband and from people in general. But I don't deserve friendship. Marcy

wanted to be friends, and she started to see the real me." She
swiped at the tears that were flowing down her cheeks. She
couldn't speak, so she fell silent. The hush of the sanctuary
pulsed against her, reverberating in her ears. It was vast and
great and she wanted to disappear into it. She jumped slightly
when Father Stasiuk spoke.

"You are ashamed of who you are?" Catie blanched. His
tone was just harsh enough to scare her tears away. "Have you
ever thought of how God would feel about that? He created
you, Catie. With love." His eyes bore into hers. She wanted to
look away, to run away, but fear held her frozen. He continued, "God has created a path for you in this life. It seems to
me that He has put you here on Earth to be a caregiver. From
what I know of you and what I heard from Father Cojocaru
from the very first time we spoke about you, you are fulfilling
your purpose in a way that is making God extremely proud
and happy." Catie couldn't help it. She smiled a small smile.
The smile faded, though, when Father Stasiuk went on, "But
do you think He is proud of the way you are caring for yourself, Catie?" After an eternity, he asked, "How do you think
He feels about you being ashamed of yourself? And about the
gift of friendship He gave you in Marcy, a gift that you are
rejecting?"

Catie was nauseated. Her head spun. She had never
thought of things this way before. She began to shake her
head. She slid onto the kneeler in front of her, clasped her
hands tightly, and said a silent prayer for forgiveness over and
over again. At last, she spoke. "No! Father, I am very sorry for
this deep sin. I have never considered this before. Do you..."
She felt acid rise up in her throat, and she had to swallow several times before she could resume. "Do you think that God
can forgive me?"

"Of course I do. I know so. But you have to show Him with your actions that you are sorry and that you will change for Him. God is loving and caring, but He wants us to do our part, too. I think He is hurt when one of his lambs says she hates herself. He will forgive you again and again, but the best thing for you to do is to stop hating yourself and to open yourself up to the people He puts in your path."

Catie's heart beat rapidly. She heard it pound in her head, and she felt it pulse in her temples and in her neck. She felt its red heat in the tips of her ears. Her ears here hot, burning, but the rest of her went frigid. Cold sweat coated her skin. She had disappointed, hurt, God. In knowing that she fell short as a human being and being very sorry for it, she was actually making things worse. Could it be true? And Marcy? Was she a gift from God that Catie had rejected because she hated herself, two grave sins wrapped into one? She nodded. "I will try, Father, but I don't know what to do or where to start." Her words were a whisper, but Father Stasiuk seemed to have heard them.

"A good start, my child, is to stop being so hard on your-self. And while you're learning to do that, let people into your life. Starting with Marcy."

"But I pushed her away. Now she hates me." The tears resumed.

"How do you know that? Never make assumptions about how other people feel. I have an assignment for you. It's for God more than it is for me. I'm just the messenger. The next time you see her, go up to her, greet her, and talk to her. Stop assuming she will reject you. Open yourself to her friendship and to God's love for you. Yes, God put you here as a care-giver. He loves you as He loves others, and He wants you to care for yourself as you care for them."

After listening to the silence around her for a great many seconds, Catie looked back at Father Stasiuk. He was leaning back against the pew, and his eyes were closed. She felt bad for keeping him at the church this long when he clearly wasn't well. She began to chastise herself for her selfishness, but abruptly she stopped herself. She was still doing it, hating herself for who she was and what she did. Now she chastised herself for chastising herself. She pressed the heels of her hands into her eyes and stifled a groan. She was thoroughly confused and still afraid of disappointing both God and people. She sighed. This was going to take a lot of time and prayer to sort out. For now, though, Father Stasiuk needed to get home. She dropped her hands away from her face and looked at the priest again. He was pale. She needed to help him get home. It's a very good thing that his house was right next to the church. "Father Stasiuk?" He opened his eyes. "Thank you so much for our talk. You have given me much to think about and a new perspective on God. I am very grateful. Now I need to go, and you might want to go home, too. Will you let me walk beside you to your home as I head home, too?" Father Stasiuk was a wonderful priest, but he was still a man. Catie didn't want to make him feel that she was telling him what to do or babying him by walking him home.

He nodded and sat up. After a pause, seemingly to gather strength, he stood. "May I escort you, Catie?"

"Of course, Father."

Catie looped her arm through the crook of Father Stasiuk's. They walked in silence out of the church. The bang and click of the gigantic wooden door made Catie jump even though she knew it would be coming. She started to berate herself for being weak, but then she stopped. She still felt weak and foolish, but this time she didn't yell at herself for it.

She didn't know if it felt any different. She still felt miserable. She sighed.

Once she had parted ways with Father Stasiuk, she headed home. She looked down. As she suspected, her feet were trudging. She couldn't get a spring into her step. Marcy would be bringing Alexandru home, probably soon, and she was incredibly anxious. So anxious, in fact, that she could hardly breathe. Her chest constricted in pain, and her vision blurred. She wiped her hand across her forehead to swipe away the sweat that was beginning to trickle down her temples and her nose. She stopped and leaned against a tree until this panic attack passed. Finally, it subsided, and she made her way unsteadily home.

# Chapter 23

······················

Catie unlocked her front door, walked in, and kept right on going out the patio doors and into the backyard. It was only after she slid the door shut behind her that she realized that she hadn't checked to see if anyone was home. She slid the door open just far enough to stick her head back inside and called, "Alexandru? Florina? Are you home? She waited. Nothing. Sliding the door shut behind her, she returned to her backyard.

She staggered to the little bench nestled among clusters of flowers and put her head between her knees. She was still shaky from the panic attack and unsteady from all that Father Stasiuk had said to her. Could it really be true? Was her self-hatred, much-deserved as it was, actually a sin? Her eyes and nose began to drip onto the ground beneath her feet, so she sat back. She leaned to the side and plucked a bunch of bloodroots out of the ground. Yanking a petal off one of the flowers, she proclaimed, "I love me not!" She turned her face skyward and shook her head. "Please forgive me, Lord. I will try to love myself the way You want me to." Returning to the flowers, she plucked petal after petal and repeated, "I love me. I love me. I love me." She continued until in her hand she held one stem with one button on the top of it and one petal

*317*

on the button. She twirled it between her fingers as she studied the ground. A carpet of petals and stems settled on the
ground between her feet. A few petals had fallen on the tops
of her shoes. She wiggled first one foot then the other, and the
petals slid down to rest on the pile. Her eyes grew wide as she
continued to stare. She gasped and covered her mouth with
the hand that held the single stem, single button, single petal.
So much destruction! And at her hands! She of all people,
who had vowed as a child when she watched the *Securitate* violently destroy her countryside home never to willfully destroy
anything, who had dedicated her life to nurturing and caring
at all costs in order to counter the pain and destruction in
everyone's life, she had been violently destroying, murdering
flowers. She had become the Dumitru of flowers! Here was
more evidence that she was a disappointment to God. These
new revelations that she was a disappointment not just to
humans but to God, too, tore at her soul. She shook her head
rapidly and squeezed her eyes shut to keep from crying again.

As she did so, she must have shaken Bunicuță loose, for
she suddenly saw her Romanian grandma, in her splendid,
peasant, glory, standing before her. "Cătălina, why are you
moping outside on the bench? What purpose does that serve?
Who would you rather be like, child? Your mother, or me?"
Then she was gone.

Catie's skin pricked with goosebumps. She wiped her eyes.
Once again she looked up to the sky and made the sign of the
cross. This time she prayed to her saint, St. Basil. She wasn't
exactly avoiding God directly, but she felt that she could use
the support of her intercessor. "Thank You for giving me so
very much to think about today. These are important lessons
about things I have never thought of in my humble humanity.
Please forgive me, and I hope it's all right to ask You for both

patience and guidance as I struggle to understand all of this and then apply it to my life. In the name of the Father, the Son, and the Holy Spirit. Amen."

Catie stared at the pathetic remnant of a flower still pinched between her thumb and forefinger. She sighed heavily. She had no idea what to say to the remaining petal. She knew she wasn't supposed to believe, "I love me not," any longer, knew she was supposed to believe, "I love me," but she wasn't quite ready. She wanted to, but she had no idea how to change her core beliefs about herself. Maybe for now she shouldn't think about having the beliefs but instead should think about what Father Stasiuk and Bunicuță believe. She could let them do the believing for her until she could figure it out for herself. She studied the remaining petal and ran her fingers gently along its smooth surface. She nodded. Then, she stood and slowly walked toward the house and inside. She removed a little drinking glass from the cupboard, filled it partially with water, tenderly lowered the almost-bare blood-root flower into it, and walked to her bedroom to place it on her nightstand.

Suddenly weary, not just physically and mentally but spiritually, too, she lay down on the bed and pulled her quilt up around her. She closed her eyes and let her spinning head spiral her ever downward, down into the welcome darkness of sleep. She bolted upright, heart pounding. What was that noise? "Mamă? I'm home! Are you here?"

Catie sighed and tried to take slow, deep breaths. She placed her hand on her chest as if the pressure would calm her pounding heart. "I..." Her voice croaked and failed. She cleared her throat and tried again. "I'm home, Alexandru! I'll be right out." She sat on the edge of the bed for a minute just to regain her composure, and then she stood. She winced.

The loom work and weaving today had clearly settled into her muscles and bones. She was already very stiff and very sore. But it was worth it. As quickly as she could, which she feared was actually very slow, she made her way to the living room to find Alexandru.

She found herself looking not just at Alexandru but at Marcy, too. She froze. Her stomach dropped. "I hope it's okay that I invited Marcy. We had a great time today, and she really helped me a lot with my reading." He smiled and looked at Marcy. "I told her she should be a teacher. She'd be awesome."

"Really? That's wonderful, Alexandru!" She turned to her coworker. "Thank you for helping him, Marcy. I truly am very grateful."

Marcy put a hand on Alexandru's shoulder. "It was truly my pleasure. He's a fast learner and an amazing student. I'm happy to help."

"So what do you say, Mamă? Can Marcy stay?"

Catie thought of Father Stasiuk's admonitions and his assignment regarding Marcy. She couldn't exactly disobey him, even though if she did he would never know. She would know, and she didn't want to deal with that guilt. Besides, how could she say no, turn Marcy away, when she was standing in her house? "Of course she can stay." Cătălina looked at Marcy. "But, well, I didn't plan anything for this and I'm not sure if I have anything for all of us to eat. Do you mind if I go to the store quickly?" It was the last thing Catie felt up to doing, but she really didn't have enough food to make something decent for the three of them, four, if Florina came home.

"No need for that!" Marcy jumped in. She rushed to the kitchen and returned with two jumbo sized take-n-bake pizzas. "Alexandru and I took care of it on the way here. Why don't we go get them in the oven?"

"Yeah, I'm starving."

"Alexandru, you're always starving."

"Hey. It takes a lot to get muscles like these." He pushed up his t-shirt sleeves so they bunched on his shoulders, and then he flexed. "Check it out. These are rock solid. See? Try to squeeze them." He slid right up next to Catie, biceps still contracted. "Come on. Squeeze."

Catie grinned. "I can tell just by looking how strong you are."

"Thanks! Now feel them."

Catie squeezed her son's arm. "Amazing, Alexandru."

"Aw, you barely even squeezed. Is that all you've got?"

"Right now, yes. I worked a loom for nine hours today, and my whole body but especially my hands are paying the painful price."

Alexandru lowered his arms and rolled his sleeves back into place. "Oh. I'm sorry, Mamă."

Catie shook her head and grasped his arms. "Don't be. It's okay." She grinned. "Your arms really are solid, Alexandru."

He beamed. "Thanks! And if it's okay, I'd like to go outside and practice juggling." He swooped down and picked up the soccer ball that was almost always by his side; in fact, if Catie didn't know better, she'd swear it was a dog following him loyally wherever he went. He bounced it off his knee several times, dropped it to his foot, and attempted to flick it back to his knee. The ball missed its mark and ricocheted to the side. Marcy lunged and snatched it out of the air before it hit a lamp. Alexandru shrugged. "Oops. I need a lot of practice. So can I go outside while the pizza bakes?"

"Please do!" Catie shooed him on his way and turned to Marcy.

"Uh, that was a great catch. Thank you for saving my lamp."

Marcy flexed her arms the way Alexandru had. "It was easy because I'm so strong."

They laughed together. Catie enjoyed the feeling. The problem was knowing what to do when the laughter faded, which it promptly did. Catie shifted on her feet. "Would you like to sit at the table while I put the pizzas in the oven and set out the plates and things? Would you like some wine as you wait? I have some red wine, but not white. I'm sorry my selection is poor." She flushed and looked down. What kind of a hostess was she? She had declined over the years, that much was certain. Early in their marriage, and even for a while after Florina and Alexandru had been born, she and Dumitru had thrown fun and exciting dinner parties. Now she could only offer her guest one type of wine, plus the guest had had to bring the food. Her cheeks were hot and certainly red, so she turned away from Marcy and busied herself with fetching first wine glasses and then silverware, plates, and cups for water. She unwrapped the pizzas and stuck them in the preheating oven.

She heard one of the chairs scrape across the floor followed by a second chair. "Catie." Marcy's voice was firm, not angry but not cheery, either. "Come sit down. We need to talk this out."

"But..." She was about to protest, to apologize again, and to refuse to sit down with Marcy, when Father Stasiuk's words, uttered just a short while ago, rushed through her mind. *"How do you think He feels about you being ashamed of yourself? And about the gift of friendship He gave you in Marcy, a gift that you are rejecting?"* She had to try to reconnect with Marcy. Carrying two wine glasses, she approached the table. "Let me grab the wine first."

Catie poured. Her pain was increasing, plus her anxiety was through the roof, so she ended up sloshing wine onto Marcy's part of the table. She gasped. "Oh no! I'm—"

"Catie, do not even think of apologizing. Wine spilled. Big deal." Marcy stepped to the sink and grabbed some paper towels off the nearby roll and returned to wipe up the wine. From where she stood, she tossed the paper towels across the room and into the sink, sat down again, and looked at Catie who stood, frozen, beside the table. "Sit." Marcy gestured.

When Catie had complied, Marcy began. "Catie. I don't want to turn this into this big thing, so I'm going to keep it simple. I love working with you. I love helping Alexandru. I was enjoying becoming better friends with you. I thought it was kind of special that you and I are each estranged from our families, and I thought we could team up and kinda be our own family. I hate this awkwardness that came between us, and if it were up to me, we'd get over it. But it's not up to just me." She stopped and took a sip of her wine, swirled it around in her glass, watched it settle down, and then took another sip. Catie didn't dare try drinking hers. She was afraid that the wine wouldn't be able to flow past the gigantic lump in her throat. Words wouldn't work their way past, either, which seemed to be fine, as Marcy quickly resumed. "What about you? Would you like to resume our friendship and get past this stupid awkwardness?"

Catie nodded and cleared her throat. "I would. I would like that a lot, actually. It's just that I'm afraid I won't be a very good friend for you, and I want to spare you."

Marcy shook her head. "Then you don't really want this friendship, do you?"

Catie felt her eyebrows shoot up when her eyes widened. "What? Of course I do!"

"You have to really want it, Catie. All the way. That means that you can't retreat. It's actually really unfair of you to just assume that I'm going to reject you or that I'm going to be abusive like Dumitru or even your family members." She stopped and looked at Catie pointedly.

"Oh. I hadn't thought about it that way." She rubbed her temples. She was dizzy and confused and heartsick from all of these profound revelations about how sinful and unfair she really was. But maybe God was suddenly sending her all of these messages for a reason. He had worked through Vasile and then Father Stasiuk to get her out of her very dangerous situation, but she wasn't acting very grateful for it. Again, though, she returned to the thought that her feelings were legitimate and she wasn't trying to be rejecting and ungrateful. She dropped her hands and toyed with her wine glass. "You're right, Marcy," she mumbled. "It really is unfair of me to assume the worst for you. My hatred of myself is something I have learned over a lifetime, and I believe that I am unworthy. But maybe like Alexandru is learning to read English better, I can learn to read myself and others better. Will you tutor me the way you tutor Alexandru?"

Marcy smiled broadly. "I'd love to. But don't think of it so much as tutoring as simply friends growing together."

Catie felt lighter than she had in as long as she could remember. She was actually able to enjoy the pizza. She didn't have to worry about what to say, because Alexandru was a chatterbox during dinner. When all but four pieces had been eaten, he asked Catie, "May I have the rest?"

"I think we'd better save some for your sister."

"What? Why? If she wanted dinner, she should have been here at dinnertime."

"She still has to eat, Alexandru. She likes pizza, so we should save some for her."

Alexandru wiped his mouth then tossed the napkin hard onto his plate. "I don't get you, Mamă. Seriously. Why?"

"What do you mean?" Catie's brows furrowed.

"Do you seriously not get it?" He stared at her for a few moments then shook his head. "You know, I guess I don't get it either. I mean, I don't understand why Florina can treat you like garbage and yet you run after, cater to her, beg and plead and try to get her to behave. I'm sure you're used to it from Dad." He paused again. When Catie still said nothing, Alexandru continued. "Do you even realize that you care more about what the people who abuse you think of you than the people who love and support you?" He fell silent. He picked up his fork and poked his napkin with it.

Catie sighed. Alexandru, too? Had these three important people in her life conspired to come down on her today, or was it a coincidence? Either way, it didn't matter. She needed to start not just listening but truly, fully, hearing. She reached over and touched her son's hand. "Alexandru. You are absolutely right. No, I didn't realize that I was paying so much attention to the wrong people. I will work on getting better, I promise." He looked at her. Catie couldn't read his expression, so she decided not to try. "Can I make you a peace offering? Would you still like the rest of the pizza?"

"Really? What about Florina?"

Catie sat back in her chair and shook her head. "I have no idea about Florina. I do know, though, that she is aware of our dinnertime. If she decides not to show up, then she'll just have to find herself something else. This food is for those of us who are here." She gestured at the remaining slices. "Go for it. They're yours."

"Awesome! Thanks!"

Catie smiled at him. She had no more to say. She had no idea how to begin moving forward with all of this new insight into herself. She was confused and overwhelmed. Maybe for a while she could fall back on her old survival tactic. She'd try it out as soon as someone asked her the magic question.

It came from Alexandru. He finished chewing a large bit of pizza, swallowed, and asked, "Mamă, are we good? Are you okay?"

Catie smiled and said, "Of course, Alexandru. I'm per-fectly fine." And to Catie's delight, the rest of the evening with Marcy and Alexandru, and without Florina, went just fine.

# Sacramento, CA
## *Two Months Later*

# Chapter 24

· · · · · · · · · · · · · · · · · · · · · ·

Catie unlocked her front door and walked in after a long day of work. She knew Alexandru wouldn't be home yet; Marcy had helped him get a part-time job at a nearby pet store. She headed straight to the backyard and visited her flowers. Spring flowers like the bloodroots had been replaced by new summer blooms. If she had wanted to play "I love me; I love me not," she could have used the white or yellow daisies that bloomed cheerily in the sunny corner of her yard. But she didn't want to. First, she was upholding her promise to never be violent again. Second, she didn't know how she felt about herself. She certainly could not say "I love me," but she was trying to work on the "love me not" part by relaxing and enjoying Marcy at work and Alexandru at home. She tried to enjoy Florina, too, but she found that increasingly hard to do. She felt guilty about that, though, and she did love her daughter, so she kept trying and failing and trying again.

She watered her flowers and then headed back to the house. She closed her eyes and listened to the silence. She wanted to see if she could capture the feeling of St. Theocharis. She hadn't stopped there after work today because she wanted to get home to work on her tapestries and sacred cloths. She had fallen into a nice rhythm of weaving on the loom on Saturdays and embroidering at home in the evenings. Creating for the church and for God had revived her passion and fulfilled a deep purpose that had been buried deep inside her since she was a child. She still felt great sorrow and loss, anxiety and panic, but her passions and purposes—her son Alexandru, her friend Marcy, and now weaving and embroidering—were helping her go slowly forward.

She inhaled deeply and exhaled slowly. While she appreciated the silence of her house, it certainly was different than the quietude of St. Theocharis. The church's silence was pure, empty of expectations but full of light, a glow that was felt rather than seen. The silence of home was more like a coiled spring. It made no sound, no movement, and instead of a peaceful glow, it held the potential to boing into action at any moment, propelled by the energy of things that needed to be done. Catie cocked her head as she pondered that comparison. She walked into the kitchen and took everything in. She had left the house before Alexandru this morning, and the kitchen was the destruction left in the wake of a teenage boy. Among the plate, bowl, cereal box, bread loaf, and crumbs was the unopened jar of peanut butter that somehow seemed to have a permanent home on the counter.

Catie shook her head. Kitchen work was work for women, but she should really get Alexandru to do some clean-up. After all, they were no longer in Romania. Even from her limited experience thus far, Catie knew that America was vastly different. She'd check with Marcy to see just how much kitchen-and house work was acceptable for men and boys here, and she'd change her expectations for Alexandru accordingly. For now, though, she'd clean up. She was just finishing when her doorbell rang. Her heart stopped, then began to throb relentlessly. Dumitru! The bell rang again. She grabbed a large knife and held it unsteadily at her side. Very carefully, very slowly, she opened the door. The creak of the hinges sounded ominous. She peeked around the door as she pulled it slowly back toward her. When she saw who it was, she exhaled in relief and leaned her head against the door. "Father Stasiuk! I'm so glad to see you. Please, step in." Catie moved out of the way so the priest could enter. She placed the knife on a living room table and then ushered the old priest to a chair. She disappeared into the kitchen to start water for tea. When she returned, she asked, "What are you doing here, Father?" Heat crept up her neck and into her face. Her hands flew to her cheeks. "Oh, I mean, I'm very happy that you are here! It's just that I didn't expect you."

Father Stasiuk chuckled. "Relax, Catie. I know what you meant. I'm here because you didn't come to St. Theocharis today. I was hoping to see you."

"I'm sorry, Father. I decided to come home right away today so I could do some embroidery work. I'm enjoying this important project so much, and I want you to know how deeply grateful I am to you for allowing me to do this."

"Catie, your work is a gift. I am grateful to you. And I know our new priest will be equally in awe and gratitude." He paused and closed his eyes. Catie braced herself. This was it. This was why he was here now. He was about to tell her that the bishop had found and finalized a replacement. She swallowed hard to dislodge the painful lump that had materialized in her throat. She didn't want to make him uncomfortable; after all, he already knew how she felt about his leaving, and dragging him through her thoughts and emotions again would neither be good for him nor change the situation. She waited quietly and patiently for him to continue. Eventually, he did. He opened his eyes and said frankly, "Catie, I wanted to tell you in person before I make the announcement on Sunday. We have a new priest, eager and thrilled to be here, and I will step down immediately."

Catie nodded. As she did, a few tears dislodged and slid down her cheeks. She smiled and wiped them away with the back of her hand. "I'm so sorry, Father. I don't want to do this to you. I truly am happy for you."

"Thank you, Catie. Will it help if I tell you that I know that you will be not just okay but very, very good? I'm not the only Greek Catholic priest who does a fantastic job." He grinned. Catie smiled weakly. "I knew you'd be a little uncertain about this," he said. *Uncertain?* Catie thought. *More like devastated, depressed, anxious, panicky...* Father Stasiuk broke into her thoughts. "So I thought that it would be good to introduce you to the new priest before Sunday. He'll deliver mass with me, and I'll formally introduce him, but if you meet him now, with me, perhaps it won't feel so strange to you on Sunday."

Catie bit her lip. She didn't want a new priest. She wanted Father Stasiuk. But this was happening regardless. It might be better to meet the new head of St. Theocharis with Father Stasiuk. She nodded slowly. "Okay. Let me turn off the tea kettle and grab my purse. I'll come with you to the church."

His chinchilla eyebrows shot up. "Oh. Actually, he's outside waiting in my car. I didn't want to just show up with him at your doorstep. I wanted to prepare you for meeting him first."

Catie looked around frantically. Two priests? In her house? Now? She hadn't thought of it before because Father Stasiuk had launched right into his reason for his visit, but now she realized that her house was unfit for a priest, let alone two. She looked at the gray blanket draped over the back of the couch, and the only thing she could see was the oval coffee stain. Her pillows, threadbare. The plant, droopy with thirst. Shame on her! The kitchen, better than before but still not good enough. Oh, no. Her heart sped up again, her ears burned, her head spun, and she thought she might be sick. She couldn't breathe. She felt Father Stasiuk's hand on her upper arm. "Catie, relax. This meeting will go well. You'll see that he's a nice man."

"But my house. It's...it's shabby. Unfit for both of you." She shook her head.

"Nonsense. You have a lovely, cozy home, fit for absolutely anybody and especially for two humble priests. So please, do make some tea. I'll go out and get him. Okay?"

Catie sighed. No, none of this was at all okay, but she smiled anyway and said, "Okay."

She went into the kitchen, poured the boiling water into a large teapot, grabbed three tea cups, a container holding a variety of tea bags, balanced it all on a tray, and carried it to the living room. She placed it on the coffee table and began to pace slightly. She forced herself to hold still. She tugged on her shirt. She fluffed her hair with her fingers. She wondered what was taking them so long. And when the door began to open, she jumped. Father Stasiuk stepped in first. He looked at the doorway, where the other priest must have stood—Catie couldn't see him because the door was in the way—and addressed him, "Please step in. I'd like you to meet one of my favorite parishioners, Catie Grigorescu."

"Really? What a coincidence. I know someone named Cătălina Grigorescu," the priest said as he stepped into the room. Catie felt her stomach drop, her blood pressure sky-rocket, her heart quicken, her skin dance with goose bumps, and her eyes fill to the brim. Her hands flew to her face as she screamed. "Vasile!" She didn't know if she had run to him or he to her; the only thing she knew was that they were embracing. She felt herself trembling and crying, and she was powerless to stop. The moment she became consciously aware that he smelled very good, she straightened up and stepped away.

"Are you…I mean…Please tell me that this isn't a joke… Are you…" Catie trailed off. She covered her mouth with her hands again and shook her head. She was too stunned to think, let alone talk.

Vasile laughed. "Are you trying to ask if I am moving here permanently as the new priest of St. Theocharis Greek Orthodox Church?" Catie nodded. He stepped closer to her and whispered, "Yes."

"Yes?"

"Yes!" He laughed again.

This time Catie knew that she was the one who flew into his embrace. Vasile!

She heard a noise and looked over at the chair. Father Stasiuk sat calmly, sipping his tea. He looked peaceful, Catie mused, but still pale and tired. She was going to miss him very much, but she saw clearly how much he needed to retire, to rest and recover. Reluctantly, she stepped away from Vasile. "Father Stasiuk, how is your tea? Are you ready for more hot water? I'm sorry I didn't pour your first cup."

"The tea is very nice, thank you. And I am perfectly capable of pouring my own cup. Father Cojocaru is, too, see?" Catie turned around to see Vasile pouring water over a teabag. He walked around and settled into the chair beside his predecessor. "See, Catie," Father Stasiuk stated smugly as he sipped. "I told you that you would be fine with the new priest."

Father Stasiuk didn't stay long. He excused himself to go home for the day. Vasile and Catie walked him to the car. Father Stasiuk approved of Vasile staying with Catie but imposed a 10:00 curfew on him. After he drove away, Catie turned to Vasile, eyes and heart brimming but words stuck inside. "I have a bench in my backyard," she managed to say.

Catie and Vasile strolled around the house and settled on the bench. This. This, she thought, was finally home. Sitting outside on a bench with Vasile. They began to talk, and it felt as though they picked up right where they left off the last time they sat on a bench together. "Oh, Vasile, I have missed you so very much."

He nodded. "And I you. Occasionally, Father Stasiuk gave me reports about you, but it wasn't the same as talking to you in person." He fell silent and reached into his pocket, pulled his hand back out, and held a closed fist in front of Catie. "I brought this for you, Cătălina, all the way from Romania. It's a little late in the year, so I hope you'll forgive my timing." He unfurled his hand. Catie gasped. Lying on his palm was a heart, embroidered from red and white string. Dangling in the middle of the heart were little embroidered dolls, a man and a woman, holding hands.

Cătălina gasped. Happy tears came to her eyes. "A *mărțișor*! I haven't had one since I lived in the countryside." She picked it up and turned it tenderly around, rubbing the dolls between her thumb and index finger. She beamed at Vasile.

"My *mărțișor* years were in the countryside of my childhood, too. Now we have an entirely new country, and I thought this *mărțișor* would be a great way to symbolize the old and the new uniting in a very good way." He touched the figures inside the heart. "We are united, Cătălina. And the *mărțișor* represents strength and health. Strength and health and so much more are ours now." He leaned forward and pinned it to her shirt, and then he made the sign of the cross over her. Catie said a silent prayer to St. Basil, to thank him and God for putting her right here, right now, and for sending Vasile to her.

"Come inside," she told him. She smiled. "I have much to tell you."

# About the Author

· · · · · · · · · · · · · · · · · · · · · · · · · · · · · ·

Tanya J. Peterson, MS, NCC writes compelling tales of the human psyche. She is the author of five critically acclaimed, award-winning novels. She is also the author of a self-help book about acceptance and commitment therapy as well as a mindfulness workbook for anxiety. She writes extensively for HealthyPlace.com and maintains her brand *Wellbeing & Words*, with all of its writing, events, and programming. She has a curriculum about toxic relationships based on her middle-grade/YA novel *Losing Elizabeth*; she takes both to schools and community programs. She speaks locally (around the Pacific Northwest) about mental health, wellbeing, and brain injury, and she participates in book readings and signings. For more information or to connect with Tanya, visit her website: www.tanyajpeterson.com

Apprentice
House Press
*Loyola University Maryland*

Apprentice House is the country's only campus-based, student-staffed book publishing company. Directed by professors and industry professionals, it is a nonprofit activity of the Communication Department at Loyola University Maryland.
Using state-of-the-art technology and an experiential learning model of education, Apprentice House publishes books in untraditional ways. This dual responsibility as publishers and educators creates an unprecedented collaborative environment among faculty and students, while teaching tomorrow's editors, designers, and marketers.

Outside of class, progress on book projects is carried forth by the AH Book Publishing Club, a co-curricular campus organization supported by Loyola University Maryland's Office of Student Activities.

Eclectic and provocative, Apprentice House titles intend to entertain as well as spark dialogue on a variety of topics. Financial contributions to sustain the press's work are welcomed. Contributions are tax deductible to the fullest extent allowed by the IRS.

To learn more about Apprentice House books or to obtain submission guidelines, please visit www.apprenticehouse.com.

Apprentice House
Communication Department
Loyola University Maryland
4501 N. Charles Street
Baltimore, MD 21210
Ph: 410-617-5265 • Fax: 410-617-2198
info@apprenticehouse.com • www.apprenticehouse.com